WITHIN THE SHADOWS

WITHIN THE SHADOWS

BRANDON MASSEY

Kensington Publishing Corp.
http://www.kensingtonbooks.com

DAFINA BOOKS are published by

Kensington Publishing Corp.
850 Third Avenue
New York, NY 10022

All Kensington Titles, Imprints, and Distributed Lines are
available at special quantity discounts for bulk purchases for
sales promotions, premiums, fund-raising, and educational
or institutional use. Special book excerpts or customized
printings can also be created to fit specific needs. For details,
write or phone the office of the Kensington special sales
manager: Kensington Publishing Corp., 850 Third Avenue,
New York, NY 10022. Attn: Special Sales Department, Phone:
1-800-221-2647.

Dafina and the Dafina logo Reg. U.S. Pat. & TM Off.

First Dafina trade paperback printing: June 2005
First Dafina mass market printing: January 2007

10 9 8 7 6 5 4 3 2 1

Printed in the United States of America

At half-past seven o'clock on the evening of May fifteenth, Andrew Wilson was riding back to Atlanta with his father, only a few minutes away from the accident that would change his life forever.

Immersed in thought, Andrew gazed out the passenger side window of the Ford Expedition. A thunderstorm was brewing. Like an advancing army, a front of dark clouds chased away the sunlight. Gusts swirled around the truck and flung dead leaves across the windshield. Far in the distance, lightning slashed the horizon.

Sighing, Andrew turned away from the window and glanced at his father behind the steering wheel.

"Looks like a storm's coming," Andrew said, stating the obvious.

"Sure is," Dad said. "We'll have to cut right through it."

Thunder grumbled, a sound that echoed in Andrew's bones.

Pondering something else to say—and hesitant to speak the thoughts that weighed on his mind—Andrew studied his father. Almost six feet tall, Raymond West was lean and muscular, with big hands that could palm a basketball as easily as a cantaloupe. He had a cinnamon complexion, laugh lines delicately drawn into his youthful face. His salt-and-pepper hair was trimmed short. His goatee was so meticulously cut it might have been sketched with a fine pencil.

Dapper as always, his father wore a tan polo shirt, khakis, and a Kangol golf hat. A sleek Movado watch glimmered on one sinewy wrist; a gold bracelet sparkled on the other.

Whenever Andrew looked at his father, he had the impression of viewing himself, twenty years older.

Sensing his scrutiny, Dad turned. His deep-brown eyes were curious. "Something on your mind, son?"

"Just wanted to say that I had fun this weekend." A knot formed in his throat. For a moment, he was unable to say another word—and he had left much unsaid.

He wasn't accustomed to sharing positive comments with his dad about their relationship.

They drove on Interstate 16, heading back to Atlanta after spending a day and a half in Savannah. They'd arrived on the coast late Friday afternoon, had dinner at a seafood restaurant, and rose the next morning for a seven o'clock tee time. After playing eighteen holes, they hung out at the clubhouse, ate an early dinner, napped at the hotel, and hit the road to return home.

It was the longest duration of time that Andrew had spent with his father in nineteen years. The experience left him with a lot that he wanted to say, but he lacked the words to adequately express himself.

It frustrated him. He was a writer; he'd published three suspense novels to growing acclaim, had ditched his computer programmer job to write full-time and had never looked back. He earned his living with words—

but right then, he felt no more articulate than a newborn baby.

A pitchfork of lightning stabbed the earth, followed by a burst of thunder. Wind rattled the elms and maples that flanked the highway.

"We had a good time." Dad grinned. "I'm not such a bad guy to hang with, am I?"

Andrew cleared his throat, breaking up the lump there. "You're all right for an old man."

"Old man, huh? This old man spanked you out there."

"You got some lucky shots. Come on, man, you had *two* eagles. That was a once in a lifetime game."

"All in a day's work for a scratch player like me, young buck." Dad smiled.

"Wanna bet it happens next time?"

"Ah, man, you know . . ."

"Thought so," Andrew said.

Dad laughed. So did Andrew. They'd done a lot of laughing together on this trip, and it felt good. It felt strange, he admitted, to be having so much fun with his father, but it was good, all the same.

"I'll just say this. Wait till you hit fifty," Dad said. "If you're in half as good a shape as I am, you better count your blessings. I know I do. Half of the cats I grew up with are dead."

"I hear ya."

On the CD player, Marvin Gaye sang "What's Going On." For their drive, Andrew had recorded a disc of classic R&B tracks.

"You got the jams on there." Dad tapped the steering wheel.

"Old school is all I mostly listen to."

"That so?"

"The music was better back then. It wasn't about dropping your booty to the floor and rolling in a

Bentley. Back in the day, they played their own instru-
ments, sang about political issues and real love, you
know?"

"Yeah, I know, but *you* don't know." Dad chuckled.
"That was before your time, man."

"You might be surprised." He had loved old-school
music for as long as he could remember, a romance
that started with his mother spinning vinyl records in
their house—Stevie Wonder, The Ohio Players, Chaka Kahn,
George Clinton and Parliament, the S.O.S. Band—all
of the greats. But, of course, his father wouldn't know
anything about his musical tastes. Shortly after Andrew
was born, his parents, who'd never married, broke up,
and his father had rarely visited—certainly, never often
enough to learn anything meaningful about him.

But that had begun to change two months ago, when
his dad had called him and asked if he wanted to play
golf.

Their newfound relationship awakened a bewilder-
ing blend of emotions in Andrew: excitement, anxiety,
confusion. He was excited to be finally forging what appeared to be a true bond with his father. He was anxious that the connection wouldn't endure, was false,
and that they'd regress to the superficial friendliness
they'd used to have. And he was confused: Why had his
father decided to reach out to him, after ignoring him
for the first thirty years of his life?

He wanted to discuss all of these things with his father. But as skilled as he was at expressing himself with
the written word, verbalizing his feelings often proved a
challenge.

Lightning opened a fissure in the bruised sky. Thunder
bellowed.

Rain began to fall from the ruptured heavens, snap-
ping against the windshield, painting the world in hues
of gray and black.

Switching on the wipers, his father leaned forward.

The time for serious discussion with his dad had passed. He needed to let his father concentrate on driving.

Once again, he'd failed to open up with his dad.

The CD moved to the next track: "Footsteps in the Dark," by The Isley Brothers. A mellow song. Andrew lay back and closed his eyes, letting the drumming rain lull him into a state of relaxation.

When he felt the truck drifting sideways, he opened his eyes.

Dad had veered onto an exit ramp.

"Where are we going?" Andrew asked. The fuel gauge hovered near the Full mark. "Do you need to use the rest room?"

"Nah, nah," Dad said. "Need to . . . see something."

His father's voice, normally energetic, had taken on a dreamy quality.

They reached the end of the rain-slick ramp. His father turned right.

It was a twisty, two-lane road, lined with tall elms and maples. Between the tightly packed trees, Andrew glimpsed rundown mobile homes and dilapidated barns.

He got that uneasy feeling that he always experienced when traveling through rural areas in the Deep South. In remote places like this, you were fortunate to get service on your cell phone. He was a city dweller, preferred to be connected and in the midst of urban civilization.

"Where are we?" Andrew asked.

"Bulloch County," Dad said in a hushed voice. "My old stomping grounds."

"Oh, yeah, you went to Georgia Southern. That's in Statesboro, right?"

"Yeah," Dad said. "A ways ahead."

"You gonna drive by the school?"

His father's response was so soft that Andrew had to lower the music's volume to hear him.

"No," Dad said. "Be quiet, Andrew."

A frown creased Andrew's face.

His dad was acting strange.

The wipers could not keep up with the hammering rain. No street lamps illuminated their path, and the headlights barely reached beyond ten feet.

Nevertheless, his father plowed down the road at sixty miles an hour.

Andrew checked that his seat belt was fastened.

The road curved to the left. They swung through the turn, wings of water sprouting from underneath the truck.

"Maybe you should slow down," Andrew said.

"Maybe you should keep your mouth shut." Dad spoke in a whisper, but his tone was firm.

Andrew blinked. What was going on here?

His dad hunched forward, gaze searching the darkness. His fingers gripped the wheel so tightly that his knuckles were pale white.

He had never seen this side of his father. This man driving was like a disturbing twin to the easygoing guy who had been boasting about his golf game only five minutes ago.

He realized how little he knew about his dad. Certainly, he knew a lot of the basics: His father was fifty-one years old, lived in Lithonia, owned a successful real estate brokerage, had been married for over a decade, attended a Baptist church every Sunday and served as a deacon, and loved golf, the Atlanta Falcons, and Heineken beer.

But he knew only surface details about his father. He didn't know what really made him tick.

Now, he felt as if he were literally on a wild ride into the unknown depths of his dad's psyche.

The Ford burrowed through the rain. His father pushed the truck hard, braking only lightly for curves.

A sign flashed past: Millville City Limits.

Millville? Andrew had never heard of the town.

A road on the left floated into view. "Dead End," a nearby sign stated.

His father swerved into the turn.

"Take it easy, Dad." Andrew braced his arm against the dashboard.

Hunkered over the wheel, his father ignored him.

Trees cloaked the road in a dark womb.

If they'd turned on to a dead end street, whatever his dad was searching for must be back there.

But what could it be?

The road twisted to the right.

Barely slowing, his father wrestled the wheel into the curve.

A hulking, white-tail deer stood in the middle of the road. The animal stared at them vacantly, nailed in place by the Ford's headlights.

Terror seized Andrew's heart.

"Stop, you're gonna hit it!" he said.

Crying out, as if frightened awake from a slumber, his father spun the wheel and pumped the brakes.

Skidding, getting no grip on the slippery pavement, the Ford tilted precariously—and tipped too far to regain its balance. The vehicle turned over with a bone-jarring crash and a squeal of tortured metal. Andrew bit his tongue, tasted coppery blood, screamed, and prayed that they wouldn't die.

Andrew awoke with a gasp.

Dull pain pulsated throughout his body, as if he'd been tumbling inside a giant washing machine. He blinked, tried to determine his surroundings.

His situation became apparent: he was in the truck. Upside down. Sandwiched between the seat and the roof.

But he was alive.

It took several seconds for him to get oriented to this upside-down world. The airbags had deployed, the puffy material pressed against his upper body. He pushed the bag away, turned his head. Pain leaped through his neck.

When he saw his dad, he forgot all about his own discomfort.

Tangled like a rag doll, thrown upside down, his father was mashed against the driver's side door. His back faced Andrew, but his shoulders rose and fell slowly.

He was alive.

Thank God for two miracles today.

"Dad?" His tongue felt like a loose piece of meat in his mouth. "You okay?"

Dad didn't respond.

The Ford's engine idled. Rain sifted inside through the cracked windshield. A rumble of thunder shook the ground.

He had to get out of there and get help.

Although it hurt to move, he contorted his body, stretched his arm and grasped the door handle. He pulled.

The door eeked open. Cold rain and wind poured inside.

He began to squirm through the door, feet first. Remembering that the engine was on, he reached behind and turned the key in the ignition, shutting the truck off.

He kicked the door open, crawled through mud and struggled to his feet.

He was relieved to discover that he could stand and walk. He had no serious injuries. He was mostly woozy, and his neck ached, too, more than any other part of his body. Probably had a minor case of whiplash.

He wiped muck out of his eyes and viewed the wreck.

The Ford had flipped over and spun into a ditch. The nose of the vehicle was buried in the trench; the rear pointed skyward. The roof was smashed as if stomped by a gigantic foot, and the front end was mangled.

It was incredible that he'd survived. He felt a distinct sense of unreality, as if he were watching an accident that someone else had wound up in.

The deer that his father had tried to avoid stood on the edge of the road, unharmed. It watched him, as perfectly posed as a gazelle on a merry-go-round.

Andrew met the animal's liquid-black gaze.

"See what you did to us?" he said. His voice was hoarse, his throat raw. "This is your fault!"

The deer only stared at him.

Did malice gleam in the animal's eyes, as if it were aware of what it had done?

No, that was impossible. Only his overactive imagination at work.

The deer sniffed, trotted into the woods.

He felt stupid for talking to the animal in the first place. He had to settle down.

The street was deserted. It terminated about a hundred feet ahead, in a wall of trees.

Perhaps thirty feet away, he saw what appeared to be an entrance to a driveway. An ornate, wrought iron mailbox stood nearby.

If there was a house back there, trees and shrubbery concealed it from view.

Was this the place that his father had wanted to visit?

Dizziness washed over him. He bent over, drew a few deep breaths, to steady himself.

What would Mark Justice do in this situation?

The familiar question came to his mind, automatically.

Mark Justice was the pen name under which he published his thriller novels. In media interviews, he referred to Mark Justice as "my heroic alter ego."

A creator of action-packed, ingenious tales that carried readers in unexpected directions, Mark Justice always knew how to steer his fictional characters out of a tight spot. When Andrew found himself in stressful circumstances, he called on Mark Justice, that clever aspect of his mind, for guidance.

It was, he figured, no different from an ordinary person listening to his intuition and common sense. Still, he'd never told anyone about how he tapped into Mark Justice. People already assumed writers were weirdos. He didn't want to validate the stereotype.

Check on your daddy, Mark Justice advised, in the brusque, tough guy voice that Andrew had given him. *Confirm his condition, then grab your cell phone and call an ambulance.*

Andrew hurried to the driver's side of the vehicle.

"Oh, Jesus," he said.

His father's face was pressed against the glass. A thread of blood inched down his chin. His features were slack, as if he were sleeping and would wake in a moment to brag about his golf swing.

Tears pushed at Andrew's eyes. Could Dad be paralyzed . . . ?

"Don't think about it," he said.

The door was dented in several places, but it appeared to be intact.

He reached for the handle. And hesitated. What if it wasn't safe to move his father? What if he'd sustained a spinal injury? Moving him improperly could disable him, perhaps even kill him. He knew a little about car accidents from his book research. But he possessed only

a layman's knowledge and wasn't qualified to determine what injuries his father had sustained, and how he
should be removed from the vehicle.

He couldn't go any farther. They needed paramedics.

By habit, he reached for the area on his waist where
he normally wore his cell phone in a holster. But it wasn't
there. It must have fallen somewhere inside the truck.

He rushed to the passenger side.

Sure enough, his phone lay inside, against the ceiling.

"All right, let's get some help here." He turned on
the phone.

The display read: *Searching for signal* . . .

"Come on, hurry up." The rain had seeped through
his clothes. He shivered.

Searching for signal . . .

He wasn't going to think about what might happen,
here in the middle of nowhere in rural Georgia. No, he
wasn't going to think about it.

Searching for signal . . .

"Hurry up!"

No service.

"I don't believe this shit!" He turned off the phone,
switched it on again. Waited. Still no signal.

He clapped the lid shut.

"Okay, don't panic," he said. "Stay cool, man, stay
cool."

Bending down, he peered inside the Ford. His father
had not moved, and was still unconscious.

Didn't Dad have his own cell phone? If so, he didn't
see it, and if his father was wearing it somewhere on his
person, Andrew would have to move his body to find it,
and that brought him back to the danger of inadver-
tently injuring him.

He swung around, looked across the road, at the driveway.

If there was indeed a house back there, the residents should have a telephone.

He started running.

Damp undergrowth clotted the driveway. Andrew fought through it, half wishing that he had a machete, like an explorer in a jungle movie.

But all he had was a light. He took his key ring out of his pocket. A mini-flashlight dangled on the ring; it was a promotional giveaway from the tour for his first novel, the title of which—*The Comeback*—was stenciled on the side.

The thin blade of light dissected the darkness around him. Through the bushes, he caught glimpses of the house. It was immense—a mansion, actually.

Did Dad really know someone who lived here?

The lane stretched on, weaving around gnarled trees, their skeletal branches overhanging the ground like groping arms. By the time he tore through the last patch of shrubbery, sweat drenched him, and scratches ran down his arms and hands.

Sitting on a hill, the house loomed before him.

Owing to the suspense novels he had written, all of which relied on a sense of place to create mood, Andrew had a decent knowledge of architecture. It was a Greek Revival mansion, built in a style popular in the antebellum South. Six massive columns fronted the house. A wide veranda wound around the front. The paint, which likely had used to be white, had faded to a dreary gray. Spanish moss festooned the walls and columns, like giant varicose veins.

All of the windows, over a dozen of them, were so dark they might have been coated with black paint. There were no vehicles parked in the circular end of the driveway.

Lightning pulsed in the sky above the mansion, threw the structure in stark relief against the churning clouds and encircling woods.

It resembled a haunted house straight out of a horror flick. He didn't want to get any closer. He wanted nothing more than to run away, get to the road and flag someone down to get help. That was a more appealing alternative than going inside this house.

He looked behind him, at the weed-choked lane. It had taken him several minutes to get this far, and his dad needed an ambulance right away.

He attempted to use his cell phone. Still no service.

"Okay, don't be stupid," he said. "There's no time to go back. It's just a house, man. Go on up there and see if they have a phone."

He approached the door.

On the veranda, a weathered, bench-style swing hung from rusty chains. It swung, as if it had been vacated only seconds ago.

It's only the wind, he assured himself.

As though in response, a breeze whispered across the veranda, caressed him.

Except for the soughing wind and the water plinking from the eaves, the area was tomb silent.

The wide oak door looked solid enough to serve as a bank vault. The doorbell was broken, the button dangling from the casing like a ruptured eye.

He grasped the brass knocker, an object shaped like an angelic woman's countenance. He knocked.

The sound was loud in the stillness.

"Hello!" he said. "Is anyone here? We've had an accident and need to use a phone!"

Silence. He watched the windows, to see if a curtain stirred, or a light flicked on. But the house remained dark and quiet.

He rapped again with the knocker, harder.

The door apparently was not shut tight. It creaked open, revealing a slice of darkness.

Someone had to be inside. It wouldn't make sense for the door of a mansion to be loose if no one lived there.

He nudged the door open a few inches.

"I only need to use a phone," he said.

Silence answered him.

After hesitating for a beat, he pushed the door open all the way.

Musty blackness greeted him. He held back a sneeze.

Shining the flashlight in front of him, he went inside.

The wide entry hall had a scarred hardwood floor. An enormous chandelier hung overhead, decorated with cobwebs. Pieces of antique furniture—chairs, tables, a mirror, vases—encased in webs and mantled with dust, lined the corridor. There were numerous rooms located off the main hallway, vast, dank chambers full of shadows.

He moved deeper inside. Paintings hung on the walls. Colorful scenes of sun-splashed meadows, long tables laden with sumptuous feasts, horses galloping through a pastoral countryside.

The paintings were skillfully done, but there were no people depicted in any of the pieces. It seemed weird to him.

"Hello," he said. "Anyone here?"

Wind drifted down the corridor. Behind him, there was a bump.

He spun.

But it was only the door. Stirred by the breeze, it had drifted shut.

He laughed nervously.

Only a house, he reminded himself. He wasn't in a horror movie.

Nevertheless, he had the sense that he was being watched. He felt a slight pressure on the back of his neck, the weight of someone's gaze.

Wetness crept down the channel of his spine.

He panned the light all around him.

The house was vacant. If someone were in there, they would have come out by now. His imagination, fed by a steady diet of books and scary movies, was running away with him. No one was watching him. It was a stupid thought.

He was about to leave when he saw a telephone sitting on a table near the middle of the hallway, at the foot of a grand spiral staircase.

Maybe there was some hope after all.

It was a rotary phone. He'd last seen one of these years ago, when he'd visited his great-uncle in Mississippi. He picked up the handset.

The line was dead.

Just as he'd worried, he had wasted his time coming there. It was time for Plan B: flagging down someone on the road.

As he hung up the phone, something scurried through the darkness in a nearby room.

He tracked the movement with the flashlight.

A large cat had perched on the arm of an overstuffed chair. Fine-boned and muscular, the feline's shorthaired coat was a lustrous bluish-gray. Crouched, it watched him. Its vivid green eyes appeared to possess unnatural intelligence.

His racing pulse slowed.

"What're you doing in here, kitty?" he said. "You live here with someone?"

The cat only looked at him. It did not meow.

So much for the feeling that he was being watched. Nothing more frightening than a plain cat had been spying on him.

Creaking sounds reached him.

This time, the cat wasn't the culprit. The noises came from somewhere above: the staircase.

The cat slipped away into the shadows.

Eyebrows knitted, he placed his hand on the dusty balustrade and shone the flashlight up the stairs.

"Is anyone there?" he asked.

A soft creak.

He imagined an old woman living there, kept company by the cat. Maybe she was upstairs, padding around slowly on a cane, planning to come downstairs to meet him.

But he wasn't going up there to see. As much as he wanted to attribute his jitters to his lucid imagination, this house was honestly beginning to creep him out.

It was time to go.

He pushed away from the railing.

A cold gust blasted down the staircase, crashed into him like an invisible freight train. He gasped, stumbled.

The Arctic gale stung his eyes and squeezed tears out of them. He flailed his arms, temporarily blinded.

Coldness poured into his mouth, rushed down his throat and flooded his stomach. The invasive chill spread throughout his body.

What's happening to me?

The freezing sensation numbed his muscles as effectively as a dose of Novocain. The flashlight slipped out of his fingers. Darkness dropped over him.

His legs lost their strength. He fell to the floor, landed hard on his side, not even feeling the pain due to the coldness that had enveloped him.

Jesus, what's happening?

Teeth chattering, he struggled to regain control of his body. He had to get the flashlight. He felt as if he was a child again, just awakened from a nightmare and terrified of the blackness in the bedroom. The darkness was too much to bear. It was like a living thing closing in on him, a monster that would consume him.

He stretched his trembling arm, extended his fingers to grasp the light.

Someone grabbed his hand.

He screamed.

A light shone in Andrew's face.

"Relax, my friend," a baritone voice said. "You are safe."

Andrew's scream died in his throat. He looked past the light and into the visage of an elderly black man.

The man's big hand covered Andrew's. He pulled Andrew upright; he was surprisingly strong considering that he looked to be at least eighty years old.

Andrew's legs steadied. The coldness had drained out of his body.

What had caused the numbness in the first place? The wind? Or maybe he was still in mild shock from the accident.

"I'm sorry," Andrew said. He bent to retrieve his flashlight. "You scared the daylights out of me. I thought I was alone in here."

The man carried a kerosene lantern, the likes of which Andrew had not seen in ages. He set it on the table beside the telephone. Golden light filled the hall-way.

Andrew got a good look at the guy. He stood at least a half foot taller than Andrew, and Andrew was nearly six feet. He was lean, straight-backed. He wore a somber black suit with a crisp white shirt and dull red tie.

His manner of dress reminded Andrew, uncomfort-ably, of an undertaker.

A virile shock of steel-gray hair flowed from the man's oval-shaped head. He was clean shaven, his skin as smooth as a pecan.

In spite of his age, the man's black eyes were hawk-sharp.

"What do you seek in here?" the man asked. He carefully enunciated each word and had only a faint trace of a Southern accent. He raised an eyebrow. "Are you ghost-hunting?"

"Huh? No, my dad and I were in a car accident on the road out front. I wanted to use the phone to call an ambulance."

"Our phone service has been discontinued for some time." He smiled. He had the whitest, straightest teeth that Andrew had ever seen, and they looked real, not at all like dentures.

"I figured out that the phone was off," Andrew said.

"Indeed. My name is Walter." He extended his hand. "I've served as the caretaker here for many, many years."

Andrew shook his hand. The brief but firm shake reinforced his perception of this old man's uncommon strength.

"I'm Andrew. Where can I find the nearest phone?"

"Perhaps in town. We have no need of telephones here."

"So someone lives here? I thought I heard sounds upstairs."

"Many live here." Walter's eyes sparkled mysteriously.

Andrew peered up the staircase. He didn't see anything. He attributed the icy gust he'd felt to an open window up there, something like that.

Walter's response puzzled him, but he didn't bother to pursue the matter. He didn't care who lived there. He cared only about getting an ambulance for his father.

"Sorry for snooping around in here, but I need to go now and get help for my dad." Andrew headed for the door. "Nice meeting you."

"Likewise," Walter said. He flashed his perfect grin.

Outside on the veranda, Andrew tried his cell phone again.

It found a signal.

"Finally!" Running away from the house, he called 911.

He didn't look back. He wanted to forget all about his odd experience at the mansion.

Standing in the doorway, lamp in hand, Walter watched Andrew leave.

He was no longer smiling.

A few minutes past eleven o'clock at night, Andrew was sitting beside his father's bed at East Georgia Regional Medical Center in Statesboro, when his dad finally awoke.

Earlier, paramedics had safely removed his dad from the vehicle and transported him to the hospital. The physician diagnosed him as having suffered a concussion and bruised ribs; he'd received stitches for a laceration on his head, too. He had been unconscious since the accident.

Andrew had been treated for minor whiplash, and had been given medication to lessen the aches.

He'd called his dad's wife in Atlanta. She was on her way and should arrive at any moment. For the time being, Andrew and his father were the only ones in the room.

When his father's eyes opened, Andrew rose. "Dad, you're up."

"Hey," Dad said in a scratchy voice. Blinking groggily, he licked his chapped lips. "How long I been sleeping?"

"Few hours." Andrew grasped his father's hand. "How're you feeling?"

"Head hurts like hell." A thick bandage encircled his father's head. Dad touched it, gingerly. "Where are we?"

"At a hospital in Statesboro. We had an accident. The truck flipped over."

"You doing okay?"

"I'm fine," Andrew said.

Rubbing his head, Dad winced.

"I'll get the nurse and ask her to give you a painkiller," Andrew said.

"Thanks."

Andrew started to press the call button near the bed, and paused.

"Dad, do you remember anything?"

"Remember . . . driving through a storm," Dad said.

"Do you remember where we were going?"

He watched his father closely.

Dad frowned. "We were heading home, right?"

"Right."

Clearly, his father did not recall taking the exit off the highway, speeding across the roads, and almost hitting the deer. Andrew had worried that the concussion would wipe away his dad's memory of the minutes leading up to the accident. Memory loss after such an injury was commonplace, the doctor advised, but Andrew had vainly hoped that this situation would be different.

But he had to ask one more question.

"Do you know anything about an old mansion in Bulloch County, off Interstate 16?"

Dad looked him in the eyes. Then, his gaze shifted.

"No," Dad said softly. "Can you call that nurse now, son?"

His father had lied to him. The truth was in his eyes.

He knew a lot about the mansion. Andrew was willing to bet on it.

But he wasn't going to push his dad for an answer. He'd pulled away many layers to his father in the past two months, like peeling the proverbial onion, but everyone kept secrets. Although his father's interest in the house puzzled him, the bottom line was that it was probably none of his business.

And Andrew wasn't convinced that he *wanted* to know his father's connection to the mansion. It was a strange place that he'd prefer to forget about. His dad's refusal to discuss it would make sweeping it under the rug of his memory all the easier.

"Sure, Dad. Forget I asked."

Andrew pressed the button to summon the nurse.

Part One

ENTRANCES

He hadn't trusted the woman at first. He never trusted anyone on sight—there were too many leeches and flat-out nuts in the world who could turn your life into a living hell if you were stupid enough to give them the chance.

But something about her was different. She quickly coaxed him to lower his guard. He hoped that he didn't regret it later.

—Mark Justice, *The Comeback*

Chapter 1

When Andrew would reflect on it later, he would realize that it all began during the Memorial Day cookout that he hosted at his house.

Monday, May 31, was a perfect day for a barbecue. The cloudless sky shimmered like a turquoise ocean. The buttery sunlight was warm and pure. Breezes tempered the Georgia humidity, keeping the outdoors comfortable and spreading the fragrance of blooming magnolias.

The official start time for the cookout was two o'clock in the afternoon, but a steady stream of people didn't begin to show up until close to three. By four, over thirty relatives and friends had arrived at his house in South Fulton County. They congregated on the two-level wooden deck in the back, lounged in the large, finished basement, and found places to relax, talk, and eat in the kitchen, dining room, and family room.

Andrew's best friend, Eric Patton, had volunteered for barbecue duty. He worked the huge Weber grill on the patio, cooking enough hot dogs, ribs, chicken, and burgers to feed a small nation. Carmen Love, another of Andrew's close friends, supervised the preparation of the other foods: potato salad, baked beans, salad, corn on the cob, and other delicious summertime dishes. Andrew handled the overall hosting duties, a task that kept him in constant motion.

Dressed in a white shirt and cargo shorts, he walked around the house like a captain inspecting a ship. His mission, which he took quite seriously, was to ensure that his guests had everything they wanted and were enjoying themselves. In the family room, which featured a sixty-inch television, he checked that those people gathered on the leather sofas and chairs were enjoying the comedy film he had selected. In the living room, he found three children gawking at the colorful fish swimming in the sixty-gallon saltwater aquarium, and he took the time to explain the species of each aquatic creature. Outside, on the upper level of the deck, a group of his friends and relatives played Spades, and he offered to replenish their drinks. In the entertainment area in the basement, a few of his cousins played a war game, *Ghost Recon,* on the Sony PlayStation, which was connected to the projection-screen TV. He offered them tips to advance further in the game.

While making his rounds, he cleaned. Grabbed discarded paper cups and plates here, swept crumbs off a table there. He'd learned that the best way to save himself from having a mess on his hands after hosting a gathering was to clean as much as possible throughout the affair—though he had to admit that he was a neat freak, anyway.

He was downstairs in the bar area, peering at the stereo system unit encased in the wall panel, mulling whether to swap his prerecorded "Cookout" CD for a disc of old school jams, when Carmen appeared in the doorway.

At certain moments, seeing Carmen made his pulse throb a little faster. This was one of those times.

Carmen was, in a word, fine. Twenty-eight years old, blessed with smooth bronze skin, she was around five-feet-four, with an athletic figure sculpted from her years as a cheerleader at Clark Atlanta. Her auburn hair was cut in a short, curly style that perfectly framed her face. Warmth and intelligence sparkled in her large honey-brown eyes.

She wore an orange halter top, a denim skirt, and sling-back sandals. It was casual clothing, but she couldn't have been more beautiful to Andrew if she'd been wearing a Donna Karan evening dress and Blahnik pumps.

If only they were more than friends . . .

"Dang, undress me with your eyes, why don't you, Drew?" Carrying two Styrofoam plates heaped with food, Carmen walked to the bar.

Andrew blushed. "Sorry about that."

Carmen laughed. "I'm kidding. Haven't you learned by now that I enjoy seeing you drool over me?"

"Okay, whatever." He laughed. She laughed, too. But he wondered what she meant by her flirtatious comment. That wasn't the kind of thing you said to someone with whom you shared a platonic relationship. Not if you wanted to keep it that way.

He and Carmen had been friends for five years. They had met at a book club meeting in Decatur, where Andrew had been invited to discuss his first novel. A member of the book club, Carmen had asked the most insightful questions about his story, shared the most thoughtful comments. After the meeting ended, they exchanged E-mail addresses and promised to keep in touch, simply to discuss books on occasion. But they became fast friends and found themselves discussing not only literature, but also everything else in their lives.

They might have begun dating shortly after they met,

but Carmen had a boyfriend at the time, and Andrew had recently broken up with someone and wanted to take a hiatus from the dating scene. By the time Carmen ended her relationship, Andrew had started seeing someone else. Then Andrew broke up with his girlfriend, and Carmen already had found another man. They always missed being available for each other as lovers. But they'd developed such a close friendship that Andrew didn't want to risk destroying it by pursuing a romance. She'd become like a sister to him.

Still, sometimes he wondered, *what if.* Carmen was smart, had a great sense of humor. She was independent, stable, a positive thinker. Had a great career she enjoyed, working as a C.P.A. with a prestigious accounting firm in downtown Atlanta. And she had a generous spirit; this was probably the fifth time that she had gone out of her way to help him host a cookout, and she never asked for anything in return.

What if . . .

His thoughts flashed on the memory of what had happened between them last month, while watching a movie at her place. He quickly forced the images out of this mind.

They had a great friendship. He couldn't risk ruining it—in spite of the flirtatious remarks Carmen sometimes made that caused him to wonder about her real feelings for him, too.

She perched on a bar stool. "Here, brought you something to eat."

"Thanks. I haven't eaten yet."

"I figured that. You're so busy making sure everyone else is taken care of, you forgot to eat."

"You know me well." Stepping behind the counter, he pulled a plate toward him, the one loaded with ribs, a hot dog, potato salad, and an ear of corn. Carmen avoided red meat so he knew at a glance which plate was hers.

On the stereo, Will Smith rapped about summertime. Digging in to her potato salad, Carmen rocked with the beat, singing softly.

"Thanks for helping me with the cookout," Andrew said. "I couldn't have done it without you, as usual."

"You know I've always got your back." She picked up a piece of chicken, took a small bite. "By the way, your dad called a minute ago. He said he's on his way."

"That's good to know."

"Why'd you say it like that?"

"Things have been weird with him lately, that's all."

"Since the accident?"

"I guess. Mind if we talk about something else?"

"Sorry." She smiled. "So, how about those Braves?"

"You don't watch baseball."

"And? You like to talk about it. I wanted to discuss something you're comfortable with. Think they'll go to the Finals this year?"

"The Finals are basketball. Baseball is the World Series."

"Whatever, you know what I meant."

He smiled in spite of himself. "You're silly."

"You need a little silliness in your life, honey. All work and no play makes Andrew a dull boy."

"What're you saying, that I'm dull?"

"As a butter knife."

"I'm not dull, I'm just serious sometimes."

"Like twenty-four seven."

"So why do you hang out with me?"

"Because you're such a cutie." She pinched his cheek. Her fingers left a smear of barbecue sauce on his skin.

"Thanks." He reached for a napkin.

"My bad, I'll clean it off." She cupped his chin in one hand, and dabbed a napkin at his cheek with the other.

He was acutely aware of the closeness of her; the sweet sexiness of her perfume; the gentleness of her touch; the lushness of her cleavage, accentuated by the gold cross she wore on her necklace.

Their gazes met. Neither of them looked away.

His breath caught in his throat.

Her full lips, colored with crimson lipstick, beckoned to him.

He remembered how it had felt to taste those lips, when they'd crossed the platonic line last month at her place . . .

Can't do that again, man. Too risky. Remember, five years of friendship, five years of friendship, five years of friendship . . .

"What the hell are you two doing?" a man's voice boomed.

Eric stood in the doorway, fists bunched on his waist. Dark-skinned, six-feet-three and lanky, he wore a white apron with words printed in big red letters: "Don't F%$K with the Cook!"

Andrew looked at Carmen. Her eyes were wide—and embarrassed. Just like he felt.

Why should he feel embarrassed? They hadn't done anything.

But you wanted to. Don't lie.

Eric's face was stern. "I leave you two alone for five minutes, and you're in here about to get freaky on the top of the bar! Don't you understand that there are children here?"

"We weren't doing anything, man," Andrew said, wondering why he was explaining himself to his friend. "Seriously, we—"

Eric broke into a grin.

"I had you two going, didn't I?" He shook with laughter. "Damn, you should've seen the looks on your faces!"

"Always the comedian," Andrew said. "Don't you have some food to grill?"

Eric spread his long arms. "All done, bro. Grill master Patton has done it again." He bowed theatrically. "Thank you, thank you very much."

"But did you clean up after yourself?" Carmen asked. "I remember what you did the last time you barbecued at my house, Eric. You left behind a mess."

Eric made an expression of mock surprise. "Can you believe this woman? How dare you imply that I, Grill master Patton, have neglected my sworn responsibilities as a grill master? Go look for yourself, woman!"

"I think I'll do that." Taking her plate, she left the room, but not before paying Andrew a meaningful glance.

Eric watched her leave, and turned to Andrew. He raised an eyebrow.

"Man, what were you guys doing, anyway?"

"Just fooling around." Andrew bit into the corn.

"You two going to finally get together?"

"We're just friends, same as always. It's not going anywhere else."

"But you want it to."

"Not at the risk of ruining our friendship."

"You've got to be friends before lovers, bro," Eric said. "Y'all have that covered, so why not go for it? Like that song by Jagged Edge—you ain't getting no younger, you might as well do it."

"You act like I'm forty. I'm only thirty-one. I've got plenty of time."

"I don't know what I'm going to do with you." Eric folded his arms on the counter. Thirty-three years old, Eric had been married for seven years, wedding his college sweetheart shortly after he graduated from Emory Law School. He never tired of praising the virtues of life as a married man. "Imagine, bro, having a woman who's got your back—for life," he'd preach to Andrew. "No more of that nonsense you get on the dating scene, dealing with those trifling females playing head games. Marriage is work, no doubt, but there's nothing in the world like sharing your life with a woman who you love. It'll make you a stronger man in ways that you can't even imagine."

Andrew had known Eric for his entire life, ever since their families had lived next door to each other in East Point. Eric was like a big brother to him and often provided wise counsel. But sometimes, he was way off base.

Like now.

"I've told you, it's not that I don't want to settle down," Andrew said. "I really do. I've been blessed with almost everything that I could want in my life—the successful career, this house, friends like you. A woman would make it all complete."

"But?"

"But I want to make sure I marry the *right* woman."

"No doubt." Eric nodded. "But if Ms. Right is already here, why wait? She's not going to wait on you forever."

"She has a man, you know that."

"That buster she's been dating for three months? Please. He's just filling time for her."

"You assume I've already met Ms. Right. What if I haven't?"

"But you have."

"You don't know that."

"Your big brother knows these things. Trust me."

"Trust you? Like the time you hooked me up with that lovely girl who'd been in jail for stabbing her ex-boyfriend?"

"Okay, you got me. She hadn't told me about that."

"Or how about the fine woman you introduced me to who tried to get me to take her *and* her mama to a movie on our first date?"

"I misjudged her, my bad."

"Or how about the last nubian princess you were so kind to send my way, who ordered two meals at dinner and said she was taking the other one home to eat later?"

"I give up!" Eric threw up his hands. "You win. I've got no business being a matchmaker."

"Exactly. Give it up. I'll meet the right woman one day, and when I do, I'll know it, and I'll marry her. Simple as that."

Punctuating his statement, Andrew picked up the hot dog and bit into it. Mustard squirted onto the front of his white shirt.

Eric laughed. "See, that's what you get for talking shit."

"Very funny. I'll be back. I'm gonna change shirts."

As he climbed the stairs to the second floor, where his bedroom was located, the party sounds faded. He heard an unexpected noise: running water.

It came from the master bedroom.

He frowned. Upstairs was off-limits to guests. It was an unstated but implicit rule that everyone obeyed.

But when he walked inside the bedroom, and from there into the master bathroom, warm mist filled the air. Hot water cascaded into the garden tub. The drain was unplugged.

He hadn't turned on the water. He had lived in this house for eleven months, and he had never bathed in the tub, preferring to use the shower stall.

Who had been in here?

Chapter 2

Andrew shut off the faucet.

He watched the water gurgle down the drain.

He had no idea who had been in there, or why. It bothered him. Although he enjoyed having guests, he invited them with the stipulation that no one would enter his private space without his permission.

"Must've been a kid, playing around," he said.

He checked to see if anything was out of place. All of the items he expected—toothbrush, colognes, lotion, and other toiletries—lay where he expected to find them on the dual-sink vanity. Nothing was missing.

Still, when he returned downstairs, he'd remind the parents to keep their children from wandering up here.

He opened the walk-in closet, located off the end of the bathroom.

The closet was meticulously organized: shoes hung on a tree; shirts and slacks, grouped by color and season, all faced the same direction; suits arranged by occasion awaited in garment bags; shelves bulged with stacks of folded jeans and T-shirts.

Whenever a friend saw his closet, they teased him,

called him an obsessive-compulsive nut. He didn't deny it. He loved the sight of order throughout his house. It comforted him.

Besides, with every piece of clothing in its proper place, dressing for even formal affairs never took longer than a few minutes.

As he was pulling the soiled shirt over his head, a knock came at the half-open bathroom door.

"Drew?" It was Carmen. She stepped inside and saw him bare-chested. "Oops, I didn't know a strip show was about to start. I better get my money."

"Bring fifties and hundreds." He was about to reach for another shirt, then said, "Hey, when I came in here, I found the water running in the tub. Someone was in here."

"Really? It was probably one of those Bebe kids, playing where they have no business going."

"That's what I figured. I only wanted to mention it to you."

"They know better than to be snooping around," she said. "I'll tell them to stay away from up here."

"Would you? I'd appreciate it."

"No problemo. The kids adore me."

"They aren't old enough to know any better." He grinned.

She cracked a smile. "I'll get you for that one later. And I wanted to tell you—your dad's here. He wants to see you."

Andrew's smile turned into a frown.

Alone at the bar with his father, Andrew lifted the caps off two Heinekens. He slid one bottle across the counter, to his dad.

"Thanks," Dad said. "I can always rely on you to have the good stuff."

His father took a long swallow of beer. Andrew studied him. He hadn't seen his father since the night of the accident, over two weeks ago.

He hadn't talked to him, either, in spite of having left him at least three messages.

He wondered what was going on. He wanted to talk to his father about why he seemed to be avoiding him—without sounding as cynical as he was beginning to feel about their faltering relationship.

But his dad didn't look good. Although he was dressed as debonair as ever in a button-down shirt and slacks, dark rings circled his eyes. Insomnia?

The bandage had been removed from his father's head, but a bruise and the traces of the stitches were faintly visible.

Dad set down the Heineken and burped. "Ahh, that was good."

"So, how've you been doing?" Andrew asked.

"Been busy. When summer hits, everyone wants to buy a new house."

"That's good news." Andrew idly curled his fingers around his beer.

Dad yawned. "How've you been?"

"All right. Working on a book, waiting on an offer from my publisher on the one I just finished."

"Getting the big money for this one?"

"I hope so." Elbow propped against the counter, Andrew sipped his beer. It tasted more bitter than usual.

"I'm proud of you. It's great to see you living your dream, prospering."

"Thanks." Andrew placed the Heineken on a coaster that had the words, "Drew's Bar" written in cursive. The customized coasters had been a birthday gift from Carmen.

"Your mother looks good," Dad said. "I haven't seen her in, what, eleven years?"

"Something like that. She stays active. Teaching and gardening and whatnot."

Nodding, Dad raised the beer to his lips.

How long were they going to lob these lazy conversational balls back and forth? Andrew had hoped that his father would take the initiative to explain why he'd been avoiding him lately, but he seemed content to chat about superficial matters.

It was time to get to the point. Andrew disliked confrontations, especially with his father, but he couldn't shy away from this one.

Andrew pushed away from the bar. "I've called you three times in the past two weeks, Dad. You haven't called me back once. What's been going on?"

Dad almost slammed the bottle on the counter. Andrew flinched.

His father's jawline was rigid. "I've been busy, Andrew. I told you that business has been jumping. Hell, I came here, didn't I?"

"Okay." Andrew dragged his hand down his face. "Sorry, I just . . ."

"You just what?"

I just thought you were serious about building a relationship with me, Andrew wanted to say. *You call me out of the blue and ask me to play golf, and we start playing once or twice a week, spending quality time together, something we've never done in my entire life with any consistency—and then, for no apparent reason, you cut me off and act like you're too damn busy to be bothered. That's what, Dad.*

But Andrew didn't share his feelings. Because deep down, he had expected that this would happen, sooner or later. His father's fickleness was the dominant theme of their relationship. He was a fool for hoping that his dad had changed. There was no point in discussing something that he already understood so well.

"Never mind," Andrew said. "Anyway, I'm glad you came."

"Been having headaches," Dad said in a softer voice. He touched the bruise on his head. "Haven't been sleeping well."

"You look tired. Maybe you should see a doctor."

Scowling at the suggestion, Dad picked up the remote control on the bar. He turned on the small television mounted on the opposite wall and flipped through cable channels until he found ESPN. The station was broadcasting a replay of a recent PGA tournament.

Dad studied the screen intently, as if the secrets to his future were being revealed on the tube.

"We'll do something this week, Andrew," he said absently. "Maybe meet at the driving range one afternoon."

"What day?" Andrew asked. He heard the eagerness in his voice, and he didn't like what it implied—that he still hoped he and his father could have a meaningful bond. But, he couldn't help his feelings, as naive as they were.

"I'll call you." Dad's gaze was locked on the TV.

"Tuesday, Wednesday?" Andrew said. "I want to put it on my schedule—"

"I said, I'll call you." Dad glared at him. "Don't start hounding me. I'm not in the mood for that shit."

Andrew bit his tongue. Counted to ten under his breath.

Dad had returned his attention to the television. A bomb exploding under his chair likely wouldn't have broken his concentration.

"Listen," Andrew said. "I have to take out the trash

and do some other stuff. There's food upstairs. Let me know if you need anything."

Dad mumbled a reply.

Andrew left the bar. At the doorway, he looked behind, at his father.

Was it possible to love and despise someone at the same time? To want to be around him even as you wanted him to get out of your life?

As much as his father puzzled him, his feelings toward him confused him more.

Oblivious to him, his father sat on the stool, staring at the television and rubbing the bruise on his head.

Chapter 3

Later that evening, around a quarter past ten, everyone had left Andrew's house except for Carmen. She helped him finish cleaning, rearranging furniture, and putting things away.

"Whew, what a day," she said. Standing at the kitchen sink, she stretched her arms above her. She picked up her foil-wrapped plate of leftovers off the counter. "I'm going home, Drew. Need anything else?"

"Nope, we're all done. I'll walk outside with you."

The night was cool and clear, the sky resplendent with diamond-bright stars. A chorus of nocturnal creatures, most of them denizens of the lake behind the house, sang their timeless songs.

He lived in a quiet, upscale community of mostly families with young children and a sprinkling of single professionals. The rambling houses sat on expansive plots of landscaped lawn. Numerous cars lined the road, barbecue scented the air, and strains of music reached him, evidence of cookouts still going strong.

Carmen had parked her silver Lexus sedan in front

of the garage. She set her plate on the roof, turned to Andrew.

Her eyes were like precious gems. He suddenly didn't want her to leave.

"Thanks again for all the help," he said.

"The bill's on the way."

"Would dinner cover it? After today, I know I'm deep in the red."

"Dinner might put you in the black again. But it depends on where we go. Waffle House won't do much for you."

He laughed. "How about Red Lobster? Sometime this week?"

"You've got yourself a deal, partner."

"I'm thinking Thursday. You free then? Or are you going out with Veggie?"

Her lips twisted. "His name is Reggie, not Veggie. I've only told you that a hundred times."

"Sorry, since you told me that he's a vegetarian, I've been getting it all mixed up."

"Whatever, Drew. I think you're jealous."

"Why would I be jealous?"

"I don't know, why would you be?" One hand against her hip, she leaned against the car. Her gaze probed him.

He couldn't answer her question honestly. He *was* jealous. But admitting it would open not a mere can, but a whole barrel of worms.

"I'm not jealous," he said. "Really."

"So stop making fun of my man's name. Or else."

He raised his hands. "Okay, I'm sorry. I was kidding!"

"So was I. Fooled ya." Smiling, she spread her arms.

He hugged her. But he knew her well enough to understand that she probably was half serious about her accusation of jealousy. Humor usually hid a kernel of truth. He was relieved that she didn't press the issue.

Her body felt good against his. Warm and firm.

"You're always picking on me," he said in her ear.

" 'Cause you always fall for it, honey." She kissed his cheek.

"Hmmm. Your lips feel good. Nice and soft."

"That so?"

He moved in closer. She turned her head away.

"Ouch," he said.

"You know we can't go there, Drew." She slipped out of his arms. "Not again."

"So it was a one-time event, huh?"

"That's right," she said, with a tone of finality. She took her keys out of her purse.

He wished he were a contortionist. That way, he could kick himself in the ass. What was the matter with him?

It was his memory of the episode that had occurred between them a month ago. That was what was the matter with him. He could recall every pleasurable second of what had happened. In HDTV quality.

His body ached with frustrated desire. He was going to need a cold shower before he went to bed.

She touched his arm. "Anyway, Thursday's fine. Call me."

Hands in his pockets, he watched her drive away.

The night felt empty without her.

The vacant house felt as desolate to Andrew as the dark side of the moon.

Part of the reason why he enjoyed hosting parties was because the house was so big. With five bedrooms, four baths, a finished basement, and a full complement of rooms, the house offered over three thousand square feet of living space. He lived alone, and worked out of his home office. The solitude sometimes drove him a little batty. He loved to fill the place with laughter, life.

Upon selling film rights to his first three thriller novels for a hefty sum, he'd moved out of his town house, rented it to a tenant, and purchased the bigger house for its investment value. Truth be told, he'd also bought it in anticipation of some day having a family of his own to share it with. Some day.

Carmen's perfume clung to his shirt, stirred a pleasurable heat in his loins. He definitely was going to need that cold shower before hitting the sack.

He made a circuit around each floor, verifying, for the last time, that everything was in order. The mere displacement of a magazine on the cocktail table was enough to send him on a cleaning binge, but everything was in its proper place. He checked that the doors were locked, too.

When he ended his rounds, he was thirsty. He found a half full bottle of chardonnay in the refrigerator. He went to the dining room, opened the china cabinet, and removed a wineglass. He took the glass and the wine upstairs, to his office.

Although it was ten-thirty and he'd been up since six in the morning, he wasn't ready for bed. He had a new book in progress, and working on it for an hour or so would be a nice way to wind down.

The sight of his organized office soothed him. He settled into the leather desk chair, filled the glass with chardonnay, and powered up the laptop computer.

Sipping wine, he logged online to check his E-mail. A few readers had sent him messages: praise for his books, which was always appreciated; and questions about how to get published, which had grown tiresome.

He zipped off thank-you notes to the readers complimenting his work, and filed away the questions to be answered later.

His literary agent had E-mailed him, too. In response to a message he'd sent her about the status of his recent manuscript with his publisher, she wrote that she expected to hear word on an offer sometime that week.

He thought about the pending deal as he opened Microsoft Word. His first three novels were selling briskly, and his latest project was more ambitious than ever. He hoped for, as his dad had mentioned earlier, big money. But who knew for certain whether his publisher would offer anything at all? It was a crazy business that had broken as many dreams as it had fulfilled.

His work-in-progress was a young-adult novel, an artistic departure for him. If he ever published it, he planned to do so under his own name. Mark Justice, his pen name for the thrillers, was a cash machine. But the books were too violent for younger readers. During the past year, he'd volunteered for a not-for-profit literacy foundation whose mission was to encourage young black boys—a group at a frightfully high-risk of illiteracy and juvenile crime—to read. The dearth of books that appealed to those kids alarmed him. So he decided to start writing the stories himself. He was having so much fun with the book that he considered retiring Mark Justice permanently.

You don't have the balls to do that, a stern man's voice whispered in his mind—the inimitable Justice himself. *That'd be like flushing a winning lottery ticket down the toilet. Plus, you need me to save your ass when you get in tight spots.*

"Sure, I need you, all right," he said, under his breath. Pacified, Mark Justice fell silent.

Sometimes, being a writer felt like being a schizophrenic.

He was rereading the pages he had written yesterday when he heard a noise come from downstairs.

A clinking sound. Like glasses falling on a table.

He cocked his head, listened.

Clink-clink-clink.

He pushed away from the desk, left the office, and went to the head of the staircase. Below, darkness reigned. He'd turned off the lights when he came upstairs.

Clink-clink.

The sound came from one of the rooms off the hallway.

He flipped a switch. Light flooded the stairs and the family room below.

No one was down there. Of course. He'd just walked through the entire house.

Clink.

But where was that noise coming from?

Blood pounding in his ears, he hurried downstairs. He searched the first floor, turning on lights as he moved.

He found the answer in the dining room.

One of the china cabinet doors yawned open. The five wineglasses—he'd taken the sixth only a few minutes ago—lay on their sides, as if they'd been knocked over by a careless hand.

Scratching his head, he stared at the stemware.

"I don't get it," he said.

There was a darting motion in the periphery of his vision.

He whirled.

There was nothing there. There was only the hallway, the walls adorned with colorful pieces of art. He was alone.

He realized that he was holding his breath. He let out a lungful of air.

He was creeping himself out. Fatigue had a way of causing your mind to play tricks on you. Instead of writing, maybe he should go to bed.

But first, he faced the china cabinet.

Unknowingly, he must have unbalanced the glasses when he'd taken the wineglass. They'd tipped over on their own. Gravity was the only culprit. He must not have firmly closed the door, either.

He carefully set the stemware upright, and shut the door. He waited.

The glasses remained standing. The door remained shut.

But it was the second strange incident of the day—the first being the water running in the bathtub, which none of the children had confessed to doing.

His writer's imagination attempted to weave a connection, and failed.

There was no link, he decided. One of the kids had been playing in the tub, and lied to stay out of trouble; gravity tipped those glasses over; and it was his fault for not closing the cabinet door tightly.

Nevertheless, it bugged him. Something didn't feel right. But he couldn't articulate the feeling with words. That bothered him, too.

He returned upstairs. Repeatedly glancing over his shoulder.

Chapter 4

Half-past midnight, Raymond sat on a couch in the den of his house, watching ESPN and thinking about how much he feared going to sleep each night.

It wasn't sleeping itself that frightened him. Hell, nothing would please him more than a good night's sleep. He feared the uninvited guest that sleep invariably brought along these days: bad dreams.

The nightmares had begun to plague him after the accident.

Absently, he rubbed the bruise on his head.

SportsCenter—his favorite program in the world—was playing on ESPN, which happened to be his favorite station, too. Although they subscribed to nearly two hundred cable channels, when he sat down in front of the boob tube, he kept it locked on ESPN ninety-eight percent of the time. Watching seemingly infinite loops of the sports news stories of the day on SportsCenter was the perfect way to unwind, and it had become his preferred way to induce sleep. He'd sit there like a world champion couch potato, watching the program till his reddened eyes slid shut. When he'd awake—usually to find that he'd been drooling on his chest like a baby—it was all he could do to drag himself to bed and collapse on the mattress in a sound sleep.

Unfortunately, the watch-ESPN-till-you-drop method failed sometimes to protect him from the nightmares. It hadn't rescued him last night. He hoped tonight would be different.

He nurtured a desperate, almost childish hope that he'd find a way to permanently end the tormenting dreams. He'd never dealt with anything like this in his life. Until the accident, his life had been normal: work at his real estate business, church on Sunday, leisure activities with his wife, and lately, golf with Andrew. Sleep had been an afterthought, something he'd always taken for granted, and dreams were merely things to be forgotten upon awakening.

He hadn't told anyone about the nightmares. He liked to confront his problems on his own and brainstorm solutions until he found one that worked. That was how he did things—he hid out in his cave and discovered answers. His wife, though he loved her deeply, tended to worry far too much about matters. He didn't see the value in sharing his troubles with her and inviting the additional stress that her involvement would create. He was going to fix this problem. On his own.

Another circuit of the day's sports news kicked off. By then, he had memorized the stories and could've provided flawless voice-over commentary, but he honed in on the screen anyway, as if he were going to be tested on his knowledge of the events at a later date.

June poked her head in the doorway.

"SportsCenter again?" she said. "You planning to start a second career as a color analyst on ESPN?"

He only grunted, ignoring her jibe. She had her own programs she faithfully followed—hell, she'd used to watch *Soul Food* like those folks were members of her own family. The least she could do was let him watch what he wanted in peace. That was why he'd set up this big, flat-screen TV in the den, just for himself. She watched her shows in the family room or bedroom.

She came inside. She was dressed for bed in a flowing red nightgown and slippers. She'd also removed her makeup and wound a scarf around her head to protect her hair while she slept, but to him, she looked good with or without makeup, in pajamas or a silk evening dress. With her cocoa skin, bright smile, and honest, almond-shaped eyes, she had a wholesome beauty that had first attracted him to her fourteen years ago, and had kept him caught up in her web ever since.

People always commented on how they made a handsome couple, but he doubted that he was holding up his side of the equation. He still wore the clothes he'd worn to Andrew's cookout earlier that afternoon. He needed to shave. And the last time he'd glanced in the mirror, the bags under his eyes had gained weight.

June sat on the arm of the couch. She smelled of soap and apple-scented lotion. Being near her heightened his awareness of how disheveled he looked and felt.

She touched his shoulder. "You coming to bed?"

"I'm watching TV."

"That's what you said last night. And the night before."

"That's 'cause I like watching TV."

She watched him closely, her face lined with concern.

She wanted to know what was going on; the question was in her steady gaze. But he kept his mouth shut. He could deal with this problem on his own.

"Okay, Ray." She kissed him on the cheek. "Have a good night, baby."

She got up to leave. He stopped her with a touch on her arm.

"Wait," he said. "Will you sit with me for a minute?"

He was surprised at the words that came out of his mouth. But right then, he simply didn't want to be alone.

She settled next to him on the sofa. She kept quiet, watching the screen like she gave a damn about the latest baseball news and NASCAR races and PGA tournaments.

Lord, this woman knew him so well. She was waiting him out. She knew that when he was ready to talk about something that bothered him, he'd initiate the conversation.

But he was prepared to discuss only part of what disturbed him.

"I snapped on Andrew today," he said. "I was out of line. I haven't been calling him like I should, either."

Her eyes were kind. "You've been stressed with work lately. Putting in long hours."

"That's no excuse. We've only started getting to really know each other."

"And you've been doing great, Ray. I'm proud of you. You've turned things around with Andrew."

"But I've got a long way to go."

"You're making progress. You're bound to hit a few bumps in the road, honey. Don't be so hard on yourself."

She was right, of course, but that didn't make him feel any better. Three months ago, after a life-changing experience, he'd vowed that he was going to finally set things right with his son. Be the father that he was supposed to be and stop making excuses. He had been progressing in small, steady steps, closing the gap that years of neglect had created between them.

Then the accident had happened, and his life had been turned upside down—like his truck on that fateful night.

"I want to do everything right with him," he said. "I've got a lot of ground to cover with Andrew, a lot of making up for lost time. I can't avoid calling him, can't snap on him like I did today. Shit like that moves me two steps backward."

She massaged his arm. "What do you think you should do?"

"I promised him we'd go to the driving range this week. I need to call him to schedule a time, keep my word."

"I'm sure he'd appreciate that, Ray."

He turned to the TV, signaling that the discussion was over. But June stayed beside him.

He couldn't fool her. Not after twelve years of marriage. She probably suspected that something else troubled him.

He was tired of keeping it bottled in. He had to admit the truth: he didn't have a solution to his problem. Denying himself sleep was only a Band-Aid fix for a deeper issue.

He needed help. He just didn't know what kind of help.

"I haven't been sleeping well," he said finally. "Been having crazy dreams."

"Nightmares," she said. "I know."

"You do?"

"We *do* sleep in the same bed," she said. "I've seen you tossing and turning, and you normally sleep like a log. I've heard the shouting, too."

"Shouting?" He had no idea he was shouting, for Christ's sake.

"Yes. Shouting. It happened a couple of nights ago. I don't remember what you said. I was half asleep myself."

"Shit." Shame flushed his face.

"What're the nightmares about?" she asked.

"I never remember," he said, quickly; not too quickly, he hoped, to disguise that he was lying. He wasn't prepared to share the details of his dreams with anyone, not even her.

"Not a thing?" she said.

"I only remember that they're scary as hell, whatever they're about. Wake up shaking."

She grasped his hand. "I want you to see your doctor."

"C'mon, you know how much I hate going to that guy."

"I want you to get a physical, and ask for some sleeping pills. Will you please do that?"

He was too tired to resist her. Anyway, when it came to matters of health, she didn't play. She'd bug him until he broke down and did what she asked.

"I'll call and make an appointment," he said. He didn't tell her when he would call. He would delay the visit as long as possible.

She smiled, as if she were aware again of his thoughts. "No, you'll get too busy and put it off. I'll call tomorrow and schedule the appointment. We'll try to get you in early this week."

He had to laugh. "You know me too damned well."

"I also know what might help you get a sound sleep," she said in a low voice. She slid her leg across his lap. Her thighs were smooth and toned, the result of the aerobics and Pilates she did five times a week. He stroked her leg. In spite of his fatigue, he felt the stirrings of desire.

She rose, and offered her hand. "Come to bed with me, baby."

Hell, a romp in the sack would beat SportsCenter.

"You ain't gotta ask me twice," he said, and took her hand.

Raymond awoke sometime later that night. Screaming.

"Ray, are you okay?" June clutched his arm, as if he might be carried away by the darkness in the bedroom.

"Jesus Christ," he said. His scream echoed in his ears. Cold sweat saturated his body.

The nightmarish visions faded out of his thoughts, and his awareness of his surroundings returned. Above him, the ceiling fan spun. Moonlight pierced the windows, blended into the shadows in the room.

He gritted his teeth. He had a fierce headache. The pain throbbed in the area of his bruise.

"Ray?" she said.

"I'm okay." He patted her hand. "Gotta use the bathroom."

His legs trembled. Standing up required a determined effort.

He shuffled to the bathroom. He splashed cold water on his face, blotted his skin dry with a towel.

He gulped two extra-strength Tylenol. Pounding headaches invariably followed his nightmares.

He'd suffered stress-induced migraines before, usually related to matters at his job. But nothing like this.

Under the glare of the lights, he examined himself in the mirror.

It might have been his imagination, but the bruise

on his head looked darker, more swollen. As if a third eye bulged underneath the skin.

"What in the hell is happening to me?" he whispered to his reflection.

A frightened man, with no answers, stared back at him.

Chapter 5

The next morning, Andrew arose at six and kicked off his workday routine.

He had been writing full-time for about nine months, after working for several years as a programmer at an insurance company, and the habit of following a routine trailed him from corporate America and into his career as a wordsmith. Some of his friends, also full-time writers, rolled out of bed whenever they felt like it, did their writing at odd times of day or night, spent months doing nothing more taxing than watching television and reading, and buckled down to work only when deadlines pressed.

But Andrew was a machine, with a meticulous routine that he obeyed like a computer following a program.

From Monday through Friday—excluding holidays like yesterday—he awoke at six and exercised in his fitness room in the basement for one hour and fifty-five minutes. He put himself through a vigorous workout of cardiovascular training and weightlifting. A wall clock kept him on schedule; dance music on the stereo kept him pumped.

Afterward, he showered. He had a routine for showering, too: he soaped himself from head to toe and rinsed off seven times. It took twelve minutes. Slathering lotion on his body and applying antiperspirant—four minutes. Shaving—five minutes. Brushing his teeth—three minutes. Brushing his close-cropped hair took another three minutes.

Dressing was quick: jeans, a casual shirt, Nikes.

Downstairs in the breakfast nook, he read *The Atlanta Journal-Constitution* in his customary order: Sports section, Business, Living, and Metro, saving the front news segment for last. While reading the paper, he ate a breakfast of bran cereal and fruit and sipped a cup of coffee.

His friends loved to tease him about his obsessive-compulsive nature. But the mocking didn't bother him, because they were right. He cherished neatness, stability, schedules, to-do lists. Those things were his means, he supposed, of imposing a sense of order on the chaos that life could so easily become. He couldn't imagine being any other way.

He finished the paper, washed the dishes and put them away, and entered his office at precisely nine o'clock.

Ordinarily, he stayed in his office and wrote for three hours, took a lunch break, then worked for another three hours. On Tuesday mornings, however, he took his laptop to a local Starbucks and worked there for the first half of the day. He slid his computer into the leather carrying case and headed to the garage. He pressed the button to open the sectional door.

It was time to wash his car again. He drove a late model Mercedes-Benz convertible, with a silver body and a black top. He'd bought it as a gift to himself when he landed the movie deal. He liked to wash it once a week, a practice he'd started with his first car, a '74 Toyota that he'd bought for three hundred dollars during his junior year in high school—and which had been a piece of junk even back then.

The door finished opening, admitting a flood of sunshine.

A large cat waited outside.

He paused.

Resting on its hindquarters, the feline sat on a curve of grass that bordered the driveway. It faced him, quiet and motionless, like a stone lion guarding a house.

He had the odd idea that the cat had been sitting there for hours, waiting patiently for him to appear.

He approached within a few feet of the animal.

The cat observed him with a detached, almost clinical interest. Its eyes were an intense green; its shiny coat was bluish-gray.

The cat triggered a vague sense of recognition, but he couldn't nail down why.

The feline did not wear a collar. If the cat was someone's pet, there was no way to know for sure.

"What do you want?" He spread his empty hands. "No food for you, kitty."

The cat cocked its head. It was so strangely calm that if he'd offered it a saucer of milk, he wasn't sure it would be the least bit interested.

"Go on, get out of there. Shoo!"

The cat remained still.

He heard a rustling, on his right.

Another cat, a twin of the first one, stalked near the shrubbery on the fringes of his lawn.

What the hell?

A crumbling noise, on his left.

Yet another feline, identical to the first two, stepped through the bed of wood chips at the front of the house.

All of the cats, maintaining a code of silence, watched him closely.

Weird.

"They're just alley cats," he said to himself. Then, louder: "You guys better hope I don't buy a pit bull on the way home."

When he backed the car out of the garage, the cats had vanished.

The Starbucks on Cascade Road was smack-dab in the middle of a thriving section of southwest Atlanta. Stores, banks, restaurants, a library, mega-churches, and pricey subdivisions lined the busy thoroughfare. Populated largely by blacks, the area could have served as a snapshot of the "Black Mecca" that metro Atlanta was billed to be; the morning traffic teemed with BMWs, Lexuses, Cadillacs, luxury SUVs—and hoopties driven by broke college students climbing their way up the ladder of the American dream.

The Starbucks was one of Andrew's favorite writing spots. Located within fifteen minutes of his house, it was a café where you were as likely to run into a corporate executive in a Brooks Brothers suit as a dreadlocked poet scribbling verse on a notepad. It was a people watcher's dream land, and more than once, Andrew had created a fictional character to resemble a person whom he had seen passing through the shop's doors.

He ordered a café mocha, and set up his laptop at a corner table. The spot provided a modicum of privacy and allowed him to keep an eye on the customers streaming in and out.

Although he often listened to music on his iPod while writing, he never brought music there. The chatter, whirring machines, and general hustle and bustle, far from distracting him, provided a soundtrack, like white noise, that allowed him to become immersed in his work.

His cell phone rang. He recognized Eric's home number on the Caller ID display.

"What's up, bro?" Eric said. "Wait, lemme guess: you're at Starbucks, sitting in the corner with your laptop."

Andrew laughed.

"Knew I was right," Eric said. "You're as predictable as Democrats raising taxes."

"Watch it, I'm a Democrat."

"So am I. That doesn't change the truth."

"Why aren't you at work? Do they pay you six figures to sit at home and bug your friends?"

"Took the day off. I got it like that. Wanna stop by later and play ball?"

A young black woman entered the coffee shop. About to answer Eric, Andrew found himself unable to speak. He did something he hardly ever did: he gaped at the woman.

She was absolutely gorgeous.

Wearing a yellow sundress and sandals, the woman strolled to the counter. The dress, swishing with her confident steps, outlined an exquisitely proportioned body. All of the men in the café, gawking at her, seemed to be holding their breaths, as if breathing too hard would blow her through the doors and out of their lives.

The woman wore a gentle smile, clearly accustomed

to making men pause whenever she entered the vicinity.

"Still there, bro?" Eric said.

Andrew swallowed. "Man, you won't believe this woman who walked in here."

"Run it down for me." Excitement crackled in Eric's voice. He was deeply committed to his wife, Andrew knew, but he loved to savor the single life vicariously through Andrew. "What's she look like?"

Andrew watched the woman place her order. She moved her weight from one foot to the other, and her shapely hips shifted, teasingly.

"Not a ten," he said.

"What?"

"Off the damn charts."

"Get out," Eric said. Then quickly: "You for real?"

"Most def. You know I don't say that too often."

"Married?"

The woman adjusted the strap of her purse. He spotted her ring finger.

"No ring," he said.

"All right. You know what that means, player."

"What're you talking about?"

"You know what, fool! Time to spit some game."

The woman received her drink, glided to the side counter. She added sugar and milk to her beverage, stirred it. She moved with fluid grace, like a dancer.

"I don't know about that," Andrew said. "I came here to write, not mack women."

"Man, if you don't talk to that girl, I'ma come through this phone and drag you to her myself."

The woman threaded between tables, found a vacant one in the corner opposite Andrew. Judging from the elegant way she carried herself, she might have been sitting down for a dinner at Spago's.

"What about Carmen?" Andrew said.

"What about her? You were the one who said Carmen might not be the one. You're only friends. Remember?"

"Yeah, but—"

"But what?"

The woman daintily sipped her coffee. She reached inside her purse and withdrew a paperback book.

Andrew could not believe his luck.

"Gotta go," he said. "I'm gonna talk to her. Later."

While Eric shouted player strategies at him, Andrew clicked off the phone.

Sweat oiled his palms. He rubbed them dry on the lap of his jeans.

Although every man in the café continued to admire the woman, none of them approached her. He understood why. She was so beautiful that the idea of stepping to her was intimidating. It was easy to imagine that she heard and rejected dozens of proposals every day. Few men possessed the nerve to possibly add their names to the Shot Down list.

He rarely initiated conversation with women he saw in public places. He'd been introduced to most of his past girlfriends by mutual friends, or had met them at work, church, or house parties. He envied men who could suavely approach any women who caught their eye. He just didn't have the nerve to hang himself on the line like that.

But this time, he had an edge: a legitimate reason to talk to her.

He drew in a deep breath. He sucked on a Certs for a minute.

Then he rose, and walked in her direction.

* * *

A few feet away from her, Andrew paused.

This close, she was even more breathtaking. Dark hair flowed to her slim shoulders in luxuriant waves. Her smooth, reddish-brown skin shone with a healthy glow.

Reading, she didn't sense his approach.

"Excuse me, miss?"

She looked up. She had large, striking hazel eyes. Sculpted cheekbones. Full lips.

He guessed that she was biracial. Probably had African American and Caucasian blended in her genes. He wasn't one of those brothers who dated only light-skinned women. He'd dated sisters from all ranges of the color spectrum. To him, beauty was beauty.

And this woman possessed it, in abundance.

Her gaze met his. But caution framed her fine features.

"Yes?" she asked, in a flat, heard-it-all-before tone. But he caught the hint of a musical voice, with a soft Southern accent.

"Is that a good book?" he said.

She measured him with a cool gaze. As if she were trying to figure out where this line was going, and if she cared to listen.

Feeling his opportunity slipping away, he pressed on: "If it's not a good book, I'd feel bad."

Curiosity flickered in her eyes.

"Why would you feel bad?" she asked.

Time for the money shot.

"Because I wrote it."

She blinked. "Pardon me?"

"Check out the inside of the back cover."

She flipped to the back. It was his second novel, *One Night,* which had been originally published in hard-cover, and had been issued in paperback four months ago. He'd supplied his publisher with a recent picture for the mass-market edition.

She examined the photo, looked at him.

She smiled, hesitantly. "You're Mark Justice?"

"I don't normally go around putting myself out like this," he said. "But when I see a beautiful woman reading my work . . . well, I had to stop by to introduce myself."

She favored him with a smile that displayed a flawless set of pearly whites.

He wanted to pump his fist in the air, like a football player who'd scored a game-winning touchdown.

"Mark Justice is my pen name," he said. "My real name is Andrew Wilson. And you are?"

"Lalamika," she said. "Most people simply call me Mika."

"It's nice to meet you, Mika." He offered his hand, and she shook it. She had soft skin, slender fingers, manicured nails. The sensation of her skin against his made him tingle. He gave her hand a firm squeeze before he released it.

"Mind if I have a seat?" he asked.

"Not at all."

He slid into the chair across from her. Her perfume reached him—a jasmine scent—and filled his head with sweet fantasies.

She tapped the book. "To answer your first question, this is an excellent novel. I'm thoroughly enjoying it."

"Thanks. Want me to sign it for you?"

"Would you, please? I'd love that."

He unclipped the pen from his shirt pocket and inscribed, *To Mika, the loveliest woman ever to grace a Starbucks,* on the title page. He signed "Mark Justice" with a bold, looping signature.

"Thanks so much. I'll treasure this."

Her eyes, radiating warmth and interest, took him in. Being the focus of her attention gave him a temporary brain freeze. She was so beautiful that he could scarcely believe he was sitting in front of her.

Get it together, man, or she's gonna boot you from the table. Thankfully, she spoke first.

"I've never met a published author before," she said.

His mind kicked back into gear. "Not surprising. Writers are generally an introverted bunch. We spend most of our time locked alone in cubbyholes, scribbling away."

"What brought you out of solitude this morning?"

"A little birdie told me that if I did go out, I'd meet a lovely woman who enjoys my books."

Her laughter was like celestial music.

"Actually, I come here every Tuesday morning to write," he said. "What brings you here?"

"I stopped in for a coffee break." She raised her cup to her lips, sipped. "Do you find it distracting to write in public? It can get rather noisy in here."

"Doesn't bother me. I need the social element sometimes, breaks up the monotony of sitting at home."

"Hmm." She ran her fingers through her hair. He wanted to lose his hands in those silky black strands. "Do you write for a living, Andrew?"

"Been doing it for nine months now. I've been blessed to be able to make a good living doing what I love."

"It's certainly a blessing. But I wonder, why do you use a pseudonym? Do you have something to hide?" Mirth gleamed in her eyes.

"You want the truth?"

"Sure."

"I don't know where the pen name came from," he said. "Really. It just popped into my head one day."

"Is that so?"

"I was trying to write stuff under my real name, for a while, and not getting anywhere—and then this idea for a thriller came to me, along with the idea that I should write it under the name of Mark Justice. That book turned out to be *The Comeback*, the first novel I published."

"Fascinating." She smiled. "I love that name Mark Justice. It makes me think of strength, bravery."

He grinned. "He's my heroic alter ego."

He wanted to transition the conversation to more personal matters. She didn't wear a wedding band, but that didn't mean she was single. And if she was single, she still could be involved in a serious relationship.

"So, Mika. What do you do when you aren't making Starbucks runs?"

"Whatever strikes my fancy. I have a broad variety of interests. Music, art, literature, films. I love to dance."

"You move like a dancer, I noticed. Graceful."

"I took lessons as a child. I suppose they've stayed with me over the years."

"That's cool. I like to dance, too."

"I love to salsa. Can you do that?"

"Matter of fact, I can. I learned a couple of years ago."

"You're an interesting man." She leaned closer. "So, can I ask you a question, Andrew?"

"Shoot."

"Why do men avoid asking the questions that are obviously on their minds?"

He sat back. She'd caught him off guard.

She laughed.

"Of course, you'd like to know if we have common interests," she said. "It's a perfectly appropriate question. But there are other topics that need to be discussed first."

"Such as?"

"Are you married?" she asked.

"You get right down to it," he said. He tried to avoid showing how surprised he was that she was interested in him. Only in his wildest fantasies had he ever imagined that he'd have a shot with a woman like her. But here she was, coming on to *him*. He half-mused that someone had hired her to play an elaborate joke on him, like in that crazy MTV show, *Punk'd*.

"I've been accused of being direct more than once," she said, in an utterly serious tone. "I stand guilty as charged."

"Well, see this?" He waved his unadorned ring finger.

"Don't take this as an insult, but that doesn't mean anything. Far too many married men walk around without wearing their rings."

"I'm flying solo," he said. "You?"

Smiling, she wriggled her bare ring finger.

"That doesn't mean anything," he said. They laughed.

"No, I'm not married," she said.

"Boyfriend?"

She shrugged. "Nothing serious at the moment. How about you?"

"Same story." He thought of Carmen, then switched off the thought. Carmen was just a friend.

"Are you gay? Are you a supposedly straight man on the down low, as they call it?" She smiled. "Don't laugh, a woman has to ask these questions these days."

"I'm strictly for the ladies. You?"

"Now that's a funny question. But I suppose it goes both ways."

"Do you?" He grinned.

"Absolutely not."

"Any kids?"

"None. Do you have any children, Andrew?"

"I've got three, and a fourth on the way."

Her smile froze.

"Relax, I was talking about my novels. They're like children to me."

She laughed lightly. "Funny man. You got me with that one."

She sipped her coffee, her gaze never leaving his face.

Stunning looks, sophisticated, down-to-earth, and intelligent. He wanted to pinch himself. It was too good to be true.

She tilted her head. "I see the gears in your mind turning. What are you thinking about?"

"I'm thinking I'd like to take you to dinner."

"We might be able to arrange that."

"Do you live in the area?"

"I'm staying in Buckhead. Near Lenox."

"That's a nice side of town," he said. "I'm about fifteen minutes south of here. We could meet for dinner somewhere in Buckhead, or Midtown. There're a lot of good restaurants in both of those areas."

"I haven't agreed to dinner yet." She crossed her slender arms on the table. "May I be direct, again?"

"Go ahead."

"I place a premium on my time, Andrew. I don't do the casual dating thing that most people do these days. It's a waste of time and energy. I know what I want, and I don't accept anything less—from the very beginning. Can you handle that?"

Could he handle it? Was she serious? She had him ready to throw his little black book in the trash.

But he stroked his chin, played it cool, as if he had to give her words some consideration.

"I can respect you having high standards," he said. "I'll make it worth your time, promise."

"How can you be so confident about that?"

"I don't play games. If I'm interested in a woman, she gets my undivided attention. I'm thirty-one, not twenty-one. I've already sowed my wild oats."

"Good answer." She leaned back in her seat, smiled. "I'll remember that you said that, too."

"Why don't you give me your number? I'll call you and we can set a time for dinner."

"I don't give out my number—not even to handsome, successful novelists." She softened her words with a smile. "Give me yours, please."

He was disappointed, but he wasn't going to let it show. He took his business card out of his wallet. "My cell number is on here. That's always the best way to reach me."

She tucked away the card in her purse, glanced at her watch. "I've got to run. It was a pleasure meeting you, Andrew."

"The pleasure was all mine."

"We'll talk again soon."

"I sure hope so."

"Count on it. *Ciao.*"

He watched her leave. When she pushed through the exit doors, the men in the café released a group sigh—Andrew included.

A young guy with a puffy Afro had been watching Andrew and Mika talk. He flashed a gap-toothed smile. "Lucky-ass Negro."

Andrew laughed and pointed at the man's Frappuccino. "Stop sipping on that hater-ade, brother."

He returned to his table. He had stopped writing in the middle of a paragraph, normally an easy place to resume his flow, but words eluded him. He couldn't get Mika out of his head.

He hoped that she called him soon.

Chapter 6

When Andrew returned home, he heard noises coming from the basement.

It was half-past noon. He hadn't managed to do much writing at Starbucks. Thoughts of Mika made it difficult to focus on his story.

He'd been fighting to keep his attention away from his cell phone. Wondering when she was going to call. Or if she was going to call. She might've only been playing a game with him, flirting. When the cell phones of people around him chirped, his heart leaped.

She'll call me, he told himself. *Give her some time.*

But it hadn't rung once.

Trying to get her out of his mind, he went home. He aimed to work for a couple of hours, and then stop by Eric's place to play basketball.

But when he walked inside, the laptop case dangling from his shoulder, the sounds coming from the basement immediately set his nerves on edge.

He laid the laptop against the hallway wall. He moved toward the door that led downstairs, opened it.

Deep shadows blanketed the staircase, layered the basement floor.

But it sounded as if someone were playing a video game down there, just out of sight. A war game. Probably *Ghost Recon,* which was in his game collection.

"That you, Eric?" he said. Eric and his mother were the only people who had keys to his house, and his mom sure wouldn't be playing games.

There was no response. He heard only simulated machine-gun fire and grenade explosions.

"Hey, are you there, man?"

Electronic blasts answered him.

Eric would never enter his home without first asking him. They were like brothers, but they respected each other's space. It couldn't be him.

What kind of burglar would break in to play games? There were no signs of disarray or forced entry. It didn't make sense that someone would have broken into his house to do this.

What would Mark Justice do in this situation?

Justice spit out a terse reply: *Arm yourself with something, and check it out.*

He owned a gun. A Smith & Wesson .38. He'd originally purchased the revolver while doing research for a novel. If you wrote about characters that packed heat, it helped if you knew your way around firearms yourself. He'd kept the handgun for security purposes.

But the gun was in his bedroom, in a locked storage case in the nightstand drawer.

If someone truly *had* invaded his home, would he make it as far as upstairs without getting into a scuffle?

He couldn't be sure. So he decided on an alternative.

He went to the garage and opened the trunk of his car, where he kept his golf bag. He slid out a Titleist

three iron. A whack with one of those would knock anyone out cold.

Club in hand, he returned inside and paused at the
basement door.

"For the last time, who's down there?"

Another explosion, followed by a computerized wail
of human agony.

He tightened his grip on the club.

He plunged downstairs.

The PlayStation console sat on the floor. A game,
Ghost Recon, was in progress on the projection-screen
TV. In the midst of a battle, the soldier on the screen
waited for direction from a human player.

But the player, whoever it was, had left.

The basement was empty.

Andrew searched the basement. In addition to the
entertainment area, the bar, fitness room, laundry room,
storage space, and a bathroom were located down there.
All of them were vacant.

The glass double doors that led to the patio were
locked, the blinds drawn against the afternoon sun. He
parted the blinds. He saw only the green swell of the
backyard, elms and pines trembling in a breeze, and a
flash of the lake beyond his property. No one running
to hide.

He stared at the PlayStation.

"I'm going crazy," he said.

Had he turned on the game that morning, and forgotten about it? Or neglected to switch it off last night,
after the cookout? A bunch of kids had been playing it
yesterday.

But he had made numerous rounds of the house last
night, putting everything in order. He'd worked out in
the fitness room that morning, too. How could he have

missed something so obvious? How could he not have at least *heard* the game before now? The volume was so high it would have gained his attention.

Before he came into the basement, the sounds he'd heard indicated that someone had been playing the game, only a minute ago.

He tapped his fingers against his leg.

A shriek burst from the stereo speakers.

He dropped the golf club. It clattered against the floor.

On the screen, a soldier had been killed. The game was programmed in one-player mode, versus the computer.

He picked up the club.

"You're jumpy as an old woman," he said. "Calm down."

He switched off the PlayStation. He unplugged the controllers, wound the cords around the console, and tucked the unit on a table in the corner, where he kept party games like Scrabble and Taboo.

He remembered, however, doing this same thing last night. He was *sure* he had.

He went upstairs. He began to verify that the doors and windows were locked. It didn't make sense that someone could have slipped inside, as he'd activated the alarm system when he left that morning; it made even less sense that an intruder would've been playing a video game. But he had to regain his peace of mind.

As he approached a window in the living room, he detected stealthy movement outside. He snatched away the curtain.

It was one of those gray cats. It perched atop the flower bed. Staring at him.

He met the feline's steady gaze. It didn't look away, as most domesticated animals did. It watched him as if they occupied equal footing on the food chain.

Strange, dumb alley cats. He refused to feed them. Sooner or later, they would leave and hassle someone else.

He dropped the curtain, tried to lift the window. It was locked. As it should be.

He confirmed that the rest of the house was secure, too.

He would have to accept that he had forgotten to turn off the video game. It was the only logical explanation.

But this was the third weird thing that had happened since yesterday. There had been the water running in the bathtub. Then the knocked over wineglasses in the china cabinet. Now this.

Was there a connection? Or were all of them unrelated incidents that could be rationally explained?

He didn't know. And it bothered him. A lot.

Chapter 7

Not quite ready to blame the game incident on a faulty memory, Andrew decided to talk to a couple of people.

First, he called his mother. There was a possibility that she'd visited his house that morning for some reason and brought his nephew, who loved to play video games at Andrew's place. But Mom said that she hadn't been there. After promising to stop by later that afternoon to cut her grass, he ended the call.

Eric was next. Andrew and Eric lived in the same subdivision. When they were kids, their families had lived next door to each other, and they had promised that, as adults, they would one day live in the same neighborhood. Eric lived a couple of blocks down the street, in a large, two-story brick house. A white Cadillac Escalade was parked in the driveway. The big yard was as neatly trimmed as the greens on a championship golf course.

For two nappy-headed boys raised by single mothers, they'd done all right for themselves.

Eric's wife, Pam, answered the door.

"Hey, Drew," she said. She beckoned him inside.

He kissed her on the cheek. "Both of you took the day off, huh? What's the world coming to?"

"When you're six months pregnant with twins, your body needs a lot of rest." Pam patted her bulging belly. She grinned.

"As happy as you look, maybe I need to get pregnant with twins, too."

"Hush. You sound like Eric."

"Where's the dad-to-be?"

"Air Jordan's on the court, says he's gearing up for a comeback."

"Lemme go out there and shame him into permanent retirement."

He found Eric in the backyard, on the blacktopped half-court that Eric had added last summer. Dressed in a red tank top, shorts, Adidas, and a layer of sweat, Eric performed post-up moves as if he were practicing for the NBA Finals. The boom box at courtside banged out a Public Enemy song, "Rebel Without A Pause."

"About time you showed up." Eric tossed the ball to Andrew. Andrew caught it and fired a jumper from fifteen feet. The shot clanged off the rim.

"A few more bricks like that and you can build me a new crib, bro." Eric mopped his face with a towel. "Anyway, what you been up to?"

"I think I'm going crazy," Andrew said. He started to tell Eric what had happened.

Eric turned down the volume of the music, and listened, without interrupting. Although he was the biggest jokester Andrew knew, he had a serious side; the all-business aspect of him had enabled him to make partner at the law firm at which he worked, in only seven years.

"First of all, I didn't stop by your place," Eric said. "I wouldn't invite myself in without clearing it with you."

"I know. So I must've forgotten to turn off the game. And that's what bothers me."

"It's no biggie," Eric said. Grabbing the ball again, he pivoted, and threw a skyhook from the free throw line. The shot swished. "You forgot to turn off the game last night or this morning. Happens to all of us sometimes. According to the wife, I forget stuff like that far too often."

Andrew got the ball. He took a shot from five feet out. That one misfired, too.

"But you know me, Eric. I don't forget things like that. Something about this doesn't feel right to me. Call it a gut feeling."

Eric snagged the ball, dribbled around the perimeter. Andrew guarded him halfheartedly.

"So who're you going to blame it on, if not your memory?" Eric asked. He whipped the ball between his legs. "The PlayStation gremlins?"

"Okay, point made."

"You forgot an itty bitty thing. I promise not to tell anyone. I wouldn't want people to realize that you, in fact, do *not* walk on water."

"And the water running in the bathtub?"

"Some rambunctious kid."

"And the wineglasses?"

"Simple gravity. Or maybe an earthquake rolled through your crib while you were writing."

"Eric, this is serious."

"So am I. Look, you're my boy and all, but sometimes you let minor shit get to you. Now if you wake up one morning butt-naked in the woods and you don't know how you got there—then we've got a problem. Until then, chill out."

Eric launched a jumper. Andrew swatted at it, missed by a mile. The ball knocked against the backboard and into the hoop.

"I guess you're right," Andrew said. "I just had to hear someone else say it. I'll let it go."

Andrew fired a shot from three-point range. It hit nothing but net.

"Nice one," Eric said. "Hey, what happened with that girl you were gonna mack at Starbucks?"

"Oh, yeah, I meant to tell you about it." He gave Eric the highlights of his chat with Mika.

"Hmm," Eric said. "Kinda interesting that she happened to have one of your books with her."

"It was a helluva coincidence. But it was too good of an opportunity to pass up."

"Maybe she was counting on that," Eric said. He stopped bouncing the ball.

"What do you mean?"

"You go to that Starbucks every Tuesday morning, right? Like clockwork."

"So? They have lots of regulars there."

"So not all of the regulars are famous authors, bro."

"I'm not famous, don't start with that."

"Oh, you're not? Let's see, *Essence* did a profile on you, you've been on Tom Joyner, your books are in every store in the country, and an actor named Will No-Last-Name-Necessary snapped up movie rights to your first three books for close to seven figs." He spread his arms. "Ladies and gentlemen of the jury, the evidence is overwhelming. Mark Justice, aka Andrew Wilson, is famous, dammit."

Andrew sat on the ground, next to the boom box. He twisted grass around his fingers.

"Maybe I'm more well known than the average brother, but I'm not gonna stop traffic," Andrew said. "Few writers are known by face. If John Grisham walked into a room, hardly anyone would know who he was."

"We aren't talking about Grisham, we're talking about you."

"What does me being a little famous have to do with Mika? You think she knew I was gonna be at Starbucks and planned to be there?"

"You've gotta consider it." Eric placed the ball on the pavement, sat on it facing Andrew. "Some of these sistas out here are so hard-up for a man, they'll scheme like the CIA to catch a good brother."

"But she didn't so much as look at me when she came in there. Acted like she was gonna diss me until I said I wrote the book."

"You used the right word, 'acted,'" Eric said. "If she thinks she's got a shot to get with you, she'll do a good enough acting job to win a damn Oscar."

"Why are you tripping? You haven't even met her. She's cool, seriously."

"I'm only looking out for you, bro. There are some serious gold diggers out there. I deal with it on the regular, and I'm married."

"All right, I can respect you looking out," Andrew said. "I'll be careful."

"Wouldn't have to be that careful about Carmen."

"There you go."

"Had to put in a good word for my girl."

"Well, who knows if Mika will call me?" Andrew said. He rose, dusted off the seat of his jeans.

Eric got up, too. "She'll call. I'll bet you a dollar that she does."

"You're on." They shook on it.

"Ready to ball?" Eric said. "Play to eleven?"

"Let's go."

Eric moved to the top of the key. "Before I forget, the wife and I are gonna have a little get together at the lake crib this weekend. You're invited. Tell Carmen, too."

"Sure thing." Eric owned a second house, on Lake

Sinclair. It was the bomb spot for parties or getting away from it all for a weekend.

Eric bounced the ball toward him. "Check."

After Andrew tapped the ball back to Eric, his cell phone chirped. He unsnapped it from the holster he wore on his waist.

The Caller ID display read, "Private Number."

"Andrew?" a soft woman's voice said. "This is Mika."

He couldn't believe she had called. Butterflies fluttered in his gut.

"Hey, Mika. It's good to hear from you. How're you doing?"

Eric grinned. "Gimme my dollar."

Chapter 8

Phone pressed to his ear, Andrew walked to the deck on the other side of the yard. He sat on a patio chair.

"Have I called at an inconvenient time?" Mika asked.

"Nope, I'm just at my boy's house. I can chat."

"Good." He heard her shifting, getting more comfortable. Wherever she had called him from, it was as silent as a soundproof room. "Did you have a productive morning?"

"Honestly, I didn't. Wanna know why?"

"Why?"

" 'Cause I kept thinking about how much I wanted to talk to you again."

"Aww, you're sweet. I hadn't planned to phone you so soon . . . but I was eager to talk to you again, too."

"You were? I'm glad this isn't a one-way street thing, then."

She giggled. It was a cute sound, and he wished he were near her, to see her smiling face.

"Have you thought about dinner?" he asked.

"I've been considering your offer, yes."

"And have you reached a decision?"

"I haven't, Andrew. I'd like for us to talk more at length before we agree to meet on such a personal level."

She wanted to take it slow. He could respect that; actually, it impressed him. She wasn't some opportunistic woman trying to squeeze a quick, free meal out of him.

"What do you want to talk about?" he asked.

"You. Tell me about you."

"What do you want to know about me?"

"Why haven't you married? You're a handsome man, quite successful in your career, and appear to be of good character. I would think that a young lady would have snapped you up by now. Am I missing something?"

"No mystery to it. I haven't found the right woman to snap me up." He propped his feet on a chair. "Nothing is crazier than the dating world these days. It's rough out there."

"I can vouch for that. What constitutes the right woman for you, Andrew?"

"It's not that complicated. Honesty, intelligence. Spiritual awareness. A sense of humor, a positive outlook on life. Ambition."

"Is beauty on your list?"

"It's on my list, but not at the top. Of course, I want to be attracted to the woman, but I've learned the hard way that inner qualities are most important. A good heart lasts long after the looks fade."

"Quite true," she said.

"What're you looking for in a man?"

She was quiet. He heard her breathing softly; it was the only noise on her end.

"Soul mate eyes," she said.

"Soul mate eyes?"

"Are you familiar with the saying that the eyes are the windows to the soul?"

"Yeah."

"When I look into the eyes of that one man, my soul mate, I will know that he and I are destined to be together."

"How about sharing common interests?" he asked. "Someone trustworthy, who treats you well—"

"My soul mate will have all of the qualities that I desire," she said crisply. "He'll possess traits that I don't even realize that I want in a man until I learn about them. He'll be perfect for me, Andrew, in every sense."

"That's deep," he said.

"I will be perfect for him, too," she said. "Everything he's ever dreamed of finding in a woman, and so much more."

She spoke with unquestionable conviction. He didn't share her confidence in soul mates—suffering a couple of broken hearts with women whom he'd thought were his soul mates had soured him on the idea. But Mika had made it clear that, for her, there would be no argument on the matter.

"Since you feel that way," he said, "then it should be easy to figure out if a guy is the one."

"How so?"

"Just look into his eyes and you know from the start if he's your soul mate."

She laughed lightly. "If only it were so simple."

"Why isn't it?"

"No one reveals his soul immediately. If the eyes are the windows to the soul, well, in most cases, we cover those windows with thick curtains. The windows are unveiled only in a moment of truth."

"A moment of truth?"

"An instant of vulnerability, of profound honesty . . . or intense passion."

"Hmm."

Had they experienced what she would qualify as a moment of truth? The idea intrigued him.

"Do you think I'm strange for expressing these views?" she asked.

"Your philosophical way of looking at things is refreshing, actually. Different."

"I'm a different kind of woman. Unlike any you've ever met."

"I'm starting to learn that."

"And in case you're wondering, we've not yet had our moment of truth," she said.

"Funny, I was just thinking about that."

"The moment will come, Andrew. In the meantime, I'd like to know more about you. May I ask another question?"

"Go ahead."

And so it went, for over an hour. She quizzed him about his past relationships, family life, friendships. She asked his opinions on a range of topics: politics, film, music, history, society. She wanted to know about his plans for his life, where he was headed and how he was going to get there.

It was the most extensive "pre-date" discussion he'd ever had with anyone. He felt as if he had been subjected to what amounted to a relationship interview.

The only downside was that she asked most of the questions; he didn't get to learn much of anything about her. Although he gained insight into her inquisitive mind by the nature of the questions that she asked, he decided that if they went on a date, he would take a more active role in the conversation. For now, he'd let her discover whatever she needed to know about him that would help her reach a decision about meeting him for dinner.

On the other side of the yard, Eric turned off the music and walked toward the house. He pointed at Andrew with mock anger as he went inside. Andrew had come over there to play ball and wound up spending most of his time on the phone.

Well, Eric would get over it. Twenty-plus years of friendship allowed a slip every now and then.

There was, at last, a lull in the conversation with Mika.

"Now, I have a question for you," Andrew said.

"Certainly."

"I don't mind your questions. But if you judge whether a man is your soul mate by the look in his eyes at a moment of truth, as you put it, why go through the trouble of covering all this ground ahead of time?"

"Simple. Engrossing conversation helps us move toward that moment of truth. You only completely reveal your soul to someone with whom you've shared much of yourself."

"I see."

"You'll get your opportunity to ask questions of me, too," she said. "When we meet for dinner."

He sat up. "You want to do dinner?"

"I'd love to have dinner with you, Andrew."

Yes, yes, yes. He felt as if he had aced a college exam.

"When are you free?" he asked.

"I'm available tonight. Are you?"

Was he available? He would have canceled a pitch meeting with Steven Spielberg to see her tonight.

"Does seven work for you?" he said.

"Seven works. Do you like Houston's, on Peachtree?"

"Definitely. That's one of my favorite restaurants."

"Is that so? Then it's settled. I'll be there at seven o'clock. Please don't be late."

"Never," he said.

In fact, he planned to get there early.

Chapter 9

Once a week, Andrew visited his mother's house to cut the grass. His mom lived in East Point, a suburb southwest of Atlanta, in a peaceful, hilly neighborhood of ranch-style houses, leafy trees, and sloping lawns.

His mother was an elementary schoolteacher. School had recently ended for the summer; it was no surprise that when Andrew pulled into the driveway shortly past three o'clock in the afternoon, he found her outdoors pursuing her favorite hobby: gardening.

"Hey, Drew." She rose from the bed of flowers near the house, set down the shears and opened her arms for a hug.

"Hey, Mom. Your lawn boy is here."

In her early fifties, Lynn Wilson was petite and short, standing about five feet tall. But in Andrew's eyes, she was a giant. She had taught him everything worth knowing about being a good man. Unlike some of his childhood friends who were babied by their moms and had grown into man-children unable to sustain themselves, she'd cut him no slack. "I'm not letting a child of mine go out into the world, shuckin' and jivin' and half-steppin'," she'd always say to him. "I'm going to teach you how to be a responsible black man, whether you like it or not. You'll appreciate it later."

Growing up, he sure hadn't appreciated it at all. He was her eldest child and only son, and it seemed that she was so much harder on him than she was on his younger sister. His list of household chores was endless; homework had to be completed to her satisfaction before he watched TV; she restricted him from hanging out with the cool neighborhood kids who she'd determined were "bad seeds"; and on it went, ad nauseum. He was convinced that she was the strictest woman on earth and had been appointed as his mom for the sole purpose of making his life miserable.

But as he grew older, he began to appreciate the lessons she'd taught him, just like she'd said he would. Many of his friends from the neighborhood—those "cool" kids she'd limited his involvement with—were either dead, in prison, or passing their days on street corners, doing nothing productive.

It frightened him to think of where he might have wound up, if he hadn't had her.

"You didn't have to come over to do the grass," she said. "I know you're busy. I can get someone else to do it."

She said the same thing to him every week. He always gave her the same response.

"I don't mind, Mom. It's my responsibility."

"I don't know what I'll do with you, boy." She smiled.

He truly believed that the yard work was his job. Although his mother had never married his father, she had been married years ago to his sister's dad, a decent guy—but after only two years of marriage, he died in a car wreck. Widowed, Mom had never remarried, though she dated from time to time. In his early teens, Andrew had assumed the "man work" of the household—keeping the yard in shape, fixing things around the house, and so on—and had been doing it ever since. During periods when promotional touring for his books kept him out of town for weeks on end, he paid a lawn service to maintain the yard. The last thing he wanted to see was his mom trimming grass. It was unthinkable.

He walked into the garage, where the Toro mower and gas can stood in the corner.

"I enjoyed the cookout yesterday," Mom said. "Hadn't seen your father in ages. He didn't look too good."

"I don't know what's been going on with him. Yesterday was the first time I'd talked to him in a couple weeks."

"He's back to his old tricks, sounds like. A leopard can't change its spots."

He shrugged. He picked up the can of gasoline and rolled the mower outside, onto the driveway.

No one knew the sad story of Andrew and his father better than his mother. She'd been there for all of the broken promises, missed birthdays, unreturned phone calls, and unexplained absences that sometimes had stretched on for years. When Andrew had told her about this so-called "fresh start" with his father, Mom had reacted, as expected, with doubt. She'd warned him to be careful with his heart.

"The ball's in his court," he said. "He said he wants to play golf sometime this week. He promised to call me."

"Promised, did he? That sounds familiar. Don't be surprised if you don't hear from him until next year."

"It doesn't matter. Life'll go on, with or without him."

She made a disgusted sound in her throat. "Without him might be best for you. As far as I'm concerned, baby, he doesn't deserve your time."

"People can change, Mom."

"Hmph. It'd take a miracle."

"Yeah." He wanted to change the subject. Bending to unscrew the gas tank cap on the mower, he said, "I've got a date tonight. With a new girl."

"You do? Where'd you meet her?"

"At Starbucks."

"Really?" Folding her arms, Mom gazed at the pine trees near the back of her property. "Does Carmen know about this date?"

"Carmen has a boyfriend, Mom. You know that. She doesn't care about who I date."

Mom smiled faintly. "I had a dream about you two last night."

"Oh, no. Not one of your psychic visions."

"It was very vivid, like those dreams usually are," she said.

For as long as he could remember, Mom had claimed to receive omens in her dreams. He was a dyed-in-the-wool skeptic, believed in rational explanations and scientific conclusions. There was a sensible answer for most things that happened; you needed only to search for it. Dreams, however, were so vague that you could twist any interpretation that you desired out of them.

But he played along, as usual, with her clairvoyant meanderings. He didn't want to hurt her feelings.

"Okay," he said. "What happened in this dream of yours?"

"You and Carmen were together, in love—and not hiding it from each other." Mom smirked.

"Yeah, yeah. Is that all?"

Mom's smile faded. "You guys were in a house somewhere, not your place or hers. It was a cabin or somewhere like that. There was a snake in there."

"I hate snakes." His lips curled. "What kind was it?"

"Something huge and mean. Like a python. It was chasing you guys, you especially. It really wanted you."

In spite of his doubts, his imagination had painted his mother's dream scene in lucid color. His stomach roiled.

"Did it get me?" he asked.

"I don't know. I woke up before that happened. It scared me so badly I didn't get back to sleep for a while."

"It was only a dream, Mom." He spread his arms. "I'm here, see? No python is wrapped around my throat."

She didn't laugh. "It was a vision of the future, Andrew. The snake is a symbol."

"A symbol of what?"

"It could be a difficult challenge coming up for you, or a person who's going to cause trouble." She frowned. "I'm not sure."

"Miss Cleo would give me a better answer than that."

Mom swatted his arm. "Don't joke about this."

"Fine. What do you want me to do?"

Her gaze drilled into him.

"I want you to be careful," she said.

"I'm always careful."

"Then be *extra* careful. Watch out for new people, new situations. Especially people. I have a feeling that someone you know or will know soon is going to be revealed as that snake, and you need to be on guard."

"All right, Mom. I'll be on the lookout for someone with scales and a forked tongue."

She sighed, exasperated. "Go ahead, crack your jokes, but promise me that you'll be careful. Okay?"

"I'll be careful, Mom. Promise."

She nodded, satisfied. She resumed working on her flowers.

Watching her, he smiled. Although she could be a little loony with her supposedly prophetic dreams, he loved her all the same.

He began to cut the grass, thinking not about snakes, but about Mika, and how seven o'clock couldn't get there fast enough.

Chapter 10

At six-thirty, Andrew finished preparing for his dinner with Mika. He wore a taupe, silk twill shirt jacket with matching slacks, tan silk crew shirt, and polished Cole Haan loafers. He'd daubed on Dolce & Gabbana cologne and used a trimmer to sharpen his hairline. He wore one piece of jewelry: an Omega watch that he sported only on rare occasions.

He'd been on dozens of first dates, but none of them felt as important as this one. Mika was special. He was determined to make a positive impression.

After checking his profile for perhaps the tenth time in his full-length bedroom mirror, he went to the garage.

The Mercedes sparkled like a demo car in a showroom. He'd gotten the deluxe package at a local car wash.

As he drove away from the house, he noted that the annoying cats were gone. Permanently, he hoped.

He stopped at a local florist and picked up a fresh bouquet of bright, summer flowers. Then he hit I-85 north, which would take him to downtown Atlanta, and into Buckhead.

Driving with the convertible top down, he grooved to the old school jams playing on 102.5 FM, the classic soul station. Sang along with Stevie and Luther and Teddy. Cool wind bathed his face, and twilight fell over the world like a great velvet sheet. It was a cliché, but he thought it was a night made for romance.

If Buckhead was Atlanta's hot spot, then Peachtree Street was its nucleus, a strip renowned for its night-clubs, trendy restaurants, eclectic stores, high-end shopping malls, expensive digs, and stylish, moneyed residents. On Friday nights and weekends, traffic could slow to a crawl as partygoers filled the avenue, wanting to see and be seen; but on a Tuesday night, the area was thinly populated with people running errands, jogging, and lounging at sidewalk cafés.

He pulled into the parking lot of Houston's at five minutes to seven. He double-checked his face in the mirror and applied a fresh coat of lotion to his hands. Sweat slicked his palms.

It's only a date, man, he assured himself. *Calm down.*

But he hoped—so much that it frightened him—that she was the One. She certainly looked as if she could be Ms. Right. But would they have that crucial yet elusive chemistry? Would she feel as excited about him as he felt about her?

He both loved and hated first dates. They were exhilarating and scary plunges into the unknown. Anything could happen. And usually did.

He heard heels clicking on pavement, somewhere close. He turned in his seat.

Mika strolled alongside the car.

The sight of her raised his body temperature a few degrees.

Behind her, a shiny black Rolls Royce pulled away.

He knew cars well; he identified it as a Silver Shadow model, manufactured in 1972 or '73. Classic, regal styling. Impeccably maintained.

The sedan had smoked windows, concealing the driver, but he was sure that she had arrived in the vehicle. It fit her style.

Grinning, he got out of his car. "Hello, there."

"Good evening, Mr. Wilson. You're on time."

"Of course. You look lovely."

She wore an elegant, strapless black dress, and pumps. A platinum necklace with a sparkling diamond solitaire in the center. Subtle, diamond earrings. Light makeup, burgundy lipstick.

Her luminous hazel eyes were hypnotic.

"You're handsome, too." She fingered the lapel of his jacket. He caught an intoxicating whiff of her perfume; jasmine, it seemed to be.

He reached inside the car and picked up the bouquet. "This is for you."

She broke into a huge smile.

"Thank you so much, Andrew!" She inhaled the flowers' fragrance.

He nodded at the restaurant ahead of them, and offered her his arm.

"Shall we?" he said.

Clasping the flowers to her bosom, she put her arm in his, and they walked to the restaurant together.

His worries had drained away. He had a great evening ahead of him. He could feel it.

Houston's was an ideal place for a romantic dinner. Dark wood paneling. Dim lighting. Spacious booths. Soft music. Attentive servers attired in black moving with calm efficiency.

Andrew and Mika sat across from each other, at a

booth in a quiet corner of the dining room. A candle glowed on the table.

They'd finished dinner—a rib eye steak for him, roasted chicken for her—and sipped glasses of Riesling. Their conversation had flowed nonstop all evening.

He satisfied his desire to learn more about her. Mika had lived in Georgia for her entire life, growing up in a small town. Her parents had died many years ago; she was the only child.

She was a painter, she said, but her focus was not on selling her work or winning accolades; she pursued art purely for the love of it. She confided that she didn't need money. Her father had been a vastly successful physician, and had bequeathed her a substantial inheritance that included the estate on which she lived. She visited Atlanta frequently, for leisure, staying in hotels for sometimes weeks at a time.

He had suspected that she hailed from wealth. Her dignified manner and speech suggested a life of privilege. Although some of his buddies balked at a woman having more money than a man, he didn't envy Mika her fortune. He had his own money, and she had hers. If they ended up together, it was more prosperity for the both of them.

Her wineglass was almost empty. He picked up the bottle and refreshed her glass.

She swirled the golden liquid in front of her lips.

"Now you've learned more about me, Andrew," she said. "But I must share a confession."

"Uh-oh. I don't like confessions. Is this the part when you tell me that you have a husband and three kids?"

"Nothing quite so dramatic. I must confess to having engineered our meeting at the coffee shop this morning."

"What do you mean? You knew I was going to be there?"

She nodded. "I'd visited a couple of weeks ago and was reading another of your novels—the first book—and one of the café employees mentioned that you were a regular there, and tended to drop in on Tuesday mornings. I decided that I wanted to meet you."

"I'll be damned." He leaned back in the booth. "Eric was right."

"Eric, your best friend?"

"Yeah. I'd told him how we met. He said it sounded too coincidental for you to happen to be there reading my book."

"Is that all he said?" Her eyes were keen.

"Pretty much." He sure as hell wasn't going to share the other stuff Eric had said, because it didn't matter. Eric had been warning him about potentially hooking up with a gold digger. But Mika had her own gold and didn't need his.

Still, it surprised him that she had gone through so much trouble to meet him.

"I hope I haven't upset you." She reached across the table and touched his hand. "I only wanted to be honest."

"I'm flattered. Really. It's not every day that a gorgeous woman goes out of her way to meet me."

She laughed. "I was relieved that you took the initiative and approached me. If you hadn't, I would've had to summon some creativity."

"Why did you want to meet me?"

Deliberating her answer, she sipped her wine. Her lipstick left a smear on the rim of the glass.

Lustfully, he wished that he were that wineglass.

"Your character," she said.

"You've read my novels, not my autobiography. I make that stuff up, Mika."

"I understand that your plots are fiction, and your story people are imaginary. But the quality of your character shines through on every page, whether you are aware of it or not."

"Well, thanks. I won't argue with a compliment."

"I knew you were a good man. A man I wanted to know better."

"But when I first stepped to you, you acted like you didn't want to be bothered. Didn't give me your number, either."

She shrugged. "Men enjoy the pursuit. The hunt. Am I correct?"

"True. But I don't like games."

"Do you think I'm playing a game with you, Andrew?" Her gaze settled on him, unwavering.

"Are you?"

"Absolutely not. A lady has to conduct herself with discretion sometimes, no matter how enamored she may be of a gentleman."

"I can understand that."

"But if we're going to pursue this further, I have to know whether I have any competition."

He set down his wineglass. "If you're asking whether I'm dating someone else, the answer is no. We talked about this earlier."

"But you spoke of having a close female friend. Carmen, correct?"

This woman had a perfect memory. He'd mentioned Carmen only once, and briefly at that, when he had talked on the phone to Mika earlier that afternoon.

"Carmen is just a friend."

"Just a friend, you say. Is she aware of that?"

"She knows."

"Is she pretty?" She examined him.

"Sure, she's attractive."

"Is she single?"

"She has a boyfriend, some guy she recently started dating."

"Then she's essentially single."

He shrugged. What was her point?

Mika leaned closer. "If she's attractive, single, and a close friend, then why aren't you dating her?"

"Because she's *just* a friend. Why're you asking all of these questions about her?"

"As I said, I have to make sure that I don't have any competition."

"No competition. You can chill."

"Good."

An alarm bell sounded in his thoughts. She was a tad bit possessive, wasn't she? This was their first date and already she was interrogating him about his friends.

He shifted in the booth. His gut had tightened.

As if afraid that he would leave, she took his hand in hers and traced her index finger across his palm. "But honestly, if I had to compete for your attention, it would not matter in the end. I do whatever it takes to get what I want. Whatever it takes, Andrew."

The sensation of her gliding finger was like cool electricity. His uneasiness faded. Lust arose in its place—his manhood stirred like an awakened animal.

"You always get what you want, huh?" he asked.

"Always. I can be relentless when I want something. Or someone."

She raised his hand to her lips. She flicked her tongue across his forefinger, as if his skin were sweet and tasty. He shivered.

Then she took his finger in her warm mouth and suckled it.

His erection stiffened.

He'd never met a woman so assertive. He felt as if the gender roles had been reversed. Normally, he was the one trying to win over the woman. But she had turned the tables. She was trying to seduce *him.*

A vivid image crashed into his brain: he and Mika on a floor, having savage, mind-blowing sex.

She released his finger. "You're thinking of something naughty. Tell me. Honestly, you won't offend me."

He hesitated. "I'm thinking about making love to you."

She only smiled, as if she'd known his thoughts all along.

"Is that so? Be more specific. Are you imagining making slow, tender love to me, or having wild sex with me?"

"Buck-wild sex."

"You wanted sex with me from the first moment you saw me. You undressed me with your eyes and wondered how I'd be in bed. Correct?"

"I'm guilty." He blushed.

She winked. "I'm fantastic in bed. Perhaps you'll get to discover it later."

"You're bold, you know that? I've never met anyone as bold as you."

"And you never will, darling. But answer me this: have you thought about making love to me, too?"

He stammered, unsure how to answer.

She flashed a smile. "Of course not. You must be in love to make love."

"Yeah."

"Am I someone you could fall in love with, Andrew?"

He faltered again. "The potential is there. Time will tell, I guess."

"That question caught you off guard."

He chuckled. "Sure did."

She leaned back in the booth. Sipped her wine. Watched him with a soft smile.

He felt as if she were measuring him, weighing a decision.

The server, a young man, visited the table to see if they wanted dessert. Andrew ordered a slice of chocolate cake that Mika agreed to share with him.

"I need to make a trip to the ladies' room," Mika said, grabbing her purse and sliding out of the booth.

He watched her stroll down the aisle. Swinging her lovely hips.

He used the napkin to wipe sweat away from his forehead.

Before she turned the corner, she checked over her shoulder and caught him staring. She blew him a kiss.

He blushed. She had him. She knew it, and he knew it, too.

When she'd asked him if she was someone he could fall in love with, he might as well have answered *yes.*

When Mika returned, she sat on his side of the booth. She pressed against him.

"Am I too close for comfort?" she asked.

"Nope," he said in a weak voice.

She snaked her leg on top of one of his. Lifting his hand, she placed it on her smooth, bare thigh.

She was so shamelessly bold. He felt as though he were dreaming.

But the closeness of her body caused a predictable reaction. His erection came back harder than ever.

She slithered her hand between them and touched him in his slacks.

"Okay, now," he said.

"What is it?" she asked, innocently. "My hand seems to have a mind of its own."

"Uh-huh."

The server brought the chocolate cake. He noted how closely together Andrew and Mika were sitting, favored them with a secretive smile.

Andrew reached for a fork. She swatted his hand.

"Let me feed you." She guided a forkful of cake to his mouth. "There."

"Delicious," he said.

"I know something that tastes better," she said.

"What would that be?"

She moved his hand from her thigh to the warm cleft between her legs.

He drew in a quick breath.

"I'm not always such a bad girl," she said. "Please don't get the wrong idea about me, Andrew."

"Do you hear me complaining?"

She fed him another piece of cake.

"I go after what I want," she said. "That's my nature."

"I like an assertive woman."

"So, then, you like me?"

"Yes. A lot."

She gave him another forkful of cake.

"I'm glad," she said. "I want you to like me."

"You're passing with flying colors."

She set down the fork. She moved her hand to his belt buckle, loosened it. Grasped the zipper of his slacks. Pulled it down with a whisper.

What was she going to do? He wasn't going to stop her, whatever she had planned for him. He sat there like a wax dummy. With a throbbing hard-on.

No one was around to stop them. They had the corner of the dining room to themselves. But to Andrew, it seemed that they were the only people in the entire restaurant. Mika's presence captured his single-minded attention.

Her fingers crept into his boxer shorts, discovered his rigid manhood. Encircled the sensitive tip.

A moan slipped out of him.

She turned. Their faces were almost nose-to-nose.

"I want to be the only woman you like," she said. "No competition, Andrew."

She squeezed him firmly, eased the pressure, squeezed again.

He gripped the edge of the table.

"You've got no competition," he said.

She stroked him.

He gripped the table so tightly it was a miracle he didn't break it in half.

"Am I the only woman you like?" she asked.

"The only one, yes."

"And if I share my body with you tonight? Will I still be the only one?"

"The only one."

"And you'll treat me like a princess?"

"A princess."

"Do you promise?"

"Promise."

With the nimbleness of a cat, she slid underneath the table.

Oh, man. Was she going to . . .

Suddenly, her lips enveloped him.

He gasped.

He couldn't believe what she was doing, right there in a public place. But he didn't stop her. Couldn't stop her.

She ran her moist tongue up and down the length of him.

He plunged his hands into her silky hair.

Placing her hands on his knees, she spread his legs farther apart. She took him in deeper.

"Oh, Jesus." He arched his back.

She sucked him, kissed him, licked him.

He clutched the napkin in his fists.

He was going to explode.

Then, before he erupted, she withdrew.

His body snapped back into place like a rubber band. As he fought to catch his breath, she emerged on the other side of the booth.

"Why . . . why'd you stop?" he asked.

She dabbed at her lips with a napkin, smiled.

"Good things come to those who wait," she said. "I'm ready to go dancing."

She signaled the server to bring the check.

They went to Havana Heat, a club on Peachtree and Pharr, in the heart of the Buckhead nightlife district. Cigar and cigarette smoke, cologne, and perfume flavored the body-heat heavy air. The crowd—thick for a Tuesday night—was a multicultural stew, heavy on Latinos, with a generous seasoning of blacks, Asians, Indians, and whites, most of the clubbers in their mid-twenties and older. People grooved on the large dance floor to the lively sounds of Latin soul, most performing salsa with varying degrees of skill, a sprinkling of them rocking lamely with a club-footed two-step.

"You remember how to salsa?" Mika asked.

"Sure do."

Two years ago, he'd taken a salsa class with Carmen, since her boyfriend at the time had no interest in dancing. He wondered what Mika would think about that— she seemed to have a jealous streak, and a keen interest in his relationship with Carmen.

Well, he figured he could deal with a little jealousy. She was so beautiful that he was prepared to deal with quite a bit. Besides, no one was perfect, right?

"Did you come here to hold up the wall?" She grabbed Andrew's hand. "Let's dance."

She guided him to the dance floor. They found a space near the middle. The pounding beat made his teeth vibrate.

She pressed against him, her hand cupping his butt. "Lead me, baby," she whispered. "I'll go wherever you want to go."

She licked his earlobe, smiled.

Hot blood sang through his veins. Pure, animal lust. It made him so dizzy he worried that he would forget all the salsa he'd learned and bungle through the steps, wind up sprawled on the floor with his legs knotted like spaghetti.

She stepped back. Took his hands in hers.

"Anywhere you want me to go," she said. Her gaze never left his face. "I'll follow you."

In a euphoric rush, his lessons came back to him, and he started to move.

Two hours later, they left the building and walked across the parking lot. After the stifling humidity of the club, Andrew breathed gratefully of the cool night air.

"You're an incredible dancer," he said.

"You've got moves, too. I'm impressed."

"It took everything I had to keep up with you."

"Nonsense, you were in perfect sync all along. As I knew you would be."

They reached his car, got inside.

She twisted in the seat to face him. "Where are we going next?"

"It's almost eleven-thirty. Tired?"

"Not at all. Are you?"

"I feel good. Full of energy, actually."

She touched his arm. "Let's go to my hotel."

He knew very well what would happen at her hotel.

"You sure about that?" he asked.

"Absolutely. Are *you* sure?"

Uneasiness clenched his stomach. This was moving faster than he'd ever imagined. Almost too fast.

But he couldn't say no and live to look himself in the mirror again. A gorgeous woman was inviting him to her hotel. What guy on the planet could turn her down?

"Sure," he said. "I'm cool."

"I sense some apprehension, Andrew. Are you man enough for me? Or do I have to go back inside that club and pick up one of those Latino hunks who isn't afraid of what I have to offer?"

"Where are you staying?" He threw the car into gear.

She laughed softly. "That's my boy. I'm staying at the Ritz-Carlton in Buckhead. Across the street from Lenox Square."

"I know where that is. Hang tight."

As he drove, she kneaded his leg. He played in her hair.

But uneasiness continued to simmer in his stomach. He wasn't the kind of guy who routinely slept with a woman on the first date. He liked to take his time and get to know a girl. Sex was more fulfilling with a woman with whom he'd established a meaningful emotional connection.

His take-it-slow philosophy, unusual among many of his buddies, also had prevented a lot of the messy drama that some of his boys always wound up in. He valued neatness and stability, in all aspects of his life.

If there was one lesson his mom had mercilessly drilled into him, it was: if you're man enough to lie down with a lady, you better be man enough to raise her baby. She'd damn near had him *terrified* to have sex. He was a freshman in college before he lost his virginity, an age so much later than his friends that it had been too embarrassing to admit. As time passed, he still preferred to move slowly to the bedroom.

But Mika had changed his game plan. His attraction to her was nearly overwhelming. Her aggressiveness only made matters more challenging.

Nevertheless, the smart thing to do was to slow down. Take a little more time getting to know her. He'd only met her this morning. Their conversation had been great, and the date was going wonderfully, but he didn't know her. Not really. The one thing he did know was that once a woman shared her body with you, you quickly became introduced to a more intimate side of her, which usually was good. But if she flipped the script and got crazy on you, it could be disastrous.

They arrived at the hotel. He cruised underneath the porte cochere, and stopped. A valet hurried to the car.

Take it slow, man. You're rushing this.

He looked at her, at her soft, full lips. He remembered the rapturous sensation of those lips on him, sucking, kissing.

The valet waited beside his door. "Sir?"

Slow down, or you'll regret it later.

Most times, it was wise to heed that quiet voice of conscience. But he felt good, overall, about Mika, about where this budding relationship might be headed. They had a powerful, mutual attraction. Fantastic chemistry. He wasn't going to back out of this situation and ruin a great thing, based solely on a voice in his head.

He opened the door.

In the hotel lobby, a doorman nodded at them. "Good evening."

"Hi, there," Mika said cheerfully. She led Andrew to the bank of elevators.

The quiet lobby was opulently furnished. Regency and Georgian antique furniture. Crystal chandeliers. Marble tables. Eighteenth-century English paintings and sculptures.

"Nice place," he said.

She shrugged, as if the sumptuous surroundings were no more remarkable than those found at a Days Inn. The nonchalance of someone accustomed to affluence.

An elevator beeped open. The car was empty.

"Go," she said.

"Huh?" He frowned at her commanding tone.

She put her hand on his back and shoved him inside. He stumbled against the back wall.

She stabbed the button for the seventh floor. The doors slid shut, and the car began to ascend.

"You didn't have to push me," he said.

"Shut up and kiss me."

Seizing his arms, she crushed her lips against his. He opened his mouth, and her tongue darted in, teasingly. Her lips tasted of sweet wine.

He ran his hands down her back, squeezed her hips.

She grabbed the front of his jacket and tore it open. Buttons popped.

"I want you so bad, baby" she said, between kisses. "You want me, too, show me how much, stop being so timid."

In response, he drove her against the wall. He grabbed the top of her dress and yanked it down, exposing more skin.

"Act like you want me," she said.

He unsnapped her bra, flung it to the floor. Her breasts hung in his face, round and full, with nipples like chocolate strawberries. He put his mouth on one of her breasts, sucked urgently.

"That's right," she said, clasping his head to her bosom.

Then she pushed him against the opposite wall. She ripped his belt buckle loose, jerked down the zipper of his slacks. She dug her hand into his boxers and cradled his manhood.

"This is gonna be mine," she said. She left a trail of kisses on his neck. "All mine, all mine."

"All yours," he said. He hiked up her dress, rolled down her panties, probed his finger inside her. She was moist. "And this is mine."

"Yours."

The elevator stopped. The doors chimed open.

"Room seven-thirteen," she said. "Hurry."

She clung to his neck. He carried her out of the elevator, kissing her.

While he held her suspended, she dug in her purse, fumbled out the room key, unlocked the door. He brought her across the threshold as if they were newlyweds. She kicked the door shut.

He took in the suite in a glance: soft lighting, lots of space, large bay windows that provided a panoramic view of the glittering city, luxurious upholstered furniture, a dining area with a mahogany table, a kitchenette. A vase of fresh orchids scented the air.

They stripped out of their clothes, left them in a sloppy pile on the floor.

She braced him against the hallway wall. His manhood stood at attention. She grasped it gently, possessively.

"Want me to finish what I started, baby?" she asked.

Without waiting for his answer, she lowered to her knees.

He cradled her head. She took him inside her mouth—completely.

It felt so good that if he hadn't been leaning against the wall, he would have fallen down.

Her fingers clenched his butt. Tightened her hold on him. Her head bobbed, drew him in and out, tongue lashing him in a sweet rhythm.

His hands roved through her hair. "Oh, Mika. Mika, Mika, Mika."

The ecstatic pressure mounted. He didn't want to come, not before he'd tasted her, repaid some of the pleasure she'd given him. He withdrew and sank to the carpet.

"My turn," he said.

She lay back, guided his head to her damp center.

His first lick was slow and tender, a stroke from bottom to top, like licking an ice cream cone.

"Oooh." She grabbed his head, gasped.

He explored her fully with his tongue and lips. Tasted her juices. Found her sensitive spot, teased it with short, quick flicks.

Crying out, she wriggled on the floor.

Pleasuring her with horizontal and vertical strokes, he chased his tongue with his index finger, creating a contrast of softness and firmness.

"Andrew, baby, yes, yes, baby, oh, Andrew, baby . . ."

He pressed his tongue flat against her fullness.

Screeching, she ground against him. Her fingernails scraped the walls.

He dove in again, quickened the pace.

Hips bucking, she rode the wave of an orgasm. He smeared his lips in her juices, lashed her with his tongue. She shrieked as another orgasm rocked her.

Finally, he slid out of her. Breathing hard, she clasped his head to her belly.

"Glad I brought you home," she said. "My goodness."

"We aim to please."

She nudged him to turn over, onto his back. Soft carpet fibers brushed his skin.

She fondled his erection. "You wanna fuck me?"

Until now, she had spoken in formal language. Hearing her talk dirty turned him on even more.

"Yeah," he said.

"Say it."

"I wanna fuck you."

"You think you can handle this?"

"Watch me." He reached for his slacks, to get some protection out of his wallet.

"Stay there." She straddled him, fished a condom out of her purse.

"Good girl," he said.

"A lady's always prepared. Although we would have beautiful babies."

"You ain't never lied."

She placed the condom between her lips. Bending, she used her lips and tongue to tenderly roll the condom over him. She laid her tongue on his belly, ran it up to his neck in a warm line.

He fondled her breasts. Traced circles across the rigid nipples.

She rose, put him inside her. Her muscles closed around him like a hot vise.

"So tight." The words burst out of him.

"You like it that way, baby?" She ground her pelvis in an excruciatingly slow figure eight. It snatched a gasp out of him.

"You've never had any pussy like this," she said. "Have you?"

"No," he said in a weak voice.

"Say it!"

"Never had any pussy like yours."

"That's my boy." She swiveled in a wide circle.

He raised his hands to massage her breasts. She snared his wrists, pinned them against the floor.

"You're my prisoner now." She kissed his neck, rose and looked at him with an intense gaze. "You're mine. I'm never letting you go."

"If being a prisoner feels this good, I don't wanna go anywhere."

She began to grind again, her muscles clenching him like a warm, damp fist. He'd never felt anything quite like it; her control was amazing. He rocked with her; they found a comfortable rhythm and kept it.

"Look at me," she said.

He looked up at her. Stared into her shining eyes.

"That's my baby." Moaning, she ground faster. Squeezed him tight.

He felt such a powerful eruption building it seemed it would shatter his body like a vase. Gritting his teeth, he closed his eyes.

"Look at me, look at me," she said. "Want to see your eyes, those pretty brown eyes."

He opened his eyes. Tears began to flood his vision, stream down his cheeks.

"Oh, Mika . . . damn . . ."

"Look at me!"

Gazing into her eyes, he thrust into her so deeply it felt as if she might suck his entire body inside her womb. She matched his thrusts and drew him even farther inside her. He was drowning in her.

"Mika, oh . . ."

"Look at me, look at me, look at me!"

Their gazes locked.

The orgasm hit him like a lightning bolt. It knocked him flat on his back and tore a cry out of his throat.

She continued to ride him, milking every ounce out of him, her gaze never leaving his face.

"Yes, yes, Andrew, baby, yes, yes, give it all to me, all of it, baby, pour into me."

He kept pumping into her, like a piston.

"All of it . . . all of you," she said.

He emptied himself at last. He dropped against the floor. Panting. Sweat slicked his body.

She finally released his wrists and slid onto the carpet beside him.

Their labored breathing was the only sound in the room.

He heard traffic in the distance, other people driving to homes and bedrooms.

Although they lay on the floor, with no cushions, he didn't want to move. He was as comfortable as if he were reclining on a plump mattress with silk sheets.

She rested her hand on his chest. He twisted his fingers through her hair.

"Never felt anything like that before," he said. "Ever."

She was quiet, contemplative.

"I saw something, Andrew," she said.

"What'd you see?"

"We had a moment of truth."

"Come again?"

"You've got them."

"Got what?"

She touched his chin, turned his face toward hers. He had been expecting a humorous comment, but her expression was serious.

"Soul mate eyes," she said.

He didn't know what to say. He answered her with a kiss. And the kiss started things all over again.

They moved throughout the suite, from the entry hall floor to a sofa, from the sofa to the dining room, from the dining room to, finally, the bedroom.

Mika was by far the best lover he'd ever had: assertive yet compliant, gentle yet firm. Intuitively, she knew what he liked, and he had a sixth sense for what turned her on, too. Together, their energy was boundless.

To think he'd considered declining her invitation to come to her room. He would've missed out on the most amazing night of his life.

They lay together in a tangle of perspiration-dampened sheets. The air conditioner churned out waves of refreshing, cool air. A jasmine-scented candle burned on a nightstand, making the bedroom flicker in light and shadow, like a place in a dream.

She curled her leg against his. "You never responded to my discovery, Andrew."

"About what?"

"Don't play the fool. It doesn't suit you. You know what I mean."

"If you think I have soul mate eyes, I just don't know how to answer that. I mean, it's flattering."

"Merely flattering?"

He sounded lame. But what did she expect him to say? That he believed she was his soul mate, too? He'd met her less than twenty-four hours ago.

"I don't have the same philosophy you do about soul mates," he said.

"Meaning?"

"For me, it takes more than looking into a woman's eyes at a moment of truth or whatever to know whether she's my soul mate. I need to spend time with her, get to know her as a friend and a lover."

"How much time?"

"As long as it takes. Can't put a deadline on it."

"Have you ever experienced anything like what you experienced with me this evening?"

He chuckled. "Hell, no."

"So doesn't that count for something?"

"It counts for a lot. But a relationship is based on more than great sex."

She sighed. "You're right. But you're wrong."

"How am I wrong?"

"Certainly, a relationship is more than fantastic sex. But it doesn't take long for a man to figure out whether a woman is the one."

"I never said you weren't the one. But I need more time to get to know you. We've known each other for only a day, Mika."

"Stop thinking so analytically. Listen to your heart. The heart has its own time frame."

"Right." He dragged his hand down his face.

She raised her elbow, propped her head on her hand. "I've upset you."

"Let's talk about this later, okay?"

"Agreed." She laid her head on the pillow. "Tell me. Have you ever been in love?"

"Yeah."

"When was the last time?"

"Couple of years ago."

"Why did it end?"

"Her job sent her to London, and she wasn't going to be coming back anytime soon, and I didn't want to move overseas. So we called it quits."

"How did you feel?"

"Terrible. Like my life was over."

"I know exactly what you mean." She shivered. "I don't know anything more painful than suffering a broken heart."

He took one of her hands in his. "What about you?"

"It's been many years since I was in love. My fiancé was murdered."

He raised his head. "Are you serious?"

Her eyes sad, she nodded.

"I'm so sorry to hear that," he said. "Who did it? Were they arrested?"

"No one was ever brought to justice. I know who was responsible for it, though he never admitted it. My father."

"Your own father?"

"As I said at dinner, my father was wealthy, a respected

physician. He paid someone to kill the man whom I loved."

"Why the hell would he do something like that?"

"I was an only child, Andrew. I was going to inherit my father's estate. If I married, of course, my husband would have substantial influence in the matters of the estate, as well. My father didn't approve of the man I loved."

"Why?"

"My father was a horrible bigot. He was a white man, the worst kind of Southern cracker, as some people call them. My fiancé was black. For a time, we hid our relationship from my father. You can imagine his reaction when he finally discovered that we planned to marry.

"He didn't want a black man marrying into his money," Andrew said.

"He was a cruel man. I know it sounds awful to say this, but I'm glad that he's dead. I'll never forgive him."

She trembled. He pulled her into his arms and held her.

She wept softly against his chest.

"All I want," she said, "is to feel love like that again. Needing love . . . hoping for it . . . it's kept me alive."

"Shhh. Everything's going to be all right." She was so beautiful that it was easy to assume she'd lived a charmed life of luxuries and endless blessings. But everyone had scars, some of which never faded.

He found himself wanting to be the one who she could love again. Wanting her to be the one for him, too. Although it had been two years since he had been in love, it felt as if it had been so long ago that it might have been in another life.

But he'd known her for only one day. He couldn't throw open the floodgates of his heart, not yet, even if he'd wanted to do so. Rushing into a relationship never had been his style. He liked to gradually move deeper inside, gaining confidence with every slow step, letting the emotional barriers fall as he progressed. The journey took time. And sometimes he decided that it wasn't worth the effort and withdrew.

He would have to be careful with her. She'd lost her fiancé, probably had never recovered from the trauma, and talked as if she craved love the same way other people craved food. She'd passionately shared her body with him. To top it off, she'd announced that he had "soul mate eyes."

The humming air conditioner couldn't produce cool air fast enough to dry the fresh sweat that beaded his forehead.

What if he wasn't able to reciprocate her feelings? He didn't want to hurt her, was loathe to lead her on.

But you slept with her. You've done a pretty fine job of leading her on, Andrew. I warned you to take it slow. It's too late to have second thoughts.

She turned onto her side. She pulled his arm across her body, placed his hand on her breasts.

"Hold me," she said.

He scooted up to her, so that they lay together like spoons. She purred, like a contented cat.

Maybe she *was* his soul mate. Maybe he only needed to wake up to a truth that she had already glimpsed, catch her vision. In matters of the heart, women usually were more intuitive than men.

Maybe he would look at her one day and realize that she had soul mate eyes, too.

The next morning, Andrew awoke to the aroma of freshly brewed coffee.

He sat up, rubbed his eyes. Grayish daylight filtered through the bay windows.

It took him a moment to recognize his surroundings. He was in Mika's suite at the Ritz-Carlton.

He was alone in the bedroom. He heard sizzling sounds; the scent of bacon wafted to his nose, making his stomach growl.

He checked the time. The clock on the nightstand read 8:12.

On any other Wednesday, he'd be finishing his workout by now and getting ready for breakfast. His schedule was shot for the day.

But it didn't bother him, since it was for a good reason. The memory of last night sent a warm tingle through his body.

He pulled away the sheets. He'd slept in the nude.

A set of blue men's silk pajamas lay on a chair beside the bed, with matching house slippers.

"Hmm, how thoughtful." He dressed in the pajamas and wandered into the bathroom.

A supply of toiletries sat on the left side of the dual-sink vanity: toothbrush, Scope Cool Mint mouthwash, Aquafresh toothpaste, Right Guard antiperspirant. The packages were brand new, unopened.

Interesting. He used the same brands at home.

Female toiletries that clearly had been used by Mika lay on the other side of the vanity.

It was coincidence that she'd bought the stuff he used all the time. Had to be.

He brushed his teeth and washed up.

He found Mika in the kitchenette, cooking. She wore a blue nightgown that ended above her knees; it was the same color as his bedclothes. Her long hair dangled in a ponytail.

"Good morning," he said. He kissed her on the cheek. "Thanks for the pjs and the toothbrush and stuff."

"Morning, baby." She smiled brightly. "The nightclothes look good on you."

"When did you buy them?"

"Oh, I went shopping yesterday afternoon." She winked. "In case a certain gentleman decided to spend the night. A lady has to be prepared, correct?"

Nodding, he went to the coffee machine on the counter. He poured some coffee in a mug. "Coffee smells good." He took a sip. "Tastes good, too."

"Does it taste familiar? It should."

"Hmm. Actually, it does."

"It's Jamaican Blue Mountain."

"Really? That's my favorite."

"I know."

"How did you know?"

"You say so on your Web site, on your biography page. Ten of Mark Justice's favorite things. I printed the list."

"You did some research."

"Yep." She transferred several strips of bacon to a platter, and began to whip a bowl of eggs with an egg-beater. "You can have a seat in the dining room, darling. The newspaper is there. Breakfast will be ready shortly."

The mahogany table was set for two. The day's edition of *The Atlanta Journal-Constitution* lay in the center, neatly folded.

But the sections had been rearranged: the Sports section was first, followed by Business, Living, Metro, and lastly, the front news page.

His eyebrows knitted together.

He read the paper in this exact order, each weekday morning.

Well, so what? She must've skimmed the paper earlier, shuffled the sections around. There was no way she could possibly know the order in which he read the daily paper; that kind of personal information definitely was not posted on his Web site.

As he read a story about the Hawks gearing up for the coming season, she came to the table carrying platters of food.

He started to rise. "Need help with anything?"

"No, no. Don't you move. I've got everything covered."

She served him a generous helping of eggs, bacon, and smothered potatoes. Two slices of toast with butter and grape jelly. A tall glass of orange juice.

"This looks delicious," he said. "You've got all the breakfast foods I love."

"Thank you. I love to cook. You should see what I can do at dinner."

"You can burn, huh?"

"I don't want to boast, but yes, I can burn." She smiled, sipped her orange juice. "Why don't we have dinner tonight, at your house? I'll cook whatever you like."

He stroked his chin. "I think I'll be free this evening. But . . ." His voice trailed off.

"But what?"

He chose his words carefully. He wasn't good at conversations like this.

"Mika, I like you a lot. I really enjoyed last night, I'm enjoying this morning, too. But I don't want us to rush things."

She stared at him, jaw clenched.

"So what are you saying?" she asked. "That you don't want to see me again?"

"That's not what I meant."

"Then what do you mean, Andrew?"

"I want us to take this slow. Take our time getting to know each other, that's all. But I definitely want to see you again."

The tension vanished from her face. She smiled.

"Oh, darling," she said. "More of that cautious man-speak." She rose from her chair and sauntered around the table. She sat on his lap, her face inches from his. She crossed her arms behind his head and wrapped her legs around his waist.

The closeness of her body was like an aphrodisiac. His erection throbbed into life.

She ground her pelvis against him, gently and insistently, as if to remind him of last night. Drawing shallow breaths, he grew brick-hard.

"That big rational brain of yours says one thing, Andrew. It says, 'Let's slow down, I'm not sure we're doing the right thing here.' But your body is speaking a different language. Do you know what it's saying?"

Her nightgown had a plunging neckline; he lost the battle to keep his gaze off the tempting swell of her cleavage. "What's it saying?"

"Your body says, 'I want to be with Mika tonight. I want to be with her all the time. Being with her is like heaven on Earth.' "

"You're bad. Using your body like this. Like a weapon."

"I've no qualms about using my charms." She moved closer and whispered in his ear: "You know you want this pussy again. I'll fuck you even better tonight, baby. Make you want to call your mama."

She raked her nails down the back of his scalp— vividly recalling for him how her fingers had skidded down his naked back last night.

He broke into a grin. This woman was something else.

"Looks like I'll be seeing you this evening, then," he said.

"That's my baby." She kissed him, and climbed off his lap. "I'll be back."

She strutted away. He admired the sensuous roll of her hips.

He took a sip of orange juice, to try to calm his body down. But it didn't help. The truth was, she had him whipped. Nose wide open. The amazing sex, the loving attention, the promise of more to come—he couldn't resist. Besides, spending two consecutive nights together wasn't a big deal. Was it?

You know the real answer, Andrew.

They were moving too fast. He knew it. Mika was in deep, convinced that he was her soul mate, and she was determined to reel him in. The wise thing to do was to slow down, not see her tonight, and wait a few days before going on another date.

But he couldn't wait. He wanted her too much.

He felt like a junkie unable to refuse a hit.

She came back to the table. She carried a small cardboard box.

"What's that?" he said.

"A gift for you." The box had been opened. She dug inside, took out a red Motorola two-way pager.

"This is for me?" he asked.

"So we can stay in touch throughout the day." She took another identical pager out of the box. "This one is mine."

"But I keep my cell phone with me all the time. You can reach me on that."

"Everyone has your cell number, baby. These pagers will be our *private* connection to each other, our secret bond." Excitement filled her voice. "Go ahead, turn it on."

He pressed the power button. Pressing buttons on her own pager, she went to the other side of the table.

His pager vibrated. A message appeared on the display.

YOU'VE GOT SOUL MATE EYES.

He looked up, smiled thinly at her. She was grinning. What had he gotten himself into?

Part Two

LOVE CRAZY

Women accused him of running from love and commitment. He never could make them understand that he wasn't running from them. He was running from the fear of losing himself in them. His freedom was all he had. Take that away, you might as well take his life.

—Mark Justice, *One Night*

Chapter 11

Of all the things in the world that Raymond disliked, going to the doctor was near the top of the list.

Doctors reminded him of illness, of his advancing age, of the looming specter of Death. Instead of dressing in white lab coats and stethoscopes, physicians, in his opinion, would have been more honestly represented wearing black robes and gripping devilishly sharp scythes.

But his wife had scheduled this Wednesday morning appointment for him, and he had promised her that he would go. He hoped that some good would come of it. He hadn't enjoyed a sound night of sleep in weeks. If nothing else, he could get a prescription of sleeping pills that might allow him to slumber without nightmares.

His longtime physician, Dr. Michael Unaeze, worked out of an office in Stone Mountain, on Columbia Drive. Dr. Unaeze was a compact, bespectacled man who spoke in a measured voice that carried a hint of his Nigerian roots.

"So your wife says you haven't been sleeping well,"

the doctor said, hands on his hips. "She's worried about you."

"She's always worried about something," Raymond said.

Unaeze smiled. "That is a wife's duty, to worry about her husband's health. Especially since her husband hates to visit his doctor!"

"Work's been busy lately, Doc." He smiled sheepishly.

The doctor waved off Raymond's excuse. "Let's start at the beginning, eh?"

While Raymond sat on the examination table, Unaeze went through the routine for a general physical, finding everything satisfactory. He touched the bruise on Raymond's temple.

"Are you experiencing any headaches or dizziness?" the doctor asked.

"Should I be?" He rubbed his grainy eyes.

"It would not be unheard of, after the head trauma you suffered."

"Been having headaches," he said. He indicated the bruise. "Feel 'em right here."

Unaeze made a note. "They began after your accident?"

"Yeah."

"How long does the pain endure?"

"Not long. Ten, fifteen minutes, maybe. But it's intense, like the worst migraine."

The doctor made another note. "Your wife says that you've been having nightmares as well."

"Christ, did she tell you everything?"

Unaeze touched his shoulder. "Sorry, I don't mean to offend you. But I must inquire, for your sake. Did these nightmares also begin after the accident?"

"Look, I've just got a little insomnia, that's all, probably get these headaches 'cause I can't get any damn sleep. Can I get some sleeping pills or not?"

Unaeze muttered something in his native tongue. He scribbled on a slip of paper and handed it to Raymond.

"This is a prescription for Ambien. It should aid your sleep, Raymond. I've given you a two-week supply."

"Thanks, Doc. That's all I needed." He slid off the table and tucked the prescription in his pocket.

"There are possible side effects," Unaeze said. "Your dreams could become more vivid than usual."

Raymond laughed bitterly. "Don't think that could happen to me, Doc."

"Other potential side effects are difficulty breathing, nausea, temporary amnesia, and in rare cases, hallucinations."

"Sounds like fun."

Unaeze frowned. He wrote another note and gave it to him.

"This is a referral to a neurologist," he said. "His name is Dr. Price, excellent doctor. I think you should see him. Your headaches concern me."

"They checked out my head after the accident. Said everything was fine. Just had the concussion."

"I'm aware of the health reports, Raymond," Unaeze said. "But I strongly believe that you should seek a second opinion from a specialist, have some tests—"

"There's nothing wrong with me that some good sleep won't cure."

Unaeze threw his hands in the air. "Why must you be so difficult? I'm only trying to help you."

"Can I go now, Doc?" Raymond jingled his keys. "I need to get back to my office."

Shaking his head, Dr. Unaeze ushered him out of the examination room.

Neurologist. Please. Going to Unaeze had been bad enough. There was no way in hell he was going to see someone else for more tests, so they could poke and prod him as if he were a lab rat and send his wife into a fit of anxiety. There was nothing seriously wrong with him. Sleep—pure, dreamless sleep—would solve his problems.

He had the prescription filled at a nearby Eckerd, and returned to his ReMax office on busy Panola Road in Lithonia. It was a quarter to eleven, early enough for him to still enjoy a productive day.

The sight of his office comforted him. It was a large, bright area, with several enclosed rooms. Sand carpeting, cream walls. Potted plants. Award plaques and photos he'd taken with community luminaries hanging on the walls.

His staff of four—three real estate agents and an administrative assistant—talked business on telephones and pounded on computer keyboards. The pleasing sounds of money being made.

Tawana, his assistant, greeted him cheerfully.

"Good morning, Uncle Ray. How did the doctor's appointment go?"

On his way to the coffee machine on a table in the corner, he spun.

"Who told you I'd gone to the doctor?" he asked.

Tawana grinned. "Aunt June, of course. She said to make sure that you went. If you came to work instead of going to your appointment, I had strict orders to call her."

This was what he got for employing family members. Tawana was his niece, his brother-in-law's daughter. Twenty-one and a junior at Spelman majoring in marketing, she was a good employee, but he could do without her intrusions into his personal life. She and his wife were always in league over some matter or another.

"I went," he said. "The doctor said I have two weeks to live."

"What?" Her mouth fell open.

"Inoperable brain tumor. I might drop dead at any minute."

Her face was so stricken that he quickly told her he was only kidding.

"That wasn't funny," she said.

"Sorry, it wasn't," he said. "About the only thing I'd drop dead of today is lack of sleep. Please hold my calls until after lunch. I want to catch up on some things."

In the privacy of his spacious office in the back, armed with a cup of steaming coffee, he booted up his computer.

Cruel humor wasn't his style. But fatigue made him irritable, and he was more tired than he'd ever been in his life.

He accessed the calendar program, his tool for organizing his days. A reminder window appearing on the screen, telling him what he needed to do today. "Call Andrew re: golf" sat at the top of the list.

The reminder had appeared yesterday, too. But he hadn't called his son yet.

Guilt pressed on him, like a physical weight.

He couldn't afford to relapse into the kind of father he used to be. Andrew deserved better.

He wanted to spend time with his son. But in the past few weeks, he'd been so damned tired.

Be honest with yourself, Ray. You're avoiding Andrew because talking to him makes you think about the accident, about that terrible place. Your boy was the only one there, and even he doesn't understand what had really been going on.

He remembered the conversation with Andrew, in his hospital room in the hours after the wreck.

"Do you know anything about an old mansion in Bulloch County, off Interstate 16?"

"No . . . Can you call that nurse now, son?"

It shamed him to recall how easy it had been to lie to his son. But years of breaking promises to Andrew had made lying to him easy, hadn't it? What was one more lie in a tall pile of them?

He had lied to Andrew to protect him. That was his justification. To keep Andrew from looking into matters that were better left alone. What Andrew didn't know, wouldn't hurt him.

He only wished there were some way for him to avoid these matters, too. But the nightmares wouldn't let him escape. They were a lucid reminder of something he thought he'd left behind thirty-odd years ago.

Pressing his lips together, he clicked the button to erase the calendar window.

He would call his son. Later.

Or so he promised himself.

Chapter 12

A ndrew spent the entire morning in Mika's suite. When she had given him the pager and started sending him lovey-dovey messages, he'd tried to give it back to her, said it wasn't necessary for them to keep in touch that way. Refusing to argue with him, she strolled into the bedroom. He followed her inside—and walked out two hours later, sweaty and worn out.

He finally left the Ritz-Carlton with the pager clipped to the waist of his slacks. Like she'd told him to do.

It felt liberating to arrive home, a place where logic ruled—not his hormones. As much as he'd enjoyed Mika's company, being with her made him feel, uncomfortably, like a puppet. Manipulated by strings of lust.

He wished he hadn't agreed to see her again that evening. Well, his rational mind wished he hadn't agreed to the date. His body already missed her.

He dropped the pager on a table in the hallway. He'd switched it off soon after he left the hotel. He'd check it for messages later.

The house was quiet. Everything appeared to be in order.

He began a familiar routine: he retrieved the mail, fed the fish in the aquarium, checked voice mail messages on his home phone, and, since it was lunchtime, prepared a turkey-and-cheddar sandwich on wheat bread, with a side of low-fat chips and a glass of Diet Coke. He took his meal upstairs, planning to eat while reading E-mail.

When he stepped across the threshold of his office, he dropped his lunch.

The lid of the laptop had been raised. Black text glowed on the white background of the Microsoft Word program:

HELO ANDREW

Stepping over the spilled food, Andrew kept a distance of several feet from the computer. As though something might catapult from the screen and bite him.

He'd turned the computer off when he left last night. He hadn't been using the word processing program, hadn't typed "Helo Andrew" on the screen. It couldn't possibly have been him.

Someone else had done this.

But who?

He gripped the back of the desk chair. The cold sweat on his palms dampened the leather.

Was he the brunt of an elaborate practical joke? Eric loved to play around, but he couldn't imagine that he'd do something like this. No one else he knew would do such a thing, either.

He found himself thinking about the other weird stuff that had happened the past couple of days: the video game incident, the wineglasses in the china cabinet, the water running in the bathtub during the Memorial Day cookout.

Intuitively, he understood that all of these things were somehow related. They weren't coincidence. Someone was behind all of this.

But who?

A current of cold air blew past him.

He glanced at the windows. They were shut.

The hair on the back of his neck rose.

He had the certain feeling that he was no longer alone.

He heard a noise, turned around.

The food on the floor was moving.

The plate turned over . . . slices of bread and turkey and cheese stacked themselves . . . the chips slid onto the side of the plate . . . the glass floated upright, half-full with ice cubes.

"I'm not seeing this." He took a step backward. "I'm dreaming. This isn't real."

The plate, heaped with food again, rose in the air as if lifted by an invisible waiter. An unseen force drew the glass upward, too.

"This is only a dream."

He squeezed his eyes shut, opened them.

The food and the glass hovered across the room, toward him.

Cold air advanced closer, too.

He screamed.

He fled into the adjoining bathroom. Locked the door. Backed away from the door as if it might explode open on its own. He nearly tripped over the toilet, managed to regain his balance before he fell.

He was breathing so hard that his lungs hurt.

He turned on the faucet and splashed cold water on his face. He dried his skin with a towel. Sucked in deep breaths.

He saw himself in the mirror. His eyes were wide and terrified.

"I'm not crazy," he said to his reflection. "What the hell did I see out there?"

Ghost, a voice in his mind answered. *It's been a ghost all along. You suspected it and didn't want to admit it.*

But he didn't believe in ghosts.

Actually, put it this way: he had never seen one before. He was willing to admit that they might exist. Several people close to him, including his mother, claimed to have witnessed apparitions. He was a skeptic on such matters, but he wasn't a bullheaded fool. He had enough imagination to believe that there was a world beyond our five senses.

But this ghost, if that's what it was, was in his house. *His* house. Not some creepy Victorian mansion in New England. His recently constructed, ultra-modern home in a booming Atlanta suburb.

How could this be happening to him?

He looked at the bathroom door.

What would Mark Justice do in this situation?

Justice didn't answer. Perhaps the supernatural fell outside his realm of expertise.

He dragged his hand down his face. Thinking.

Then, before he lost his nerve, he unlocked the door, yanked it open.

The sandwich, chips, and glass sat on the desk beside the laptop.

But a chill had settled over the room. The presence? In horror movies, coldness in the air often announced the nearness of a spirit.

His heart jackhammered.

He noticed that new text had appeared on the computer screen, underneath the first message.

DONT BE SCARD

He laughed, a bit maniacally, at the misspelling of the word and the absurdity of the message.

Don't be scared. Shit.

He was getting the hell out of there.

Chapter 13

Rain tapped on the roof of Carmen's Marietta town house. Somewhere in the far reaches of the night, thunder rumbled.

At the kitchen table, sipping from a bottle of water, Andrew told Carmen the story of why he believed his house was haunted. He needed her advice to help him decide what he should do next. He was an independent thinker and preferred to find solutions to his own problems. But he couldn't solve this one on his own.

After rushing pell-mell out of his house, he had busied himself driving around, completing errands, browsing at the shopping mall—and trying to avoid thinking too much about what he'd seen in his office. He didn't want to think about it until he could share the story with someone he trusted, because with his tendency to overanalyze things, he feared he would drive himself crazy. He wanted to tell Carmen the story first; he was anxious for her to arrive home from work so he could share his experience with her face-to-face and make sure she understood that he wasn't imagining things.

Which was one reason why he hadn't told Eric about it. Eric, like him, was relentlessly rational. No doubt, he'd attempt to persuade Andrew that he'd dreamed the entire episode while taking a nap. Andrew didn't want that kind of feedback, not with his own thoughts so tangled over what had happened.

Carmen, on the other hand, was open-minded, intuitive, and clear thinking. The kind of friend he needed right now.

"Wow," she said, when he finished his story. She pulled her hands back through her curly hair, and whistled. "Wow, Drew."

"Do you believe me?" he asked.

"Of course I do. You're not the kind of guy who would make up something like this. You're, like, Mr. Logical. I totally believe you."

He breathed a sigh of relief. "Thanks, Carmen. I needed to hear that. This has been driving me nuts. I never expected something like this to happen to me."

"Who would? When I saw a ghost, it surprised me, too."

"You've seen a ghost before?"

She nodded. "I was seventeen. My granddaddy visited me, a few days after he passed. He'd moved in with us when he got up in age, and I became really close to him. When he died, it hit me hard. One night, not long after the funeral, I was in bed, not able to sleep . . . and I felt this weight sit on the side of the mattress, and a cool touch on my cheek. I *knew* it was my granddaddy. I was surprised, but I wasn't scared. He was visiting to let me know that he was doing fine, and that I shouldn't be sad any more, 'cause he was in a better place. And you know what? After that night, I started to feel better."

"Glad to know that something like this has happened

to you, too," he said. "Makes me feel better about my own sanity. Unless we're both crazy."

"You're the writer, so that means you're probably the crazy one." She smiled.

"Always got jokes."

"Seriously, we've got to put our heads together and figure this out," she said. "For that, I need brain food. I'm starved. Want me to order a pizza?"

"Pizza's cool."

"Pepperoni on one half, veggie on the other?"

"Sounds good." It was the style of pizza they always shared. The pepperoni was for him, and the other half was for her.

While she called Pizza Hut and placed an order for delivery, he went to the bathroom. In there, he turned on the pager that Mika had given him.

He wondered why he was hiding in the bathroom with the pager, where Carmen would not see him. Wondered why he hadn't mentioned Mika to Carmen at all. His behavior was that of a guy who was cheating on his woman, which was ridiculous. They weren't romantically involved.

Still, he'd rather not tell Carmen about her.

Throughout the day, Mika had sent him eleven messages. BEEN THINKING ABOUT YOU; HEY, DARLING; CAN'T WAIT TO SEE YOU TONIGHT; and so on.

He had finally responded about an hour ago with, "HAVING VERY BAD DAY, CAN'T COME FOR DINNER TONIGHT. SORRY, WILL SET ANOTHER DATE." He simply couldn't deal with Mika, and the strangeness that had invaded his house, simultaneously. Until he found out what was going on at his home, he'd be unable to focus on anything else. Mika would have to wait until later.

But as he scanned the list of messages that Mika had sent, he saw that she hadn't responded to his date cancellation. She hadn't called his cell phone, either.

She probably was pissed at him. Pissed that he wasn't coming to see her, pissed that he wasn't within arms' reach so that she could seduce him into changing his mind. Well, she would get over it.

Back in the kitchen, he took a seat at the table. Carmen poured herself a tall glass of iced tea.

His gaze wandered over her. She'd changed from the conservative navy-blue business suit she wore to her accounting job into casual wear: red shorts, a white tank top, and flip-flops. She'd washed off her makeup, too.

But it didn't matter what she wore: she was fine. He found himself comparing her to Mika. Mika was perfection personified, like a woman straight out of an exotic fantasy. Carmen was beautiful in a girl-next-door way.

And Carmen, though she could be a flirt, didn't need to use sex to get what she wanted. You wanted to please her because she was such a sweetheart.

He shook his head. Why was he comparing the two of them? He knew Mika as a lover, and Carmen as a friend. He shouldn't be doing this.

Carmen noticed his attention. "What're you looking at?"

"Uh, can I have some tea, too?"

"Sure. But you might want to finish off that water first, since ogling me's got you all hot and bothered."

Heat flushed his face. He drank the rest of his water.

She laughed. "I was only joking. Jeez, you act like a guilty man. Should I change clothes? Throw on something grungy?"

"No, you're fine."

"Am I? That's so sweet for you to say that, Drew."

"You know what I meant." But he blushed again. She had an uncanny knack for embarrassing him.

She came to the table with two glasses of tea and slid into the seat next to him.

"Back to business," she said. "Take out your notebook, honey. Time to talk about this ghost of yours."

"Okay," Carmen said, "as far as we know, we're assuming that the haunting began Monday, at the cookout. With the water running in the bathtub."

"Right." He scribbled, "water running in tub" on a spiral notepad.

"Next, the ghost knocked over some wineglasses, left the cabinet door open," she said.

Nodding, he wrote her words down.

"Then it turned on the PlayStation, popped in a game, had the volume cranked up," she said.

He wrote, "video game incident, volume high."

"Lastly, it left not one, but two messages on your computer. Said 'hello, Andrew' and 'don't be scared.' Picked up the food you'd spilled on the floor, too, right in front of your eyes."

"Yeah." The memory sent a shiver down his back.

She snapped her fingers and grinned. "My dear Watson, I think I've got it."

"What is it?"

"This ghost has been trying to get your attention. But you weren't picking up the hints, so it came right out and did something bold today. Something that you couldn't write off to a bad memory or coincidence."

"It's definitely got my attention now. But why? What does it want?"

"Don't know. But I bet I know how you can find out."

"How?"

"You've got to ask it, Drew. Ghosts are usually trying to communicate stuff to us, warn us about things, or comfort us, like my granddaddy did for me. You've got to start a dialogue with this spirit. Find out who it is, what it wants, and why."

He put down the pen. "You've gotta be kidding me. I don't wanna *talk* to this ghost. I want it to get the hell outta my house."

"Okay." She shrugged. "Then call Ghostbusters."

"Very funny."

"I don't know what else to tell you. I think you need to talk to it. I don't think it plans to hurt you. Why else would it say, 'don't be scared'?"

"But, Carmen . . ." He dragged his hand down his face. She didn't understand how badly the experience had rattled him. His life had been invaded by the supernatural. Things like this simply did not happen to him. He was a rational guy, with an orderly life. And here she was, telling him to chat with a ghost? It was crazy.

She touched his hand. "You don't want to go home, do you?"

"Not tonight. I want to get some distance, sort this out some more. I wouldn't sleep for a minute knowing that there's a presence or whatever in my house."

"You can spend the night here," she said. She added: "In the guest room."

"Thanks, I appreciate that."

"But later, I want you to follow my advice. Talk to it. We can sit up here all night spinning theories, better to get some direct answers."

"I agree, and I'll do that," he said. "Later."

She smiled, squeezed his hand.

He smiled at her, too.

He didn't want her to take her hand away from his.

The doorbell chimed.

"That should be the pizza," she said. "My, that was quick." She rose and walked out of the kitchen.

He watched her leave. Thoughts about her that went

far beyond the boundaries of their platonic friendship
flitted through his brain.

Let it go, man. She's just a friend. Leave it at that.

Sighing, he returned his attention to the notepad.
He wrote, "next step: talk to the ghost," and underlined
the words.

Talk to the ghost. Had he entered the twilight zone
or what?

"Andrew, can you come here, please?" Carmen said
from the doorway.

Mulling over what he could possibly discuss with a
ghostly visitor, he got up, entered the hallway.

He stopped.

Holding a red umbrella and wearing a sugar-sweet
smile, Mika waited at the front door.

Chapter 14

When Andrew saw Mika waiting at the door, a swarm of questions buzzed through his mind in a matter of a few seconds.

How did Mika know he was there? Had she followed him? What did she want? Was she going to think he was sleeping with Carmen and cause some drama? What was Carmen going to think of this?

And again: how did she know he was here?

He'd lost his ability to speak. A lump as large as a golf ball had lodged in his throat.

"Andrew, you have a guest," Carmen said. She addressed him as Andrew only when she was upset with him.

Mika's saccharine smile never wavered. Twirling the umbrella, she said, "Goodness, I need to get out of this cold rain," and stepped inside.

Closing the door, Carmen shot her a look of thinly concealed disgust.

Mika acted as if she didn't notice. She was dressed for a night on the town: black miniskirt, red silk blouse, pumps, platinum jewelry. Her long, wavy hair was freshly styled; her jasmine perfume teased his nostrils.

She gave him a megawatt smile.

At last, he found his voice. "Mika, what are you doing here?"

Mika came forward and grasped his hand. "Oh, darling, don't you remember that we had dinner plans for this evening? We discussed it this morning—after you left my suite."

He blinked. Was she serious?

"I sent you a message on the pager," he said. "I won't be able to make it for dinner. I've had a really crazy day and—"

"Which is why you need to come spend the night with me again, baby," Mika said. She stroked his arm. "I'll make it all better."

"I don't need to see any more of this," Carmen said. Glaring at Andrew, she turned to walk away.

"Carmen—" Andrew said.

Mika's face brightened. "Oh, so this is Carmen? Andrew has told me so many great things about you."

"Has he?" Carmen asked. "Funny, he hasn't told me about you."

"He hasn't?" Mika said. "That's not too shocking, I suppose. We met only yesterday. My name is Mika." She extended her hand.

Carmen shook her hand quickly. She rushed away, saying, "I'll let you two chat. You must have so much to discuss since you've already spent the night together." She didn't even look at Andrew.

Damn. He was in trouble now.

Mika watched Carmen leave, and pivoted to face Andrew. Her smile fell away.

"What are you doing over here?" she asked.

"I need to be asking you that question. Did you follow me here?"

"I have my ways, especially where my man is concerned."

My man? Had he heard her correctly?

He cleared his throat. "Listen, Mika, it's not like that between us. I'm not your man. I've known you for one day."

"How can you say that, Andrew? We had such a fabulous time together, packed months of passion into a few hours."

"But it was only one day! That doesn't give you the right to follow me around."

"Why are you being so mean to me, baby?" Her eyes glimmered wetly. "I only wanted to see you. After last night, I thought that you cared about me."

He wiped his hand down his sweaty face. He wasn't good at dealing with emotional conflict. It was messy, unpredictable, stressful. His natural inclination was to avoid drama and hope that the problem faded away, took care of itself. But he had the unsettling feeling that Mika wasn't an issue that was going to be so easily resolved.

"It's her, isn't it?" Mika said. Her gaze sharpened like a knife. "That bitch, Carmen. You're in love with her."

"First of all, she's not a bitch. Don't disrespect her like that. And I told you, she's only a friend."

Mika laughed hollowly. "Only a friend? Walking around in high-cut shorts and a tank top that shows off her titties? Are you going to make love to her tonight, Andrew, or are you just going to fuck her, like I guess you did to me?"

He paused. Stared at her.

Mika's eyebrow twitched, as if currents of dangerous energy had overloaded her nerves. At that moment, she seemed capable of anything, and he was afraid of what she might do.

He looked at her tiny black purse, wondered if she had concealed a gun or a knife in there.

He backed up a couple of steps.

"You promised me that I've no competition." She stepped closer.

"I was telling the truth. We're only friends."

"You better not be lying to me, Andrew. I don't like liars."

She was about five-feet-seven, several inches shorter than he was, and he outweighed her by probably fifty pounds. Physically, she was no match for him. But the steel glint in her gaze promised a fight.

"Mika, I'm not lying. Really. We're only friends."

Her face softened. "Then come with me tonight, darling."

"I can't, not tonight. We'll talk about this later. Okay?"

"I want you tonight." She draped her hands around his neck, stroked the back of his head.

The memory of last night's passion sparked an awakening in his groin. As if they had a mind of their own, his hands moved to her hips.

She smiled, knowingly. "You want me, too. Your little friend has perked up."

He wanted to curse. His body had betrayed him again.

"I've got what he wants," she said. She moved her hand to his crotch and massaged his erection, which, in spite of himself, was growing more rigid by the second.

"Mika—" he started.

"Come with me tonight, baby," she said. "Please don't make me beg."

"Listen, Mika, I can't."

She lowered to her knees. Tugged his belt buckle.

He backed away.

"Not here," he said. "Not in my friend's house."

"Afraid she'll get jealous? She's in love with you. It's all in her eyes."

"I'm sorry, but you need to go. I'll see you later."

Her head drooped forward suddenly, hair falling over her face. She knelt there like that, silent, for at least ten seconds. Like a wind-up doll that had lost power.

A frown crinkled his features. Something wasn't right about this woman. He'd told her that he'd see her later, but that was only a delaying tactic to make her leave. He didn't think it would be a wise idea to see her anytime soon—if ever again. There were so many red flags waving in his face that he'd be a fool to ignore them, no matter how strongly he was attracted to her.

She finally raised her head, and rose.

"Fine, Andrew." She smiled blandly. "We'll see each other later. Unless we see each other in our dreams tonight."

"'Bye, Mika."

"Good night, soul mate eyes." She picked up her umbrella and let herself out.

The Rolls Royce waited for her at the curb. A chauffeur—a hat pulled low over his head hiding his face—opened her door, and in seconds, they glided away into the stormy night.

He closed the door and leaned against it.

Talk about a helluva day. A ghost was haunting his house. A woman he'd just met had become a borderline stalker.

The predictable, routine-dominated life he'd created was coming apart at the seams, like an old coat. He longed for a return to normalcy, as boring as it had been sometimes.

The doorbell rang.

Afraid that it might be Mika again, he cautiously peered through the peephole.

But it was only the pizza delivery guy.

Carmen sat at the kitchen table, reading an issue of *Essence.*

He brought the pizza into the kitchen and placed it on the counter. "Time to eat."

The cheer in his voice sounded false, but he didn't know what else to say to her.

Her eyes punctured him like needles.

"I don't believe you, Drew."

"What do you mean?"

"You didn't say a damn thing about meeting a new woman. Whatever, though, I can deal with that. But you slept with her on the first date?"

He leaned against the counter, folded his arms. "Carmen, that's personal."

"The first date?"

"Listen, I didn't plan it, things just happened. When did I claim to be a saint?"

"Never." She closed the magazine. "But it disappoints me. I thought you were better than that."

Hearing those words from her hit him like a blow to the stomach.

Carmen held him in high regard. She always bragged about him to her friends, used him as an example of how there really were some nice guys left in the world, said he was proof that not all men were sex-crazed animals who dropped their drawers at the earliest opportunity. He cherished her admiration and respect for him. He felt as though he had failed her.

"I'm sorry to disappoint you," he said.

"Whatever, like you said, that's your personal business. But I think you could've chosen better. Did she follow you over here?"

Lips pressed together, he nodded.

"That's some crazy shit, Drew. You've known this girl for a day and she's following you?"

"Honestly, I never thought this would happen. She seemed normal at first."

"Has she been to your house?"

"No."

She smiled ruefully. "I bet. If she trailed you over here, you better believe she knows where you live, too."

He didn't want to think about it, but he suspected that she was right.

"I don't want to tell you how to handle your business," she said, "but I think you need to kick her to the curb. Like, ASAP."

"Yeah, I know."

"If you string her along, it'll only get worse. When someone starts obsessing over you, they can be like a pit bull. Lock their teeth on you and you can't ever shake 'em loose."

"She's a nice girl," he said. "She's only needy, I guess."

"That's how psychos are, Drew. Nice and needy—and nutty."

"She's had some bad experiences, stuff that's damaged her."

"Sure she has. So have all of us. That's life, deal with it."

"That's harsh."

"You're a softie, and I love that about you, but you can't be like that with this woman," she said. "She'll use that to take advantage of you. Manipulators recognize your weaknesses and use them to get what they want."

He didn't like the way she spoke about Mika as if she

were some femme fatale, some psycho stalker. Mika wasn't *that* bad. Carmen wasn't being fair, and he wasn't going to give her more ammo so that she could continue to attack Mika's character.

Part of him, however, questioned whether he was letting his physical attraction to Mika soften his opinions about her. He knew from experience how easy it was to make excuses for all kinds of behavior after someone had rocked your world.

"Anyway, I've got it under control," he said, his cue to change the subject.

"Was she jealous of me? I bet she was."

He recalled Mika's venomous comments. *It's her, isn't it? That bitch, Carmen . . .*

"It doesn't matter," he said. "I told her the deal between you and me."

"Told her we're just friends? She'll never believe that. She's going to push harder now that she thinks she's got some competition."

"Doesn't matter, it's over," he said. He opened the pizza carton. He put slices on plates for himself and Carmen.

But the scent of Mika's perfume remained on his skin. Sexy jasmine. Yeah, she was way out of line for following him—but he couldn't help wondering what they might have done if he'd spent the night with her again. His imagination cooked up a dizzying mélange of erotic scenarios.

Let it go, man. She's crazy.

Later, he'd have to take a thorough shower to scrub all traces of her fragrance from his body. Or else, his mind would persist in churning out forbidden fantasies.

He returned to the table with the pizza.

"I still can't believe you slept with her," Carmen said.

He paused with a pizza slice near his lips. "Carmen, will you please let it go?"

"Forget it, it's none of my business." She took a bite of her pizza, flipped through the magazine.

Carmen was jealous. She probably was "disappointed" in his poor judgment in sleeping with Mika on the first date, but her jealousy likely loomed larger in her mind than anything else. He didn't know why he didn't see it before now.

"So, does Mika have any competition?" he asked.

She didn't look up. "Not from me she doesn't."

Her reluctance to meet his eyes only verified his suspicion.

The other day, he'd admitted to himself that he was jealous of her dating other men; she obviously was jealous of him dating other women. What did that say about them? Was their "we're just friends" categorization of their relationship merely a front for what they really felt for each other?

It was an awkward subject that he wasn't quite sure how to approach—and he wasn't sure that he wanted to. He liked what they had together, whatever it could be called. He didn't want to drag it into the spotlight, subject it to examination, and risk spoiling it.

Carmen made it easy for him by changing the subject. She finished her pizza, pushed aside the magazine and said, "Let's get back to the ghost stuff."

They discussed how he might go about opening a dialogue with the ghost, when he decided that he was ready for that step. He suggested that since the ghost had typed a message on his computer, using the laptop might be the best way to begin the communication. He could present a question to the spirit in his word processing program. Carmen agreed that it was a good idea.

"Maybe if I ask, the ghost will write my next book for me," he said. "Gives new meaning to the term 'ghost writer,' doesn't it?"

"Good to see you're keeping your sense of humor, Drew." She stored the leftover pizza in the refrigerator.

"If I couldn't make fun of it, I'd have to check into a padded room somewhere. The whole situation is totally crazy, you know?"

"You know what gets me? The timing of it."

"I don't follow you."

"The haunting started a couple of days ago. Then you met psycho chick yesterday."

He'd let her "psycho chick" comment slide. "So?"

"So doesn't it seem a bit too coincidental to you? Two weird things starting at the same time?"

"I don't see how Mika could have anything to do with a ghost, or vice versa."

"Me, neither." She wiped the counter with a dish towel. "It was only a thought. I think everything happens for a reason. I don't believe in coincidence."

She'd raised an interesting idea. But he couldn't go anywhere with it. Mika was only a woman who was eager for love. He didn't know yet what the presence at his house wanted from him, but he doubted it had anything to do with her. It was an intriguing, but moot, point.

Outdoors, a peal of thunder shook the night. Gusts wailed around the windows, sounding like the cries of a lost child.

Chapter 15

Courtesy of five milligrams of Ambien, Raymond finally enjoyed several hours of peaceful, dreamless sleep.

He'd left his office early and slid into bed at three in the afternoon. He awoke around eleven. Eight hours of quality sleep. He felt invigorated.

Beside him, June slumbered quietly. He'd slept so deeply he'd never heard her get into the bed.

He kissed her on the cheek. Although he disliked visiting his physician, the sleep aid prescription had been exactly what he needed. He loved her for being concerned about him. Especially when he lacked the good sense to take proper care of himself.

He quietly left the bedroom. He planned to review some business documents, watch ESPN for an hour or so, and return to bed. He didn't want to throw his sleep schedule completely out of whack.

He tied the belt of his house robe, got a glass of water from the kitchen, and went to the den. His leather briefcase lay on the coffee table. A Post-It was stuck to the top. "Call Andrew, re: golf" it read, in his chicken-scratch handwriting. He'd scribbled the note to himself before retiring to bed.

Now that he'd found a solution to his nightmares and had gained some rest, he felt better about talking to his son. He called Andrew's house. It was late, but his boy was a night owl, like him.

There was no answer; Andrew was probably out chasing women. Chuckling at the thought, he left a message asking Andrew to meet him at the driving range tomorrow afternoon.

Smiling to himself, he unlatched the briefcase and raised the lid.

He expected to find a collection of manila file folders within. He didn't.

He found, instead, darkness.

Blackness completely filled the bottom half of the briefcase, as if he'd raised the cover of a manhole that dropped into a subterranean world of endless depth.

A powerful force, like gravity, drew his hands toward the darkness.

He yelped. Tearing his hands away from the pull of the mysterious energy, he slammed the lid shut.

What the hell had he just seen? Was he still asleep and dreaming?

When he reached out to get the glass of water, his hand trembled so badly that water slopped over the rim. He gripped the glass in both hands to steady it, drank deeply.

He studied the briefcase.

"You imagined that, Ray," he said aloud. "There's no way you really saw what you thought you did, and you know it."

Slowly, he leaned forward. He popped open the case.

Impenetrable darkness yawned inside.

Again, he felt that strange, invisible tug.

He smashed the lid down and kicked the briefcase. It flipped off the table and thudded against the floor, out of sight.

"Out of my mind," he said. "Going out of my damn mind."

Maybe he'd defeated the nightmares, only to be plagued by something even worse: hallucinations.

He remembered Dr. Unaeze's words about the sleeping pills: *Other potential side effects are difficulty breathing, nausea, temporary amnesia, and in rare cases, hallucinations.*

Hallucinations. Seeing crazy shit that wasn't real.

It was a frightening thought that he dared not consider further.

He decided that work could wait until morning. Instead, he would watch television. Not in here, though. He didn't want to be around the briefcase, didn't want to touch it and move it out of the room, either.

In the family room, he settled into his recliner—he called it "The Captain's Seat"—picked up the remote control off the armrest, and clicked the power button.

He feared that instead of a cable channel, the set would be tuned in to the same velvety darkness that had claimed his briefcase. With great relief, he saw ESPN's SportsCenter fill the wide screen.

His stomach rumbled. He shuffled into the kitchen to get a snack. He hadn't eaten since the afternoon.

Pulling open the refrigerator, he peered inside cautiously.

No darkness lurked inside there, either. Food and drink filled the shelves.

He laughed at his foolishness. His imagination had really run away with him. There was nothing to worry about. The blackness in the briefcase had merely been . . . well, he didn't know what it had been, but he needed to forget about it.

He removed a carton of milk, set it on the counter, and turned to the pantry to get a box of cereal.

The pantry door opened to a pitch-black void.

A scream flew up his throat, came out of his mouth as a choked gasp.

Like the darkness in the briefcase, the black hole in the pantry exerted a strong gravitational pull. He tried to backpedal to the counter, move out of the energy's orbit. But he felt himself drawn, inexorably, to the doorway.

Not happening to me, this is another hallucination, can't be happening . . .

The darkness sucked him inside.

The darkness vanished in the twitch of an eye.

Blinking, Raymond realized that he was in a familiar place.

He stood at the mouth of a weed-choked, gravel driveway. The narrow path led to the mansion.

The same mansion he'd driven to a few weeks ago, when returning from Savannah with Andrew. The mansion that had haunted his dreams ever since.

Although he knew this world wasn't real, iciness spread through his veins.

Thunder boomed across the land. The night sky bulged with storm clouds. A drizzle fell, the cold droplets as penetrating as sand.

Behind him, his Ford Expedition was crashed in a ditch, upside down, roof smashed and windows busted. Just like the actual accident.

The difference was that here, in his dream, he had somehow scrambled out of the vehicle after briefly losing consciousness.

He heard movement ahead, in the underbrush. Someone hacking his way along the drive. He knew who it was, without needing to look.

It was his son, Andrew. Going to the house in hopes of getting help for him.

He had to stop his boy from reaching the mansion. It wasn't safe for him to go inside.

He hurried along the driveway, beating back bushes and twigs.

"Andrew!" he said. "Don't go up there, son! Wait!"

But Andrew moved much faster than he did. He couldn't catch him. Raymond's movements were slowed, as if he were fighting through sludge.

By the time he stumbled out of the undergrowth and into a clearing, Andrew approached the veranda of the house.

His son wasn't a grown man of thirty-one. He was short, maybe seven years old. He wore a red Atlanta Hawks T-shirt and matching shorts.

In the dream, Andrew was always a child. Raymond didn't understand it.

"Andrew, stop!" he said. "Stay the hell outta that house, boy!"

But Andrew didn't hear him. He pushed open the front door and disappeared inside.

Panting, Raymond dropped to his knees. Tears ran down his cheeks.

This was his fault. He never should have taken the exit off the highway and brought them to this godforsaken place.

But he hadn't been in control of himself at the time. Someone—*something*—had piloted his body and brought him here.

The estate towered ahead of him, like a forbidden house in a fairy tale. Moss twisted around the thick columns. Dark windows stared blankly, like dead, giant eyes.

Then, a soft, greenish light brightened one of the upper rooms. The light pulsated rhythmically, like a luminescent heart. It had an indefinable, alien quality.

Always, the same questions about the light came to him. What was it? Where did it come from? Why did he have the sense that it was calling him toward it? What did it want with him?

Like a sleepwalker, he began to trudge forward through the mud.

He mounted the veranda steps, walked across the rotted floorboards. He approached the large oak door.

The door was locked.

He pounded his fist against the wood. "Andrew? You in there? Let me in!"

No answer.

Andrew couldn't help him. His son had walked into a trap. Raymond understood that intuitively.

The thing that had captured his son didn't want Raymond to reach the light in the upper room, either. Somehow, he knew that intuitively, too.

He didn't know how he knew these things, but he *knew* them, as surely as he knew his name.

He had to find another way inside the house.

Although wooden chairs stood on the veranda, he didn't bother attempting to shatter a window with one of them. He'd tried that before, in another instance of the dream. The windows were unbreakable.

Remembering what he had done in nightmares prior, while he was in the current nightmare, made him briefly question his sanity. What in God's name was really going on?

The weird part was that in all of his bad dreams, he found himself at the locked front door of the estate, like this, needing to get inside to save his son. But at this point, the action always diverged in a different direction.

It was as if he were immersed in some weird, hyper-realistic video game. The particular circumstances changed. But the setting and the goal always remained the same.

The same opposition inevitably appeared, too.

He turned, putting the door at his back.

The caretaker, Walter, rounded the corner of the veranda.

The tall black man was an actual person. Raymond had encountered him when he originally visited the estate, over thirty years ago. He'd looked the same back then. Old yet strangely youthful, with a shock of iron-gray hair fluttering from his pate. Dressed in a somber black suit that recalled a funeral director.

Walter marched to the foot of the veranda steps.

"You don't belong here, Raymond," he said, in his baritone voice.

"I'm here to get my son. I'm not leaving without him."

Walter advanced to the first step, long arms spread.

Raymond's gut tightened.

"We are keeping Andrew here with us," Walter said. "We are grateful to you for bringing him. Your work is now done. Go home in peace."

"I'm not going anywhere without my boy."

Walter hustled forward. He moved with the speed of a young man.

Raymond sprinted across the veranda.

That was when he saw the large bluish-gray cat crouched on the railing in front of him. Its vivid green eyes glimmered with cold intelligence.

He raised his arms to protect himself, but too late.

Screeching, the feline leapt at him.

*   *   *

Raymond clawed at his face, to tear away the cat.

But there was no cat. He wasn't running across a veranda, either.

He was in the kitchen wearing a house robe, facing the shelves of the pantry.

He exhaled explosively. Slumped against the counter.

It had all been a dream, a hallucination.

A sharp pain flared in his head, like a steel spike driving into his brain. He winced. The throbbing ache was concentrated in the area of his bruise.

Tears came to his eyes. He'd never felt pain like this. It felt as if his skull were being pulverized into mush.

June hurried into the kitchen. "Ray, what's wrong? I heard you shouting. Are you okay?"

"I . . . I thought I saw . . ." He was going to lie about seeing a mouse in the pantry, to throw her off the truth.

But as his headache intensified, he realized that he couldn't lie anymore. Something was seriously wrong with him, and denying the truth of the problem could be deadly.

"You thought you saw what?" June asked.

"June . . . I," he said. "I think I want to go to that neurologist. I'm . . . scared."

He began to tremble uncontrollably.

She took him in her arms, and held him.

Chapter 16

In the guest room of Carmen's town house, freshly showered, Andrew prepared for bed.

Before leaving his house earlier that day, he'd packed an overnight bag. He was determined to sleep elsewhere that night, whether it was at Carmen's, his mother's, or in a hotel. Although his discussion with Carmen influenced him to believe that the presence in his house might harbor no malicious intent, he wasn't ready to go back and face the ghost. He'd see how he felt about it tomorrow.

Sitting on the edge of the twin-size bed, he used his cell phone to check his messages at home. His father had left him a voice mail asking if he were interested in meeting him at the driving range tomorrow afternoon.

Dad had kept his word. Considering how badly their conversation had ended at the cookout, Andrew was happily surprised. He hadn't expected his father to call him again for a long time.

A familiar blend of anxiety and hope churned in his stomach. Those warring emotions had tormented him when he was a kid, awakening whenever his father called

or visited. Over the years, he'd learned by painful experience to harden his heart and expect nothing from his
dad. But the past two months of regular phone calls
and golf outings had turned him into a child again. In
spite of his persistent worry that he was setting himself
up for disappointment, he dared to believe that his father truly had changed.

It was a quarter to midnight, so he'd return his dad's
call in the morning. It would be nice to do something
that would take his mind off his "ghost problem," and
Mika.

Mika, thank God, hadn't left any messages on his cell
phone, or the pager. Had she realized how crazy she'd
acted earlier? He hoped that she'd gotten herself together. Still, after what she'd pulled, he'd be worse than
a fool for pursuing a relationship with her. Carmen
probably would slap him silly if he did.

There was a knock at the door.

"Come in," he said.

Carmen opened the door. She was dressed for bed
in an oversize T-shirt with "National Black Arts Festival
2004" printed across the front in bright colors. The
shirt ended just above her knees.

He purposefully avoided checking out her legs. But
it was hard to ignore the way her breasts nicely filled out
the shirt.

He'd changed into baggy boxers and a T-shirt. He
noticed that her gaze did a quick sweep across his legs.

Inwardly, he smiled. Women thought they were so
slick sometimes.

Crossing her arms over her bosom, she leaned against
the doorjamb. "Going to bed soon?"

"In a few minutes."

"Need anything?"

Only you, lying here beside me.

"I'm cool."

"I'm going to turn on the alarm system, then."
She yawned. " 'Night, Drew."

"Carmen?"

She turned. "Yeah?"

"Thanks. For letting me stay here, and, well, every-thing."

She smiled. "Don't mention it."

They stared at each other, silent.

Then, she pulled the door shut. A few seconds later, he heard the beeps of the engaged security system.

He stretched out on the bed.

Carmen had wanted him to make a move. He'd felt it. But he'd let the opportunity slip away.

How could he act so boldly with Mika, whom he'd known for only a day, yet behave like a meek choirboy with a woman he knew so well? He didn't know the an-swer to the question, and it frustrated him.

As he reached to the lamp on the nightstand to cut off the light, the pager, which he'd set beside the digital clock, vibrated.

There was a message from Mika.

YOU'LL DREAM ABOUT ME TONIGHT, BABY.

"Whatever," he said. "If I do dream about you, it'll probably be a nightmare."

He snapped the pager shut and turned out the light.

An explosive orgasm blew Andrew out of sleep.

"Oh, shit," he said, as the last ecstatic wave spasmed through him. Trembling, he sat up. The bedsheets en-tangled his legs; his boxer shorts were rolled under his hips.

He smelled a trace of jasmine, like the perfume Mika wore.

But it had to be his imagination. It only made sense

that he'd imagine such a scent, after all—he'd just had a wet dream about her giving him an amazing blow job.

He wiped cold sweat from his face with the edge of his shirt.

The dream had been so *real*.

In her last pager message, she'd promised him that he would dream about her. Her words must have acted upon him like a post-hypnotic suggestion.

The digital clock read 2:21. It was a long time until morning. He needed to get all the rest he could, as he had a full day ahead of him tomorrow.

First, he wanted to clean himself up. He switched on the lamp. He checked to ensure that he hadn't stained the sheets—Carmen would never let him live that down if he had—then pushed out of bed and padded to the adjoining bathroom.

A red silk thong hung on the knob of the bathroom door.

It hadn't been there before he'd retired to bed. He was absolutely certain of it.

And it looked like the same thong Mika had been wearing last night.

He lifted it off the knob, sniffed it.

It had the fragrance of jasmine on it, too.

In the bathroom, Andrew laid the thong on the vanity, and cleaned himself up.

He didn't know where the thong had come from. His first thought was that it belonged to Carmen, but she would've had to sneak inside his room and drop it on the doorknob while he was sleeping, and he couldn't imagine her doing such a thing. She was a flirt, and he suspected that she liked him as more than a friend, but this didn't seem to be her style.

And Mika? It looked like hers, smelled like hers . . .

but how could she have gotten in the house? Carmen had turned on the security system. The alarm would have wailed like crazy if someone had broken inside. It couldn't have been her.

The logical explanation was that Carmen had done it. Maybe she was more assertive than he'd assumed. It wouldn't be the first time that a woman had surprised him.

He smiled to himself. Carmen was a nice girl, but she had a little freak in her, didn't she? It turned him on.

He changed into a fresh pair of boxers. Twirling the thong around his fingers, he crossed the hallway and went to Carmen's bedroom. The door was partly open. He spied her in the darkness, wrapped in sheets.

A bright light flashed in his face. Carmen asked, "Who's there?"

Shielding his eyes against the glare, he said, "It's just me."

"Oh." She lowered the flashlight. "What is it?"

"Can I come in for a sec? Want to show you something."

She murmured a yes. He sat on the side of her bed, and dropped the thong between them.

"You forgot this," he said.

She spot-lit the garment with her heavy-duty flashlight. She always slept with the light nearby, she'd confided to Andrew once. As a single woman living alone, it made her feel safe.

"What're you talking about?" she asked. "This isn't mine."

"It has to be yours. It was hanging on the doorknob of the bathroom."

"I'm telling you, it's not mine." She pushed the thong away as if it were something filthy.

"Stop playing, girl."

"I'm *not* playing . . . what's that noise?"

He heard it, too. It sounded like people talking and laughing.

"Must be the TV," he said.

She clicked on a lamp, flung back the sheets and swung her legs over the side of the bed.

"But I turned the TV off before we went to bed," she said.

Both of them looked toward the hallway.

He suddenly knew that they had a visitor in the house.

Chapter 17

They checked the control panel of the security system, located on the wall beside the door of her bedroom. The red "Secure" light burned.

If someone were in the living room watching television, the motion detector component of the system would have picked up the movement and triggered the alarm.

Unless the visitor was not an ordinary, flesh-and-blood person.

"You sure you turned off the TV?" Andrew asked.

"Positive," she said.

Dampness lay across the back of his neck, like a cold towel.

What would Mark Justice do in this situation?

Justice must have become acclimated to the weird things happening to Andrew, because he promptly replied: *Don't be a punk. Go check it out, brotherman.*

"Okay," he said, sounding braver than he felt. "I'll check it out."

"I'll go with you. You lead." She placed the flashlight in his hand. "This makes a good club."

He almost told her that, due to the nature of the suspected intruder, he doubted any weapon whatsoever would offer any help. But he kept his mouth shut. He didn't want to frighten her. He was scared enough himself.

She punched in the code to disarm the security system. He led the way down the hall, Carmen close behind.

The living room was around a bend. He reached around the wall, flipped the light switch. Light illuminated the area.

The television was on. The movie playing struck him as comically ironic: *The Sixth Sense.*

The room was empty.

He released a pent-up breath.

Carmen left his side and entered the kitchen, turning on lights.

Nothing else appeared to be out of place in the living room.

Maybe a power surge had turned on the television. It had been storming for much of the night. Stuff like that happened, didn't it?

Although his intuition gave him a different explanation for the TV, he was determined to find a logical answer.

"Drew, you better come in here," Carmen said. Her voice was troubled.

Dread lay heavy on his shoulders. He walked into the kitchen.

She pointed to the refrigerator.

A collection of colorful alphabet magnets clung to the refrigerator door. Carmen had bought the magnets months ago to entertain her nephew, who was learning how to read.

The letters had been arranged into a phrase.

CAINT RUN ANDREW

His heart whammed like a bass drum.

The ghost had followed him.

Carmen looked at him, her eyes haunted.

"Looks like you're not the only guest at my house tonight."

Andrew never imagined that the first time he'd share a bed with Carmen would be under circumstances like this.

The discovery in the kitchen had put both of them on edge. The message was clear to him: there was no escaping his ghostly companion. Whoever it was, and whatever it wanted, it was following him. There was little point in staying at Carmen's house, or anywhere other than his own home, again.

But tonight, he didn't want to be alone, and neither did Carmen. Nothing unusual had ever happened in her house, she said, and it creeped her out. In spite of the ghost's earlier message telling Andrew that there was nothing to fear, an almost primitive anxiety, like a child's fear of the dark, held sway over both of them. Sleeping in the same bed was probably the only way either of them would feel safe enough to shut their eyes that night.

Earlier in the evening, they had talked about him attempting to talk to the ghost. But he'd been too frightened to try anything when they found the message on the refrigerator. Perhaps tomorrow, in daylight, he'd summon the nerve.

They kept the bedside lamp on, placing it on its dimmest setting. Neither of them wanted to sleep in the dark. Not tonight.

Beside him, Carmen burrowed under the sheets.

"Never thought something like this would land us in bed together," she said.

"I was just thinking about that."

"I bet. Don't think you're gonna get some."

"Damn, I'd gotten my hopes up." He was kidding—partly. He had to admit to a healthy curiosity about what might happen between them in such close quarters.

"I'm not that easy," she said. "Unlike some women you know."

"Ouch. You're still upset about that, huh?"

She closed her eyes, didn't respond.

"Now I get the silent treatment?" he asked.

She looked at him. "Go to sleep, Drew."

"Come on, I wanna talk about this."

"What's there to talk about? You slept with a woman you hardly knew, a woman who turned out to be a psycho, and it's none of my business, like you said."

"You're definitely acting like it's your business."

She yawned—a bit dramatically. "I need to get some sleep, Drew."

"Are you jealous?" he asked.

"What do you think?"

"I think you are."

"Are you jealous of me dating other men?"

He paused. "Maybe . . . a little."

"All right, so maybe I'm a *little* jealous of you seeing other women."

It was as close as they'd ever gotten to confessing their true feelings for each other. Would they finally cross over the line, come clean about their emotions?

"Then what're we gonna do about it?" he said. "Both of us being a little jealous and all?"

"What do you want to do about it?"

She was putting the onus on him. Waiting on him to

initiate. She was old-fashioned like that, he knew. No matter how much she liked a man, she wasn't going to chase him. In her opinion, a real man would have the guts to make the first move.

He wanted to take their relationship to the next level. Truly, he did. But with all the crazy things going on in his life, was this the right time? He was scared to death of making a mistake with her. He cherished her too much to ever want to hurt her.

"Listen, Carmen, can we have this conversation later? I don't think this is a good time."

She sighed. The sigh was full of disappointment.

"Yeah, Drew. You're probably right. Bad timing."

"When things settle down, though, I want us to have a heart-to-heart about it."

"Well, until then, I just want to make it clear. All flirting aside, I don't do the friends-with-benefits thing."

"Understood," he said. "And respected."

"Good."

"Good night, Carmen."

" 'Night, Drew."

She rolled over, away from him.

She was upset. It bothered him, but he was trying to handle this as best he could. He didn't want to rush into something and wind up regretting it. Like he'd done with Mika.

But Carmen was different. He'd known her for years. He already loved her as a friend. He didn't doubt that he could love her as more than a friend.

But he was scared. Carmen offered the possibility of something deeper than he'd ever had before. A soul-to-soul connection. The promise of such intimacy, while exciting, frightened him. What if he wasn't ready to give up the freedom of the bachelor life? What if he wasn't good enough for her? What if, God forbid, they got bored with each other?

Too many questions. No satisfying answers. He shoved the thoughts aside, to be revisited later.

His mind turned back to the red thong he'd discovered in the bedroom.

Carmen denied that it was hers, and he was inclined to believe her. Could the ghost have been responsible?

That didn't feel right to him, either. The ghost was concerned with leaving messages and getting his attention in a more straightforward manner.

How about Mika? After all, it looked like hers, smelled like hers.

But that would mean she'd gotten into the house. Slipped in and out with the stealth of a ninja, evading detection by the alarm system. Which seemed highly unlikely.

But he had to admit that it was possible.

He'd known Mika for only one day. He sure as hell hadn't expected her to trail him to Carmen's house. The truth was, he knew so little about her that she could be capable of anything.

Anything.

It took him a long time to get back to sleep.

Chapter 18

On Thursday, Raymond and June had an early lunch at Gladys and Ron's Chicken and Waffles, near Stonecrest Mall in Lithonia.

That morning, he'd had an appointment with Dr. Price, the neurologist to whom his physician had referred him. Since it was on short notice, Dr. Unaeze had called on his behalf to book the visit, stressing the urgency of Raymond's situation.

June accompanied him to the neurologist. He underwent a cranial CT scan, a test to evaluate the brain for abnormalities and to visualize vascular masses. The scan results indicated that there was nothing wrong with him. Dissatisfied with the test results in light of Raymond's complaints of intense headaches, the doctor scheduled an MRI for next Monday. The MRI promised to provide a more detailed picture of his brain—and what might be wrong with him.

At the rate his life was deteriorating, Raymond wondered whether he'd still be sane by next Monday.

Sitting at the restaurant table, they perused the lunch menus. After a moment, he put down his menu and gazed vacantly outside the large front windows. He didn't have an appetite.

What he did have was a growing anxiety that science would fail to diagnose and solve his real problem—the recurring dreams. Brain scans . . . MRIs . . . sleeping pills . . . none of them would help him. Maybe he should talk to a shrink. Or a psychic.

That he was even considering such things was unusual for him. He'd never been to a psychiatrist, never called a psychic hot line. But he was running out of options. He was open to almost anything that might help him.

June looked up from her menu. "What's on your mind, honey?"

His evasive response was automatic: "I'm supposed to meet my boy at the driving range this afternoon. Just thinking about seeing him again."

"Ray? Honestly."

He dragged his hand down his face. Avoiding the truth was pointless. June knew him well enough to know what really bothered him.

"June, I don't know what the hell's wrong with me. I'm worried."

Her eyes were kind.

"We're going to get help for you. The MRI next week—"

"It won't help. Got nothing to do with the problem."

"The dreams?"

Lips tight, he nodded.

He didn't like to talk about the dreams anymore. He was beginning to feel superstitious about the nightmares, as if discussing them aloud would guarantee their return.

The server arrived to take their orders. June ordered

fried chicken and a waffle; Raymond asked for the same entree. If he didn't at least attempt to eat, June would worry.

"You still don't remember what the dreams are about?" she asked.

He shook his head. Wished she would change the subject.

"Last night, before you screamed in the kitchen, I thought I heard you shouting," she said. "You said something about Andrew going inside a house. It's like you were warning him to stay out. Does that trigger anything?"

He felt the blood drain out of his face.

Her words brought the dream images crashing into his thoughts, with terrifying clarity.

Noticing his sudden anxiety, June leaned forward.

"What house, Ray?" she asked. "I know you remember, I see it in your eyes. Will you please tell me?"

Ordinarily, she allowed him to confide in her at his own pace. Now, she was determined to pry the truth out of him.

He slumped in his seat.

He was too worn out to keep up the lies. And too worried.

She waited for him to speak. Her hands were clasped together, her knuckles milky white.

He'd thought he was the only one going through this hell. But she was suffering, too. He had been so focused on himself he hadn't realized how badly his problems had affected her.

He felt like an ass. She had always been in his corner. He was wrong to block her out.

But could she help him?

He didn't know, but he was weary of shouldering the burden on his own.

He hunkered forward and planted his elbows on the table.

"All right," he said. "This is what's been going on . . ."

Fifteen minutes later, Raymond finished talking.

The food sat on the table, growing cold. Neither of them had touched their meals.

"So am I a certifiable nut case?" he asked.

"Of course not. Don't joke like that, you're fine."

"Fine? How can you say that I'm fine?"

She picked up her silverware and sliced into a chicken breast. "These visions you've been receiving are messages. Someone is trying to tell you something."

"Who?"

"Don't know exactly. My guess is that it's something from a spiritual plane."

"You believe in stuff like that?"

"Certainly. Don't you?"

It was funny. They had been married for over a dozen years, and he'd never known about her belief in the supernatural. It wasn't something that had ever been a subject of conversation between them. He had unpeeled another layer to his wife, and it was a surprising discovery.

"Since I don't have any other explanation, I guess I do believe," he said. "But why is this happening to *me?*"

"Because you're responsible," she said.

"Responsible for what?"

"Saving your son," she said.

Her words sent a shiver through him. She was right. He knew it in the very core of his being. He was responsible for saving Andrew. Hearing her say it to him drove the truth home, deep into his soul.

How ironic. He'd neglected his son for his entire life. Now he had to rescue him.

"But what am I supposed to save him from?" he asked.

"I've no idea. Has he told you that anything unusual's happened to him lately?"

"No. I'll ask him when I see him this afternoon." He sighed. "I wish I understood all of this better."

"We're going to find out the answers," she said. "Together."

She was so confident that his spirits lifted. He took a bite of chicken, chewed with gusto.

"Where are we going to start with this?" he asked.

"Research," she said in a crisp tone. She had been a research librarian at Georgia State University for almost twenty years. But he never would have thought to seek her help decoding the mystery that had consumed his life.

"We should start with the house," he said. The image of the mansion flashed in his thoughts; gooseflesh popped up on his arms. "I don't mean going there. That's the last thing I want to do. Let's see what we can find out without setting foot on the property."

"I was going to suggest the same thing. I can pull public records, dig into the background of the owners and the estate. It should give us a good start."

"Can we start today?"

"You couldn't stop me from starting today, honey. I want to get to the bottom of this as much as you do."

She smiled at him; he returned her smile.

His wife had his back. He was so grateful to have her that he wanted to drop on his knees and thank God for blessing him with her.

"You'll start with the research, then," he said. "And I'll talk to Andrew today and see what's going on with him."

He spoke the words smoothly, but what he proposed was easier said than done. Open, direct communication with his son had always been a problem for him. Often-times, he was tongue-tied around the boy. Or he'd say something, and it would be the wrong thing, or something superficial and meaningless, like a joke. He couldn't remember the last time he'd had a serious, personal conversation with Andrew.

He realized, then, that there was one thing in the world that scared him far more than his nightmares ever could.

Fatherhood.

Chapter 19

Thursday morning, Andrew busied himself by browsing at a Borders in Buckhead. He was supposed to meet his father for golf at two o'clock, which gave him a few hours to burn.

His first step upon entering the store, as always, was to check on his books. He made a beeline to the "J" area of the fiction section. The store stocked all three of his Mark Justice novels; he turned the copies of the newest one so that they were face-out, a little trick to gain some extra visibility on the shelves.

As he walked the other aisles, he frequently swiveled to survey the edges of his vision. Looking for a darting motion or a blur—any sign of his ghostly accomplice. Each time, he spotted nothing.

Sitting at a table in the café, he cleared his mind and drew deep breaths, trying to fine-tune his extrasensory awareness and tap in to whatever psychic wavelength the ghost occupied, as if it were the equivalent of locating the right channel on a radio station. But after sensing nothing whatsoever, he started to think the whole thing was stupid.

"This is how the journey to the nuthouse begins, man," he said to himself. "Next thing you know, I'll be listening for voices, too."

He left the bookstore, but avoided going home. Returning to his house would mean establishing a dialogue with the entity. He both anticipated and dreaded the encounter and delayed it for as long as he could. Instead, he cruised through Atlanta's neighborhoods and retail districts, whittling away time. Being prevented from following his daily routine bothered him, but if he had to choose between annoyance and the sheer terror of facing something supernatural, he'd choose a little frustration any day.

At two, he arrived at Atlanta International Golf, a course in Decatur, a city near the eastern edge of Atlanta. Since he and his father lived on different ends of the metro area—he on the south side, his dad in the far eastern suburbs—the location was close to a middle point for both of them.

He'd been looking forward to the golf outing all day. It would be a nice break from the madness that had stormed into his life.

His dad was already there. Swinging away, he wore sunglasses and a Kangol hat to block out the brilliant afternoon sun.

Andrew took a driving iron out of his golf bag in the trunk and went to meet his dad.

They shook hands.

"Good to see you, young buck," Dad said. "I got here early."

"I know. I saw you flailing away from the road."

Dad grinned at the good-natured ribbing. He was in a much better mood than when Andrew had seen him at the cookout.

"Got a bucket of balls for you," Dad said. "Try not to land all of 'em in the trees."

"There you go."

Things were back to normal between them. Andrew didn't know what had been going on with his dad over the past couple of weeks, but he seemed to have gotten over it. If he wasn't, he sure acted as if everything was cool.

Andrew wished he could say the same about his own life.

He set up on the spot beside his father. He stretched, took a few practice swings without the ball. Then he lined up, swung, and sent the ball soaring.

"So you were out when I called last night," Dad said. "Sowing those wild oats, huh?"

Dad loved to talk about women. In addition to sports and work, girls were a frequent topic of discussion for them. It had probably been that way since Andrew was thirteen.

"I stayed over Carmen's last night," Andrew said.

"Is that right? Now she's a sweetie, cute as all get out, too. You and her finally getting together?"

"We haven't talked about it yet."

"It's coming up, trust me. Women like to have those talks, young buck."

"You called it," he said, thinking of how Carmen had been expecting him to initiate a where-is-this-going chat last night.

"You'll know when the time's right," Dad said. "But don't wait too long. I want me some grandkids before I'm too decrepit to enjoy them."

"Judging from how you're swinging that club, I'd say you're already there," Andrew said.

Dad laughed. He pulled off his sunglasses.

Setting up for a swing, Andrew hesitated.

The bags still hung under his father's eyes. But even worse, he looked disturbed, too.

No, not disturbed. Haunted. That was the right word. His dad looked haunted by something.

"Is anything else going on, Andrew?" Dad asked.

He wasn't going to tell his father about the ghost. He'd sound like a fool. His dad was a no-nonsense kind of guy, a man's man. And he respected Andrew—admired him, even. He didn't want to lose his dad's respect by telling him a nutty story about being followed around town by a ghost who couldn't spell. Hell, it sounded like a crazy story to him, and he was the one living it. He didn't know his father well enough to be confident that he would react with anything other than complete disbelief.

"Nothing much going on," Andrew said. "Working on a new book, you know?"

"Nothing else?" Dad asked. "Business as usual?"

He wasn't going to tell his dad about Mika, either. Although they often discussed women, they typically kept the conversation lighthearted and funny, like guys in a locker room swapping stories about girls. He never told his dad about *real* problems he had with women, never sought his dad's advice about dating, and definitely never cried on his shoulder. It had been the pattern of their talks for as long as Andrew could remember.

"Business as usual," Andrew said.

"Just wanted to make sure things were okay, since we haven't talked lately."

Why did his father appear so troubled, and why had he asked these probing questions? What was the deal with him?

"How have *you* been doing, Dad?"

Dad slid on his sunglasses and prepared to strike the ball. "I've been all right. Finally getting a little more sleep. I had a touch of insomnia for a minute, made me cranky as hell."

"Glad you're feeling better. Now I can get back to making fun of you on the greens."

"And I can get back to schooling you."

They spent the next hour cracking jokes and knocking balls across the range. Andrew had a lingering suspicion that his father hadn't given him the full story about his condition—he couldn't forget his haunted gaze and curious questions—but he didn't say anything about it. If there was one thing he knew for certain about his father, it was that he didn't like to be pushed. The last time Andrew had pressured him, at the cookout, Dad had bitten his head off. He'd learned his lesson.

After they had exhausted several buckets of golf balls, Dad said, "I'm ready to head out, son. Want to play this Saturday? Eighteen holes?"

"Saturday's good. Bring your best game."

"Bring yours, too—once you find one," Dad said.

Laughing, they went to their cars.

As Andrew pulled out of the parking lot, his good mood faded.

He couldn't avoid it any longer. He had to go home. To face whatever awaited him there.

Sitting in his Ford Expedition, Raymond watched his son speed out of the parking lot.

One of his biggest regrets was how he had largely missed Andrew grow up to become a man. These days, he was trying to make up for lost time. But the painful truth was that the past was forever lost to both of them.

He'd asked Andrew about what was going on lately, seeking to learn about any problems that his son might be dealing with, a clue of something that could confirm his own nightmares. But Andrew had given him only a bland "business as usual" answer.

The thing was, he believed Andrew was lying to him.

But what was he going to do? Strangle the truth out of his son? He was in no position to demand anything of Andrew.

His boy didn't trust him enough to be honest with him. That was the bottom line. And Raymond couldn't blame him one bit. Until recently, he hadn't acted like a father who deserved to be trusted. Building a bridge of trust between himself and his son would take years.

He admitted that he hadn't been forthcoming with Andrew, either. When Andrew had pointedly asked him about what had been going on with him, he'd been only half truthful. He wondered if his son picked up on that, too.

They were two grown men, father and son, and they couldn't have an open talk with each other. It saddened him.

The past wasn't lost to them. The past was here and now.

And both of them were prisoners to it.

Chapter 20

The cats were back.

When Andrew pulled into the driveway of his house, he spotted the trio of felines. They cavorted around the garage and the lawn as if they owned the place.

Why were these cats hanging around? He hadn't fed them a thing. Did he have an infestation of rats or something?

He pressed the remote control to raise the garage door. One of the felines crouched beside the door and watched him pull the car in. Its green eyes reflected an almost unsettling intelligence.

Welcome home, Andrew. We've been waiting for you.

In his imagination, he'd given the cats an eerie voice like Vincent Price, the star of those old Hammer horror movies.

The cat was still watching him when he got out of the car. It didn't venture inside the garage, however. He was glad. The idea of getting close to the creature made him uneasy, though he didn't know why—it was just a cat, after all. But it was yet another of those strange but powerful gut feelings that he'd been experiencing lately.

He pressed the button to lower the door.

The cat stared at him until the door closed.

We'll be watching you, Andrew.

Andrew did a quick walk-through of the house, to see if anything had been disturbed in his absence. Everything was as it should be.

"Of course it is," he said. "Casper the Friendly Ghost spent the night with me at Carmen's."

Before fleeing the house, he'd dared to turn off the computer. The laptop sat on the desk, lid shut, just as he'd left it yesterday.

He settled into the office chair and turned on the computer. He drummed the desk as the machine progressed through its boot-up cycle.

He couldn't delay any longer. It was time to try to communicate with the ghost.

He blotted his sweaty palms on the lap of his jeans.

He couldn't remember ever being so nervous. During his last book tour, he'd delivered a speech to a group of two hundred people gathered at a public library in Phoenix, and as much as the event had stressed him, it was nothing compared to the anxiety that currently twisted his stomach. He was getting ready to reach out to something in the Beyond, and he had no idea what to expect, no written speech to follow, no scheduled time to do his talk and get off the stage. Anything could happen.

He opened Microsoft Word. He'd viewed the plain white screen thousands of times, but now it looked as mysterious to him as a smoky crystal ball that might convey a message from another dimension.

He typed a question.

WHO ARE YOU?

He gazed at the screen. Waited.

The telephone rang.

He jumped so fast that he nearly fell out of his chair.

The call was from Sandy Clark, his literary agent in New York.

"Hey, Sandy," he said.

"Hi, Andrew. Is this a good time? I wanted to give you an update on your book."

He glanced at the screen. Still no answer.

"I can talk." Speaking to Sandy would be a welcome reprieve to waiting for a response from . . . well, whomever he was trying to establish a dialogue with. Due to the drama that had colored his life the past few days, he'd become disconnected from the world of his writing career. A nice chat with Sandy would ground him in the ordinary world again.

"I spoke to Tina this morning," Sandy said. Tina was his editor at the publishing company. "She promised that they'll have an offer ready by tomorrow. A very lucrative offer. She wanted to make sure that I told you that."

"All I can say is, show me the money, baby. Talk is cheap."

"No kidding," Sandy said. "But I have a feeling that they're going to do right by you this time. They know that your stock has risen quite a bit. They don't want to lose Mark Justice to another house."

Her words made him smile. It was funny how things had changed.

When he reflected on the growth of his career, it amazed and humbled him. He'd started out as a self-published novelist who couldn't get so much as a personalized rejection letter from an agent or publisher;

he spent his weekends driving around the country to expos and festivals, peddling his book out of the trunk of his car and doing book signings whenever stores agreed to allow him in. Then, Sandy Clark—one of the few New York agents whom he hadn't already queried and gotten a rejection letter from—happened to pick up a copy of his novel from a street vendor in Harlem. She E-mailed him, said she loved his writing and wanted to represent him. Flattered and ecstatic with her confidence in his talent, he signed on with her. She sold his book to his current publisher in less than three months. For peanuts, really. He was one of the few African American writers who wrote thrillers, and as such, his publisher had regarded him as an experiment.

The first novel sold decently, but not spectacularly. The second one performed better, but didn't light up the world. Then, after he had written the third book but before it was released, he sold film rights to all three novels for almost a million dollars. The national media discovered him, which led to soaring sales for his third book when it was published six months ago. His first two novels experienced a dramatic sales boost, too. At long last, his publisher had stopped viewing him as an oddity and hopped on the bandwagon.

As he talked to Sandy about the impending deal and other business matters, he went downstairs to get a bottle of water. A glance over his shoulder as he left the office only confirmed that no answer awaited him.

He began to feel stupid. Typing a question to a ghost. What could be dumber than that?

Sipping water, he returned upstairs.

Someone was typing on the laptop. Letters appeared on the screen.

But the room was empty.

"Sandy, gotta go. Call you later."

Coldness filled the air, as if a freezer door yawned open somewhere nearby.

He shivered. Slowly approached the computer.

The keys stopped moving.

But there was an answer to his question.

MY NAME IS SAMMY

Chapter 21

He stared at the words on the screen.

My name is Sammy.

He blinked, opened his eyes again. The sentence was still there.

He wasn't dreaming. This was real. He was talking to a genuine spirit.

A pocket of cold air had gathered around the computer. The coldness had weight, too, as if the very ether had thickened into syrup.

Gooseflesh pimpled his arms.

Wonder and fear flushed through him in equal amounts, immobilizing him. He stood there, still, for perhaps thirty seconds, staring at the computer screen.

Confusion clouded his thoughts, but he knew one thing for certain: his life was never going to be the same again. This was going to change everything with him, forever.

My name is Sammy.

His thought processes shifted into gear. Sammy, Sammy. He didn't know anyone named Sammy, not who had died. The name drew a blank.

He settled into the chair again. Stroked his chin.

He typed another question.

WHY ARE YOU FOLLOWING ME?

He lifted his hands off the keyboard, and waited.

Ghostly fingers tapped the keys.

I WAS LONLEY

He was lonely. Jesus.

He asked another question: WHERE ARE YOU FROM?

The ghost responded: SAD PLACE

He didn't think it was possible for him to feel any colder, but a bone-numbing chill seeped into him.

He asked: WHERE IS THE SAD PLACE?

NOT HEAR

"Good to know that it's not here," he said under his breath. One of the things he had feared was that his house had been built on an old Indian burial ground or something, like a plot device out of a Stephen King book.

He typed: WHERE IS IT?

FAR FROM HEAR

"Good to know that, too," he said. But it frustrated him that Sammy hadn't given him a specific answer. The ghost had limited language skills.

He decided to cut to the chase.

He wrote: WHAT DO YOU WANT?

TO HELP

"To help?" he asked aloud. He typed: YOU WANT TO HELP ME WITH WHAT?

HELP WITH HER

"You've lost me. I don't know what you're talking about. Who's this person you want to help me with?"

He remembered that he had to type the questions. But the keys moved before he touched them.

SHES HEAR

The doorbell rang.

Chapter 22

He dashed to his bedroom and lifted the curtain.

A black Rolls Royce Silver Shadow idled in the cul-de-sac in front of his house, sun rays coruscating across the windshield, as if the interior of the sedan was afire.

Mika was here.

How did she know where he lived?

He answered his own question: The same way she'd learned that he visited Starbucks on Tuesday mornings. The same way she knew that he loved Jamaican Blue Mountain coffee. The same way that she found him at Carmen's house last night.

She'd studied him well enough to earn a Ph.D. on the subject of his life.

It wasn't flattering. It was downright creepy.

But how did the ghost know about her, and how did he plan to help him with her?

He couldn't fathom the answers to those questions.

The doorbell chimed again.

He didn't relish a confrontation with her. But he had no choice. Undoubtedly, she knew he was home. Ignoring the door wasn't going to solve anything.

He went downstairs.

Be firm with her. Don't let her think there's any chance of us still seeing each other. Cut it off.

He opened the door.

Mika stood outside, hands full of bulging, plastic grocery bags. She wore a red tank top that showed off her cleavage and flat stomach, a hip-hugging denim miniskirt, and sandals that displayed her perfectly pedicured feet.

"Hey, baby!" She flashed a diamond-bright grin.

Her beauty momentarily threw him off his plan, made him hesitate.

It was the only opening she needed. He didn't intend to let her inside, but she bustled through the doorway before he could act to stop her. She dropped the bags on the floor, wrapped her arms around him, and kissed him full on the lips, her tongue sliding eagerly across his.

The old battle with his libido began anew.

Emotionally, she repulsed him—even scared him a little. As his grandma liked to say, she wasn't wrapped too tight.

But his body hungered for her.

He moved his hands to her narrow waist. Knowing he shouldn't but unable to draw back.

Kissing him hungrily, she guided his hands to her hips.

"You've missed me, haven't you baby?" she whispered. "I can feel it."

She pressed against his hardness.

"I've missed you, too," she said.

Over her shoulder, he saw a photograph sitting on a table in the hallway. It was a picture of him and Eric on the golf course.

What would his boy think of him right now, ignoring

his common sense to be with this woman who might be hazardous to his health?

Another photo, beside the first one, showed him, Carmen, and Eric posing together at a cookout.

What would Carmen say if she walked in on him at this moment?

Thinking of it, he finally untangled himself from Mika's arms.

"What're you doing here?" he said. "I never told you where I live."

"Haven't I told you before, Andrew? I make it my business to know everything about my man. I'm here to cook for you, since we didn't have dinner together last night. Carry one of these for me please, will you, darling?"

She handed him a grocery bag. Grabbing the other groceries, she strutted down the hallway, to the kitchen.

She navigated the house confidently, as if she had visited many times before.

He looked dumbly at the bag in his hand. It was full of strip steaks and baking potatoes.

Had this woman lost her mind?

He caught up to her as she was placing the bags on the countertop.

"We can't do this," he said. "Please stop."

"Oh, we don't have to eat dinner quite yet, Andrew." She busied herself removing items from bags. "I know, it's not yet evening. But I'd like to marinate these steaks, and afterward perhaps we can go for a walk."

"Are you serious?"

"Of course I am! It's such a lovely day and you've got a beautiful lake behind your property. I'd like to stroll along the bank, holding hands. It sounds rather romantic, don't you think?"

His head pounded. He couldn't take this anymore.

"Dammit, will you listen to me?" he said. "If you want

to come over and cook dinner, you call me first and offer. I say, 'Yes, Mika, that sounds good, come on over.' Then we agree on a time, and then I give you directions to my house. You don't follow me around and find out where I live and show up with groceries whenever you feel like it. You're going about this wrong, Mika, all wrong. You're acting like a nut."

An uncertain smile flickered on her face.

"I'm going about this wrong?" she asked. "I must admit that I can be aggressive sometimes. I can try to change—I can slow down if that would make you happy. Is that what you would like?"

"Mika, listen—"

"I'll do whatever makes you happy, baby," she said quickly. "Tell me what you want me to do."

He dragged his hand down his face.

She watched him, eager.

She was gorgeous. But her neediness tainted her beauty. Why was she so desperate? With her looks and money and sophistication, she didn't need to run down a man like this. He didn't understand it.

Although she offered to change her approach, he saw that for what it was: a ploy to calm him down and prevent him from pushing her away. In truth her obsessive streak was part of her nature. It would inevitably spring back. As his mother said, a leopard can't change its spots.

He had to do the smart thing and cut this off. Permanently.

"Listen, we can't pursue this," he said. "I'm sorry."

"Oh, don't talk like that, baby." She reached for him.

He moved away.

Tears shone in her eyes. "Please don't leave me, Andrew. I only want to be with you. Is that so terrible? I'm only guilty of loving you."

"Loving me?"

"Yes, baby. Loving you." She wiped tears from her eyes. "I love you so much that it hurts. It's like an ache in my chest."

"You can't love me. We just spent one night together!"

"An unforgettable night." She gave him a sly smile. "Wasn't it unforgettable for you, too?"

"One night together doesn't mean we're in love."

"It doesn't? How about the fact that you told me you'd never felt anything like what you felt with me? Was that a lie, Andrew?"

"No, but—"

"How about the fact that you wept like a baby and cried out my name until your voice cracked? Were you putting on an act?"

Embarrassment heated his face. "I never said the sex wasn't great. But it was only sex—lust, not love. There's a difference."

"There is *no* difference!" she said. He flinched, took another step away from her.

"No difference," she said, in a softer tone. She came closer to him. "When we first met, I told you that I don't believe in casual dating, and you said that you didn't, either. You promised me that dating you would be worth my while."

He remembered what he had said. He felt like shit.

"Our first night together, you promised that if I shared my body with you, you would treat me like a princess. Do you remember that, Andrew?"

Slowly, he nodded.

"Is this how you treat your princess? Like a two-dollar whore? Is that the kind of man you are?"

"No." Guilt weighed on him. He lowered his head.

He was partly to blame for this mess. He'd acted without considering the potential consequences. Normally, he was slow and methodical in his relationships, but he'd blown it this time, and he had no excuse whatsoever.

"I know in my heart that you're a wonderful man," she said. "Know what else I know?"

He only looked at her.

She smiled. "I know that you love me, Andrew."

He nearly choked.

"Come to me, baby." She raised her arms, to hug him.

He gently nudged her away.

"Mika . . . look. I misled you, said some things I shouldn't have said, just because I wanted to get to know you. I'm sorry. I don't feel the way you do."

"Oh, yes, you do. You share my feelings, deep down. You love me, too."

"Mika, I don't love you. I'm sorry."

"Sometimes, you can be such a typical man." She ran her fingers through her hair and shook her head. "Running from your emotions, like men always do. But I anticipated this reaction from you. I'm not going to allow you to push me away and hide in your little mancave until you figure out your feelings and realize that you truly love me. No, I don't have the patience for that nonsense. I know what's best for us. We're meant to be together."

"Listen—"

"No, *you* listen!" She pointed at him. "I'm not playing games with you. You're my soul mate, whether you realize it or not. I'm not letting you get away from me. Absolutely not. I've waited too long to find you and I'll be damned if I let you go."

Her eyes flared dangerously.

She truly was a bonafide psycho, like that woman in *Fatal Attraction*. He couldn't talk her out of her obsession, couldn't reason with her. It was useless.

He stepped away from her and moved around the glass dinette table, putting it between them.

He wanted to get her out of his house. But how could he do that, short of picking her up and carrying her out, kicking and screaming?

"Come here, Andrew," she said firmly, as if she were addressing a child.

"I want you to leave," he said. "Right now."

Her face tightened like a fist.

She charged across the kitchen. He backed up, hit a chair and would've fallen if she hadn't seized a handful of his shirt. She yanked him upright with a mighty jerk and shoved him into a wall. The collision knocked the breath out of him.

Jesus, she was strong. He'd never seen a woman so strong.

She pounced on him like a hungry animal. Ripped his shirt and planted her mouth on his chest. Licking, sucking, nipping with her teeth.

He grabbed her arms. "Get. Off. Me!"

He pushed her, hard.

She crashed onto the top of the dinette table. Salt and pepper shakers clattered to the floor.

She lay still. Breathing hard.

"I'm sorry," he said. "I didn't want to hurt you, I just want you to leave."

Roaring, she rebounded to her feet. Her disheveled hair hung in her eyes.

He backpedaled to the counter.

Shaking her head, whimpering, she gripped tufts of her hair and pulled at it. She wept loudly.

"I only want you to love me. Please, please, please love me. I love you so much, baby. Only want us to be together." She sniffled.

He was sickened and saddened by how she was acting. She seriously needed psychiatric help.

Keeping his distance, he said, "Please, Mika. Go. Go home."

"Oh, honey baby, sweetie pie, darling, soul mate eyes, don't leave me, please—"

"Go!"

She raised her eyes to the ceiling and screeched, a piercing cry that he was convinced would shatter every glass in the house. He clapped his hands over his ears.

Spinning, she grabbed the edge of the dinette table and flung it off its base. It crashed against the floor, a jagged crack running down the center.

The tabletop had required two people to balance it on the table legs, but she had thrown it as if it weighed no more than a trash can lid.

She brushed her hair away from her eyes. She wore a sly smile, clearly pleased at how her display of unusual strength had shocked him.

"I'll leave, Andrew," she said. "But only to give you time to regain your common sense. This isn't over— and you can't hide from me. Remember the thong?"

He remembered. The red thong hanging on the doorknob at Carmen's place. He hadn't wanted to believe that she'd been able to get inside the house and then slip away, undetected by the security system. But somehow, she had done it.

She watched him, smiling, as the realization sank in.

Then she strutted out of the house, swinging her hips.

He locked the door—both the dead bolt and the chain.

His hands shook.

On weak legs, he made his way upstairs to the office. A new line of text glowed on the screen.

YOUR IN BIG TRUBEL NOW

Chapter 23

Eric let out a whistle as Andrew finished telling him what had happened.

"Damn, bro, I'm sorry to hear that. Sounds like you've got a seriously psychotic female on your hands."

They were on the deck at Eric's house. It was half-past six in the evening; Andrew arrived there almost immediately after Eric got home from work. He'd been a package of nerves for the past few hours and had been eager to share his story with his friend.

Still dressed in his dark brown Armani suit, silk tie loosened, Eric paced the wooden planks, hands buried in his pockets. Eric the Comedian had vacated the premises and been replaced by his identical but solemn twin, Eric the Attorney.

Andrew had told him everything that had occurred. He wanted his advice. Eric worked as an employment law attorney at a boutique firm in Buckhead; he'd litigated numerous cases of workplace sexual harassment, which Andrew figured was close to what he'd been experiencing with Mika—with the unfortunate exception being that his situation wasn't limited to an office. Mika was harassing him everywhere he went.

In his retelling, he'd left out the parts about his communication with the ghost, Sammy. He wanted to keep his talk with Eric in the realm of the real world, for now. He still didn't understand how the ghost knew about Mika. Upon discovering the last message from Sammy, which warned him that he was in big trouble, he'd typed a question asking Sammy to elaborate. But the ghost never responded.

"Mika's psychotic all right," Andrew said. "Strong, too. She doesn't look like she could harm a fly, but she flipped that table across the room like it was a paper plate."

"Could be on drugs," Eric said. "PCP, something that amped up her nerves. Or she's just flat-out crazy."

"And she knows everything—I mean *everything*—about me," Andrew said. "This woman could write a book on my life."

"She's taken her time to plan this," Eric said. "That's typical of stalkers. They have an ability to gather information that could shame the NSA."

He reflected on the time he'd spent in Mika's hotel suite, the morning after their date.

"But she's taken this to another level," Andrew said. "When I woke up the next morning, she'd laid out the same deodorant and toothpaste and stuff that I use. Cooked the breakfast foods that I liked. Eric, *even the newspaper* was arranged in the exact order that I read it every day."

"Whoa," Eric said. "Gotta admit, that's impressive. Disturbing as hell, but impressive."

"I thought it was all coincidence." He shook his head, leaned back in the deck chair. "But none of it was. I feel like an idiot for ignoring the signs."

"Don't blame yourself. You were letting the other head do the thinking, for a minute. Wouldn't be the first brother guilty of that, you know."

"But as much as she knows about me, I hardly know anything specific about her. I don't even know where she lives."

"That's right, you spent the night with her at the Ritz." Eric tapped his lips. "She's *really* been planning this."

"The hotel should have some info on her. Her home address, for sure."

"As detail oriented as this chick seems to be, I wouldn't count on it," Eric said. "How about that Rolls Royce she takes around town? Ever seen the plates?"

"I never thought of that. Never seen the driver, either, actually."

"You've got to pay attention to that stuff, bro. Didn't I tell you that you have to be more careful in your personal life?"

"Don't lecture me right now, man."

"Sorry, my bad."

"I admit it—I screwed up," Andrew said. "But I need to know what to do about this. I want your legal advice."

Eric sat on the railing. He folded his arms, his gaze serious.

"Legally, your only recourse, initially, is to get a temporary restraining order. You know what that is?"

"Yeah, the cops'll tell her to stay the hell away from me."

"That's the basic idea. The problem for you is that matters haven't moved along far enough for you to request one yet. There has to be an established pattern of stalking and threats before you have a decent chance of getting a TRO. No doubt, Mika's tripping, but she's just started, bro."

"But this isn't gonna end anytime soon. She told me that herself."

"Then you need to keep a record of everything she does and says," Eric said. "Every uninvited visit, every nutty phone call or crazy E-mail message, every threatening word or harassing signal—write it all down. Write down the innocent seeming stuff, too, like if she sends you flowers or something. You've kicked her out of your crib already, and if she keeps dropping by and getting in touch with you, that's harassment."

"What about this?" He raised the pager that Mika had given him.

"Keep it. Save all of the messages. Could be helpful later."

"Will do."

"The bottom line is this. The more documentation you have, the easier it'll be for you to get a TRO—and if things get worse and you have to press criminal charges, those records would be a gold mine for a prosecuting attorney."

"I hope it doesn't get to that point, but I'll take your advice."

Eric cocked his head. "Want some more advice? Switch up your routines."

"Why?"

"I know, that's the last thing you wanna hear, but you've gotta do some things differently. Stop going out for walks every evening and to Starbucks on Tuesday morning and all of that. Make it harder for her to keep track of you."

"Makes sense, I guess."

"Just watch your back, bro. At all times. You're probably going to feel paranoid for a while, but that's all right. It's necessary until we get this under control and can cool this chick down or throw her in the joint."

"Thanks, Eric. I appreciate the tips."

Eric waved off his words. "Have you told Carmen the latest on this?"

"We're having dinner tonight. I plan to tell her then."

"Ah, you and Carmen are kicking it two nights in a row? Need to tell me something?"

Andrew smiled for the first time in hours. "I'm taking her to dinner to thank her for helping at the cookout."

"Uh-huh. I was sweating like a pig at that grill. You ain't offered to take me to dinner."

"Wanna go? I'll take you to Waffle House."

"You're planning to make a move on her. You ain't slick."

"We're just friends. Nothing's changed yet."

"Not yet. But it will if you've got anything to do with it."

"I plead the fifth."

"Whatever, bro. All I can say is, it's about damn time."

Andrew wanted to play it cool, but he couldn't stop smiling.

Eric grinned, too, but then his face drew into a taut expression.

"Want another tip? Every stalker I've ever heard of is jealous as hell. You and Carmen both need to be careful now."

Chapter 24

Later that evening, Carmen and Andrew went to dinner at Red Lobster.

Over platters of fried shrimp and glasses of white zinfandel, he filled her in on everything that had happened. He'd had a whirlwind of a day, but her comforting presence anchored him on stable ground. He hoped that discussing the latest developments with her would give him more ideas on what he should do to regain control of his life.

"Jeez, you've had a day out of a nightmare," she said. "Psycho chick proved my theory."

"What theory?"

"That's she's straight-up crazy, that's what. I had a bad feeling about her the minute she showed up at my door. Call it female intuition."

"Has to be female intuition, 'cause I sure didn't expect her to act like this when I met her."

"Of course not. No *man* would—he'd be too busy drooling over her."

He only nodded. He couldn't disagree at all with her assessment.

She dipped a shrimp in cocktail sauce. "But you're holding up well. I'm kinda impressed."

"Impressed?"

"To see Mr. Robotic rolling with the punches like this? Yeah, I'm impressed. Didn't know you had it in you."

"Being around you helps. If I didn't have you and Eric, I don't know what I'd do."

"That's what friends are for." She popped a shrimp into her mouth. "I'm really curious about how Sammy plans to help you with Mika."

"Me, too. I wish he'd been more specific."

"Remember what I said last night? That there has to be a connection between him and psycho chick, because it seemed too coincidental that all of this would be happening at the same time?"

"Maybe Sammy's a dead relative of hers. Or how about a guy that she stalked and killed? Maybe he wants to help me so she doesn't murder me, too."

"She's not going to hurt you. We'll get her crazy ass thrown in jail first."

"I'm only brainstorming. Sammy has to have *some* kind of history with her."

"Agreed," she said. "Next time we talk to him, we've gotta get him to tell us more about his background, where he knows her from."

"It's not gonna be easy. Sammy's got the writing skills of an eight year old. It's hard to get a clear answer out of him."

"What do you think of this sad place he mentioned? Any ideas at all on that?"

"None," he said. "I tried to get a detailed answer out of him, but he wouldn't give one. Frustrating."

"Something'll break. We'll do the best we can."

He noted her frequent use of the word "we." He liked that; she wasn't abandoning him to deal with this on his own. She was partnering with him. He had never been more grateful for her friendship.

And what about taking their friendship to the next level? Although they were having a good conversation, the timing still felt wrong to him. He wanted to wait until he'd restored a semblance of order to his life. Then, with his mind at ease, he could talk to her about moving away from the platonic zone and into the realm of a relationship—and hope that she shared his feelings.

He rose to visit the rest room. On the way across the restaurant, he spotted Mika, sitting at a corner booth. She watched him.

He halted in mid-stride, nearly causing a waiter to crash into him with a tray of food.

"Sorry." He stepped aside.

It wasn't Mika. The woman in the booth, dining with a man, bore only a faint resemblance to her.

He was getting paranoid. Eric had warned him that he would, had said it was a good thing because it would keep him on his toes. But it bothered him. With his vivid imagination, a touch of paranoia would go a long way. Too much of it would send him to the loony bin.

Keeping his eyes straight ahead, he hurried the rest of the way to the washroom.

After dinner, they went to Andrew's house. One of the cats sat on the hood of Carmen's Lexus. The other two cats lounged near the shrubbery, green eyes shining in the evening's deepening twilight.

"Damn cats," Andrew said. "I don't know where they came from."

"Have you fed them?" she asked.

"Never. They've been hanging around for days. They never meow, they just watch me."

"That's kinda weird." She unbuckled her seat belt as he nosed the car into the garage. He got out, carrying a take-home box from the restaurant.

He headed for the door that led inside the house, but Carmen wandered outside the garage, approaching the cat that rested on her car.

"How ya doin', kitty?" she said in a coaxing voice. She loved cats. "My car make a warm little resting spot for ya?"

The feline stared at her. It didn't move.

"He's a Russian Blue," she said.

"Blue? I guess I can kinda see the blue in the fur, but I would've just called them gray cats."

"I know, but cat folks call them blue," she said. "Gimme some food, please."

"If you feed it, then I'll never get rid of it."

"Come on, Drew." She snapped her fingers.

He opened the Styrofoam carton. She plucked a shrimp from inside. Stepping forward, she waved the morsel in the air.

The cat showed no interest in the food. Its watchful gaze shifted from Carmen to Andrew, back to Carmen.

Who is this woman that you've brought home, Andrew? The ominous Vincent Price voice he'd given to the animals had kicked into his mind again.

"Maybe it's not hungry," Carmen said. She placed the shrimp near the feline's front paws. "Here's some food, kitty. Nice, juicy shrimp. Want it?"

The animal ignored the morsel and stared at them.

"Since when does a cat not even sniff some food like that?" he asked.

"What's wrong, kitty?" she cooed. She reached to stroke the cat's fur.

The cat bared its teeth. It hissed.

She drew back. "All righty, then."

He heard a rustling sound behind them. The other

two cats had crept closer. Muscles tensed, they also glowered at Carmen.

We don't like this woman of yours, Andrew. She doesn't belong here.

He wondered if he was attributing overly human thoughts to the cats. Why would they dislike Carmen on sight? It was a ridiculous notion.

But the creatures' threatening body language was unmistakable.

He put his hand on her shoulder. "Let's go inside."

She didn't argue. She came into the house with him.

When he looked one last time at the cat sitting on the car, it swept its tail across the hood and batted the shrimp to the pavement.

Chapter 25

He had left the computer on, in case Sammy opted to type another message while he was away. He and Carmen gathered in front of the laptop. There were no new messages. Andrew's last question—*Why do you say I'm in big trouble now?*— remained on the screen, unanswered.

Carmen scanned through Sammy's misspelled sentences. "Vocab of a kid is right. I wonder if he *is* a child."

"That's another question we can ask him whenever he shows up again."

"He'll be back soon, I bet," she said. She yawned. "What time is it?"

"Half-past ten."

"I need to run. Gotta work tomorrow."

"You have to leave so soon? Hang out for a while, watch a movie with me."

He kept his tone playful, but he seriously wanted her to stay longer—to spend the night, in fact. Romance wasn't on his mind. Fear was on his mind. With Mika roaming in the night dwelling on her deranged, obsessive thoughts about him, he no longer felt secure in his own house.

This isn't over—and you can't hide from me.

His anxiety had a good basis. He recalled how, last night, Mika had prowled through Carmen's place and left behind her thong, undetected by the security system or either of them, as if she were as elusive as a disembodied spirit.

"You've talked me into it," she said. "I'm not too keen on you being alone here anyway, with psycho chick running around. Not to say that you can't take care of yourself, but you know what I mean. Strength in numbers and all that."

"Does that mean you're gonna spend the night, too?"

"We'll see." She smiled.

He smiled, too—to conceal his relief. For Carmen, "we'll see" meant "yes." Although, like virtually all women, her language was as mysterious to him as ancient hieroglyphics, he'd managed, over time, to decipher the true meaning of a handful of her statements.

In the entertainment area of the basement, he dimmed the lights and put a film on the projection screen: *Love and Basketball.* It was one of Carmen's all-time favorites.

He reclined on the sofa and rested his feet on the leather ottoman.

"Wow, I can't believe you put on this movie," she said. Sitting next to him, she propped her feet on the ottoman, too. "What have I done to deserve this?"

"Helped me cope. I really mean that. Thank you."

She patted his leg. "I got your back, honey. Anyway, you need me right now. I can tell you how psycho chick thinks."

"How's that?"

" 'Cause I'm a woman. It takes a woman to understand a woman."

"But you said she's crazy."

"She *is* crazy, but in a way that makes a twisted kinda sense."

He turned to face her. "Break that down for me."

"Okay," she said. "You and her slept together—"

"Carmen—"

"Let me finish, there's a reason why I'm telling you this. I'm not judging you, only stating a fact."

"All right."

"For most women, sex is the most intimate act in the world. When a woman has sex with a man, she naturally starts to feel attached to him, in more than a physical sense. She bonds with him emotionally, mentally, spiritually. It's like a soul connection."

"Not all the time. Some women can hit and run like men."

"True, but women who do that are only looking for fun, a little tune-up. If the woman is in a frame of mind of wanting to have a serious relationship with you, and then she sleeps with you—she's gonna feel that soul connection, Drew."

"I knew I was going to regret it," he said. "Before we got to that point, I was having second thoughts. But I ignored that little voice in my head telling me to slow down."

She touched his arm. "That was your intuition. Part of you knew that you were walking into a bad thing."

"She called me her soul mate, too. How could she say that after knowing me for one day?"

"You said yourself that she was needy. You know how it feels to want something so bad that it hurts?" Her gaze searched him.

"I've felt that way sometimes, yeah."

"We all have," she said. "When you give someone

hungry for that certain thing a little taste of it, well, they can lose control—especially if it seems that they might lose that thing after waiting for it for so long."

"So I give her a taste, and she decides that I'm her soul mate."

"It's like love at first sight. Think about your last serious girlfriend. I remember you told me that after your first date with her, you knew you wanted to have a relationship with her. You *knew*."

"Good point. But I don't feel the same way about Mika that she feels about me. She said she knows I love her."

She frowned. "The knowing you love her part—that's a touch of her craziness there, something I don't understand. But I know why she keeps chasing you. Did your ex-girlfriend know after the first date that she wanted you to be her man?"

"It took a couple of months. I had to pursue her, convince her."

"In Mika's warped mind, she sees it the same way. She thinks she has to pursue you, and that you'll finally come around one day, let your guard down, and be her man. The big problem—and it's *our* problem—is her way of going about winning you over."

"Yeah, following me around, throwing temper tantrums and flipping over furniture—definitely a big problem for us."

" 'Hell hath no fury like a woman scorned,' " she said. "But I bet she'll be super-sweet the next time you see her, apologizing for how she behaved. The classic nice-and-nasty pattern."

"Doesn't matter how sweet she acts. Nothing's gonna make me change my mind about her."

"Yup, you gotta stand firm. I hope I'm wrong, but I think this is a long way from being over. Psycho chick ain't gonna give up easily."

Her words evoked his worries again. Bands of tension squeezed his chest. The projection TV was the only light source in the basement; the shadows in the room appeared darker than before, as if hiding something malevolent.

He edged closer to Carmen.

Barefoot, she wore shorts and a halter top. Delicious warmth radiated from her body.

Nonchalantly, he placed his hand close to her leg.

Desire bolted through him. He didn't know whether the lust came from a reflex reaction—his seeking a calm oasis of intimacy in the midst of his fear—or was a natural expression of his growing feelings for her. He'd felt attracted to her countless times before, but not usually as strongly as he did now.

She crossed her legs on the ottoman. He looked at her pedicured feet, slender ankles, toned calves, firm thighs.

He'd never forget how it had felt, the one time they'd crossed the platonic line, to hold her close and kiss her.

Nope, man. Forget it. You can't go there with her again. Not now.

It was the same voice that had warned him about going to Mika's hotel suite. The whisper of intuition. He knew he had to listen to it. He couldn't touch Carmen until he was prepared to come clean about his feelings. It wouldn't be fair to her, and she probably wouldn't tolerate another just-friends-kissing episode without demanding a serious talk about the direction of their relationship.

He clasped his hands in his lap and watched the movie with her in friendly silence.

As Andrew had assumed, Carmen decided to spend the night. By the time the movie concluded, it was after midnight. She said she was too weary to make the thirty-minute drive home to Marietta. She would sleep in the guest room.

While she prepared for bed, he checked to ensure that all of the doors and windows were locked. It was a nightly habit for him, but in light of Mika's invasion of his life, the task had taken on greater importance.

In the living room, he peeled back a curtain.

Outside, a pair of small, glowing green eyes watched him from the bushes.

Those damned cats. They were getting on his last nerve.

And they'd threatened Carmen, too. That pissed him off—and concerned him.

Something about these animals wasn't normal. He couldn't put his finger on exactly what it was, but they made him uneasy.

Tomorrow morning, he would call the city's animal control unit. Maybe they would pick up the cats and take them to a shelter. The felines had to be strays.

Upon finishing his circuit of the house, he returned upstairs and activated the security system from the control panel in his bedroom. Then he checked the laptop in his office.

Still no message from Sammy. But he left the computer on.

In the guest room, Carmen was pulling back the sheets on the twin-size bed. Her back was to him. She wore one of his Atlanta Braves T-shirts, the fabric ending just beneath her hips.

It was impossible to ignore how well the shirt displayed her lovely figure.

She looked over her shoulder, smiled. "Caught ya."

If he'd had a lighter complexion his skin would have turned as red as a tomato.

"I wanted to ask if you needed anything," he said in a low voice.

She slid onto the mattress, one leg tucked underneath the other. She wore a faint smile.

Although she wasn't wearing lingerie, she looked as sexy to him as a model in a Victoria's Secret catalog.

Before he knew what he was doing, he crossed the room. He rested his hands on her shoulders and leaned closer to her.

She stopped him with a hand on his chest.

"No friends with benefits, Drew," she said.

He stiffened. "Can a brother at least get a good-night kiss?"

She rose off the bed. She wrapped her arms around his waist, stood on her tiptoes.

He tried to kiss her on the lips. She turned her head and gave him a chaste peck on the cheek.

"Good night," she said. She patted his head, as if he were a little boy whom she was sending off to bed.

"That's cold, Carmen."

"You get up at six, right?" she asked. "I'm gonna set the alarm in here, but please check on me to make sure I'm up. I'll need to go home to get ready for work."

He sighed loudly. She only looked at him, arms crossed over her bosom.

"All right, I get the point," he said. He backed up to the doorway. "I'll check on you at six. Good night."

She smiled sweetly and waved.

In his bedroom, he lay on his bed in the darkness.

Carmen had made it clear: she wasn't going to fool around with him any more, not as long as they continued to call themselves just friends. It frustrated him, but he had to respect her hard-line stance. She was doing what was necessary to preserve their friendship. He couldn't fault her for that—especially at those times when he lacked the willpower to rightfully keep his hands off her.

Nevertheless, the other side of the mattress was cold as he drifted to sleep.

Chapter 26

Night. A roiling charcoal sky and a fine, cold drizzle as abrasive as broken glass.

In his dream, Raymond stood in front of the mansion again, in the muddy driveway. A child version of Andrew approached the front door.

He shouted the same command that he'd said in vain, countless times: "Stay outta that house, boy!"

Ignoring him, Andrew pushed open the big door and disappeared inside.

Raymond screamed in anguish.

In the upper room of the house, the strange green light throbbed, with the perfect rhythm of a ticking clock.

The light was summoning him, for reasons unknown. Promising to help him find his son, maybe. He didn't know. All he knew for certain was that he needed to get inside the house.

He ran toward the veranda. Then, before reaching it, he stopped.

He had done this before, he realized. The door would be locked.

To have any hope of saving his son, he had to find another way inside.

He wiped rain out of his eyes with the heel of his hand. Looked around.

He didn't see a door, but he would try another side of the house. On an estate of this size, there had to be another entrance.

He ran around the left corner of the veranda, his shoes squishing through wet grass.

Over there, a weeping willow drooped, boughs laden with rain. As he moved past the tree, the leaves eeled like slimy tentacles across his shoulders and back.

Beyond the willow, a wrought iron, arched opening stood. Spanish moss wreathed the archway. Mist obscured the enclosure beyond the entrance.

What was in there?

It would lead him away from the mansion, but he was drawn toward it, reeled in by curiosity.

He stepped underneath the archway.

"Jesus," he said in a soft voice.

Soupy fog thickened the air, but he saw, clearly, that he had entered a graveyard. It contained dozens of graves, each one marked by a foot-high, wooden crucifix.

Who were the people who lay buried here? Former residents of the estate?

At the nearest grave, he searched for a headstone, some indication of the deceased's identity. But there was nothing, and the crucifix that jutted from the earth offered no information, either.

He went to another plot, and found the same thing. Moved to another, then another, and yet another. He discovered the same at each.

It was a cemetery of nameless corpses.

It made no sense. If past residents were buried here, wouldn't their surviving relatives have wanted to honor them with something more significant than a flimsy crucifix?

Yes . . . unless the people buried here were not prior residents.

Fog skirted his legs, slithered along his arms.

There was something very wrong about this place. His curiosity had faded. Dread had replaced it in full, constricting his lungs.

He turned to leave.

His foot slid into a soft depression in the earth. He tried to move, but the ground crumbled away beneath him.

Shouting, he fell into a pit several feet deep. He landed hard on his side, the impact rattling his teeth.

Although it was a dream—and he knew it was a dream—the pain felt no less real.

He lay there for a few moments, panting, letting the pain in his body fade to a dull ache. Then he reached out, touched smooth earthen walls.

As he'd suspected, he'd fallen into an empty grave.

It was about six feet deep, four feet wide, and maybe seven feet long. A good fit for him.

Don't think about that, Ray.

The opening above gave him a rectangular view of the turbulent night sky.

He pulled himself upright. Fortunately, the sides of the grave were dry, packed tight. He should have no problem hauling himself out of there.

He raised his arms and hooked his hands in the turf over the lip of the pit. He started to pull.

You can do this, Ray, it's like doing a pull-up, remember those?

A boot mashed onto the fingers of his right hand.

He yelped, lost his grip, fell back into the grave.

His fingers throbbed painfully, but didn't feel broken. Could you even break a bone in a dream? If you did, would you wake to find your bones shattered in real life, too—like the old saying that if you died in your dream you died for real?

As he gingerly massaged his fingers, Walter, the tall caretaker, appeared above him.

Standing at the edge of the hole, he looked down at Raymond with disgust. He balanced an enormous shovel on his shoulder, like a fishing rod. Patches of dirt smudged his somber black suit.

He's not a caretaker. He's a goddamned undertaker is what he is.

"You don't belong here," Walter said in his baritone voice. "But we'll let you stay here with the rest of them."

"To hell with that." Raymond scrambled to his feet. He jumped and snagged a tuft of grass with his good hand. He struggled to lift himself out of the hole.

Walter hefted the shovel in both hands, like a lumberjack preparing to split a log with an axe.

"No!" Raymond shouted. He was almost out.

Grinning, Walter raised the shovel high and brought it down on Raymond's head . . .

Raymond burst out of the dream, shouting.

But he was in his bed. At home. Safe.

He dropped back onto the mattress.

His head ached, as if he'd been whacked upside his skull with the caretaker's shovel—struck precisely in the same area as his bruise. He rubbed his head, a moan slipping out of him.

Beside him, June stirred.

"Ray? Are you okay?"

"Another dream. Saw a graveyard this time."

"A what?" She sat up.

"There's a graveyard at that house." His mouth was dry; he snatched the bottle of water from the nightstand and took a sloppy gulp. "Lots of graves . . . but no names, not a name on a damned one of them."

She found his hand, squeezed it. He needed the reassuring contact as much as she did.

"Ray, what in the hell *is* that place?" she asked.

Chapter 27

Carmen awoke thirsty.

The bedside clock read 3:34 A.M. She'd have to rise for work in less than three hours. It felt as if she'd barely slept at all. Sleeping in an unfamiliar bed often had that effect on her.

But her mouth was cotton-dry. She needed a drink of water before she could return to sleep.

The house was hear-a-pin-drop silent. She wondered, not for the first time, how Andrew could live alone in this huge place. She loved her cozy, two-bedroom town home. But this place, with all of these vacant rooms and quiet, open spaces, felt more like a museum than a house.

What Andrew needed was a wife and kids to liven up things.

Smiling at the thought, she pushed off the mattress and padded into the hallway. Dim copper light came from a street lamp outside, filtered through the arched window set above the two-story entry hall, softening the shadows around her.

The door to Andrew's bedroom was half open. She heard him inside, snoring softly.

She went to the door; she needed to go there anyway, to deactivate the security system so she could walk downstairs. But her gaze lingered on him: he lay on his side, pillow clutched to his stomach, somehow managing to look both innocent and virile all at once. A soapy scent emanated from his body, mingled with the faint, primal odor of masculine musk.

What would he think if she climbed into bed with him and kissed him awake?

The thought made her tingly. But she would never, ever act on it. Not while they occupied the just-friends zone. She'd rebuked herself for letting down her guard once before with him, allowing things to progress farther than they should have without a discussion about what they wanted to do with this friendship of theirs.

Years of dating and heartbreak had taught her a painful lesson: never assume anything with a man. Don't think that because he called you every day, as if you were his woman, that you really were his woman. Don't believe that if he showered you with attention as if you were the most special woman on earth meant that he viewed you as any more special than the woman he'd seen the night before. Don't presume that making love to a man meant that he had any love for you.

She'd made all of those mistakes before with men. She had the scars on her heart to prove it.

A smart woman assumed nothing. She'd demand that a guy state exactly what he felt for her and expected from her. Men hated to be pinned down like that— most of them would prefer taking an enema to disclosing their feelings and expectations—but it was the only way that she would deal with men these days. Andrew included. Especially Andrew. Their friendship was too valuable to risk losing over some ill-considered and spontaneous sexual adventure.

He had to tell her, in clear terms, that he wanted them to take their friendship to the next level. Although she was currently dating a guy, it wasn't serious at all; it was one of those superficial, enjoy-the-moment relationships that had no real future.

But Andrew . . . she believed they would be as great as lovers as they were as friends. He had to initiate it, though. She didn't believe in chasing men. In her experience, when you chased a man, he'd feel cornered, and he'd either run—or tell you what he thought you wanted to hear, which could be completely at odds with what he genuinely felt.

The challenging part was that she knew they could really get down in the bedroom. That heavy-petting episode made it obvious to her that they shared a rare physical chemistry. Making love to him would send her scaling the walls.

Andrew shifted, his hand sliding down the pillow protectively.

It was easy to imagine her body in the place of that pillow he held so closely.

Sometimes—like now—she wished she could throw her principles to the wind and give in to what her body craved. Damn the consequences.

But she was twenty-eight. She'd left behind that reckless style of living years ago. It had made for some lonely nights in an empty bed, but she was holding out for something real and lasting. In spite of articles in magazines such as *Essence* that made it seem as if finding a good black man who wanted a monogamous commitment was as improbable as discovering a five-carat diamond in a garbage dump.

Sighing, she looked away from Andrew. She punched

in the code to disarm the security system. She was one of the handful of people who knew the access code to his house; he knew the code to hers, as well.

After five years of friendship, she and Andrew had shared so much of their lives, probably the only things left for them to share were their bodies.

Damn him for being so confused right now.

Don't be selfish and impatient, girl, she scolded herself. *He needs you now, as a friend. Be a friend for him, and be open to whatever blessings the future may bring.*

Although the disengaged system sounded a quick beep, Andrew continued to slumber. She pulled the door half shut behind her.

She went inside the office. The white computer screen glowed in the darkness. A glance confirmed that the ghost hadn't answered Andrew's question about why he was in trouble.

A ghost and a psycho chick. What a weird combination. But there had to be a link, and she was determined to help Andrew discover it.

She quietly walked downstairs, to the kitchen. She switched on the ceiling light.

The kitchen sparkled, like the rest of the house. But as clean and stylish as it was, it had an austere air that begged for a woman's touch.

She'd given him some decorating tips before, and he'd followed them. The live plants, decorative throw pillows, and colorful vases in various areas of the house were her idea, and she'd bought him other accessories as housewarming gifts. It amused her to think that she'd been staking out her territory here, months ago. But, the things she could do to this house if they ever got married . . .

Slow your roll, girl.

She removed a bottle of water from the refrigerator.

Unscrewing the cap, she bumped the door shut with her hip.

A large cat stood on the edge of the kitchen. Watching her.

Cold sweat dampened her brow.

This was one of the mean-assed cats she'd seen sitting on her car earlier that evening.

Movement past the doorway, on her left.

A second feline was walking through the dining room.

What was going on? How had they gotten inside?

A hissing, above her.

She looked up.

A third cat sat atop the refrigerator, glaring at her with dilated pupils.

Too terrified to breathe, she instinctively raised her arms, dropping the water bottle to the floor.

The cat pounced.

A scream snatched Andrew out of sleep.

Oh, God, that was Carmen. Had to be her. What was going on?

He rolled over and yanked the drawer of the nightstand so hard that it crashed to the floor. Normally, he kept the gun case therein locked; tonight, he'd left it unlatched, so that he could open it at a moment's notice.

He closed his hand over the cool handle of the Smith & Wesson .38 revolver. The gun was already loaded.

He'd never fired the .38 in a real-world situation, but he was more than willing to use it to protect her. This was one of those times when he didn't need to ask Mark Justice for advice. His response was automatic.

He leapt out of bed, flung open the door, and raced down the hallway, calling her name.

* * *

Like an uncoiling cobra, the cat sprang onto Carmen's head. Claws and teeth tore into her upraised arms and ripped through her hair.

She screamed.

The animal's furry tail swung in her face, like a noose.

Terror gripped her heart in a stranglehold. She staggered, stumbled. Trying to fling the cat off her, trying to keep it from gouging her eyes out with its wicked claws.

She felt another cat attack her calf. Teeth sank into her flesh. She kicked, wildly. But the feline held fast.

Another cat leapt onto her back and attached itself to her T-shirt. It pawed at her neck.

Jesus, they were going to kill her.

Tears flooded her eyes. Each claw and tooth opened a searing wound. She felt warm blood streaming down her skin.

Gotta get them off me, dammit!

She finally got ahold of the tail of the feline crawling on her head. She whipped it around and flung it across the kitchen. The cat landed nimbly on the counter. It flashed its teeth at her.

Through her tears, she saw the knife block, and yanked a blade out of there. She swung it at the cat mauling her leg. The blade lopped off the animal's ear. Howling, the cat fell away.

The feline clinging to her back raked its razor-sharp claws down her spine.

She drove into the refrigerator backwards, crushing the cat against the door. Bones crunched. Wailing, the feline fell off her, slumped to the floor.

She was dizzy with pain, felt blackness tugging at her,

trying to drown her. But she didn't dare lose consciousness.

The feline on the counter hissed, muscles bunched.

God, this wasn't over yet.

The cat launched itself at her again.

She thrust with the knife and swiped the cat's throat.
The cat dropped like a stuffed animal.

She backpedaled to the far counter.

The injured felines clustered together and faced her.
Their eerily intelligent eyes burned with malice.

She waved the blood-spattered knife in front of her.
She bled from multiple bites and scratches, and her
body was a throbbing pulse of agony, but she'd be
damned if she let some cats get the best of her.

"Bring it on!" she said.

The cats hissed in unison, their fur standing on end.

These weren't normal cats. No way. They were too
synchronized in their movements, too purposeful in
their violence. These animals behaved as if they were
under the influence of a single, malevolent mind.

Andrew rounded the bottom of the staircase. He had
a gun. "Carmen!"

As one, the cats spotted him. They streaked into the
dark dining room across the hallway.

"Follow them!" she said. She hurried into the room
and switched on the lights, no more than a second behind the creatures.

But the cats had vanished.

She glanced beneath the dining room table and
chairs. No sign of them.

Cats couldn't vanish like that. It was impossible.

A spell of dizziness hit her. She gripped a chair to regain her balance.

Andrew arrived in the doorway, scratching his head.
"Where'd they go?" he asked.

* * *

In the family room, Carmen lay on the sofa in her bra and panties, while Andrew sat beside her and applied ointment to her scratches and bites, to disinfect the wounds.

Although she lay in front of him, nearly nude, sex was the farthest thing from his mind. Other, disturbing thoughts took precedence.

It pissed him off that she'd been hurt at all, but it made him especially angry that it had occurred in his house. Although he couldn't have predicted what had happened, he felt responsible for her safety. Maybe it wasn't fair for him to accept the blame, but he blamed himself anyway. He'd been asleep when she'd come under attack. Thank God, she'd been capable of fighting back.

She was precious to him. If the assault had been worse . . . he didn't want to dwell on it anymore. The idea made him almost ill.

Once he'd confirmed that she was okay, he had spent a few minutes searching for the felines. He hadn't found so much as a fur ball to verify their presence inside his house.

It couldn't have happened. But it had.

As he attended to her, she sipped a cup of chamomile tea. She'd been trembling and the tea helped to calm her.

"I knew they didn't like me," she said. "That was obvious when we got back home from dinner. One of them hissed at me, remember?"

"I just don't understand how they got in the house. Or how they disappeared like that."

"Me, neither, but they did," she said in a don't-argue-with-me tone.

"Still think we should take you to the hospital, in case

they have rabies or something. Stray cats could be carrying anything."

"I'll go to the doctor later today, but those weren't ordinary, disease-carrying stray cats, Drew. They're something else, something scary and weird."

She shivered. The coldness she felt must have jumped to him, because a shudder rippled through his body, too. She had voiced his same worries.

"I don't know what they are, where they came from," she said, "but they hate me. And they didn't want to hurt you."

That was another point that bothered him. Why did the cats attack her, but run when he arrived?

"They've been watching me for days," he said. "But this is the first time they set foot in the house."

"That you know of. They could've come in here while you were away."

"Good point. But the real question is, why? I'm thinking the cats belong to someone, someone who commands them. They seem to be acting out of some purpose, know what I mean?"

She sucked in her lip, nodded. He dabbed ointment on a scratch across her cheek.

"I can think of only one person who'd be pissed at me right now," she said. "Psycho chick."

Squeezing the tube of ointment, he stopped. "What?"

"You know she's jealous of me. My spending the night with you would be the kind of thing that would set her crazy ass off. She's the only one who has a motive."

"But we're talking about her commanding some, I don't know, supernatural cats to attack you? How could she do that?"

"Don't know, but doesn't it make sense? You just said those cats have been spying on you for days. She's the only one who'd want to constantly keep an eye on you."

"But Mika is only a regular woman. Yeah, she's been

obsessing over me, but it's a helluva jump to go from calling her a psycho chick to believing that she's got some trained attack cats that can vanish into thin air."

"It wouldn't be the first jump you've made lately. Last week, did you really think you'd be chatting with a ghost on your computer?"

He pondered her words. He rubbed ointment into a cut on her leg, and taped a bandage across the affected area.

He wasn't ready to admit that Mika owned the cats. If it were true, it would change everything—for the worst. He wanted to hold on to his optimism for as long as he could.

"Let's talk to Sammy," he said. "He said he wants to help me, and he's been quiet all night. It's time for him to give us some answers."

He brought a folding chair into the office so that Carmen could sit beside him while he attempted to communicate with Sammy again.

His last question—*Why do you say I'm in big trouble now?*—remained unaddressed. Perhaps, at this point, it was moot. Mika had thrown a violent fit in his house and the weird cats had attacked Carmen. Obviously, he was in big trouble of some kind.

He erased the question and typed a new one: SAMMY, ARE YOU HERE?

"Might take him a few minutes to reply," he said to her. "It did the first time."

"Guess it's a long walk to here from the other side," she said.

"Or he could be sleeping," he said, playing along. They desperately needed some humor to lighten the bleak mood.

"Doubt it," she said. "Haven't you seen the movies?

The other side is always full of bright light. How could a ghost sleep somewhere like that? Bet he's got bags under his eyes."

He chuckled. Then he looked at her, solemn.

"I'm really glad you're okay, Carmen."

"Come on, I'm a tough chick, Drew. Your girl ain't one of those damsels in distress that can't run across a room without falling on her ass."

Sudden coldness in the room brought their conversation to a halt. The frigid air swirled around them, and gathered near the laptop.

Both Andrew and Carmen's breaths frosted in the ether in front of them.

"Sammy's here," Andrew said.

Carmen's eyes shone with awe.

The laptop's keys moved. Sluggishly—as if the ghost had been pulled from slumber, like they had joked.

I HEAR TYPENG MAKE TIRED

"Typing must be hard for him," Carmen said. "We better get right to it."

Andrew typed: WHO OWNS THE CATS?

He received the answer that he feared. The answer that changed everything.

HERS SENT THEM TO SEE YOU

"So Mika owns the cats," he said. "She sent them to watch me."

"Like I thought," Carmen said, but without the usual glee that she had whenever she had the correct answer.

Sammy's response triggered a batch of questions. Who was Mika—really? How did she have the ability to command the extraordinary cats? If the cats were not ordinary cats, then in what way was Mika not an ordinary woman?

Most important of all: Why had she chosen him?

"Ask something else," Carmen said.

He typed: TELL US MORE ABOUT HER.

The keys moved, slowly.

VEREY SCAREY

Such iciness fell over him that the temperature in the room felt as if it had dropped thirty degrees. Carmen, too, looked frightened.

He typed: WHY DID SHE CHOOSE ME?

SEEN YOU

"Seen me?" he said. "I don't get it. Of course she saw me, we met at Starbucks."

"Ask a different question," Carmen said.

He typed: WHERE IS SHE FROM?

SAD PLACE

"He told me earlier that he was from a sad place, too," he said to Carmen.

She leaned closer to the screen. "So they must be from the same place, then."

He asked: IS SHE A GHOST, LIKE YOU?

SAD PLACE HERS

He glanced at Carmen. Her face was as confused as his thoughts.

He asked: WHAT IS THE SAD PLACE?

MORNENG

He typed: WHAT DO YOU MEAN?

Half a minute passed before the answer came.

GO TYPENG MAKE TIRED

"Wait!" Andrew and Carmen said.

But the coldness in the air dissipated.

Sammy was gone.

Chapter 28

The next day, Andrew visited Southwest Regional Library. The library was located on Cascade Road, in a stylish, reddish-brown brick building that stood far back from the busy thoroughfare. On this sunny Friday morning in early June, only a handful of cars sat in the parking lot. He parked in the corner, in the cool shade of a blooming dogwood.

He planned to do research on Mika. She knew an awful lot about him, but he knew little about her. Sammy, though he had tried to assist them, didn't possess the language skills or the knowledge to clearly answer all of their questions. Until they understood who Mika was, they would be incapable of protecting themselves against her and her feline minions.

Although he had Internet access at his house and could've begun his research in the privacy of his office, the library subscribed to expensive, members-only databases that he couldn't tap into from home. Using their resources was the surest and quickest way to get the information he sought.

The librarian at the checkout counter greeted him.

She was a stout, middle-aged black woman with beautiful jet-black braids that flowed to her shoulders. Her name tag read Elaine.

"Hi, Mr. Andrew. Visiting us to do some research for a new book?"

The library staff had assisted him with research for his previous two novels. He'd thanked them in the acknowledgments, which had pleased them to no end. At some point they'd decided that his name was Mr. Andrew, too. Correcting them had never worked, so he let it slide.

"Something like that," he said. It was easier to let her assume he was doing book research than it was to explain that this was for personal reasons; besides, he was loathe to put his private life in the public eye. "Do you have some time to help me out?"

"I certainly do." Grinning, she came around the counter. "What do you need?"

He dug into his book bag and fished out his spiral notebook. He'd scribbled a list of what he knew about Mika: name, the fact that she was raised in Georgia, age, and the few details he'd learned about her family. He didn't have much information at all, and everything he knew was based on what she had told him—and she could've fed him a serving of lies.

"In my book, the main character needs to dig up information on a woman," he said. "But he doesn't know much about her. He knows her name and has some idea of where she's from, and a few other general things, but not much more. He wants to learn as much as possible about her background. I need to know the steps he'd take, the databases he'd use—that sort of thing."

Elaine clucked her tongue. "Sounds like a toughie. You say he knows her full name and where she's from?"

"Yep."

"That's a good start. Come with me."

She led him to a bank of computers. She sat in front of a PC and started tapping keys.

"By the way, I love your novels," she said. "What's this new one about?"

"Ah, you know I don't discuss a book until it's written. Might jinx myself."

"Can you give me a little hint?" She smiled winningly.

She charmed a smile out of him. "Well, it's about this guy who's, uh, being stalked by this woman who he met. He needs to learn about her to get a better idea of who he's dealing with."

"Sort of like *Fatal Attraction*, is it?"

"I guess you could say that." He chuckled uneasily.

She shook her head. "I tell you, honey, that's why I'd never want to become famous. So many psychos out there. You hit it big and become a target for every nut in the country."

He hadn't fooled her one bit. She knew that he was conducting this research for personal reasons. He saw no reason to continue the charade.

"Elaine, I really need to find out more about this woman," he said. "I'd appreciate any help you can give me."

Nodding, she quickly accessed a Web site. She started clicking on links.

"Looks like this is gonna take a while," he said.

"I'll show you enough to get you started," she said. "But you're right, there are hundreds of resources out there, some public, others private. These days, if you know where to look, you can find out almost anything on anyone. We'll dig up the info you need, Mr. Andrew."

"Thanks. That's exactly what I wanted to hear."

* * *

After he'd spent over three hours in front of the computer, combing subscribers-only databases and public records, he had discovered only one noteworthy detail. And he wasn't certain what he thought of it.

His finding: Lalamika Renee Woods was a fictional character.

His search had led him to a Web site that detailed characters and plot lines in novels, stage plays, television programs, and films. Lalamika Woods was the heroine in a romance novel entitled *Soulmate Eyes;* a writer named Alexia Forrest published the book in 1981.

You've got them . . . soul mate eyes . . .

The flesh at the nape of his neck tightened as he recalled Mika's words.

Could this book contain clues about her? It was such a far-fetched notion that he almost believed that it would.

Fingers tingling, he scanned the online card catalog.

Score. The library had one copy of *Soulmate Eyes* available for checkout.

He hurried to the shelves and found the paperback. It was dog-eared, the pages yellowed, but it was readable.

The cover art depicted an exotically beautiful young woman in the foreground, and in the background, glowing like a full moon, the countenance of a dark, handsome man with haunting eyes.

There was no photo or bio of the author, Alexia Forrest. But Mika couldn't have published the book. He placed her age at around twenty-five, and with the novel seeing print in 1981, she would've been an infant at the time.

In college, he'd taken an Evelyn Wood speed-reading class, and he still used the techniques sometimes. The book was two hundred pages long; he could zip through it in about an hour.

He moved to a study carrel in a quiet corner, settled in, and started to read.

A little over an hour later, he set aside the novel and reviewed the notes he'd scribbled while reading.

The plot of *Soulmate Eyes* revolved around a young woman, an heiress to a New England estate, who'd lost the man she loved to a tragic accident. Devastated, she plunged into depression. Almost thirty years later, her fortunes changed when she met a younger man who reminded her of her deceased lover. It was the look in his eyes, his "soul mate eyes," that fueled Lalamika's belief that he was her long-lost love, returned.

Due to the age difference, he resisted her, preferring to seek the company of a woman closer to his own age. But Lalamika would not be deterred; she pursued him with the full force of her fortune and charms.

Near the end of the story, through various clues, she proved to the man that he was, in fact, her former lover—reincarnated into a new body. When she succeeded in helping him remember his past life and their old love, he ditched the other woman, and he and Lalamika lived happily ever after.

The book, though rife with purple prose and a predictable storyline, had riveted him.

On their first night together, Mika had related the story of losing the man she loved to murder at the hands of men her bigoted father had hired to kill him.

And she'd told Andrew that he possessed "soul mate eyes."

It chilled him.

Mika wasn't the author, and obviously, she wasn't the actual character in the story, either.

But perhaps she'd read this book, and, finding parallels to her own life, had patterned herself after the heroine. Assumed the character's name and beliefs. And had decided that Andrew was her lost love. Reincarnate.

It was crazier than anything he had imagined.

But all of this stuff had ceased to be logical. His world had slid full-tilt into madness.

He was willing to bet that his theory about Mika's connections to this novel was right.

Nothing in the story explained Mika's other characteristics—such as her apparent power over the strange cats. Her real name, true nature, and capabilities remained a mystery. But he had gained insight into her beliefs, as bizarre as they were, and that was better than nothing.

He approached the checkout counter with the book. He planned to keep the novel for a while, for future reference.

"I wanted to ask you," Elaine said, "have you thought about going to the police?"

"If it comes to that, I will," he said, though this was becoming so weird he wondered how helpful the cops would be.

Elaine scanned the paperback through the library loan system and then studied the cover, curious.

"Don't ask," he said. "This situation is more bizarre than you think."

"Well, please be careful, honey."

Carrying his book bag over his shoulder, he pushed through the revolving doors and walked into the summer heat. It was twenty after one. His stomach growled for lunch.

He headed to the corner of the parking lot, where he had parked.

His car was missing.

Chapter 29

Andrew spun around in the sun-drenched parking lot. About a dozen vehicles occupied the lot. But none of them was his. Which left only one possibility.

Someone had stolen his car.

"I don't believe this shit," he said. He was short of breath, as if he had been punched in the stomach.

He dug into his jeans pocket. He still had his key. The thief must have hot-wired the vehicle.

"Shit, shit, shit."

There was never a good time to have your car stolen— but he didn't think there could've been a worse time. He already had enough problems.

Shit.

Cursing under his breath, he took his cell phone out of its holster.

As he was about to dial the police, a horn bleated behind him.

Mika cruised toward him. Driving his car.

* * *

She had lowered the convertible's top. She wore sunglasses—*his* Oakley sunglasses—and a wide grin. She looked happy and carefree, as if she'd been on a leisurely excursion in the country.

An old-school song played on the stereo: "I'm So Into You," by Peabo Bryson.

His face burned hotter than the June sun.

Once again, she had found him. Had this woman tagged him with a GPS tracking unit or something? He'd read articles about stuff like that—cutting-edge gadgets based on global positioning technology that allowed one to track a person wherever he went, without his knowledge. It was as simple as concealing a tiny antenna on someone's car. The antenna then transmitted signals to a handheld unit that displayed your target's precise location on a digital map.

She had to be doing something like that to him. Her ability to find him was uncanny.

But this time, she'd gone too far.

"What the hell are you doing in my car?" he asked.

She giggled. "Oooh, I love this car, Andrew. The ride's so smooth and powerful. A lot like you, baby." She smiled lasciviously.

He spotted the key in the ignition. He kept the spare at home, in his bedroom. How had she gotten it?

He answered his own question: she had invaded his house while he was gone. Searched through his belongings. At this point, he put nothing past her.

"Get out," he said. He grabbed the driver's side door handle.

She laughed, inched the car forward. "Oh, shut up and get in. Ride with me and let's talk about us."

"There is no *us.* Don't you get it?"

"Hop in and let's chat," she said. "Or I'll drive off and who knows where I may ditch this fine automobile?"

The sun shone mercilessly. Salty sweat leaked into his eyes, compounding his frustration.

"I'm calling the cops," he said. "I'm sick of this shit."

She shrugged. "So call them."

He lifted his phone, to punch in the speed dial number for the police, which he had added since talking to Eric about Mika's disturbing obsession with him.

But the phone had shut off. The display indicated that the battery had run out of juice.

Only two minutes ago, the phone had been fully charged, ready to go.

"Doesn't make any damn sense," he said. He pressed several buttons, to no avail.

"Technical difficulties?" she asked.

Why did he have the gut feeling that she had somehow disabled his phone?

But she can't do that, she's only a regular woman, for God's sake.

Waving, she began to roll away. "*Ciao*, darling."

"Wait!" He raced to catch up to her. He grabbed her hand on the steering wheel.

She screamed. "Someone, help me!"

Remembering that they were in a public area, he snatched his hand away from her.

An older woman, shuffling to the library, watched him with narrowed eyes.

"Do you want me to cause a scene?" Mika asked. "It would be a shame if someone believed that a big man like you were assaulting little ole me."

"You're crazy as hell," he said. But he knew she was right. Trying to take his car back by force would land him in handcuffs. In situations like this, the cops usually assumed the man was at fault.

She reached across the seat and pulled the passenger door handle, nudged the door open. She pushed out her lips like a pouting child.

"I only want to talk," she said. "I won't bite."

He dragged his hand down his sweaty face.

Could he handle talking to her? Did he even have a choice anymore?

"Fine, but make it quick," he said.

She was dressed to kill, as always. She wore a skimpy yellow top that exposed her cleavage, a white miniskirt, and open-toe sandals. Her hair ran to her shoulders in lustrous waves, her red lips as ripe as cherries.

Although she was gorgeous, he no longer felt desire for her, didn't want to even touch her. She was like a Bengal tiger in its deadly prime. Magnificently beautiful. But so dangerous you didn't want to venture within twenty feet of it.

He kept close to the passenger door.

She didn't appear to notice how she repelled him. Singing to herself, she steered the Mercedes out of the parking lot and onto a side street that intersected Cascade Road. At the stoplight, she flicked on the left-turn signal.

"Where are we going?" he asked.

"For a little spin."

"Why are you doing this to me?"

"Doing what to you, Andrew?"

"You know damn well what I'm talking about—stealing my car, making me talk to you, the whole nutty nine yards. Why?"

"Because I love you, of course." The light switched to green. She turned onto Cascade Road.

"Could've fooled me after that temper tantrum you threw at my house."

"I apologize. I was upset and lost my composure. Do you accept my apology?"

He stared at her, unable to believe her nerve. A casual apology for flipping over a freakin' table?

"If only you understood how much I love you," she said. "If only you knew, you would understand why I was so angry when you rejected me."

They neared the exit for Interstate 285. She turned onto the northbound ramp.

"I've been trying to understand you." He unzipped the book bag on his lap, removed the copy of *Soulmate Eyes*. "Look what I found at the library, Lalamika Renee Woods."

He didn't know what reaction he had expected from her, but he certainly didn't anticipate the one she gave him.

"Oh! That's a wonderful book! My absolute favorite, ever. Have you read it, what did you think of it, weren't you surprised when Lalamika—?"

"Listen! I know you're basing yourself on this woman or whatever, okay? Lalamika, Mika—that's not your real name. You took it from the book."

"You're a fine one to condemn me for using an alias, *Mark Justice*." She smiled.

"That's not the same thing, and you know it."

"Oh, so what? Of course I took the lady's name. She and I share a similar predicament. Her story resonates with me."

She spoke as if it were the most common thing in the world.

They merged onto the highway. She fed the gas. The speedometer climbed to seventy miles per hour.

They already had exceeded the speed limit of fifty-five, but as anyone in metro Atlanta knew, I-285 was the equivalent of the Daytona 500. You had to zoom at seventy-five merely to keep up with the flow of traffic.

"What's your real name?" he asked.

"Truly, it doesn't matter. All that matters is that I love

you, and that we're finally together again—soul mate eyes."

"So you think that I'm the reincarnation of this guy you used to love?"

"I don't think you are. I know you are. I have proof, Mark Justice."

"Listen, it's Andrew. And what proof are you talking about?"

"You'll see, very soon, I promise."

A few years ago, he had watched a segment on *Dateline* or *60 Minutes;* he couldn't remember which show. Y2K was nearing, and the news journalist had interviewed the leader of a religious cult who had convinced his followers to leave their homes and jobs behind and seek refuge in an underground bunker in the Arizona desert, to await the Apocalypse that he believed would strike the world on New Year's Eve. The shaggy-haired leader spoke of the imminent end of the world with unshakeable confidence (and evident glee), and no amount of probing questions from the journalist could rattle his poise.

Mika was like that crazy cultist. Utterly convinced of her bizarre beliefs. Arguing with her was a waste of time.

She continued to press the accelerator. The needle climbed to eighty.

He checked that he had engaged his seat belt.

"What about the cats?" he asked.

"Their names are Circe, Iris, and Eos. Know where those come from?"

"I don't know, Greek mythology or something."

She squeezed his leg. "You're so smart, baby. Yes, I always loved to read about the Greek myths when I was a child. Wonderful stories."

"But what about the cats?"

"What about them? They watch over you. My little guardians." She giggled.

"They attacked Carmen."

"She had no business staying at your house last night. I sent them as a warning."

"How can you control them?"

She frowned. "Because they're mine, Andrew. Obviously."

"But they just disappeared!"

"They have a tendency to do that." She chuckled.

It was too much madness. His head felt as though it were going to burst.

The speedometer moved to ninety. She veered into the far left-hand lane.

"Mika, you need to slow down."

She mashed the accelerator. The engine moaned.

The speed climbed to ninety-five . . . one hundred.

They were in the danger zone. If a highway patrol officer clocked them now, both of them might be carted off to jail.

"Slow down!" he said.

"Admit that you love me, Andrew. Then I'll slow down."

"What?"

"Tell me you love me."

The needle hovered at one hundred and five miles per hour. The wind howled in his ears, buffeted his face.

"But I *don't* love you," he said.

"Be honest, darling. Tell me you love me. Confess it."

One hundred and ten.

The Mercedes vibrated. Trees and cars flew past in colorful blurs.

He swallowed dryly.

As they bore down on vehicles ahead of them, she

began to zigzag through traffic. She nearly clipped a Chevy's bumper. Horns blared.

She was going to cause an accident. At this speed, hitting another vehicle was a sure trip to the morgue.

"Dammit, slow down!" he said.

"Say you love me! I won't slow down until you say it!"

He gnawed his lip.

One hundred and fifteen.

The rocketing car felt as if it floated on a ribbon of air.

She veered through traffic, recklessly. His stomach flipped.

"Say it, baby!" she said.

"I love you," he said. "Okay, I said it, now slow down!"

"Louder. Scream it for the whole world to hear!"

"I love you!"

"Again, baby!"

"I love you!"

She shrieked with pleasure.

"Was that so hard?" She patted his leg. "I love you, too, Andrew. I love you so much."

He slumped in the seat. His intestines churned, as if he'd digested something rotten.

Decreasing their speed, she steered the car into the far right-hand lane.

"Want to drive now?" she asked.

Silent, he nodded.

She parked on the gravel shoulder of the highway.

"All that invigorating, high-speed driving has awakened my appetite." She patted her stomach. "Let's go somewhere and get something good to eat."

"Okay." His body felt limp, as if he had been subjected to heart-stuttering g-force on a wicked roller coaster.

But the gears of his mind spun.

What would Mark Justice do in this situation?

Justice spoke to him, gave him a plan.

She climbed out of the car. He got out, too. His knees trembled.

Feet, don't fail me now.

She walked to the rear of the Mercedes, to come around to the passenger side. He met her at the vehicle's flank.

Only a few feet away from them, cars whizzed past on the interstate.

He touched her arm. Tried to hide his disgust.

"What is it, darling?" Her eyes sparkled.

Seizing her arm, he swung her around and pitched her into the weeds lining the highway's shoulder.

She screamed.

He sprinted to the driver's side door and scrambled behind the wheel. He mashed the gas pedal and roared away in a frenzy of grit and dust.

He glanced behind him. Mika had gotten to her feet. She shouted, arms waving wildly.

"Crazy ass," he said.

He had gotten away from her. This time.

Chapter 30

Andrew's appetite had returned. After he'd put several miles between himself and the place where he'd ditched Mika, he exited I-285 and drove to a Chick-Fil-A. He ordered a chicken sandwich, waffle fries, and lemonade. He requested extra napkins, to dry his sweaty face and hands.

Sitting in the car with the convertible roof shielding him, running the air conditioner at full blast, he devoured the food. He couldn't remember ever being so starved.

Maybe fear had that kind of effect on him.

He didn't know what to do next. Report Mika to the cops? And say what? He didn't even know her real name.

As he deliberated his next step, his cell phone chirped. He checked the display. The battery had returned to full strength.

Weird. He hadn't recharged the phone.

The call, thankfully, was from his agent.

"I've got some wonderful news," Sandy said. "The publisher's made an offer."

Sandy loved to be dramatic. Under ordinary circumstances, he would be clutching the phone, excitement crackling in his voice. But his voice was flat as he asked, "How much, Sandy?"

She paused, for emphasis.

"They're offering five hundred thousand dollars, Andrew. Congratulations."

He concluded his phone call with Sandy. He barely remembered what they discussed after she told him the sum of money that the publisher had offered. He did recall that he told her to accept the deal.

A half-million dollars, for one book. A jackpot.

What an unbelievable day.

In a daze, he started driving.

He figured he should celebrate. Pick up a few bottles of champagne and invite his family and friends over for an impromptu party.

Or maybe not. Inviting people to his house probably was a bad idea right now. Instead, maybe they should go out to eat somewhere classy, like Chops or Maggianno's.

But as he thought about Mika's knack for finding him anywhere he went, he nixed that idea, too.

Here he was, with so much to celebrate, and he couldn't do it the way he wanted. Paranoia ruled him.

He drove to his mother's house in East Point. She was always the first person with whom he shared good news. But she wasn't home, and he didn't call her on her cell phone. This publishing offer was the kind of stupendous announcement he wanted to make face-to-face.

While parked in his mom's driveway, he thoroughly searched the interior and exterior of his car, seeking the device that he suspected Mika was using to track his whereabouts. He found nothing.

How was she managing to find him? It baffled him.

Maybe she was psychic, could concentrate on him and locate him anywhere he went.

It was a crazy idea, like something out of a horror movie, but he was beginning to believe that anything might be possible.

After hanging out at his mom's place for a half hour or so, he gave up waiting and left. He stopped by a package store on his way home. He could use a drink, just for himself. He bought a six-pack of Heineken.

He pulled into the driveway of his house. With relief, he noted that the cats were not around.

But the front door was open.

Warily, he stepped inside the house. He hefted a golf club in his hands.

He wished he had the gun, but it was upstairs in his bedroom. He wanted to kick himself for not carrying it with him.

"Hello!" he said. "Who's in here?"

No answer.

As he surveyed the first floor, he groaned.

It looked as if a mini-hurricane had torn through the place.

Artwork had been ripped off the walls, tossed to the floor, and smashed. Tables and chairs were overturned, their cushions slashed. Glasses and vases had been shattered.

The aquarium had been knocked over, underwater plants bristling from the tank like spilled guts. The fish were missing.

It was Mika. No one else would have done this. She was pissed off because he'd deserted her on the highway.

The crazy bitch.

He rushed through the house, to see the extent of the damage.

In the kitchen, her three cats sat on the counter. Circe, Iris, and Eos, or whatever the hell their names were. They were eating the fish from his tank.

They stopped and looked at him as if he were an uninvited guest at a dinner party.

"Get the fuck out of here!" He swung the club and knocked one of the felines across the room. It screeched.

The other cats scattered.

He chased them, swinging the club.

"Come back here, you motherfuckers!"

The cats made a beeline into the bathroom. He hustled after them.

But the bathroom was empty.

The animals had vanished.

They have a tendency to do that.

Cursing, he threw the golf club to the floor and went through the rest of the house. She hadn't neglected a single room. Every area had been trashed.

In his office, the laptop screen had been busted. A hammer lay nearby.

His link to Sammy. Destroyed.

The pager she had given him, which he still wore on his hip, vibrated.

IT'S CALLED TOUGH LOVE, BABY.

He flung the pager to the floor, grabbed the hammer, and pounded the pager to bits.

Later, he called Eric.

"I need your help, man. I want to get a restraining order."

Although he doubted it would do any good against Mika.

Chapter 31

Eric dropped off Andrew at home. They'd visited the Fulton County courthouse, where Andrew had submitted a request for a temporary restraining order.

Without being able to provide Mika's permanent address or legal name, he wasn't optimistic that the police would be able to offer much assistance. The only concrete detail he had was the room number of her suite at the Ritz-Carlton. The police promised to follow up on it. They offered no guarantees, and echoed the advice Eric had given him earlier: record everything that happened, and watch his back.

On the drive back to his house, he'd told Eric everything, including the parts about Sammy. He was too tired and scared to keep any more secrets.

Eric didn't express any skepticism, which surprised and relieved him. "You've been my boy my whole life, I know you aren't making this shit up," Eric had said. "I had a bad feeling about that female from the start, bro."

Eric wanted him to spend the next few days at his house on Lake Sinclair, about a hundred miles southeast of metro Atlanta. To lie low and let Mika cool off.

Andrew declined the offer. He wasn't going to let Mika run him out of his own place. It would be like accepting defeat.

Besides, he wasn't convinced that running away would help. Mika found him no matter where he went.

It was early evening when they arrived at Andrew's home. The setting sun cast a crimson-orange glow across the sky. The deep, lengthening shadows promised an especially dark night.

He got out of Eric's SUV and shuffled around to the driver's side.

"Still think you should go to my lake crib for a while," Eric said. "Take Carmen with you and chill."

"Listen, anywhere I go, this woman finds me. Like she's got a tracker on me or something. If I'm gonna be stalked, I might as well be in the comfort of my own home."

"I hear ya, bro. If you change your mind, the keys to the place are yours, you know that."

"I appreciate that."

"Got your piece?"

He patted his side. He wore the revolver in a shoulder holster, concealing it with an oversize Atlanta Falcons jersey. He'd vowed that he wouldn't be caught defenseless again.

"Cool," Eric said. "What're you about to do now?"

"The locksmith should be over in a half hour. I need to finish cleaning up, too. Got a helluva mess in there."

"Want any help?"

"Nah, I can handle it."

"I'll check on you later this evening. But call me if you need anything, all right?"

"Will do. Thanks, man."

Eric pulled away and drove to his home down the street.

Andrew faced the house. This wonderful place for

which he had labored for years to be able to attain. He felt a surge of the same, fierce pride he'd experienced when the real estate attorney at the closing had handed him the keys to the front door.

And Mika had violated it.

As his pride gave way to righteous anger, he clenched his hands into fists.

His outrage didn't really stem from her vandalism of the house; most of the items and furniture she'd broken could be repaired or replaced. He was angered because she was wrecking what his house symbolized to him. Freedom. Stability.

She'd robbed him of his freedom, had him nervous to sleep in his own bed. At any time, her or her cats might be watching and scheming.

And his stable life of comforting routines had been destroyed. He never knew what might happen next, what fresh terror would strike him. Chaos had taken over.

All because a woman he'd met in a coffee shop had fallen in love with him and wouldn't take no for an answer.

He squeezed his fists so tightly that his knuckles popped.

He wasn't going to give up the life he'd earned for Mika. Never.

He'd rather die than give up.

The locksmith arrived around six-thirty and replaced the locks on the front and patio doors. Andrew called the security company and changed the access code to the system, too.

Tomorrow, he was taking his car to the dealership to get it outfitted for new keys.

Switching the locks and the passwords probably would

not keep Mika out of his house or his car. She possessed unusual talents that might grant her entry to wherever she desired to go. But in the absence of detailed proof regarding exactly what she was capable of, it was logical for him to take basic steps to secure his possessions.

He kept the revolver in the shoulder holster as he cleaned up the mess Mika and her cats had left behind. If she showed up again, he wasn't sure he'd be able to shoot her. The only thing he'd ever fired at were targets at shooting ranges. But keeping the gun on him made him feel safer.

Tidying the entire house would take days; he limited his efforts to the kitchen, bedroom, office, and bathroom, the areas that he frequented.

As he swept broken glass across the kitchen floor, the telephone rang. It was a cop.

"Mr. Wilson, we've run into a problem trying to serve this restraining order," the officer said in a gruff voice.

His stomach plummeted. "What's wrong?"

"You say that a Lalamika Woods was staying at the Ritz-Carlton in Buckhead? That you spent time with her there this past Tuesday night, June first?"

"That's right. Let me guess: the room's listed under a different name."

"Sure is, buddy. It's listed under your name."

"Excuse me?"

"Hotel says Mr. and Mrs. Andrew F. Wilson checked in on Tuesday, June first at two o'clock in the afternoon. You checked out the next morning."

"That's impossible."

"Is it?" the officer's voice held a note of sarcasm. "You having marital problems, buddy?"

"Huh? I'm not married!"

"The police department ain't the place to vent your troubles with your wife. On top of that, filing a false police report is a crime—"

"Listen, I'm not lying. You've gotta believe me, she must've checked into the hotel under my name—"

"With your credit card, too, huh? American Express?"

"I don't have an American Express card."

"You used it to book the room at the Ritz."

"It wasn't me!" He pounded his fist against the counter. "She must've stolen my identity, gotten a card under my name, used it to book the hotel—"

"Why the heck would your wife go through all that trouble?"

"She's *not* my wife!" he said. "Don't you get it? This woman is nuts and she's ruining my life."

"Buddy, I usually wouldn't do this, but I'm going to keep this TRO request on the desk here over the weekend, give you some time to reconcile with your wife. I'll check back with you Monday and see if you're ready to stop playing these silly games with us."

"Wait, I really need your help!"

Click.

He slammed the phone onto the cradle. He paced the house.

Going to the cops was useless. As he'd feared.

Mika had set him up perfectly. He had no way to catch her. It was like trying to capture smoke.

Chapter 32

He called Carmen and told her what had happened. "Wow, psycho chick is a schemer and a half," she said. "She's really covered her trail."

"There's gotta be something I can do," he said. "But I don't know what."

"I'm sorry, Drew. Wish I knew what to tell you. Is there any way you can talk to Sammy again?"

Standing in his office, he glanced at the smashed computer screen.

"Computer's shot," he said. "I'll have to get a new one. I'd planned to go to Best Buy first thing tomorrow."

"You saved your manuscripts to disk, right? Wouldn't want the mega-author to lose his masterpieces."

"Saved them to disk and uploaded the files to an on-line storage site, too. I do that for everything all the time. A few years ago I read about Toni Morrison losing some of her important manuscripts in a house fire, and that scared me to death."

"I'm glad that's covered, then."

"Wish I could upload myself to a Web site right now,

escape this madness. I'm not gonna sleep tonight, Carmen."

"I'd love to be there with you. But I know you don't think it's safe for me. Can I at least drop off my computer for you?"

A crashing sound came from downstairs.

An icy wave of dread washed over him.

"I'll call you back," he said. "I need to check out something."

"Be careful, Drew."

He rushed downstairs. He was certain the noise had come from the basement.

Poised at the top of the basement staircase, he flipped the light switch, chasing away the blackness.

Silence lay over the area below.

With a shaky hand, he drew the .38 from the holster. He held the gun in both hands, muzzle pointed at the ceiling, and slowly descended the steps.

He saw what had caused the noise. In the corner of the room, a board game had been tossed to the hardwood floor: Scrabble.

Cold air wafted toward him and caressed his face. The coolness felt as welcome as a breeze on a sizzling day.

"Sammy." He smiled. "You're a genius, man."

In the kitchen, he spread the crossword game board on the dinette table and dumped a couple dozen wooden letter tiles out of the sack.

The board overlapped the jagged crack caused when Mika had flipped the table. The fracture served as a vivid reminder of how much was at stake.

"Sammy, I need some answers," he said. "I need to find out how to deal with Mika."

He remembered that during previous communication, Sammy had answered questions that he presented verbally. He decided to try the same approach now, to save time.

The air around him thickened, cooled.

Sammy was nearby.

He leaned over the game board. "Earlier, you said that you and Mika are from the same place—you called it a sad place. Do you know the name of the town or city?"

The letter tiles began to slide across the board and form a phrase.

FAR FROM HEAR

"Okay, you told me that before," he said. "But what's the name of the city, Sammy?"

DONT NO

He sighed, tried to hide his frustration with the ghost's inadequate answers to basic questions.

"Is the sad place a house?"

YES

Okay, this was progress. Until now Sammy hadn't told him exactly what the "sad place" was.

He flipped through his notebook and looked at his notes. Earlier, Sammy had said, "sad place is hers." Mika therefore owned this house, and Sammy had dwelled there, too.

"Good, Sammy. Where is this house located?"

MORNENG

That puzzling word again. Morneng. What the hell did he mean?

Hunkered over the table, he decided to temporarily change the line of questioning, and hope that he could lead Sammy back to this subject and a more coherent answer.

"Let's talk about Mika," he said. "What is she?"

WOMAN

Was Sammy trying to be a smart-ass? Or was he merely simple-minded?

"Listen, she can't be an ordinary woman, not with the stuff she's able to do." He drummed his fingers on the table. "Is she some kind of psychic—meaning, she's got lots of weird powers?"

CAN DO LOTS OF STUF

"Okay, I can believe that, then. She's always able to find me, wherever I go."

SEE FAR

"See far? You mean, she does some kind of remote viewing thing, can sort of focus on me in her mind and know where I am?"

YES

It was perfectly unbelievable. And perfectly sensible.

"That means I can never get away from her, Sammy. Is that true? Will she always be able to find me?"

CANT SEE VEREY VEREY FAR

His answer seemed to indicate that Mika's ability to detect his location had limitations. But what was the extent of her talent? How far away did he have to run? A hundred miles? A thousand? Ten thousand?

He doubted Sammy would be able to provide a more quantitative explanation. Back to the house.

"Sammy, is the sad place very, very far from here?"

YES

"Where?" He was so eager to know he asked the question without realizing that it would take them back to conversational ground they had already covered.

MORNENG

Morneng, morneng, morneng.

He wanted to pull his hair out. What did that word mean?

He got an idea.

"Wait here, Sammy, I'll be right back."

He ran upstairs to his office and dug a state road atlas out of a desk drawer, where he kept some of his reference materials.

He checked the names of cities and towns in Georgia. Mika had told him that she lived somewhere in the state, hadn't she?

But in the entire state of Georgia, there was no town called Morneng.

It might be a misspelled word. Sammy sure wasn't going to win a spelling bee competition.

Morning, maybe?

He examined the atlas. There was no town named "Morning," either.

He returned to the kitchen. The spectral coldness waited near the table.

"Morning?" he asked. "Is that the name of the town, Sammy? Morning, like 'good morning'?"

SAD PLACE IS MORNENG

"The sad place is called morning?"

Sammy rapped the board, causing the tiles to jump, but the message remained the same: SAD PLACE IS MORNENG

Andrew gnawed his lip. Maybe he meant "mourning" as in grieving. But a check of the atlas confirmed that no city named "Mourning" existed in Georgia.

"Sammy, I don't understand."

Sammy tapped the board again, like an impatient teacher: SAD PLACE IS MORNENG

"Mourning like crying? The sad place is crying?"

Another knock: SAD PLACE IS MORNENG

Andrew dragged his hand down his face. This was going nowhere.

"Listen, how can we get rid of Mika?" he asked.

DONT NO

"What can we do to stop her?"

A tap: DONT NO

"Can we make her quit?"

Another tap: DONT NO

"Don't you know anything at all?" he asked. "Damn, you sound like a stupid kid!"

The cold, coagulating air grew thicker.

"I didn't mean that, Sammy. I'm just confused and scared. I'm sorry."

The ghost spelled another message.

AM A KID NOT STOOPID

And the coldness faded away.

He pleaded for Sammy to come back. He repeatedly apologized. But the ghost did not return. He was angry with him, apparently.

"Good job, man," he said to himself. "Pissed off the only one who could help you."

He wrote down what he recalled of their communication. He read through his notes, tried to make sense of what Sammy had told him about the sad place, which he considered the linchpin of understanding Mika's background. But the meaning of Sammy's cryptic statements eluded him.

One thing had become clear: Sammy was a kid. It explained his poor communication skills.

"Why couldn't I have gotten a grown-up ghost?" He laughed bitterly at the absurdity of the situation.

He took a Heineken out of the refrigerator. He sat at the dinette table, drank deeply, belched.

The thought of drinking himself into a stupor appealed to him. It would take the edge off the anxiety that chewed at his guts.

Even as he considered the thought, he knew he wouldn't do it. Drunk, he would lose full control of his mental and physical functions, and with Mika on the prowl, he couldn't afford to be vulnerable. One or two beers would have to be the limit.

As he sipped the brew, Sammy's baffling messages spooled through his mind.

Sad place is morneng.

He was missing something. A vital link that would explain all of the clues. But what was it?

Sad place is morneng.

Why was he convinced that it was something obvious? Sammy wasn't Shakespeare, crafting intricate and metaphorical language. He was a kid, almost painfully simple and direct.

He worried that he was analyzing this too rigorously. The logical left side of his brain doggedly attempted to grind out a solution—but inhibited his creativity and intuition.

Sad place is morneng.

He took another sip of beer and let his thoughts settle. From his experiences writing fiction, he'd learned that the muse often visited unexpectedly, after he had given up trying to wrestle an idea to the surface.

He went to the pantry, opened a can of Planter's almonds, and poured out a handful. He munched on almonds and sipped the Heineken.

Without any purposeful effort, his mind circled back to what Sammy had told him.

Mika and Sammy hailed from the same place. The sad place. A house. What kind of house would an heiress to a fortune own?

An estate, probably. Like a mansion.

A mansion . . .

He stopped eating.

The beer bottle felt much colder in his hand. Like a brick of ice.

He had an idea. An idea that frightened and excited him simultaneously.

He needed to talk to Sammy. Immediately. The ghost was his only hope of proving what he suspected.

He ought to knock himself upside the head for insulting the kid.

Loud music struck up in the basement. The kitchen floor started to throb.

He placed the beer on the counter.

It had to be Sammy down there, fooling around with the stereo. Throwing a temper tantrum. Just like the child he was.

He went to the basement door.

A disco song played downstairs: "Dance With Me," by K.C. and the Sunshine Band.

"That you, Sammy?" he said. "I said I'm sorry!"

The music increased in volume. The walls vibrated and the door trembled.

"Turn it off!" he said. "Stop messing around!"

The banging music played on.

Feeling like a parent needing to discipline a boisterous child, he pounded down the steps.

But Sammy was not there.

Mika was.

Chapter 33

Mika was dancing.

Standing at the base of the stairs, Andrew froze.

On the other side of the room, the patio door was half open, allowing an evening breeze to whisper inside. The locksmith had changed the lock on the door only an hour ago, and he had made sure that it was secured.

It proved his fears: locks were useless against Mika.

Twirling around the hardwood floor, she waved at him. "Hey, baby. Come on and dance with me!"

Laughing, she whirled. Snapped her fingers to the beat.

As she neared the furniture, it moved out of her path; the sofa, chairs, and end tables, pushed by an invisible force, glided to the walls.

She barely noticed.

Fear covered him, like a blanket of ice.

What would Mark Justice do?

Justice answered: *You can't fight her, Andrew. She's got unbelievable powers. Get the hell outta here.*

But terror had rooted his feet to the floor.

"We've got plenty of space to boogie," she said. "I

loved salsa dancing with you. Get your booty out here, darling."

"Where are you from?" His voice was hoarse.

"You'll find out, baby." Grinning, she shimmied toward him, hands extended to entice him to dance with her.

He finally broke his paralysis. He drew the revolver out of the holster. His hands shook as he aimed the gun at her.

"Stay the fuck away from me," he said.

"Put that down, Andrew." She stopped dancing. Her eyebrow twitched.

He curled his finger around the trigger.

"Get back," he said. "Or I'll shoot. I'm not playing with you."

"I warned you." She raised her hand, as if to signal someone to stop.

An ice-cold sensation clamped over his wrists. He gasped in surprise and pain. The strange force wrenched his wrists downward with almost enough savagery to break them.

He cried out. The gun popped out of his hands and clattered to the floor.

As swiftly as it had seized him, the coldness faded.

He examined his wrists; red blotches burned on his skin.

"Don't ever do that again, Andrew," she said. She smiled, faintly, as if pleased by his horror. "Now get out here and dance!"

He stood immobile. Wanting to run. Afraid to run.

She grasped his hands and pulled him closer to her. She wriggled her body **against** his, spun and bounced her hips against his crotch, every sensuous movement in sync with the pounding disco beat.

Like a robot, he started to dance—on sagging legs that threatened to drop him on his face at any second.

He watched her shiny mane, whipping across her back and neck. He wanted to grab her neck and choke the life out of her.

But he didn't dare try it. It was as unthinkable as sticking his hand in a buzzing wasp nest.

The disc moved to the next track: "Super Freak," by Rick James. He realized that she had put his old-school party CD into the player.

He remembered that party, which he'd hosted at his house last New Year's Eve. Carmen had dressed in a puffy Afro wig and corduroys; Eric had worn a polyester suit and platform shoes. It had been a great time.

Would he ever see his friends again?

Mika jumped around and gyrated, losing herself in the music. There was no doubt: the girl could jam. If he weren't terrified of her, he would've been dancing as energetically as she was. But it took all his effort to move his limbs as woodenly as the Frankenstein monster.

They danced around the room. In his peripheral vision, he noted two objects: the small brass lamp that stood on a nearby end table, and the gun that lay at the foot of the steps, across the basement.

He didn't need to ask Justice for advice. He knew what he was going to do.

When Mika whirled, putting her back to him, he grabbed the lamp and smashed it against her head.

On impact with Mika's head, the lamp's light bulb exploded.

Mika shrieked and fell.

Move, move, move.

He sprinted across the basement and plucked the gun off the floor. He glanced over his shoulder.

She was getting up. Her eyes blazed.

Hot breath whistling in and out of his mouth, he began to charge up the steps.

Something grabbed the waist of his jeans. Rudely jerked him backward.

He snagged the staircase railing just in time to prevent a backward fall down the steps.

Coldness lashed his hand, like a whip.

He yelped, lost his hold on the railing. He teetered, lost his balance, and bumped down the stairs, each thump sending a painful rattle through his tailbone. He tried to stick out his legs and arms to halt his tumble, but he couldn't gain any leverage.

But he kept his grip on the gun, like a man lost at sea clutching a life raft.

When he hit the bottom of the staircase, Mika stomped toward him, arms swinging, eyes fierce.

At that instant, there was nothing tender and loving about her. She might have been a vengeful goddess, descended to earth to punish him for his transgressions.

He didn't hesitate.

He aimed at her and pulled the trigger.

It was only a .38, but in the confines of the basement, the gun boomed like a cannon.

The bullet plowed into her chest. She screamed, staggered backward several feet and crashed to the floor.

He lowered the revolver. Warm, gritty smoke filled his nostrils.

He couldn't believe that he'd shot her.

I had no choice. It was self-defense.

Still, his stomach quivered sourly.

The CD player moved to the next track: "You Dropped a Bomb on Me" by The Gapp Band.

He got to his feet. His tailbone ached, drew a hiss of pain from him.

The gun felt like a fifty-pound dumbbell in his hand.

He dreaded the next step, but it was inevitable: he had to call the police and report what had happened. And hope that they didn't slap him with criminal charges.

Across the room, Mika stirred.

He'd plugged her square in her chest. A fatal shot.

But as he watched, the bullet pushed out of her gunshot wound and clinked to the floor, like a misshapen coin.

Oh, shit. That's impossible.

She sat up. Her gaze drilled into him.

"I warned you about that gun, Andrew," she said, her voice as clear as ever. "You've pissed me off now."

He turned and ran.

He streaked up the stairs, leaping past two and three steps with each frantic stride.

Mika chased him.

He hit the top of the staircase and scrambled across the hall.

He had to get out of the house, as far away from her as possible.

He threw open the door to the garage, slammed it behind him, locked it. He mashed his fist into the button to raise the sectional door.

It began to rise, with infuriating slowness.

Come on, come on.

The trio of cats waited outside the garage. Screeching, they came after him.

Shit. Those damned things again. They were turned against him now, serving their angry mistress.

He bolted to his car. As he hustled behind the wheel and went to shut the door, one of the cats slipped inside. It leaped onto his lap and clawed at his face.

He raised his arm to protect himself. Claws ripped into his forearm. He screamed.

Remembering the gun in his hand, he hammered it against the feline's head. The animal howled as something in its skull cracked. The cat slumped against his chest.

He grabbed it by the scruff of the neck and flung it to the floor.

The other felines pounced on the windshield. Hissing. Clawing at him through the glass. Fury boiled in their alien eyes.

Behind them, the door blew open.

Like a human tornado, Mika stormed into the garage.

He stabbed the key in the ignition and turned it so fast it was a wonder it didn't break off in the casing.

The engine roared. He slammed the gearshift into reverse and jammed the accelerator. Tires squealed.

The cats jumped off the car.

Mika raced to the nose of the vehicle, bent, and snagged the bumper in both hands, like a weightlifter preparing to do a dead lift.

Halfway out the garage, the car rocked to a halt. The tires spun uselessly.

Face hovering above the hood, she grinned.

He pressed the gas pedal full to the floor. Acrid smoke plumed in the air as the tires screeched against the concrete.

But the car was stuck.

She was inhumanly strong.

Thinking fast, he switched gears, into drive.

The sudden change of direction propelled him forward quickly enough to cause whiplash.

The Mercedes plowed into Mika. She wailed in pain as the vehicle drove her against the wall. She flopped onto the hood, lifelessly.

He knew better than to assume she was dead.

He threw the car into reverse again and zoomed out of the garage. She dropped to the ground.

He reached the end of the driveway. He was so busy watching Mika that he almost ran over the mailbox.

She began to push herself up.

"Dammit, why won't she die?" he said.

She raced out of the garage and chased after him. Her cats flanked her, eyes gleaming.

He barreled out of the driveway and shot down the road.

His neighbors had left the big blue BFI garbage bins standing on the curbs, to be emptied in the morning when the sanitary crews made their weekly rounds of the neighborhood. One of the cans careened toward him, like a giant pinball.

He whipped the steering wheel, narrowly avoiding a collision.

Mika was doing this. Trying to prevent **him** from getting away.

There seemed to be no limits to her powers.

Another garbage can hurtled toward him. He swerved, but the can thudded against the windshield and rocked the car, spilled trash across the hood.

He nailed the gas pedal to the floor.

Several garbage containers clustered across the street ahead, forming a wall.

He gritted his teeth and burst through the makeshift barrier, like a bowling ball knocking down pins. The bins tumbled end over end. Loose trash soared like confetti through the air.

Mika's scream echoed in his ears. In the rearview mirror, he saw her standing in the middle of the road. Nowhere near dead or even injured.

Ahead of him, the street was clear. He kicked up his speed, slowed to veer around the corner. He left the subdivision.

He blew out a deep breath. He had been breathing so hard that his lungs hurt.

On the floor beside him, the cat's tail danced like a cobra.

He had crushed the feline's skull, but it wasn't dead. Nothing surprised him anymore.

He lowered the window, grabbed the cat by the tail, and tossed the creature out into the night. It rolled across the pavement, yowling.

His hands shook on the steering wheel. So much emotion churned through him that he didn't know whether to cry, or collapse. He felt like doing both.

Chapter 34

He drove to Carmen's house. He didn't know where else to go. Eric's home, located in the same neighborhood as his, was off limits with Mika being in the vicinity. Going to the cops would be fruitless; ridiculously, they thought he and Mika were married, and they sure as hell wouldn't buy his story of her getting up uninjured from a gunshot wound and lifting the front end of his car like some mythical Amazon woman. They'd probably throw him into a rubber room at the nearest psychiatric ward.

Thirty miles away in Marietta, Carmen was his best option. Only she would understand what he was going through.

"Drew, what's wrong?" Carmen said at the door. "What happened?"

"Tell you . . . in a minute," he said weakly. He plopped onto the sofa in the living room. "Got some water?"

She brought him a glass of water. He gulped half of it, then poured some on his hands and splashed it on his flushed, sweaty face.

Sitting beside him, she noticed the ragged scratch

on his forearm, from the cat's claws. Anxiety darkened her eyes. "Let me take care of that."

As she cleaned and dressed his wound, he told her what had happened.

"Jesus," she said. Eyes wide, she said it again. "Jesus."

She offered to let him use her computer. She kept a Hewitt Packard laptop on a desk in her bedroom.

"I know you followed me here, Sammy," he said. He accessed a word processing program. "I need your help. Badly."

She watched over his shoulder as he typed: ARE YOU HERE, SAMMY?

They waited.

He had told Carmen his theory about the "sad place." She agreed that he was probably right. But to prove his suspicion, he needed to talk to Sammy.

They waited.

"Please don't be mad at me still." He chewed on his knuckle.

On the screen, the cursor blinked. But no coolness manifested in the air, and they received no reply.

"Please, Sammy," Carmen said. "We need you, honey."

Sammy ignored them.

Andrew paced back and forth in Carmen's kitchen. He was as fidgety as if he'd swallowed a handful of caffeine tablets and chased them with strong cups of coffee.

He had checked the front windows perhaps five times. He hadn't seen any sign of Mika or her attack cats.

But she was out there. Most likely, she knew he was

here, too. It was only a matter of time before she made her next move.

While he paced, Carmen cooked a quick meal of angel hair pasta, marinara sauce, and ground turkey.

"Need to think about what to do next," he said. "We've gotta learn what her weaknesses are—if she has any—and fight back."

"She's got a weakness all right," she said. "You."

"Me?"

"She's lost her mind over you. She's willing to do anything to have you, to please you. Got to be a way we can use that to our advantage."

"How?"

"Don't know yet. We'll figure it out."

"I'm about to lose it, for real." He finally sat in a chair at the dinette table, dragged his shaky hand down his face. "Wish we could hop on a plane and fly somewhere, somewhere she'd never find us."

"Eat, honey." She set a plate heaped with pasta in front of him. "You've burned up a lot of energy. You'll crash if you don't get some food in you."

"Thanks." He began to shovel pasta in his mouth. "You eating?"

"Ate earlier." She sat across from him and sipped a mug of peppermint tea. She touched his hand. "God, I'm so glad you're okay."

"I don't know how I got away from her. Luck, I guess."

"There's no such thing as luck. Someone's looking out for you, and I don't mean Sammy."

"I wish someone would tell me what to do next."

"We'll find answers, Drew. But you know what we've gotta do in the meantime?"

"What?"

"Stay together. I don't want you out there alone anymore."

A frightening vision returned to him: Mika rising from the floor, unharmed, after he had shot her almost point-blank with the .38.

He held Carmen's hand tightly.

"I don't want to be alone, either," he said.

After he finished eating, they moved to the living room. They reclined on the sofa, a fluffy throw pillow separating their bodies; but each of their hands massaged the pillow, the paths of their fingers frequently intersecting.

Carmen had turned off the electric lights and lit a few ylang-ylang-scented candles. The rich, floral fragrance suffused the room; the flickering flames slowed the flow of the adrenaline coursing through his veins, relaxed his tense muscles.

The large entertainment center standing against a wall housed a TV, and a stereo. He had shut off the television and inserted a CD in the stereo system, the closest album at hand. It happened to be Will Downing. Downing was singing, "If I Ever Lose This Heaven." Mellow, soulful music.

Sliding across the pillow, his hand trailed over hers. The feeling of her silky skin sent a pleasant buzz through him. On impulse, he took her hand in his, brought it to his lips, and kissed her fingers.

He expected a prompt, "no friends-with-benefits" rebuke. But she didn't pull away, or speak. Shifting to face him, she gently traced her hand along his cheek.

He leaned forward and kissed her on the lips. Soft, tender kisses. Her mouth tasted like delicious peppermint.

She slid her arms around him, encircling his back. Pulled him close. Rubbed her hand along his back, from his shoulder blades to the base of his spine. He moved his arms around her, too, drew her against him tighter. Their chests were pressed so close it seemed their hearts had unified into one, slowly beating organ.

"Feel so good I never want to move," he whispered, his lips near her ear.

"Hmmm," she said.

"I love you," he said. He'd never spoken those words to her before, but they tumbled out of him, unexpectedly. And he immediately knew he meant them. He loved her body, of course, loved the feel of her, the taste of her, the electrifying sensation of being physically close to her; but much more than those things, he loved her caring soul and generous spirit, loved her sharp intellect and sense of humor and easygoing nature and unwavering support of him, no matter what he was going through. He loved even her flaws, because they formed the complete, one-of-a-kind, wonderful woman who was Carmen.

She drew back and looked at him, blinking. Surprised at his confession.

"I love you, Carmen," he said, and added: "As more than a friend."

She blinked again. Then smiled. "I love you, too. In all the same ways."

He pulled her into his arms again, and held her.

Cuddled together on the sofa underneath a crisp blanket, they lay in companionable silence.

The candle flames encased the room in a soothing glow. Night breezes soughed around the windows.

They had switched off the stereo, to savor the tranquil night, the lub-dub of their heartbeats, and their hushed breaths.

Andrew felt their love for each other like a tangible presence in the room. Not like the coldness that heralded a spirit, but like a soul-hugging warmth that would comfort them on even the coldest night.

Although they had professed their love for each other, he was in no rush for them to *make* love. Being with Carmen comforted him, but he was too tense to initiate lovemaking, too anxious about Mika to risk exposing either of them to what could be a very real physical threat. As long as they stayed together, he believed they would somehow beat Mika. Afterward, when they were safer, there would be plenty of time and opportunity to explore a deeper level of passion together.

Besides, waiting to make love to Carmen gave him something to look forward to, something to live for. In the meantime, he was happy to hold her and bask in the warmth of her presence.

Carmen finally spoke. "What's on your mind, honey?"

"You."

"What're you thinking about me?"

"All the stuff we've been through together over the years. How we somehow managed to stay platonic for so long. Wondering why we waited."

"Hmm. I think it's timing. We weren't ready for each other as more than friends, till now."

"Not until the rest of my world is collapsing, huh?"

"We'll get past it," she said. "Anyway, I don't wanna talk about bad stuff, Drew."

"Neither do I. I'd much rather talk about us. Where this is going."

She rubbed his chest. "Ah, a man is bringing up plans for the future. I'm impressed. Usually guys hate to talk about that stuff."

"We're normally commitment-phobic. I can't front, I've been that way myself, in the past. But this is different—I wanna do this right."

"You want an exclusive with me?"

"Most definitely."

"Want me to be your *numero uno* girl?"

"Yep."

"Your ace-boon-coon chick?"

"The Bonnie to my Clyde." He grinned.

She grinned, too. "Sounds tempting. I'll give it some thought and get back to you."

"What?" He looked at her.

"Drew, Drew." She giggled. "Always so gullible."

"And you've always got jokes. But seriously, what do you think? Do you want the same thing?"

"This is what I think." She grasped his chin, guided his mouth to hers, and kissed him, repeatedly and tenderly.

"I take that as a yes," he said.

"I've always been your lady," she said.

As they lay together, both of them half asleep, his cell phone rang.

"Who can this be?" Groaning, he got up, Carmen rolling off him.

It was Eric.

"Drew, you've gotta get over here now!" Eric said. "Your house is on fire."

Chapter 35

Flames devoured Andrew's home.

The ravenous fire swallowed the roof, ate the walls, and chewed the windows and doors, belching a stream of acrid, gray-black smoke into the cloudy night sky.

One arm draped loosely around Carmen, Andrew watched the conflagration from a safe distance across the street. A team of firefighters battled to save his house. But they had arrived too late, and the fire had spread too quickly, for them to prevent most of the devastation.

Earlier that evening, he had stood in the driveway and regarded his home with protective pride.

Now, everything he owned was going up, quite literally, in smoke.

He had homeowner's insurance, but that wouldn't replace everything. Photos, memorabilia special only to him—they were lost forever.

Most of all, insurance could never replace the sense of violation that had numbed him to the deepest core of his being.

Eric was beside him. Talking to him. He might as

well have been speaking in a foreign tongue. Dazed, Andrew couldn't comprehend his words.

Although it was past ten o'clock in the evening, half of the neighborhood had clustered nearby to gape at the gigantic torch that was Andrew's house. Many of his neighbors had offered supportive words, had given his shoulder a reassuring squeeze. But he could read the thoughts lurking beneath the friendly surface of their eyes, and the thoughts were: *I'm sorry, man. But I'm sure as hell glad that's not my house.*

He probably was imagining things. But he couldn't help it. He had never in his life felt so hollow. When the wind occasionally picked up, he felt as if he could just be carried away on the breeze and spun through the night like an empty soda can.

A grim-faced fire investigator approached, holding a clipboard. "Mr. Wilson?"

Andrew looked at him. Fuzzily realized the man had spoken to him. Said nothing.

"We're very sorry about your home, sir. We'll do a full investigation to find out what caused the blaze. Could've been electrical, chemical, natural or—"

"She did it," Andrew said flatly. "She's punishing me."

"Who?" The investigator clenched his pen.

Andrew shrugged. "I filed a restraining order against her. But it doesn't matter. You won't catch her."

"Pardon me?"

Tears came to Andrew's eyes. He wiped his eyes quickly, almost savagely.

Carmen stepped in. "He means a psycho bitch burned his house down. But she's too slick for you guys to catch."

"Ma'am, I promise you, we'll investigate this and if an arsonist is responsible, we'll see that justice is served."

"Do whatever you want, follow your little procedures," she said. "We'll handle our business, thank you."

The investigator pursed his lips, offered a card and told them to call him in the morning to answer more questions, and walked away.

Carmen gave Andrew a handkerchief. He blotted his damp eyes.

He couldn't remember the last time he had cried. Probably when his grandfather had died, seven years ago. Shedding tears wasn't his style. But he couldn't stop them from flowing out of him, lava-hot.

Carmen rubbed his back, murmured words of comfort. Eric rested his hand on his shoulder.

"Thanks, guys," he said. He drew in a hitching breath. "I'll be okay."

His cell phone rang. The call was from a private number.

He knew who was calling. He didn't want to talk to her.

But he did.

"Mika," he whispered, in a voice that, if it were a weapon, could have killed.

"See what happens when you make me angry?" Mika said.

She sounded cheerful. Triumphant.

If he could have channeled his rage through the phone lines, it would have struck her down like a lightning bolt.

"I love you, Andrew, but you had to be taught a lesson," she said. "Stay away from that bitch. Stop hiding from our love."

Fury had strangled him, made it nearly impossible to draw the breath necessary to speak.

Eric and Carmen watched him. His body language had transmitted itself to them. Their eyes had narrowed and their jaws had clenched, as if they were striving to contain explosive rage.

It went without saying that they realized who had called him.

"You don't need that hovel you called a house, anyway," Mika said. "Soon, you'll come to our home, and you'll scarcely remember that miserable, third-rate place of yours."

He clutched the phone so tightly the handset's edges pressed red indentations into his palm.

"And I know all about Sammy, that pathetic little soul you've been talking to about me," she said. "I pay him no mind, and neither should you—he can't help you hide from the truth. No one can. Your only choice is to give in to our love, accept our joyous future together. Tell me that you love me, baby. Say it how you said it earlier, when we were driving—"

Shouting, he hurled the phone into the night.

A young boy who lived across the street retrieved his phone. Andrew accepted it reluctantly.

Mika had hung up. But a text message awaited him.

CAN'T RUN FROM R LOVE I WON'T LET U

He deleted the message. He glanced at his burning house, and turned to Eric.

"We've got to get away from here," he said. "Guess I'll be moving into your lake house after all."

Chapter 36

Raymond sprang out of sleep with a scream on his lips. Accustomed to his eruptions from nightmares by now, June automatically touched his arm. "Ray?"

He licked his dry lips, touched his aching temple.

"Had another one," he said.

"What happened?" she asked.

"Nothing new, more of the same craziness."

She lay back on the mattress. "Head hurt?"

"Like hell. Probably got a brain tumor."

"Hush with that. Whatever it is, we'll find answers, just like we're finding answers to that awful house."

"Go back to sleep, sweetheart. I'm going to stay up for a while, do some reading."

He kissed her cheek, sat up, and swallowed the two Tylenol capsules that lay on the nightstand, beside a tall glass of water. The pounding headaches so reliably followed his nightmares that he'd begun to keep Tylenol at his bedside.

The clock read 1:31 A.M. He'd slept less than three hours. He had stopped taking the Ambien pills that his doctor had prescribed. Fighting for every scrap of sleep was preferable to the waking-nightmare hallucinations that the drug had apparently induced.

Thankfully, tomorrow was Saturday. He could sleep in a bit, though he still planned to go to the office and put in a few hours.

He slipped on his house robe and shuffled into the kitchen.

He boiled water in a tea kettle, to brew tea. You knew you were getting up in age when hot tea became your preferred nighttime drink. In the wild days of his youth, he'd wake up to Budweiser and go to bed with Crown Royal. What a reckless young buck he'd been. It was a wonder that he'd fathered only one child out of wedlock and not a whole litter of them.

Considering how much he'd struggled with Andrew, he supposed it proved that God never gave you a burden heavier than you could handle—but he'd sure as hell strained under the weight of being Andrew's dad. Had pushed him to his limits. But it motivated him to become a better man.

Thinking of his son and their golf outing tomorrow afternoon, he took a mug of Earl Grey tea to the study and settled in the comfortable leather chair. Tried to ignore his throbbing headache and concentrate.

A thick manila folder lay on the cherry wood desk. It contained the results of the research that he and June—well, mostly June—had conducted for the past couple days. He'd labeled it, "The Nightmare File."

It was an apt name, for more than one reason.

He pushed up his glasses on his nose and opened the folder. He paged through the documents, most of which they'd printed from the Internet, others of which they had copied from library resources.

His wife, a professional researcher, had done a splendid job. They'd learned enough about the mansion that haunted his dreams to write a short book.

If he ever decided to pen such a work, it would be the equivalent of a horror novel.

They'd acquired information about the land on which the estate resided, the original owner and his family, and the town in Bulloch County in which the house was located. Colorful stuff. Crazy stuff.

Especially the things about the heiress.

But as fascinating and informative as the data was, it failed to answer his pressing question: why was he having these recurring nightmares?

He was missing something. An important connection awaited his discovery that, he believed, would coax all the pieces into their proper place.

A framed photo stood on the corner of the desk. Taken two months ago, it depicted him and Andrew standing together on a golf course, clubs propped in front of them like elegant canes. They grinned.

He took the photograph in his hand.

Andrew had something to do with all of this; his appearance in Raymond's nightmare proved it. But when he'd asked his son if anything unusual had been going on with him lately, he said no. He thought Andrew was lying. But he had no proof.

The years had created a chasm between them as wide as the Grand Canyon, inhibiting their ability to communicate honestly and openly. But they were going to have to bridge that gap. Somehow. And soon.

He was beginning to believe that their lives depended on it.

Part Three

HIDE

Whether he wanted to admit it or not, whether he wanted to discuss it or not, whether he wanted to deny it or not, the nasty truth remained the same. He couldn't hide from it. It would follow him wherever he went. He might as well learn how to deal with it.

—*Mark Justice, The Surrender*

Chapter 37

Late the next morning, Andrew and Carmen left for Eric's home on Lake Sinclair, located in the town of Eatonton, Georgia, over one hundred miles southeast of metro Atlanta.

Sunshine brightened the lush blue sky, showering the world in golden rays. The temperature was in the low eighties, accompanied by a cool wind that moderated the humidity.

It would have been an ideal day to begin a vacation if they weren't running for their lives.

Most of his belongings had been destroyed in last night's fire; the items that remained reeked of smoke. They'd stopped at Wal-Mart, and he had stocked up on clothing, toiletries, and groceries. Enough supplies for a week. He planned to be away for at least that long, and longer if necessary. Carmen planned to use vacation time from her job to be with him.

He still had the .38, for all the good it had done against Mika. He'd purchased a Buck hunting knife, but he had doubts about its usefulness, too.

They packed Carmen's laptop, in case Sammy

decided to reappear. Optimistically, Andrew hoped to do some writing, too—if he could clear his mind to focus on something other than the nightmare in which he now lived.

To reach Lake Sinclair, he took I-20 east for about fifty miles, and then exited on US-129, which eventually turned into Milledgeville Highway. Traffic was light; he spotted a few trucks pulling boats to lakeside residences.

But he didn't see a black Rolls Royce, either ahead of them, or trailing them.

He turned onto Crooked Creek Bay, a hilly, two-lane road that wound around the densely wooded lakefront properties. Eric's place was ahead, at the bottom of a steep dip in the road.

He braked at the mouth of the driveway. Pines, maples, and head-high shrubbery concealed the house from view.

"Why'd you stop?" Carmen asked.

"Hold on."

He climbed out of the car and stood beside the road. And watched. And waited.

Birds chirped. Somewhere far away, an airplane soared.

The Rolls Royce did not appear. In fact, no vehicles at all passed.

He got back in the car. "Wanted to be sure no one followed us."

"Good idea."

He turned into the gravel driveway and burrowed under the canopy of trees. Shadows cloaked them on all sides—as if they were being hidden from the world.

Andrew slowly rolled down the driveway, toward the house.

A basketball goal with a tattered net hung from a thick pine tree in the middle of the driveway. Even here, Eric loved to play ball.

Farther ahead, a wooden sign was posted to a maple. "The Pattons" was carved in the sign, in big, cursive letters.

He parked at the end of the driveway, near the house.

It was a white clapboard, two-bedroom home, with a reddish roof blanketed with leaves and twigs. The door was on the left side, accessed by a short flight of wooden steps. A storage shed stood beside the house.

He shut off the car.

The only sounds were chattering birds, the sighing breeze, and the murmurs of rippling water.

"This place is pristine," Carmen said. "We've gotta be safe here."

"Let's hope so. Hang tight. I want to take a look around."

While she waited in the car, he walked around the perimeter of the house. Pine needles crunched beneath his feet.

Beside the house, an air-conditioning unit hummed. A stack of chopped wood leaned against a tree, reminding him that Eric kept an axe—a potential weapon—in the shed.

At the back of the property, a grassy slope descended to a dock, a path of smooth circular stones providing a walkway. A pontoon boat, moored to the dock, floated in the water.

The lake gleamed in the sunlight. Numerous piers and boats dotted the banks; he saw a couple of people across the lake, fishing. A gaggle of Canadian geese quietly swam the waters.

He returned to the house. A large deck wound around the back, reachable by a set of sturdy steps. He climbed the stairs and walked across the floorboards, which were layered with acorns, pinecones, and brittle leaves. A big gas-powered grill and wicker patio furniture sat on the patio. The glass patio door was locked.

But of course, locks didn't mean anything. He smiled sardonically.

The deck curved around the side of the house, to the main door. He unlocked the door and stepped inside.

The still air was cool, scented with a lemony fragrance. He checked out each room—one hand resting on the butt of the revolver he wore in the shoulder holster.

The house was full of no-frills furnishings and minimal decor. The bedrooms were tidy, each bed neatly made. The bathrooms, living room, and kitchen were spotless, too. When Eric or his friends were not present, he leased the house to renters, and he hired a housekeeper to clean up after every guest. The place was sufficiently well kept to meet even Andrew's obsessive-compulsive standards.

Most importantly, he saw no signs of Mika or her cats.

He returned to the porch.

Leaning against the car, Carmen looked at him.

"All clear?" she asked.

"Looks like it. Let's unload."

They unpacked the car. Inside the house, while Carmen put away the groceries and familiarized herself with the kitchen, he set up the computer in an alcove off the living room, and left a word processing program on the screen. Then he walked around, locking windows and doors.

It was a waste of time. No locks could keep Mika at bay. He secured the house out of what had become an illogical, paranoid habit.

Afterward, he walked to the dock.

The dock always had been his favorite feature of the property. He loved to sit there and watch the sun rise, and set. But this time, he ignored the beautiful panorama and focused on the boat.

It was a Premier Marine pontoon boat, twenty feet long, built to accommodate up to eight individuals. As he climbed onto the deck, the cream-colored bimini top shielded him from the sunlight.

Sitting in the helm chair, he inserted the key in the ignition and twisted.

The motor caught, and purred. He checked the fuel gauge. Three-quarters full. Good.

Eric had only ever used the boat for fishing the plentiful bass and catfish that swam in the waters, or relaxing on lazy summer days. Andrew had an altogether different and far more serious purpose in mind for the vessel: it was a last-resort means of escape.

He turned off the engine and hopped onto the dock.

As he walked back toward the house, his cell phone rang. It was his mother.

"Hey, Drew. Did you get to the lake yet?"

Including Eric and Carmen, his mother was the only other person to whom he'd told the full story of what had been happening to him. She believed him, wholeheartedly. She'd always been more inclined than him to accept phenomena that stemmed from what she termed, "the world beyond our five senses."

"I'm here, safe and sound," he said. "We're settling in now."

"Good," Mom said. "Please be careful out there. Remember my dream . . ."

He'd forgotten all about his mom's dream, which she'd related to him a few days ago. It crashed back into his consciousness.

Mom had dreamed of him and Carmen taking refuge in a cabin—and later being attacked there by a deadly snake. The dream did not reveal the outcome of the struggle. But it had terrified her.

He'd dismissed her dream as meaningless. Made jokes about it, too.

He had no idea that a snake—which he now realized was Mika—had been waiting to slither into his life.

His chest tightened, as if he felt the pressure of a real serpent wrapping around him and constricting his lungs. "I'll be careful, Mom. Very careful."

"Who else knows where you are?" she asked.

"Eric. And he's the only one who knows how to get here, too. He knows better than to tell anyone."

"Talked to Raymond?"

"Not in a couple of days. Oh, I forgot—we were supposed to play golf this afternoon. I'll have to call him and cancel."

"Don't tell him where you're hiding out. The fewer people who know, the better."

"He's got no clue what's been going on with me, anyway."

"Hmph. What else is new?"

He ignored her jab at his father. She was right, but he wasn't in the mood to talk about it.

Mom evidently picked up on his feelings, because she changed the subject. "How's Carmen?"

"Carmen's great. She's in the house."

"So was my dream about you guys right?"

He heard the smile in his mom's words. He smiled a little, too.

"On the money," he said.

"Y'all take care of each other," she said. "I'm praying for you."

"Thanks, Mom. I'll call you later."

As he climbed the deck's steps, Carmen flung open the patio door.

"Come in here, quick," she said.

"What's wrong?"

She grinned. "It's good news. Sammy's back."

Chapter 38

Cold, syrupy air had gathered in the alcove, where Andrew had set up the computer on the desk.

He and Carmen sat in chairs in front of the laptop. A message waited on the screen: GESS WHO

"Could it be Mr. Sammy?" Andrew chuckled. "Thanks for coming back, man. And again, I'm sorry for what I said earlier."

OK

"I'm curious," Carmen said. "How old are you, Sammy?"

AM EIGHT

"Eight years old when he died," she said softly. "God, that's so sad."

"Can I ask you . . . how you died?" Andrew asked.

IN SAD PLACE

Sad place is morneng.

Before, Sammy had told him that the sad place was a house. A house Mika owned. A wealthy heiress, Mika could conceivably own a mansion.

He'd been nursing a theory about the mansion. It was time to test it.

Carmen watched him, waiting for him to speak.

"I want to ask you about the sad place, Sammy," he said. "Have I been there before?"

YES

A thrill coursed through him. He felt the same way he did when he was writing and he had discovered the perfect words to express himself. Inspired.

"Was I there when my dad and I got in the car wreck?"

YES

Carmen's eyes were bright, excited.

Adrenaline flooded his veins. It took a concerted effort for him to sit still.

"It's all starting to make sense," he said. "I went in that house when my Dad's truck turned over. My cell phone didn't get a signal so I wanted to find a phone. Talk about creepy. That place was something out of a horror movie."

"Did you see anyone in there?" she asked.

"Not at first. But I felt . . . cold. There was this wind that came from upstairs, practically knocked me down."

ME

"You?" he said. "That was you, Sammy?"

I WAS LONLEY

"My goodness," she said. "I bet he came home with you. Rode you piggyback out of there."

YES

Awed, Andrew could only shake his head.

"What else did you see in there?" she asked.

He stroked his chin, casting his thoughts back to that strange place.

"One of those cats," he said. "It was in a room, watching me."

HERS

Carmen's face soured; she absently touched the

scratch on her cheek from her battle with the felines. "Anything else?"

"I met an old, tall black man, too. Said he was the caretaker. I can't remember his name."

WALTR

He snapped his fingers. "Right. Walter. Eccentric guy. Anyway, he told me they didn't have a phone. After that, I left—hell, almost ran out of there. Like I said, the house was creepy. The whole time I was in there, I felt like I was being watched."

WERE BY LOTS US

"He was being watched by lots of you?" she said. "There are more ghosts in there?"

LOTS OF US

A shudder passed through Andrew and seemed to travel to Carmen, because she shivered, too.

"What about Mika?" he said. "Was she there?"

YES SEEN YOU

He nodded. In light of what he'd learned about Mika's talent to view him from afar, it didn't matter whether he had encountered Mika face-to-face at her mansion or not. He had been on her turf, and she had been observing him. And that was when she'd decided to pursue him.

Sad place is morneng.

Still, as much as he'd learned, he didn't understand everything Sammy had told him. Some pieces of the puzzle eluded his mental grasp.

And then it hit him.

Dad.

His father knew something about the estate. He never would forget the shiftiness in his dad's eyes when, at the hospital in Statesboro, he'd asked him whether he knew anything about the place he'd driven them to on that fateful, rainy night. Dad had claimed not to know anything about it, swore to have forgotten why he'd taken that bizarre, wild excursion off the highway. Andrew had sensed that his father was lying. But he had left it alone. It hadn't seemed to matter, and he'd disregarded it as one of those secrets that his father might never share with him.

Until now, he hadn't realized how important it was to know the complete truth.

He fumbled out his cell phone.

"Who're you calling?" Carmen said.

"My dad. It's time we had a chat about some things."

Chapter 39

On Saturday, Raymond was making deals. In the real estate business, the weekend was the busiest time of the week for showing houses and closing sales.

Working allowed him to take his mind off his tumultuous personal life, granted him a few hours of peace. However, he'd brought The Nightmare File with him to the office. In case inspiration visited him.

It was a busy day, but he planned to leave soon, to play golf with Andrew. He hadn't talked to his son since they'd met at the driving range a couple of days ago, but he assumed that they were still on for their three o'clock tee time at Hidden Hills Country Club in Stone Mountain.

As he was ushering a young couple out of his office, after having them sign paperwork expressing their intent to purchase a property, Tawana ran up to him, eyes flashing.

"Uncle Ray! Have you heard the news?"

"What news?"

"Someone burned down your son's house. It's in the paper. Cops think it was arson."

Shock hit him a kick below the belt.

"You're kidding," he said.

She gave him the day's edition of *The Atlanta Journal-Constitution*. The story was in the Metro section. "Writer's Home Destroyed, Arson Suspected."

The reporter had briefly interviewed Andrew. His son said that a woman was stalking him and that he was certain she was responsible for the fire. The authorities stated that they were investigating the claim.

"He hasn't called you?" Tawana asked. Her tone made it clear that she would be upset if he'd talked to Andrew about this and hadn't shared the news with her.

"No." He took the paper into his office and threw it on the desk.

He couldn't believe something like this had happened to Andrew, and he hadn't told him a goddamn thing. Here he was, expecting to play golf with him this afternoon, and his boy's house had been burned to the ground.

Didn't he matter to Andrew? Wasn't he important enough to inform about something like this?

Get over it, Ray, a voice in his head chided him. *You've got a long way to go before you join your son's inner circle. You've recently started spending time with him after years of neglecting him. Why the hell would he tell you?*

The Nightmare File lay on the corner of the desk.

He'd suspected that something had been going on lately with Andrew. Could this be it? Was this the connection that he had been seeking?

For all of their sakes, he hoped that he was wrong. But he had to find out for sure.

He reached for the phone.

As he did, it rang.

Incredibly, it was Andrew.

* * *

As Raymond pressed the handset to his ear, a powerful frisson gripped him, as if something vital yet frightening had clicked into place, at precisely the right time. Every nerve in his body shouted that his nightmares were on the verge of being explained by revelations soon to come.

But first, he launched into safer territory.

"I heard about what happened," Raymond said. "Very sorry to hear about the house."

"Yeah," Andrew said. He sighed; he sounded far older than his thirty-one years. "Still can't believe it. But the past week's been full of craziness."

"The story in the paper said a woman's been stalking you?"

"They printed that, huh?"

"I wish you'd told me about this earlier, son. I . . . I might be able to help you."

"Funny, I was thinking the same thing, Dad."

Gooseflesh appeared on Raymond's arms. This was the strangest conversation he'd ever had in his life.

He opened The Nightmare File. His fingers twitched.

Andrew didn't speak, but he was breathing hard. Something was eating his son alive inside. It was obvious that his son wanted to talk, but wasn't sure of himself.

I'm the father. Time for me to act like it and take the initiative to tear down this damn wall between us.

He cleared his throat.

"Andrew, this may sound like a crazy question, but answer it for me, anyway. Does the name Mourning Hill mean anything to you?"

Chapter 40

Andrew couldn't sit still any longer. He bounded out of his chair and paced through the living room.

"What is it?" Carmen asked.

He held up his finger, signaling her to be quiet. He needed a moment to think.

Does the name Mourning Hill mean anything to you?

Sad place is morneng.

His heart boomed like thunder.

"What is Mourning Hill?" he asked his father slowly.

"It's a house—a mansion, actually," Dad said. "It has a long, twisted history. Probably means nothing to you, but I figured I'd ask. After all, we were there."

"I know."

"You . . . you do?"

"When we were driving back from Savannah. We flipped over across the street from the place. I asked you about it later, but you said you didn't know anything about it."

"Christ," Dad said. "I'm sorry. I didn't know . . . shit, this is a mess."

"That's an understatement." He had to bite his

tongue to keep from cussing his dad out with every four-letter word he could think of. Why the hell had his dad lied to him?

"I'm sorry for lying about it," Dad said. "But we've gotta help each other now. Tell me where you're staying, son. It's time you learned the full story."

Andrew gave Carmen the highlights of the discussion with his dad.

"He's on his way," he said. "We've been pulling our hair out over this shit, and all along he's had info. The liar."

"Drew, maybe you should give him the benefit of the doubt. What would you have thought if he'd told you about this mansion two weeks ago?"

He shrugged. He didn't want to admit that she had a good point. It felt better to hold on to his anger. Directing anger toward his dad was a comfortable—and familiar—feeling. He had years of practice with it.

"You wouldn't have believed him, and you know it," she said.

"Okay, probably not," he said. "But he should have let me make the decision about whether I chose to believe him. Don't try to sweep it under the rug."

"But you guys have just started getting to really know each other. Stands to reason that he'd hide something that might make you doubt his sanity, maybe push you away from him. Right?"

"All right. Yeah. Come to think of it, last time I saw him he *did* ask me whether anything was going on with me. He had this strange look when he asked, too."

"What did you tell him?"

Shame flushed his face. "I lied and said nothing. Didn't want him to think I was a nut."

She only folded her arms over her bosom and nodded slightly. She didn't need to say anything else. The point was made.

"I've always had a hard time telling him what's really on my mind," he said. "He acts like that with me, too. It's like we're handicapped or something."

"But you're working on it. This stuff might actually bring you guys closer."

"Wouldn't that be ironic?"

"Does your dad know about Mika?" she asked.

"He didn't say, but he has to know about her. He promised to share the full story, and hey, she owns Mourning Hill."

Just to confirm, he sat in front of the laptop. The chill of Sammy's presence lingered in the air.

"Is the sad place called Mourning Hill, Sammy?"

Ghostly fingers plucked the keys: YES

"Sammy's been telling me all along, 'sad place is morneng'," he said. "He was giving me the name of the mansion. Damn, I feel like an idiot." He dragged his hand down his face.

She sat next to him, massaged his shoulder. "Don't be so hard on yourself, honey. You'd told me everything, and I hadn't put it together, either. And I know I'm not an idiot."

He smiled thinly. Returned his attention to the screen. The cursor blinked, waiting.

More questions boiled to the surface of his consciousness.

"Sammy, you said there were lots of ghosts in that house," he said. "Correct?"

LOTS DED

"Lots of them dead," Carmen said. "Jesus."

"Who killed all these people?" he asked.

HER DID TO ALL

His stomach turned.

"Why, for God's sake?" she asked.

NEDS US

"She needs you for what?" he said.

LIKE FOOOD

"Like cannibalism?" Carmen asked. Her mouth twisted in disgust.

Terrible understanding came to Andrew.

"Not cannibalism," he said. "She's feeding on souls, people's energy, something like that. Maybe that's how she's so powerful. She's eating people's souls like freakin' energy bars."

YES

"But how could she *do* that?" Carmen asked.

"No idea," he said. "You know how she does it, Sammy?"

NO

"When Dad gets here, maybe we can figure it out," he said. "But there's one more thing I want to know right now. Sammy, are we safe in this house?"

CANT SEE HEAR TOO FAR

"She can't see us here," he said. "We're outside of her range. Like I hoped."

"Thank God," Carmen said. "Now that's good news if I ever had any."

GO TYPENG MAKE TIRED

"Talk to you soon, buddy," Andrew said.

The iciness evaporated. They rose from their chairs.

"We can finally relax, at least until your dad gets here," she said. "One of those beds in the back looks pretty comfortable . . ." Her words trailed off as she smiled.

Taking her in his arms, he smiled, too. "Sounds like a plan."

But anxiety weighed on his shoulders. Sammy had proclaimed that they were safe here, but it couldn't be so easy to thwart Mika. She was too cunning. He couldn't silence his worry that she had another trick up her sleeve.

But perhaps he was letting paranoia get the best of him. Maybe they really were safe.

Outside, dark clouds began to gather in the sky.

Chapter 41

Raymond parked his Ford Expedition behind Andrew's car in the lake house's driveway.

It was half-past three in the afternoon. When Andrew had given him directions to the place, he'd advised him to expect a ninety-minute drive from Raymond's office in Stone Mountain. Raymond violated the speed limit and made it there in nearly an hour.

On the way, he'd called June and told her that he was going to see Andrew and believed they were on the brink of a breakthrough. She wanted to come, too, but he gently convinced her to stay home, assured her that he'd call if they needed her help. He didn't divulge his true reason for keeping her away: he was afraid to endanger her.

Combining the contents of The Nightmare File with what he'd learned of Andrew's troubles made him feel as if he sat on a ticking time bomb. He didn't want his wife to be around when the inevitable explosion hit.

He didn't want to be around, either, in fact. But his involvement was no longer a matter of choice. It was mandatory.

His son needed him. It was as simple as that. For so many years, he had failed to have his son's back. He could never erase his mistakes with Andrew, but he could do the right thing when it counted the most. Like now.

Purple-black thunderclouds made it appear as if night had fallen over the world. Blades of lightning lacerated the false twilight. Cold rain had begun to fall, driving into his face like bits of ice as he climbed out of the truck.

Clutching his briefcase, he hurried to the door.

"Hey, Dad." Andrew let him inside. Carmen hovered behind him. Both of them wore hopeful expressions.

They thought he could solve their problems. Little did they realize that he sought answers from them, too.

They moved to the living room. He unlocked the briefcase, removed The Nightmare File, and laid it on the center of the oak coffee table, amongst other assorted papers.

"Anyone want some coffee?" Carmen asked. "Something to fire up our brain cells?"

"Coffee's good, but this here will probably get your nerves popping." He tapped the bulging folder. He shucked off his jacket, felt biting air. "Cold in here."

Andrew and Carmen exchanged a look.

"That's probably Sammy," Andrew said. "He's been hanging out with us, on and off."

"Sammy?" Raymond frowned.

"Our resident friendly ghost," Carmen said casually. "He met Andrew at Mourning Hill, decided to come home with him. He's only a kid. He said he was lonely."

"We've been chatting with him via computer," Andrew said. He indicated the laptop in a partly enclosed corner of the living room. "He types answers to us."

"I see," he said carefully. He pursed his lips.

Under usual circumstances, he would have called the

authorities to have his son and girlfriend committed to an institution. But these were, he had to admit, far from usual circumstances.

He studied the computer screen and the lines of text. He didn't know the questions that had elicited these responses from the entity, but a reasonably coherent picture formed.

This was as bad as he'd worried it would be.

"We've got a ton of questions, Dad," Andrew said. "But let's cut to the chase. Who is she?"

Raymond sat on the sofa. Carmen brought coffee for everyone. He waited until she and Andrew were seated before he opened the file. He slid on his reading glasses.

"Of course, you're talking about the heiress of Mourning Hill," Raymond said. "Ready for this, kids? According to the records I've found, she's one hundred and eighteen years old."

Chapter 42

Eric spent Saturday afternoon at one of his favorite stores: Home Depot. He picked up lawn fertilizer, weed killer, and other landscaping supplies. The pursuit of the perfect lawn was a challenging mission, and stores such as Lowe's and Home Depot offered an abundance of products that never failed to satisfy a home improvement fanatic such as himself.

Driving back to his house, he passed the charred ruins of Andrew's home, the area enclosed within crime scene tape. He clenched the steering wheel a little more tightly.

Psychotic broad. He hoped the cops found her and threw her in the joint for a long time. Andrew believed that she would forever elude the law, but Eric's deep commitment to the legal system led him to hope that justice would be served, and crimes would be punished. Andrew claimed she was some kind of superwoman— like a wacko Wonder Woman with psychic powers—and while Eric tended to believe his boy was telling the truth, no one was above judgment. Even if said judgment only came from the Man upstairs.

He reminded himself to call Andrew and check on how things were going. Andrew had called when he and Carmen had arrived at the lake house that morning, but Eric wanted to touch base with him again. Just to be sure. When someone was stalking your friend, you never could be too careful.

He parked in his garage. His wife's spot was vacant. She'd gone shopping with her sister, to buy yet more clothes and baby items for the twins.

It was amazing to think that in three months, he'd be a father to twin girls. He still felt like a big kid himself.

He climbed out of the Cadillac Escalade, popped open the rear cargo door. As he lugged the bag of fertilizer to the corner of the garage, he noted that the inner door, which led from the garage to the house, was ajar a few inches.

He'd left the house after Pam, and he was certain that he had locked this door.

Or had he? He was forgetful sometimes. Thirty-three years old with occasional memory lapses. Years of toiling seventy hours a week at a law firm could have that effect on you. It wouldn't be the first time he'd forgotten to lock up. He was only fortunate that, this time, Pam hadn't arrived home first, or she'd give him an earful.

He took his time unloading the vehicle. He went to the door.

Before he could touch the door, it opened all the way.

On its own.

Chapter 43

Outside the lake house, thunder rumbled. Lightning flashes shattered the darkness, and winds sniffed around the windows, like creatures eager to come inside.

Dad had paused, letting Andrew and Carmen absorb his stunning revelation.

"She's one hundred and eighteen?" Andrew said. "I can't believe it. She looks—"

"Twenty-five?" Dad said. "I know. She looked to be in her mid-twenties when I met her, too."

"You've met her?" Carmen asked. "When?"

"When I was in college at Georgia Southern," Dad said. "Junior year. That would've been about, what, thirty years ago?"

Nervous energy propelled Andrew to his feet. He paced across the living room.

"What happened?" he asked his father.

Dad stroked his chin, remembering.

"I met her on campus. At a frat party. Wild place. Cats were doing their stepping thing, hollering, trying to impress the ladies. She was there, sitting in a corner away from the action. She was the finest woman I'd ever seen in my life, but hardly any of the cats there were hitting on her—well, only the drunk ones were, and she was brushing them off like flies. She had the kind of looks that can intimidate a cat."

Andrew nodded. He'd initially been hesitant to approach Mika, too.

"Anyway, I'd knocked back a couple of Buds myself, so I was a little loose. I talked to her, said I hadn't seen her around campus and knew I would've remembered her. I'd never forget a girl like that, man. She talked to me; she was polite, friendly. 'Sophisticated' is the word I'd use to describe her. Said her name was Tina— name'll make sense later.

"I thought she was out of place at this loud party. I asked her if she wanted to go for a walk outside. Wanted to get her to myself for a while and really lay down my game, know what I mean? She was fine with that. We ended up going to her place. Mourning Hill."

"Wow, you guys didn't waste any time," Carmen said.

"No kidding," Andrew said.

Dad smiled a little. "Must say, my game was pretty strong back in the day. But I found out later that my macking didn't have much to do with why she took me home with her. She had chosen *me*. It was only a matter of me making the first move."

"Sounds familiar," Andrew said.

"The estate blew my mind," Dad said. "It was huge, full of antiques and period furniture. But a lot of the rooms were dusty, didn't look like they'd been lived in for a long time. She said that her parents had died and left the house to her, so she didn't use many of the rooms. A caretaker looked after the place for her. I met him. Tall, thin, older gentleman with white hair."

"Walter," Andrew said. "I met him, too. He looked old back then?"

"Like he was eighty if he was a day," Dad said. "But he carried himself like a young man."

"Sure did." Andrew recalled the caretaker's unexpectedly firm grip and hawk-sharp eyes. "Maybe he's been sipping from the fountain of youth, too."

"Could be," Dad said. "Anyway, we went to her room . . . and, let's just say that we got close."

Blushing, Andrew avoided Carmen's gaze; he didn't want to remind her of the intimate episode he'd had with Mika.

"While she was asleep," Dad said. "I got up and explored the house. Found out very quickly that there was a lot of strange stuff going on there. I heard whispers, screams, footsteps. Saw doors that opened and closed on their own. Ghosts, man. I never believed in that shit, but I couldn't deny what my eyes were telling me. That place was *full* of ghosts."

A cold breeze swept through the living room; Sammy, making his presence known.

Dad had paused, his eyes spooked. Then he went on: "And I saw cats, too. Big, gray cats that would run into rooms and vanish into thin air."

"We know all about the cats." Carmen fingered a long scratch on her forearm.

"What'd you do?" Andrew asked.

"What do you think? Grabbed my clothes and got the hell out of there. She woke up when I was leaving. I apologized for rushing out but told her that her crib was haunted and I couldn't take it."

"What did she say?" Carmen asked.

"She laughed. She said that she was happy to see me go, since I wasn't her soul mate anyway. Said she'd selected me for this close encounter, but had seen in my eyes that I wasn't the one. For once in my life, I was glad to be rejected. I split and never went back—and tried to forget everything about that weird-assed house."

Dad quieted. Sipped his coffee. The mug shook slightly in his hand.

Andrew finally sat down again, in front of his father.

"Guess what, Dad? She thinks I *am* the one. She's been stalking me like you wouldn't believe."

"What's been going on?" Dad asked.

He gave his father an abbreviated version of what had happened.

"I'm so sorry we didn't discuss this sooner," Dad said. He lowered his gaze to the floor. "Could've helped you out."

"It's not your fault," Andrew said. "I could've been more open with you, too."

An awkward silence came over them. He looked away from his dad and studied the raindrops streaming like a flood of tears down the glass patio door.

He sensed that his father wanted to say more. He wanted to say more, too, wanted to delve into an honest and profound exploration of his feelings. But his tongue felt stuck to the roof of his mouth.

The silence might have stretched on interminably if Carmen hadn't broken in and said, "We know that Mika found out about Andrew when you guys had the accident and he went into the house to find a phone. But I've been dying to ask you a question, Mr. West. Why did you drive there in the first place?"

"I've been meaning to ask you that, too," Andrew said. "We were on the way home from Savannah, then you got off the highway and went there and wouldn't tell me where we were going. Why?"

Dad dragged his hand down his face—a gesture familiar to Andrew. He unconsciously did the same thing when he was confused or stressed.

"I was in a trance, that's all I can figure," Dad said. "I don't remember anything about it. *She* must have drawn me there, somehow, as crazy as that sounds."

"After what I've seen her do, that doesn't sound crazy at all," Andrew said.

Thunder bellowed, shaking the house. The lights flickered, and then steadied.

Andrew glanced at the light fixture. Although Sammy had said they were safe there, he'd hate to be caught in a dark house without power.

Dad continued, "Over the years, I managed to convince myself that none of the things I thought I saw at Mourning Hill had ever really happened. Hell, I pretty much forgot about her, too. Then we had that accident. And after the accident, I started to have nightmares about that place."

Andrew noted the shadowy rings under his father's eyes. "You'd said something before about not being able to sleep."

Absently, Dad touched his temple, where the bruise had faded to a faint, thumb-size imprint. "I'll tell you about the dreams in a bit. But man, they got so bad that I realized I had to learn more about the house, see if I could figure out why I was having the dreams." He tapped the manila folder he'd placed on top of his briefcase. "The Nightmare File here is the result of my research. Credit goes to my wife for digging up most of the info."

"The Nightmare File?" Carmen said.

"The name fits in more ways than one," Dad said. He opened the folder, and shuffled the papers. "Let's start from the beginning. . . ."

Chapter 44

Eric watched the door open on its own.

Immediately, he rationalized how it had happened: the wind must've pushed the door. He or Pam must've left a window open, and air currents drifting through the house made it appear as if an invisible force had opened the door. That had to be the answer.

But cold pincers seemed to squeeze the flesh at the back of his neck.

Andrew's stories about the psycho broad with super powers had creeped him out. He was overreacting to completely ordinary phenomena.

He stepped into the hallway and shut the door behind him. The door remained closed.

See? Just wind.

Chuckling at himself, he headed toward the kitchen. He stopped when he found someone sitting in his living room.

A young, beautiful woman reclined on the sofa, legs crossed prettily. She wore a black cat suit that hugged every curve of her shapely, taut physique. Polished black boots with silver buckles and pointy toes. Like an actress on her way to an audition for an ill-advised *Catwoman* sequel.

She had cats, too. Two large bluish-gray felines flanked her on either side; another lounged on her lap. She idly stroked the animal's fur.

Eight intelligent eyes watched him. He went rigid.

He knew who this woman had to be, but the question burst out of him: "Who the hell are you?"

"You know who I am," she said. "Where is Andrew?"

"I don't know where he is. Since you burned down his damn house, guess he had to find somewhere else to live."

She clucked her tongue. "You're his best friend, Eric. You know full well where he's gone. He's outside my range. I can't sense him."

Can't sense him? This woman was as weird as Andrew had said.

"That's too bad, isn't it?" he said. "Get out of my house."

Mika lifted the cat off her lap and placed it on the sofa cushions. The three felines watched him, as if he were a tasty mouse.

She rose. She was not physically imposing at all. But Eric, remembering Andrew's tales of how dangerous this woman was, steeled himself for a fight. Or to cut and run.

"Oh, Eric," she said. "Why do you have to make this difficult for yourself? Simply tell me where my man has gone, and I'll leave."

"Number one: he's not your man. Two: I don't know where he is. Now get out." He pointed to the door.

She began to strut across the living room. She carried herself with icy poise, as if she were running the show and he was merely a minor piece in her game plan. He swallowed. He wasn't easily intimidated, but her self-possession was frightening.

"You're lying to me," she said. "I can't tolerate liars. I'll ask you one more time, and if you don't answer honestly, this is going to become messy: where is Andrew?"

Energy emanated from her body. He felt it in the air, like static electricity crackling through the distance between them.

Andrew's warnings echoed in his thoughts. Although he was much bigger than this woman, she was no ordinary person. There was no shame in fleeing to avoid disaster.

He ran to the door.

A large vase that stood on the table in the entry hall flew through the air and crashed into the side of his head, shattering into dozens of pieces.

White pain blossomed in his skull. He spilled onto the foyer's hardwood floor.

Bitch threw a vase at me, he thought dimly. *Without even touching it . . .*

He blacked out.

Eric awoke to a nightmare.

He was in the dining room, sitting in a chair at the head of the long cherrywood table. Wrists tied behind him with what felt like an extension cord. Ankles bound to the chair legs with the same.

He had been stripped to his boxer shorts. Sweat dripped down his face in cold rivulets, spattered his lap.

His head throbbed from where the vase had struck him.

The cats sat on the table, aligned in a row like little soldiers. Crouched, they stared at him with their unnaturally aware green eyes.

A carving knife lay on the decorative runner in front of him. It was taken from his own cutlery collection.

He'd used that same knife last Thanksgiving to carve the roasted Butterball turkey.

Mika was nowhere to be found.

He tried to break his bonds. But he was strapped in tight.

"Help!" he said, praying that a next-door neighbor would hear. "Someone help me!"

Music turned on, coming from the stereo system that distributed music throughout the house. It was a Public Enemy song, "Fight the Power."

Hearing the banging music made his headache pound harder, but it answered his question, too: Mika was still around.

He shouted louder: "Help!"

The volume increased, muffling his voice to whatever helpful ears might hear it.

He closed his mouth. Sweat ran into his eyes, stinging them. He blinked to clear his vision.

Mika appeared in the doorway that led to the hall. She sauntered into the room and knelt beside him.

"I see that you've awakened, Eric. You were unconscious for almost ten minutes."

"Let me go," he said. "Please. I'll tell you where Andrew's staying." He was thinking that he'd tell her, get her out of there, and then call Andrew and warn them to get out of the lake house. Anything to keep from dying. He couldn't die. He had twin girls on the way.

She picked up the knife on the table.

He sucked in a sharp breath. Tried furiously to break free. But it was useless.

She straddled him, and sat on his lap. Her face was inches from his, her hazel eyes beautiful, but cold, calculating.

Her jasmine perfume tickled his nose. Being so close

to her would've turned him on if he hadn't been terrified out of his mind.

She placed the tip of the knife on his chest. Above his heart.

"I know you'll tell me where Andrew is staying. Didn't Andrew share with you that I always get what I want?"

Chapter 45

As Dad spoke, he spread documents across the table, like puzzle pieces. But a clear picture slowly began to form, and it was beyond anything Andrew had imagined.

"Mourning Hill was built in 1855," Dad said. "It was constructed on land sacred to the Creek Indians, who used to occupy the area. The mansion actually was built on one of their old ceremonial centers, the *pascova*, where the Creeks would kindle what they called the 'sacred fire' at the Green Corn Festival each year. Now, I don't know if this has anything to do with what happened later, but the sacred fire stuff sounded interesting . . . especially considering the nightmares I've been having. I'll explain more about that in a bit.

"George Mourning owned the mansion, named it after himself and the hill the house stands on. He was a physician from North Carolina, and he ran his medical practice out of the estate. An unusually successful practice. He acquired a reputation for being something of a miracle worker. Folks came from all over to visit him.

During the Civil War, wounded Confederate officers begged to be taken to his clinic for treatment."

"She'd told me her dad was a doctor," Andrew said.

Dad showed them a copy of a black-and-white photograph. It depicted a solemn, bespectacled white man with a mane of black hair. And piercing, hypnotic eyes.

"She's definitely got his eyes," Andrew said.

Dad continued, "As successful as Dr. Mourning was, he couldn't cure his first wife. She had a nervous breakdown, apparently, and he committed her to an asylum. She'd never given him any children. So he took up with one of the house servants, a black woman named Etta."

"He was one of those men, huh?" Carmen said. "Had to hook up with the sister who mopped his floors."

"She was high yellow, too, light enough to pass for white when necessary," Dad said. "But she bore him only one child. A daughter, named Celestina. She was born in eighteen eighty-six."

Born in 1886? Andrew had to remind himself that they were discussing the same woman whose nubile body had pressed against his only days ago. It was unbelievable. But true.

"Yeah, you heard me right, young buck," Dad said, aware of his thoughts. "Eighteen eighty-six. Makes her one hundred and eighteen."

"And her real name is Celestina?" Andrew said. "I see where she got Tina from when you met her."

Dad passed him another photo. It was a black-and-white portrait of a family: the stern physician, the beautiful, light-skinned black woman whom he'd taken for his wife, and a little girl of five or six. The daughter's resemblance to Mika was undeniable.

"All was well in the Mourning household, for a while. The good doctor continued to work his miracle cures and amass his fortune. Things went smoothly, until Celestina hit her teen years. When she was thirteen, a hail of stones fell on the village of Millville, about a mile away from the estate."

"A hail of stones?" Carmen said.

Dad gestured to a microfiche document. "That's what was reported. Stones—real rocks—the size of baseballs, fell from the sky. Three people died."

"What did that have to do with the Mourning family?" Andrew asked.

"People saw Celestina in town the night that it happened. They believed she caused it."

"But she was just a teenage girl," Carmen said. "Why would they suspect her?"

"I get the feeling that in spite of all the people her dad was curing, the townsfolk were scared of them," Dad said. "You know how suspicious people can be, especially in the South. People accused the doctor of working roots, of being in league with the devil, all kinds of odd stuff. They were scared of Mourning's 'mulatto daughter' most of all. They talked about her as if she were some kind of demon child. I doubt that the hail of stones was the first bad thing that happened that the town blamed her for, but it was the first to make the papers."

Thunder boomed, and something—a branch, maybe—clattered onto the roof and cascaded across the area above the living room with the brittle sound of rolling bones.

"And it sure wasn't the last," Dad said.

As Andrew and Carmen continued to listen, Dad ran down a long list of disturbing incidents that had plagued the unfortunate town of Millville, over the years.

"Flash floods," Dad said. "People struck by lightning. Pets—especially cats—attacking their owners. Vats of fresh milk turning to blood, overnight. Bizarre stuff. Folks blamed the Mournings for it, Celestina in particular. They were ostracized from the community. And Mourning, though his services were still sought by outsiders, started to lose business from all of the bad press. People were too afraid of the girl to visit the house."

"Like she was evil incarnate," Andrew said. "But did anyone know *how* she could do these things?"

"Nope," Dad said. "There were plenty of rumors. Some said she was born with a veil, which is an old sign of special gifts. Others said her dad had made a deal with the devil to be successful—but had to pay by giving the devil his daughter, to do with as he wished."

"That's crazy." But Andrew shuddered.

"When Celestina turned eighteen, things got even worse," Dad said. "Her father went berserk. Blew his head off with a shotgun. But not before he'd murdered his wife."

Carmen recoiled. "Why?"

"No explanation given," Dad said. "It bugs me, too. Why would this highly regarded physician lose his mind, kill his wife, and take his own life? What triggered it? Makes no damn sense."

"Unless he did something that made his daughter angry," Andrew said. "Like kill the man she'd secretly been engaged to marry."

Dad and Carmen regarded him curiously. Briefly, he told them Mika's story of how her bigoted father had disapproved of the black man that she loved, and hired someone to kill him.

"You're probably right," Dad said. "Sounds like it could've been the trigger for her to go off. And somehow screw with her father's head, drive him to kill."

"What about her mom?" Carmen asked. "She was murdered, too."

"Maybe her mom took her father's side about the

marriage thing," Andrew said. "So Mika decided to punish both of them."

"That's cold-blooded," Carmen said. "But at this point I wouldn't put anything past her."

"At any rate, the town was shocked, but not overly sympathetic," Dad said, shuffling through more old newspaper articles. "Again, there was some insinuation that Celestina was responsible."

"Jeez, they don't show her any mercy," Carmen said.

"After that, Celestina falls off the map," Dad said. "She's never mentioned again in any articles or public records. Well, only once. In 1981, she transferred the deed to the estate. Guess who got it?"

Dad watched them, with a gentle smile.

"Who?" Andrew and Carmen said at the same time.

"Lalamika Renee Woods," Dad said. "Celestina would have been ninety-five years old in 1981. Although it seems that she completely isolated herself from the public, she likely thought it best for her to change identities, keep people from getting too curious about her true age and wondering if that young lady who lived in the big house in the woods was really Celestina, that old demon child."

Andrew paced again. His brain felt as though it were bulging with all of the information he'd learned.

"Over the years," Dad said, "after her father's suicide, it seems Celestina toned down her activities. There were no more reports of hailstorms of stones or anything wild like that. But there have been disappearances."

Andrew thought of Sammy. The look in Carmen's eyes conveyed to him that she shared his thought.

Cool air danced around the living room.

"The folks in Millville have been spared," Dad said. "But there have been numerous instances of people traveling through the area who are never seen again. Single adults, runaway kids, couples, entire families—it runs the gamut."

"Sammy said she uses them," Carmen said. "Feeds on their energy."

"But what is she *doing* with them?" Andrew said. "Where is she putting the bodies?"

"I think I've got the answer to that. " Dad placed the folder on the table. "Let me tell you guys about my dreams."

Chapter 46

Sitting on Eric's lap, Mika pressed the tip of the knife against the flesh near his heart.

Eric bit his tongue to stifle a scream. The scream that boiled in his throat didn't come from the feeling of the blade piercing his skin—it was no more agonizing than an ordinary pinprick—but from the terrifying thought of what this might lead to. And how he was powerless to prevent it.

A bead of bright blood appeared on his chest.

She regarded the droplet of blood, her gaze intense yet oddly detached, as if she were a biology student studying a specimen under a microscope. She dabbed her finger in the blood. Tasted it. Smiled with evident pleasure.

His intestines knotted.

This woman was sick.

Her gaze shifted to his face. "Do you love your wife?"

"She's my everything." He nodded vigorously.

"She's pregnant. With twins. I watched her leave your house earlier today. She's going to have little girls, I sensed it."

"Please, leave my wife out of this. I'll tell you where Andrew's staying. Please."

"You're a loving husband, Eric. Your wife is very fortunate. You're committed to her, through and through."

He didn't understand where she was going with these disturbing comments, and he wasn't sure that he wanted to know.

God, please let me live. Give me a miracle, Lord.

She flicked her tongue across the edge of the knife. "Andrew loves me. Did you know that?"

He shook his head.

"He shares everything with you, but he hasn't told you how much he loves me?"

"He doesn't tell me everything."

"He loves me, but he's afraid to admit it. He's hiding from his feelings."

"You could be right." He'd agree with her if it would spare his life.

"He's running from commitment, like you men so often do."

"We do that a lot, yeah."

"It infuriates me, Eric. It forces me to do things that I don't want to do—but that I *must* do, to teach Andrew that there are consequences to his actions."

Troubled by the turn in the conversation, he kept his mouth shut. Air whistled in his nostrils.

He was aware, distantly, of a new song booming on the house stereo. "Bring the Pain" by Method Man. She'd slipped one of his hip-hop compilation CDs into the system.

"Men are like puppies," she said. "If you urinate on the carpet, your nose is squashed in the mess and you're scolded. If you retrieve a ball, you're given a treat. That's how men learn to behave properly. The pain and reward system. Do you agree?"

"Train us like dogs," he said hoarsely.

She rapped his chin with the knife. He flinched.

"Give me the location of where my man is staying, and directions from here."

He told her the address of his house on Lake Sinclair, and gave her detailed directions. She didn't write anything he said, but her eyes were alert. He believed that she stored his words verbatim in her memory bank, like a computer.

"Thank you, Eric." She smiled sweetly. "Now, you'll have to blame your best friend for what I'm about to do next. He's been a naughty puppy and needs to be taught."

She slid the knife from his chin, to his throat.

"No, no, no." He strained to free his hands, couldn't. Tried to rock the chair, but couldn't gain any leverage.

"It's Andrew's fault, dear," she said. "You were a loyal friend to him and deserved better. I'm sorry it has to end this way."

"No!"

She plunged the blade into his throat.

Chapter 47

Andrew and Carmen listened to Dad explain his recurring nightmare. Seeing a child version of Andrew ignore his warnings and enter Mourning Hill. Witnessing a green glow in an upper room of the mansion. Trying to get inside and encountering resistance from Walter, the caretaker, and the cats. The graveyard beside the house . . .

"I believe they have a cemetery hidden somewhere on the property," Dad said. "These unfortunate people who get drawn to the house . . . they're buried there."

Andrew heard a frenzied clicking sound. At first, he thought it was rain, tapping against a window. Then he realized that the sound came from the computer.

All of them rushed to the laptop.

Sammy typed: YES YESSS YYES YEEES YESS YESSS

Andrew looked at his father. "I think he's saying that you're right."

Sammy stopped tapping the keys, his message communicated.

"The house is full of ghosts, I remember that much,"

Dad said. "Could be the ghosts of the poor folks she's drawn to that place over the years."

Sammy typed once: YES

"But some other stuff in your dreams confuses me," Andrew said. "Why am I, like, six or seven years old when I go inside the house?"

"Don't know," Dad said.

"You can't always take dreams literally," Carmen said. "It might not mean anything. Or it could symbolize, I don't know, how that little boy Andrew was lost to you, since you weren't around when he was growing up."

Shame stamped Dad's face. "Could be."

Andrew wanted to change the subject. This wasn't the time to poke old, tender wounds.

"What I really want to talk about, Dad," he said, "is this green light you saw in a window upstairs. You said something earlier about the Creek Indians, who used to have a ceremonial site on the property of Mourning Hill and would kindle their sacred fire there?"

"Yeah," Dad said. "Could be a stretch, but I think it might have something to do with that."

"Me, too," Carmen said.

Andrew went to the coffee table and rifled through papers. He found the documents about the medical practice that Dr. Mourning, "the South Georgia miracle worker," had run at the estate.

"I think I've got something," he said.

Dad and Carmen waited for him to continue.

"I know a bit about sacred sites, or what some people call places of power," he said. "Don't ask me how. You learn about the damndest things when you do book research."

"Go on," Dad said. Carmen nodded eagerly.

"The Native Americans' religions are earth-centered," he said. "In other words, they're really in tune with

Nature. There's a theory that's been around for a long time that certain spots in the world are special, that these areas give off energy—magnetic fields, natural radiation, psychic currents—whatever you want to call them. You get the idea."

"Still with you," Carmen said.

"Stonehenge is a good example," he said. "That ring of huge rocks in England? Some people think it was built by aliens, others think people constructed it, thousands of years ago, for ritual purposes. At any rate, it's widely considered a place of power. There's a unique energy to the area that you can supposedly feel on your skin, like a tingling in the air.

"So then let's say these Creek Indians, who would've been in sync with the energy of a natural place, selected the area of Mourning Hill for their sacred ceremonies because it resonated with earth power. What if the green light Dad sees in his dreams actually represents a power reservoir of some kind, that exists right there on the property, maybe in the house? And—what if Mika's father was *tapping into it*, somehow, consciously or unconsciously, when he was running his medical practice? It could've enabled him to work his miraculous healings."

"And what if Mika uses that same energy?" Carmen said. Excitement sparkled in her eyes. "She channels the power, uses it how she wants."

"Then feeds it or something by taking other people's energy," Dad said. "Like Sammy told you guys."

"Exactly," Andrew said. "She's probably used this energy to keep herself youthful. And to do all the other amazing things that she does."

"But how does she harness this power?" Carmen said. "It's not like you can buy a Psychic Power Channeling Kit from Wal-Mart, guys."

Andrew tapped his lip. "I think she has some genuine psychic talents of her own. It gives her the ability to draw from this other energy source. Which then turbo-charges her, so to speak."

"Now the big question is," Carmen asked, "how can we use this against her?"

All of them fell silent. Rain beat a steady tattoo on the roof.

Andrew was convinced that their theories were correct. They had made a lot of progress toward filling in the gaps in their knowledge. But Carmen's question exposed the major issue that gnawed at all of them. How could they use what they had learned to put an end to Mika's relentless stalking campaign for good?

The quiet stretched on.

"You know what I'm thinking, kids?" Dad said at last. "To get all our answers, I think we'll have to pay a visit to the source. Mourning Hill."

Chapter 48

Like a stealth submarine cruising turbulent ocean currents, the Rolls Royce Silver Shadow cut through waves of rain and gusting wind.

Her obedient cats gathered around her, Mika sat on the plush leather seats in the rear of the sedan, gazing out the side window.

Although her eyes took in the rain-blurred countryside, she was looking inward; viewing other times, places, and people with her mind's vivid eye.

She reflected on chapters of her life; different times, divided like scenes in a novel.

She thought about the beginning . . .

She was her mother's first and only child. She was born with a veil, as was her grandmother, and many ancestors before her. It was proof that she had inherited the gift that had run through her mother's bloodline for generations. Second sight. The sixth sense. Extraordinary talents. She was special.

Her mother named her Celestina, after her grandmother, a free mulatto woman from Louisiana who used her talents to become a revered root worker.

Her father, a solemn man, had wished for a son, to carry on the Mourning family name. But he quickly warmed to her, adored her. Called her his princess. And used his considerable resources to indulge her every whim.

Nothing in the world is too good for Daddy's princess. The world is yours, darling. Whatever you desire is yours.

He bought her expensive little girl dresses custom-tailored in London. Gave her a horse from a renowned breeder, when she was barely old enough to sit in the saddle. Had an ornate, elaborate dollhouse constructed for her that was large enough for a full-size adult to comfortably inhabit. Built a boxwood garden for her, containing life-size, stone statues of her favorite Greek goddesses: Aphrodite, Athena, Artemis, Hera. Hired private instructors to teach her piano, dance, painting, French, and Latin.

She always got what she wanted, and always would. Because Daddy taught her that that was her right as a princess. She deserved only the best.

Her mother, predictably, resented the attention her father showered upon her, declared that she was spoiled and would grow up to be unbearably selfish. Her father ignored her protests; he was so taken with his daughter that he'd apparently forgotten that he had a wife.

Mama knew all about the teachings that a special child such as she needed to acquire, in order to properly handle the gifts with which she'd been born. But embittered, Mama taught her nothing about her talents.

Therefore, Celestina learned all by herself.

She was four years old when she saw her first ghost. When she was out in the yard playing, a short man in overalls, with graying hair and a wrinkled, tanned face, leaned against a Georgia pine, scratching his protruding belly and staring at her. His image wavered like a reflection on a pond.

She wasn't afraid. She was fascinated. When she mentioned the apparition to Mama, her mother, who knew better, told her to stop imagining things. Daddy didn't believe her, either.

But she instinctively knew nothing was wrong with her; she was seeing real people who weren't in the same place as her anymore. As she grew older, seeing ghosts became as frequent and ordinary as watching butterflies flitting around the flower garden.

She quickly graduated to more interesting activities.

Her cats, Circe, Iris, and Eos, pedigreed Russian Blues from the same litter, always had been excellent companions. One day, when she was six, she discovered that she could bond with her cats in a manner that went far beyond playing simple games with balls of thread. She learned that she could summon the cats—without speaking a word or making a gesture, even if they were in a different section of the mansion. They came running to her, unfailingly loyal, willing to please. Soon, she taught them to do anything that she desired, solely by her issuing telepathic commands.

Once she mastered the cats, her skills developed at a rapid pace. Making silverware rise in the air and turn end over end. Causing her mother's dresses to dance around the room, like ladies at a debutante affair. Starting fires, merely by focusing on a small pile of twigs and visualizing a cone of flame . . .

She'd learned to hide her burgeoning abilities from her mother. Her mother would try to convince her that she was just an ordinary little girl and needed to stop playing foolish fantasy games. But she was far from being a common girl. She was a princess, like her daddy said. A particularly special princess.

When she was ten, she ventured into the upper room of the mansion for the first time.

She'd long believed that there was something unusual about the attic. On numerous occasions, she'd watched as, late at night, her father stumbled out of the doorway that led to the attic, his hair frizzy and eyes bulging, as if he'd been given a jolt of electricity. He would always secure the door with a heavy padlock. He was hiding something important inside.

One night, concealed around the corner, she saw her father stagger out of the attic and latch the door, and then amble off to bed. She went to the door and concentrated on the lock for several seconds . . . and it popped open and clattered to her feet.

Locks could no longer keep her away from what she wanted. But it had taken her years to screw up the courage to enter the attic.

Her palms tingling, she climbed the steps and emerged in the chamber.

A big, greenish orb revolved in front of her, sparks crackling across the translucent surface.

She moved forward, into it.

It was like walking into the sun.

Afterward, her life was never the same.

Pure, soul-searing psychic energy resided in the upper room. It had no consciousness, no malicious or positive intent. It was the equivalent of a fire that would never die; an ancient, limitless power source that had broken through a wall that separated the physical plane of existence from the world of the unseen. Indeed, the power was so transforming, so awe-inspiring, that one likely could have employed it to resurrect the dead.

And it was hers, to use as she desired. She was, after

all, a princess. She could have anything in the world, do anything she wanted.

Her daddy already had been using the power, for his medicine work. He didn't possess her gifts. But the energy aided him, all the same.

Working in tandem with her innate abilities, the power boosted her to a superhuman level, made her almost like the Greek goddesses she loved to read about. She expanded the uses of her talents far beyond anything she'd done before.

Invoking storms was an especially pleasing activity. A hail of stones. Nineteen inches of snowfall in southeast Georgia. Flash floods.

She did other stuff, too. Varied acts. Whatever caught her fancy.

She never exercised her powers to hurt anyone—though sometimes, people got hurt or died. For her, it was all about fun and discovery. As a princess, she had the right to have her way with the world, which she'd begun to consider as her own, gigantic dollhouse.

Then, when she was eighteen, she fell in love.

He was a tall, well-muscled young man with smooth cocoa skin, a new member of the crew that landscaped the grounds of their estate. Watching him work barechested in the summer sun, seeing his sweat-slicked muscles flexing, gave Celestina a warm, tingly sensation all over.

She decided that she would have him, at least to fulfill her sexual needs. It wouldn't be the first time she'd taken one of the laborers for her own uses. She'd lost her virginity at fifteen; her body, deliciously ripe at that age, had enticed one of the virile, young gardeners to knock off work and spend the afternoon with her in the woods on a remote region of the estate. She quickly learned that sex was a powerful means to get a man to comply with her wishes. No man had ever been able to resist her. She often liked to use her beauty and charms to get attention, to drive a man to do anything to win her favor.

But her new prospect was different. He had a sharp mind, something she rarely encountered in the men who worked at the house. He possessed the imagination of an artist, such as a painter or writer. He was more like one of the high society men that she'd met at formal functions—but those stuffy men feared her, and spread nasty rumors behind her back. This man, however, this handsome manual laborer, displayed no fear of her.

He understood her. Knew she was special. And like her daddy, he called her his princess.

She fell in love fast and hard. So did he. He was her soul mate. She'd seen it in his eyes, when they first kissed in a meadow on a sweet August day.

But they kept their romance secret. Her father regarded black men as inferiors, and would likely disapprove. Nevertheless, after three dizzying months of exchanging secret love letters and sharing clandestine dates, her lover could hide his ambitions no longer. He wanted to ask her father for her hand in marriage. She tried to talk him out of it, said that she would agree to marry him and didn't need her father's approval and they could elope, that she would renounce her inheritance to be with him. But he was a proud man and refused to keep his love for her in the shadows.

He met with her father. And was driven out of the house, her father chasing him with angry fists and a stream of threats.

She talked to her father, too. She confessed her love

for this man and begged for his blessing. Her father had never denied her anything. How could he deny her this, the greatest gift she'd ever received?

But he vehemently opposed her wishes. Eyes swollen in their sockets, he shouted that he would never allow a Negro man to marry his precious daughter—and inherit his estate.

Her mother, smiling smugly, pleased to see her daughter's hopes crushed, sided with her father, too.

She hatched a plan to elope with her lover. But only two days later, while lounging on the lake, fishing, a rifle shot to the back of the head dropped her lover to the sandy banks. The authorities ruled his death a hunting accident.

She knew better. Her father had hired someone to kill him.

His murder plunged her into the most profound grief she'd ever known. She dressed in black and tore plugs out of her hair.

She would kill herself. Death was preferable to living another day without her love.

She climbed into a half-filled bathtub. With a razor, she slit both of her wrists. Blood flowed from the gashes . . . but within seconds, the wounds healed. Screaming, she slashed herself again, with the same result. And again . . .

But after years of drawing upon the power in the upper room, her body had developed powerful defenses against injury. Her suicide attempt was futile.

Soon, her grief gave way to rage.

Damn *anyone* for denying her what she wanted.

She vowed to give her father the same punishment he'd administered to her soul mate.

All her life, she respected the mental space of people around her. But she blew like a psychic tsunami into her father's thoughts, and pushed him to madness.

He took a shotgun and killed her mother, then put the warm barrel in his mouth and pulled the trigger.

Revenge is a meal best served cold.

As expected, she inherited her father's fortune, and Mourning Hill. Townspeople speculated about the successful physician, flying into a senseless, murderous rage. She ignored them and went about her affairs as usual.

Her primary—indeed, her only—purpose for living was to unite with her soul mate again.

He had been killed, but she believed he would return. Spirit was eternal. His spirit would cycle through the planes of existence, and eventually return to an earthbound life.

She had to be ready for her groom's return. Had to keep herself looking young and beautiful for him. He wouldn't want a decrepit old woman as his bride.

She discovered a method to preserve her youthful appearance: soul energy. Not the power in the upper room. Only harvesting the energy of others worked.

She lured travelers, runaways, and the lost to her estate, as she needed them.

Walter, the longtime caretaker, was helpful in that regard. He did the dirty work. In return for his services, she granted him a dramatically lengthened lifespan and the strength of a young man.

Of course, she kept her cats around, too. Gave them special talents. Her little guardians.

She realized that in absorbing the energies of innocents, she was, in effect, killing them. But it was for a worthwhile purpose. She was staying attractive for her soul mate, her prince.

No cost was too high for her happiness. Her father,

may his soul rot in hell forever, had taught her that lesson.

Over the years, she searched for her soul mate. Visited countless nightclubs, parties, and social gatherings. Combing the crowds for a man with a sparkle in his eye, a man who just might be the one. Drawing prospects to her estate, for a closer look. In seeking her prince, she'd kissed hundreds of frogs. Never losing her faith that, one day, at a moment of truth, she would gaze into a man's eyes and see the soul of her long-lost lover.

And when she saw Andrew's eyes, those soul mate eyes, she realized that, at last, her wait was over.

Sighing, Mika looked away from the window.

She'd lived such a long life, full of varied chapters. She was nearing the end of an old chapter and the beginning of a new one. A much happier one.

Andrew wasn't going to hide from her anymore. She wasn't going to let him. She knew what was best for him. Even if he didn't yet realize it himself.

The cargo in the trunk would convince him of the grave seriousness of her mission.

She needed him; she was incomplete without him. So be it that it was her responsibility to unite them in everlasting love.

She was going to show him irrefutable proof of the love they once shared, too. To break down the final barriers in his heart.

As they rolled down the highway, the storm clouds parted, and the golden sun beamed down on her, like a beneficent father.

Smiling, she snuggled into the seat cushions with her cats, and sat back to enjoy the rest of the ride to retrieve her soul mate.

Chapter 49

The thunderstorm passed. Late-afternoon sunlight pierced the venetian blinds.

They talked about visiting Mourning Hill. Andrew declared that going there today would be foolish. Dad and Carmen agreed with his contention that they needed more time to plan a strategy.

"In my dreams, getting inside that house is like trying to take a fortress," Dad said. "I don't think it'll be easy for us."

"We'll need to stake out the place," Andrew said. "That should give us some ideas."

"But we do it during daylight hours, guys," Carmen said. "I'm not too keen on going there at night. Nighttime and haunted houses—not a good mix for me."

"We can do it tomorrow morning," Dad said. "It's about a three-hour drive from here."

"If we're ready by then," Andrew said. "We've got time to brainstorm. Remember—Mika doesn't know we're here. We can take our time, prepare to do this right."

"Good point," Carmen said. She clasped her hands

together. "Okay, anyone hungry? I'm starvin' like Marvin."

"Could use a bite," Dad said.

Andrew rose. "I'll fire up the grill."

Outdoors on the deck, Andrew cooked chicken breasts and hamburgers on the gas grill. Carmen worked in the kitchen, whipping up potato salad and baked beans. Dad leaned against the deck railing, sipping a Heineken and gazing at the lake.

For several minutes, neither of them spoke. They quietly admired the shimmer of sunshine on the water. Listened to the honking of geese and the rustle of windblown leaves.

"Nice place Eric's got here," Dad finally said. "How deep's the water?"

"Three or four feet around the dock," Andrew said. "You wouldn't want to dive in. Gets deeper as you move farther away from the banks."

Dad bobbed his head. "Quiet out here, too. Good place to collect your thoughts."

"It's a nice hideaway." Andrew used tongs to flip a burger. "I'm glad Eric was able to let me stay here. I've no idea when we'll rebuild my house."

"That was an awful thing." A frown wrinkled Dad's face. "Lose any of your books?"

"No, I always back 'em up online. I keep the first editions in a safe deposit box, too."

"That's good. At least your livelihood's intact."

"Speaking of livelihood, I forgot to tell you. I got a new offer from the publisher."

"Really? How much?"

"Five hundred."

"Thousand?" Dad grinned. "I'll be damned, that's great. Congrats!" He clapped Andrew's shoulder.

"Thanks. Of course I haven't been able to celebrate yet, not with everything that's been going on."

"Of course not." Dad's face tightened. He stared into the depths of his beer bottle. Scratched his head.

The silence hung between them, thick as smog.

I'm tired of this. I've got stuff I want to say to this man. Why the hell can't I have a real conversation with my own dad?

Idly, Dad stroked his chin. It was another one of those gestures that Andrew shared with him. He stroked his chin like that when he was pondering what he wanted to say.

Maybe Dad wanted to have a heart-to-heart conversation, too.

Andrew placed the tongs beside the grill, rubbed his palms on the apron he wore around his waist.

Go ahead and talk to him. He's your father, man.

It wasn't Mark Justice speaking; it was the wise voice of his conscience. He'd learned the hard way to listen to that voice when it offered advice.

"Can I . . . can I ask you something, Dad?"

"Huh?" Dad put down his beer. "Sure. What's up?"

"I'm not sure how to say this. But . . . why can't we talk?"

Wearily, Dad settled into one of the wicker chairs. Studied the floorboards as if the words he wanted to say were engraved in the wood.

"I don't know, young buck. I've wondered the same thing. Guess the years have messed us up."

"But I don't want it to be that way." Emotion clutched Andrew's throat in a vise grip. "I want to be able to talk to you. But I can't."

"Do you resent me, Andrew?"

"Resent you? I used to *hate* you, for ignoring me. Why'd you ignore me like that?"

Dad looked up at him. Redness outlined his tired eyes.

"I was scared, son."

"Scared?" Andrew suddenly—and he hated to admit it to himself, but it was true—wanted to punch his father in the face. One roundhouse slug in his dad's mug to express all the anger he'd kept bottled inside for so long. "Scared of what?"

"Scared of what? Shit. Let me tell you. Scared of trying to raise a son and fucking it up, like my daddy fucked up with me. I know, you don't know a damn thing about your granddad, but that man . . . shit, he was like a robot, never showed any emotion, just worked himself to death and grunted half the time. I never felt like I knew *how* to be a father, Andrew. Didn't have any good examples. That's a sorry-ass excuse, but it's the truth."

It was the first time his father had ever given an explanation for his behavior. It was almost childishly simple. *I was scared.*

As if Andrew had never been scared while growing up without his father around.

Andrew struggled to find words. To keep a lid on the rage that boiled in his heart.

Dad looked at him, watery-eyed, like a guilty criminal awaiting a verdict.

"You could've at least tried," Andrew finally said.

"I know that now," Dad said. "Hindsight's twenty-twenty. Know what made me call you a few months ago and invite you to play golf?"

"I've been wondering, yeah."

"My dad—your granddad—died," Dad said. He wiped his eyes. "I hadn't seen him or talked to him in at least twenty years. But I went to his funeral. When I looked at him in that casket . . . Christ, it was like looking at a goddamn stranger. I didn't feel anything. Didn't shed a tear. And I hated that, hated that this was how we'd ended up, me walking by his casket and feeling nothing. This was my *father*, Andrew. My flesh and blood. But he was nothing to me.

"I decided, on the spot, that I was going to get off my sorry ass and start being a father for you, 'cause when I die, I don't want you to look in my casket and feel like you're staring at a stranger."

Andrew gaped at his father. Speechless.

He realized that tears had begun to flow down his cheeks.

Dad sniffled. "I need to ask you something."

"Yeah?" Andrew blinked back tears.

"I need to ask you to forgive me. For not being there. For everything."

"Dad, I . . . I . . ." Tears had completely blurred Andrew's vision.

His voice faltered. He couldn't grant his father the forgiveness he sought. Not yet. He wanted to; forgiving his dad would roll away the weight on his own heart. But he couldn't honestly speak those absolving words. Not until he learned to trust his dad. And he couldn't trust him yet. He was scared that he would abandon him, as he'd done so many times before.

"Can't," Andrew said, shaking his head.

Dad got up. He gripped Andrew's shoulder.

Andrew trembled so violently it seemed he would shatter into pieces like a ceramic figurine.

"You don't have to say it yet, son," Dad said in a soft voice. "I've got to earn your forgiveness. We can't erase the past so easily. It's gonna take us some time. But I *will* be here for you, from now on. I'll lay down my life for you, if it comes to that."

Dad pulled him into an embrace.

Not accustomed to a hug from his father, Andrew was as limp as a rag doll in his Dad's strong arms. Hot tears streamed down his face.

Finally, he lifted his arms, which felt as heavy as logs, and hugged his father back.

Watching them from the kitchen window, Carmen smiled.

They had dinner on the deck. Hamburgers, chicken breasts, potato salad, and baked beans. They sipped icy glasses of sweet tea, which Dad had brewed, claiming that it was his specialty. Andrew was doubtful at first, but his dad was right; the tea was delicious.

He learned something new about his father all the time.

As they ate, his attention continually wandered to his dad. His father's confession had forced Andrew to evaluate him anew. The old, familiar box into which he'd placed his father no longer fit. In a sense, he felt as if he were getting to know his dad for the first time. And he liked what he was learning.

Getting to truly know his father was the first step toward forgiving him, and developing his trust in him.

By unspoken agreement, at dinner, they avoided mention of Mika, ghosts, and the estate. Their conversation touched on a diverse range of ordinary topics—music, movies, sports, current events, politics—everything except the extraordinary circumstances that had drawn them to the house in the first place.

Andrew welcomed the lighthearted conversation. It was a major stress reliever. Part of the human survival instinct, he reasoned, depended upon our ability to find optimism and pleasure even in the midst of the most desperate situations.

As the afternoon edged toward evening, the shadows

deepened. Andrew lit the two torches posted on the deck railing, to provide light and keep insects at bay.

"I want you guys to answer me one thing," Dad said, as Andrew returned to his chair. "When am I gonna need to put on my tux?"

Carmen giggled. Andrew shrugged.

"Depends on when you plan on going somewhere that requires you to wear a tux, Dad," he said.

"You know what I'm talking about."

Andrew smiled.

Dad touched Carmen's arm. "Look at this girl here. She's fine, smart, has a good job, knows how to cook—"

Carmen was laughing.

"—and puts up with you!" Dad said. "Aren't gonna meet another one like her. You need to get to it. I want some grandkids while I'm young enough to enjoy 'em."

"Honestly, I don't know if I want kids, Dad."

"Hey." Carmen bopped his arm. "You better be kidding."

"I was kidding, man." He rubbed his arm. "Are you gonna abuse me like that if we get married?"

"Only when you deserve it," she said.

"There you go, girl, lay down the law." Dad chuckled. "Take it from me, son. Do whatever your woman says. Your woman is always right."

"I like you," Carmen said.

"Even when she's wrong," Dad said, and both he and Andrew burst into laughter.

Out on the lake, the geese suddenly took to the air in a frenzy of flapping wings and squawking.

Andrew's laughter died in his throat. Dad and Carmen quieted, too.

Everyone felt it. Something was wrong.

Andrew's plate flipped over. The half-eaten hamburger and a gob of potato salad splatted to the floor.

"What the hell?" Andrew got to his feet.

A breeze had been drifting across the yard, but the air around them abruptly grew cold.

"Sammy?" Carmen said.

The patio door slid open, whammed shut. Opened and banged shut again.

Dad's eyes were haunted. "Let's get inside."

They hurried inside the house and went to the computer.

Sammy's invisible fingers raced across the keyboard. GO SHES COMENG HEAR GO SHES COMENG HEAR GO SHES COMENG HEAR

Chapter 50

Andrew opened the front door.

The Rolls Royce was parked in the long driveway, headlights burning like predatory eyes.

Shit. What would Mark Justice do now?

Justice answered immediately: *Do you need to ask me, buddy? Get your ass outta there!*

He didn't see Mika, but he quickly slammed the door, bolted it.

Fear shone in the eyes of his father and Carmen.

"We were supposed to be safe here," Andrew said. "How did she find us?"

"Doesn't matter now." Dad gathered the papers on the coffee table and stuffed them in his briefcase. "We've got to move. Can we take the boat docked in the back?"

"Checked it earlier today. It's ready."

"Then let's go," Carmen said. She slung her purse over her shoulder.

Andrew snagged the holstered revolver from an end table in the living room and slipped it on. The gun hadn't worked against Mika, but arming himself had become a reflex reaction.

Someone pounded on the front door.

Dad raced across the kitchen to the patio door, Andrew behind him, Carmen close on his heels.

The front door blew open.

Clad in a tight black cat suit, wild hair matted on her head like a warrior's helmet, Mika stood in the doorway. Her eyes appeared to glow like molten jewels.

She was beautiful. And terrifying.

Andrew tore his attention away from her. Dad scrambled outside onto the deck. He followed him.

But like a leash jerking a dog, something snatched Carmen away from the doorway and back inside the house. She screamed.

"No!" Andrew lunged to grab her.

The door clanged shut in his face. The lock snapped into place.

Carmen was trapped inside with Mika.

Mika's invisible power had hooked Carmen into the kitchen and tossed her across the floor. She tumbled over the tiles, her shoulder rapping against a cabinet. A hiss of pain escaped her clenched teeth.

Rubbing her shoulder, Carmen rose on wobbly legs.

Mika marched into the kitchen.

"It's you and me, bitch," Mika said. "You're not keeping my man away from me anymore."

Fear pinched Carmen's guts. Mika possessed powers that she didn't comprehend, had talents that she could never match. She was, to put it bluntly, superhuman.

But Carmen had never been a quitter, and she sure wasn't going to start now. She'd be damned if she rolled over and died for Mika.

Adrenaline flooded her nervous system, electrified

her muscles. She'd taken a kickboxing class several months ago, and felt the same jittery energy now that she experienced back then when she plunged into a bout. But this time, the consequences of losing were fatal. That cold truth only heightened her intensity.

Looking around, she snagged the knife off the counter that she'd used to peel potatoes, only a short while ago. It was long and sharp. Crouching, she brandished the blade.

Outside, Andrew hammered the patio door, tried to force it open, to no avail. No doubt, Mika had locked it. To guarantee a showdown between them.

She wanted to tell Andrew to run away, but she didn't dare take her attention away from Mika for a second. This woman was like a rattlesnake that would bite you if you took your eyes off her.

"You're not standing between us," Mika said. "I won't let you. He's mine."

"Get a clue, Mika, okay? Andrew doesn't want *you*. He wants *me*."

Mika's eyes narrowed to dangerous slits, her eyebrow twitching.

Carmen clutched the knife. Prayed under her breath.

Roaring, Mika charged forward.

Perhaps she underestimated Carmen, because she didn't raise her arms to defend herself. As she surged forward, Carmen swiped at her. The knife sliced across Mika's forearm, opening a long, thin cut.

Mouth contorted in pain, Mika cradled her wounded arm. Blood leaked between her fingers.

If she can bleed, then she can die, Carmen thought.

"You bitch," Mika said.

"Bring it on." Carmen raised the blood-streaked knife. "I'm not running from you."

Resolve shaped Mika's face into an iron mask.

Lowering her head like a bull, she came at Carmen.

Chapter 51

Raymond sprinted across the path of rocks that led to the dock. Ahead, the pontoon boat awaited in the water, shrouded in the evening's growing darkness.

If they could reach the boat, maybe they could get away.

He didn't know where they would go once they boarded the boat. Across the lake, presumably. Somewhere far away from the insanely powerful woman. Although it seemed that no matter where they went, she could find them.

After the breakthrough he and his son had experienced earlier, there was no way this night could end in disaster. That would be the cruelest joke life could play on them—to rob them of the newfound closeness that had escaped them for so long. No, they *had* to live.

Behind him, Andrew was shouting.

Raymond stopped. Turned.

His son was still on the deck. He was at the patio door, straining to open it, failing, pounding against it.

Through the kitchen window, Raymond glimpsed Carmen inside, with Mika.

Dammit, no.

The girl didn't stand a chance against that fiend. But neither did any of them.

Still, he couldn't leave Carmen behind to die.

He started back toward the house.

A mechanical roar came from somewhere ahead. A car. Getting closer.

He spun—directly into the arc of a pair of bright headlights.

A Rolls Royce sedan thundered across the backyard and bore down on him, grille gleaming like a mouthful of steel teeth.

Vainly, Andrew tried to get back inside the house to help Carmen. But the door would not open.

He didn't know how to kill Mika, or even how to hurt her. But he couldn't leave Carmen in there to fend for herself.

Finally remembering his revolver, he pulled it out and aimed at the lock.

A bellowing car engine, and his father's bleat of terror, distracted him.

He turned in time to see Dad dive out of the path of the Rolls Royce, which had plowed across the backyard like a bulldozer.

As Dad got to his feet, the sedan braked. The driver's side door swung open.

Walter, the ageless caretaker, climbed out of the car.

Andrew's eyes widened.

I'll be damned. I bet he was driving Mika around town all along.

Standing well over six feet tall, Walter towered over Dad. He looked at Andrew. And winked.

Remember me? that wink said.

Walter moved toward his father.

Although Andrew had a gun, he didn't trust his aim at the distance of twenty or more feet that separated him from the caretaker.

So he shouted at his father: "Run, Dad!"

Dad didn't need to hear him say it. He dashed toward the lake.

Moving with the agility of a much younger man, Walter chased after him.

Indecision froze Andrew.

Should he help his father? Or help Carmen? Both of them were caught in dire situations.

He noticed that the Rolls Royce's trunk had popped open. Something was inside.

Or rather, *someone.*

That can't be who I think it is, my eyes are fooling me.

Dazed, temporarily forgetting everything else, he walked off the deck to look closer.

Mika came at Carmen, hard and fast.

Letting out a battle yell, Carmen thrust with the knife.

The blade sank into Mika's belly. Deep. All the way to the hilt.

Mika screamed—a ragged, blood-choked sound. She collapsed against Carmen, expelled a seemingly final sigh.

Gagging, Carmen pushed Mika off her, somehow having the presence of mind to pull out the knife, too.

Mika dropped against the floor on her back. Her eyes, glassy as a doll's, gazed sightlessly at the ceiling.

A heavy flow of dark blood seeped from her abdominal wound.

"Jesus," Carmen said. She shuffled to the counter, threw the knife down. Blood stained her fingers. Hurriedly, she used a dish towel to clean her hands.

Mika lay on the tile, a circle of blood widening beneath her.

She had killed the woman.

She felt a strange mixture of elation, and nausea. Wanted to whoop with joy and vomit at the same time.

As it was, she simply hugged herself.

Mika wasn't invincible, as they had thought. Andrew said he'd shot her earlier, but perhaps she'd been wearing a bulletproof vest or something.

It didn't matter. She was dead now.

She looked through the window. Andrew had walked off the deck and was plodding toward the Rolls Royce, which somehow had ended up in the backyard. What was he doing?

"Bitch."

Terror lanced Carmen's spine.

She turned.

Mika was getting up.

She was no longer bleeding.

Dear Lord, help me.

Carmen reached for the knife. But as if it were an arrow shot through a bow, the blade flew off the counter and across the room, where it clattered to the floor.

"I've had enough of you," Mika said. Standing, she balled her hands into fists.

Carmen made fists, too. She lowered into a fighter's defensive stance.

Time for those kickboxing classes to pay off.

Slowly, she and Mika circled each other in the middle of the kitchen.

Mika was a few inches taller than she was. Long-limbed. Impossibly fit. With supernatural regenerative powers. She owned every advantage, physical and otherwise.

But Carmen wasn't backing down. She couldn't.

Make a move. Let's tangle.

Outside, Andrew screamed.

Automatically, Carmen looked toward the window.

Mika took advantage of the interruption. She backhanded Carmen across the face. Hard.

Carmen cried out and stumbled, her hands going to her struck jaw. She'd never been hit so hard in her life. She half-expected to see a loose tooth on the floor.

"Slapped you like the bitch that you are," Mika said. She grinned.

Carmen lunged at her. She seized Mika by the fabric of her cat suit and drove her against the refrigerator. She rammed punches into Mika—one-two-three slugs to the body.

"Get off me, bitch." Mika grabbed Carmen's hair and savagely yanked her head back. Carmen yelped. Mika drove her knee into Carmen's stomach.

"Uuuhh." The air blew out of Carmen's lungs. It took all of her fortitude to keep from passing out.

Carmen swung a wild fist at Mika. Mika blocked the punch and shoved Carmen across the kitchen. The edge of the counter stabbed Carmen's back. She winced. Panting.

This psycho bitch was strong. Inhumanly strong. She couldn't fight her.

She glanced at the doorway, wondering if she could make it out of the kitchen.

Mika tracked her gaze. "You're not running away, bitch."

She came at Carmen again.

Grabbing the handle of a skillet—the nearest thing at hand—Carmen heaved it in a wide arc.

The skillet *boinged* off the side of Mika's head almost comically, as if they were a couple of battling cartoon characters.

But it didn't slow her. Driving forward, she smacked Carmen in the face. The pop of open hand against soft flesh was like a firecracker.

Carmen's legs sagged. Her face was on fire; blood dripped from her lips.

Gathering all her remaining strength, she rushed Mika. Mika pushed her away as if she were a child. She smacked her again.

Woozy with pain, Carmen fell onto the floor.

"Bitch." Mika kicked her in the ribs with her pointy-toed boot. It felt like a spike.

Gagging on her screams, Carmen pulled herself into a ball. Wished she could curl up so tightly that she would vanish. She couldn't win this fight—it was hopeless.

Mika roughly turned her over. She sat on Carmen's stomach, her knees pinning Carmen's arms to the floor.

"Bitch." She slapped Carmen again.

Carmen's head drooped sideways. Blackness tugged at her.

"Stop," Carmen said weakly. "Please . . . you win."

Mika shook her head. Maniacal glee shone in her eyes.

She burrowed her hands underneath Carmen's blouse, slipped them under the cups of her bra. She grasped Carmen's nipples and twisted.

Carmen cried out. Tears washed down her cheeks, mingled with the blood running from her mouth.

Mika laughed. Twisted again.

"How's it feel, bitch? Was trying to take my man worth it, bitch? Was it?"

Another brutal twist.

"Was it worth it, bitch? Answer me!"

Carmen was weeping. But she formed a glob of saliva and spat in Mika's face.

"Damn right it was worth it. And I'd do it again!"

Spit dripping from her nose, Mika gritted her teeth. She extended her hand.

The knife spun through the air like a boomerang and landed in her grasp.

Chapter 52

The Rolls Royce's open trunk mesmerized Andrew. Someone terrifyingly familiar awaited him in there. He trudged toward it like a sleepwalker, oblivious to his father and Carmen and everything else around him, as if the trunk was the glowing end of a long, narrow tunnel.

At the bumper, he froze.

Inside, Mika's three cats sat on a dead body.

Eric's body.

Bundled in a blue house robe, Eric lay inside, his tall, lanky body twisted to fit the dimensions of the trunk. Blood dampened the robe's collar; his throat was slit from one side to the other, as if someone had drawn a bloody grin across his flesh.

His lolling head was turned so that that his dead eyes bore into Andrew. Accusingly, it seemed.

It's your fault this happened to me, bro. I warned you about that crazy female.

The cats glowered at Andrew, as if confirming the guilty charge.

As though from a great distance, Andrew heard himself scream.

* * *

Raymond fled across the big backyard, heading toward the dock.

Walter pursued him. He was an old guy, but he was supernaturally fleet-footed. He gained steadily on Raymond.

Not gonna be able to outrun this bastard.

Raymond hadn't been in a fistfight since he was a teenager. It had been a bench-clearing brawl at a high school football game. He'd given a kid a black eye and had only wound up with swollen knuckles.

But that had been decades ago. He didn't feel optimistic about his chances in a fight with the giant, strong caretaker.

Ahead, the boat bobbed in the water.

There was no way he'd have time to get in the boat and start it—he didn't even know how in the hell to start a boat—before the caretaker caught him.

Walter's footfalls clapped behind him. Closing in.

He prayed that the old guy couldn't swim or was afraid of water. If not, he was done.

Remembering Andrew's comment about the water's shallow depth near the banks, Raymond ran to the end of the dock and leaped into the lake.

Eric's dead. Mika killed him. To get to me.

Like a blow to the cranium, shock had dulled Andrew's thoughts. He gripped the edges of the trunk. Head lowered, he stared at a body that surely could not be real. This body was like a figure in a wax museum. A perfect replica of Eric Patton. But not real.

The cats had scattered when he had screamed.

This can't be happening.

But Eric hadn't blinked once. His chest hadn't risen

or fallen. His mouth hadn't opened to form words in his achingly familiar voice.

Andrew's thoughts were as disordered as leaves in a windstorm. Didn't know whether to believe Eric was dead or not, whether the corpse in front of him was real or not.

Before he knew what he was doing, he was running back to the house. Alternately crying and cursing. Finger on the trigger of the .38.

He fired at the patio door, destroying the lock. He flung the door open.

Inside, another vision out of a nightmare awaited him.

Mika was crouched above Carmen, on the floor. She had a knife.

The knife was buried in Carmen's throat.

No, no, no.

Mika turned. "Andrew, darling!"

Andrew didn't hesitate. He shot her.

The bullet tore into Mika's shoulder. The impact knocked her off Carmen's body and sent her rolling across the floor.

He hurried to Carmen.

The blade jutted from her throat. God, it was buried so deep in there. Blood pumped from the wound, drowned the edges of the knife.

He was afraid to pull it out. Had the insane, frightening thought that yanking out the knife would be like unplugging her from life support, and he would lose her forever.

Carmen's clouded gaze found him. She smiled weakly. Blood leaked from her lips.

"Sorry . . . Drew . . ."

He held her hand. "You're not going to die, baby. No, no, you're not gonna die. Not like this."

More blood streamed from the wound, ran down her neck in fat rivulets.

He grabbed his cell phone.

They needed help. An ambulance. They could fix this. Someone could.

As he fumbled to push buttons on the phone, Carmen gently grasped his hand, guided it to the knife handle.

"Take . . . it out," she whispered.

"Can't do that," he said. "No, baby, I can't do that, I'm calling for help, we're going to take care of everything, okay, just hang on, all right? Hang on."

She blinked, slowly. Her hold on his hand loosened.

"Can't die, you can't, you've gotta hang on, please, baby, just hang on!"

The light in her eyes dimmed, sputtered.

"Just hang on, baby!"

Her light went out.

She was dead.

No.

Keening wordlessly, he cradled her body and rocked back and forth, as if the movement could nudge her back to life. He buried his face against hers. Her warm blood smeared his cheeks, blended with his tears. Sobs shook him.

"Stop crying, Andrew. That bitch isn't worth it."

Mika was on her feet, loathing twisting her face. Her shoulder wound had healed.

Blinded by tears, he groped for his gun.

A boot stomped on his fingers. He yelped in surprise and pain. Looked up.

Like an evil giant, Walter towered above him.

"My apologies for this, sir," he said, and clouted Andrew upside the head with a blunt object.

*   *   *

When Andrew swam back into consciousness, Mika and Walter stood above him in the kitchen, talking.

"His father escaped," Walter said to Mika, with the deference of a child addressing an elder. "He jumped into the lake. You understand how water frightens me."

"It doesn't matter," she said. "Andrew scarcely knows the man. Let him go."

Andrew's head ached where the caretaker had struck him. A moan slipped out of him.

"He's awake!" Mika said, her eyes brightening. Smiling, she knelt beside him. "Hello there, darling." Tenderly, she touched his head.

He jerked away from her touch. "Get the fuck away from me."

"We're going to go home now, Andrew." Her face had drawn into a stern expression. "No more running, no more hiding. It's over."

"Not going anywhere with your crazy ass."

Rising, she nodded at Walter.

"Hold still, sir," Walter said in his gravelly baritone. He knelt beside Andrew and placed his gigantic hands on Andrew's arms, pinning them to the floor.

"Let go of me!" Andrew squirmed to break free, but the old guy's hands were like iron clamps.

Walter grinned at him, showing a mouthful of big, white teeth. Teeth like a horse, his mother would have said. He easily held Andrew down.

Mika opened a small, black leather carrying case. She removed a syringe.

"This will relax you during our drive home," she said. She punctured the crook of his arm with the needle and injected a silvery fluid into his bloodstream.

Andrew spat curses at her.

"We'll be home soon, baby." She caressed his face.

As the sedative took over, he sank into darkness.

* * *

As Raymond had hoped, the caretaker didn't follow him into the water. After he jumped into the lake, feet-first, he waded several yards away from the shore, until the waves came up to his chest, to put a safe distance between himself and his pursuer.

Walter stood stock-still on the edge of the dock. He regarded the water fearfully.

In the backyard, at the rear of the Rolls Royce, Andrew screamed—a sound not of physical pain, but of soul-wrenching grief.

What the hell had his boy seen?

Maybe it was something that he didn't want to know.

Andrew ran to the house, shattered the patio door with a gunshot, and burst inside.

Another shot rang from the kitchen.

Spiders of anxiety crawled across Raymond's neck.

What was going on in there?

Walter's gaze went from the house, then back to Raymond—and then he shrugged and stalked toward the house.

Raymond stayed in the water.

He wanted to help Andrew and Carmen, but he didn't know what he could do to aid them against these monsters. Something—intuition, maybe—cautioned him to keep his distance from the main action. Although he wondered if he were just being a coward.

Several minutes later, Mika strutted outside. He marveled at how beautiful and youthful she looked. He had last seen this woman thirty years ago, and for how she appeared, it might as well have been yesterday.

Mika didn't look toward the water. She waited beside the car while Walter carried two people out of the house, limp bodies slung like garbage bags over his broad shoulders: Andrew, and Carmen.

Raymond's blood turned colder than the water around him.

She couldn't have killed Andrew. She was in love with him. Right?

But he wasn't as optimistic about Carmen's fate.

Walter put Carmen in the trunk; he placed Andrew in the backseat. Mika climbed in the back, too, and Walter shut the door behind her.

The sedan sped out of the yard, spitting leaves and grit in the air, and disappeared around the corner of the house. The echo of the rumbling engine faded.

They could be going to only one destination: Mourning Hill.

He had been left behind. They knew he was hiding in the lake. Probably, they figured he was too insignificant to bother with any more.

They'd underestimated him. Dismissed him as a non-factor.

But this was the event of which he'd been dreaming for the past few weeks. The nightmare had been a message; it also had been prophetic.

It was time to save his son.

Chapter 53

As the night extended its hold over the world, Raymond frantically moved around the lake house.

In a bedroom, he found clothes in Andrew's suitcase. He changed out of his damp gear and slipped on jeans, a T-shirt, and low-cut Adidas. Fortunately, he and Andrew wore the same sizes.

Next, he searched for a suitable weapon. He found numerous knives in the kitchen, but disregarded them. He wanted something more lethal than an ordinary piece of cutlery. A gun would be ideal.

He didn't find any firearms, but in the storage shed, he discovered a heavy-duty wood axe, nearly three feet long from the bottom of the handle to the tip of the head. The broad, wedge-shaped blade gleamed, evidence of a recent sharpening. This would do just fine.

He didn't hold any misconceptions about what he had to do. Someone would likely end up dead before the night ended. The blood that stained the kitchen floor was proof of the high stakes for which they were playing.

Calling the police wasn't an option. What was he

going to do—tell the cops that a hundred-something-year-old woman who looked twenty-five and possessed extrasensory powers was taking his son to her haunted mansion? Sure, that would guarantee their assistance—hauling him to the local psychiatric hospital, that is.

Giving the authorities a more reasonable story—maybe saying that Andrew had been abducted—while it would likely secure the police's involvement, wasn't a much better option. What were the cops going to do when they faced Mika? Shoot her? It would never work. Conventional tactics bound the police.

But not him.

This was not a matter to be settled by ordinary thinking, commonplace methods. Which meant involving other people would be a waste of time. This was his responsibility. He had to go at it alone.

But in fact, he really wasn't sure what he was going to do. All he was certain of was that he needed to get to Mourning Hill. By the time he arrived, he hoped that a plan presented itself.

Carrying the axe over his shoulder and his briefcase in his hand, like some weird lumber-chopping executive, he hastened to his Ford.

The driver's side door sprang open.

He paused.

A coolness that couldn't be attributed to the evening breeze danced around him.

"Sammy?" he said. "You with me, son?"

A cold sensation, not unpleasant, folded over his hand. Ghostly fingers gently pried the briefcase out of his grasp and carried it inside the truck, placing it on the passenger seat.

"I'll be damned," he said.

He wasn't alone after all.

Chapter 54

After a deep sleep rife with disturbing dreams, Andrew awoke.

He lay on his back on soft, burnished leather seats. Groggy, he tried to figure out where he was.

He was inside a car. The fragrance of jasmine hung in the air.

His breath snagged in his chest as comprehension came over him.

Mika's beatific face floated into his line of sight. She cradled his head in her lap.

Looking down at him, she smiled. "Hi, baby."

He opened his mouth to scream. But he couldn't draw enough breath to do so. Bolting upright, he gasped, hyperventilating like an asthmatic child.

Mika was unconcerned. "We're home, darling. At last! I can hardly wait to give you a tour of our estate."

He finally found his voice. "Get the hell away from me!" He scrambled to the other side of the car and grabbed the door handle, not knowing or caring whether the sedan was moving. He shoved the door open and rolled outside, onto the damp earth.

The Rolls Royce was parked at the end of a long, winding gravel driveway. Mourning Hill stood before him on the crest of a mound, wide roof framed by tattered clouds and a bone-white moon. The dreary mansion, its massive columns wreathed in Spanish moss, was every bit as forbidding as he remembered from his first time there.

This had to be the worst nightmare he'd ever had in his life. Someone had to wake him up before he lost his mind.

The sedan's trunk yawned open. Fear made his legs watery, but he dragged himself to the rear of the vehicle, and peered inside.

The trunk was empty. There were no traces of blood or hair or clothing—nothing to indicate the terrible cargo that had been stored in there the last time he'd looked. The trunk was as clean as it probably had been on the day the car rolled out of the dealership parking lot.

He thought of Eric and Carmen. Dead. Gone forever.

Crippling grief buckled through him. He sagged against the bumper, hugging himself tightly.

"Walter has taken care of them," Mika said, coming around the car's flank. She put her hand on his arm. "Don't worry about such nasty things, baby. We're home now. Let me hold you." She stepped closer, arms spread to embrace him.

He knocked her hands away and backpedaled, squishing through mud. "I'm getting out of here."

"That isn't possible. You can't leave. Ever."

"Bullshit." He sprinted along the driveway, away from the house.

"I'll be waiting for you on the veranda, baby." She laughed, and began to sing happily, a song about lovers reunited.

He ignored her maddening singing and concentrated on running down the narrow lane.

Carmen and Eric were alive. They had to be. They were alive, and he was stuck in this nightmare, and the only way for him to wake up was for him to get away from Mika and this lunatic place.

After he'd run a couple of dozen yards, he reached a head-high wall of shrubs that completely blocked his path. Pines and maples crowded the area, their leafy boughs interwoven like an immense net.

The last time he'd been here, he'd had to force his way through the shrubbery.

How had Mika's Rolls Royce gotten through this? Could there be another way out?

In his mind's eye, he envisioned Mika commanding the bushes to part, like Biblical sea waters, to allow the car to nose through. Nothing seemed impossible anymore.

The thicket certainly didn't move aside for him, and he didn't see a way around it, so he began to clear a path. He ripped aside branches and kicked down bushes. Cold sweat coated his face. Thorns scratched his arms and hands, but he didn't register the pain. Desperation had numbed him to any distractions from his goal of escaping.

He fought through the last patch of shrubbery, and emerged in a clearing, underneath a canopy of trees.

Beyond the trees, Mourning Hill loomed like an old, abandoned fortress. He'd arrived at the back of the house.

This was impossible.

He'd been running *away* from the mansion.

You can't leave. Ever.

It was as if he'd been magically teleported to the rear of the property.

He ran to the boundary of the vast lawn, on another

side of the yard. A tall line of shrubbery formed the perimeter; black woods grew beyond. He plunged into the bushes and drove through them, pushing into the forest.

Nocturnal creatures croaked, hissed, and scampered around him. Bugs buzzed against his face. He batted them away, and pressed on.

After he'd run for at least a quarter of a mile, the woods thinned, and gave way to a high wall of bushes. He fought through them and stumbled into a clearing.

The broad, moss-covered side of Mourning Hill stood ahead of him.

Again, he'd been transported to another location on the estate grounds.

He shouted a wordless cry of anguish.

His lungs burned from the running he'd done. He sank to his knees in the thick, wet grass, drawing deep breaths.

He could no longer avoid the truth, as unbelievable as it was to his rational mind.

He was like a tiny mouse in a big maze with no exit. Trapped.

He found Mika on the veranda. She swayed on the wooden bench swing, clicking her heels together like a schoolgirl on a playground.

She cocked her head, eyes amused. "Tired of running, Andrew?"

"I want to go home," he said. "Please."

"You *are* home." She hopped off the swing, and offered her hand. "Come inside with me."

He didn't want to go inside this madhouse. But what was the point of resisting? He couldn't escape. He didn't have the energy to continue what seemed to be a pointless fight.

However, he nursed a delicate hope that, once inside the house, he would discover something that would give him an edge over her.

He took her hand, like a child.

She led him inside Mourning Hill.

Chapter 55

The interior of the mansion looked nothing like the dusty, cobweb-filled estate that Andrew remembered from his initial visit, or that his father had described.

This was an utterly contemporary, fantasy place, like something from the MTV show, *Cribs*.

"This is . . . amazing," he said, as Mika led him down the entry hall.

"This is your home now," she said. "I redecorated and furnished it to please you."

Gaping at his surroundings, he could only shake his head.

There were polished marble floors in the hallway, which was wide enough to accommodate driving a Hummer across its length. The creamy walls were adorned with dramatically lighted, framed artwork, with numerous insets full of Greek sculptures and ornate vases. Near the middle of the long corridor, an enormous crystal chandelier hung overhead, illuminating a grand spiral staircase; the staircase featured a gold balustrade and marble steps, with nary a cobweb in sight.

He peeked inside the living room. A vast space. Soaring cathedral ceiling. Snow-white carpeting. Humongous, flat-screen television. Plush, Italian leather furniture. End tables gilded with gold. A black grand piano. An aquarium large enough for he himself to swim in, full of shimmering water and stocked with exotic, colorful fish. A marble fireplace sufficiently spacious to contain an inferno.

A song played in the background, piped to his ears from hidden speakers: "Fantasy" by Earth, Wind, and Fire. They were one of his all-time favorite bands.

"When did you do all of this?" he asked.

"When I knew you were the one," she said. She grinned. "Come, Andrew. I'll show you more of our home."

A door off the hallway opened to a theater that put the entertainment area in his house to shame. It had a massive, wall-size screen, seating to accommodate fifteen people, and even an old-fashioned popcorn machine.

The library was next. Pure light filtered from another crystal chandelier. The chamber contained a labyrinth of mahogany bookshelves, every one packed with hardcover volumes penned by all of his favorite authors: Stephen King, Dean Koontz, Tananarive Due, Steven Barnes, Walter Mosley ... thousands of books, books he'd read and books he wanted to read one day, all collected here. Comfortable leather club chairs were positioned near large bay windows that provided a view of the rolling, manicured estate grounds. The colorful Persian rugs on the floor were so soft he could've slept on them.

"And here's the kitchen," she said, gesturing to a room beyond another arched doorway. It could have served a restaurant staff: a big marble island, double-ovens, two gigantic refrigerators, a collection of shining pots and pans dangling from hooks, a cappuccino machine, and more, every culinary device he could think of neatly stored on the sparkling counters.

He opened one of the refrigerators. It was packed with food—fruits, vegetables, meats, cheeses, beverages, and much more, enough food to feed a family of ten for a month.

He removed a ripe peach and held it before his eyes, squeezed it to test its firmness—as if it might dissolve in his fingers like a cloud. He still struggled to accept the reality of what he was seeing. It was like a lucid dream.

He bit into the peach. It was juicy, sweet. Real.

Mika was smiling at him. "There's much more down here, but I'll show you the upper level. Follow me."

On the second floor, another crystal chandelier showered them in golden light. There were more vases and sculpted works displayed on decorative stands. Lush oil paintings on the softly hued walls.

A floor-to-ceiling mirror with a gold-leaf frame hung at the end of the corridor.

She pushed open a door. "Your office, darling."

The room was at least five times as spacious as his home office. A walnut desk stood in the center of the room, on which sat a computer and a flat-screen monitor. Office quality laser printers and copier machines lined one wall. Blown-up, gold-framed covers of his books decorated the other walls. A bookcase contained every edition of his books that had ever been published, in four languages. Large windows overlooked a rose garden, and a gazebo.

"I can't believe this," he said. He ran his hands over the smooth desktop. "This is like my dream office."

Mika took his hand. "Wait until you see the bedroom."

She led him farther along the hall, opened another door.

"Wow," he said.

The master bedroom was bigger than the entire first floor of his old house. A hand-carved, four-poster bed dominated one side of the room. He stroked the sheets, recognized the high thread-count, Egyptian cotton bedding. A luxury he'd hoped to have one day.

Another immense, flat-screen TV hung suspended from a wall. There was a roomy sitting area, with leather chairs, tables edged with gold, and another marble fireplace. A mini-bar sat against another wall, stocked with top shelf liquors and glasses for every purpose.

She showed him the walk-in closet. It was larger than the main bedroom at his other house. Dozens of designer suits—Armani, Hugo Boss, Versace, and more— for every conceivable mood and season, waited on hangers. There were so many pairs of shoes he could've worn a different pair every day for three months without rotating them.

"I know all your sizes," she said. "Every piece of clothing will fit your handsome body like a glove. Come on."

Winking at him, she strutted across the room, and through a doorway. He followed her.

Into the master bath. Tons of space. Polished Italian tiles. Marble counters. Twenty-four-karat-gold faucets. A shower stall so roomy you could practice somersaults inside of it.

There was a Jacuzzi, too, full of steamy, gurgling water. A gold ice bucket stood at the edge of the tub, chilling a bottle of Moët champagne and two flutes.

The feeling that he was trapped in some kind of fever dream gripped him more tightly than ever.

Part of him railed against everything that he was seeing, believed that he was imagining these fantastic sights and needed to shatter the illusion and see the mansion as it really was—a place of torment and death.

But another part of him was seduced. Had accepted

that there was no escape and wanted to enjoy this heavenly prison. Wanted to surrender his soul to this beautiful woman once and for all . . .

She handed him the champagne. "Would you do the honors?"

Like a robot, he popped the cork. She held the flutes, and he poured the bubbly into each. She gave him a glass.

"Let us toast," she said. "To our eternal, youthful love."

He clinked his flute against hers. Raised the glass to his lips.

His gaze wandered to the window behind her.

The glass gave a view of a side of the property. He spotted Walter below, in a big garden full of boxwoods and stone, life-size statues. Walter was digging.

He's digging a grave . . . Carmen, Eric . . . oh, Jesus . . .

The glass slipped out of his hand and shattered against the floor.

"What's wrong, baby?" Mika asked.

What was he doing, sharing a toast with the monstrous woman who had murdered his friends?

Nausea wormed through his guts. *Symptom of critical stress,* a remote, rational side of his mind theorized. He bent over, gagged.

Murmuring words of comfort, Mika rubbed his shoulder.

As dizzy as if he'd stepped off a spinning carousel, he pushed her away, staggered across the room.

Suddenly, he saw cobwebs on the walls, not colorful oil paintings. Dusty antiques everywhere, not shiny gold tables and big TVs. A grimy, claw foot tub, not a Jacuzzi . . .

He blinked, eyes filling with tears. Separate realities wavered before his watery eyes like heat mirages.

Groaning, he fell onto the bed, and passed out.

Chapter 56

Driving as fast as he dared without risking a wreck, it took a little over two hours for Raymond to reach Mourning Hill. As he drove, he played a CD of old-school jams that Andrew had recorded for him, weeks ago. Roberta Flack, Donny Hathaway, The Emotions, Sly and the Family Stone, Minnie Ripperton, so many other classic artists. Although listening to the soulful cuts usually brought back memories of what he'd been going through in his life when those melodies first hit the radio airwaves, this time, he thought only of his son, and how badly he wanted to see him again.

The ghost rode shotgun with him. He didn't see the entity, but coolness occasionally tapped his hand, as if the spirit wished to reassure him that he was not alone.

It was the kind of night during which you no longer questioned what was possible.

He didn't call anyone, and didn't accept any calls on his cell. His wife would've tried to talk him into doing something more sensible than what he planned to do. But he could not be moved from the task ahead of him.

Around a quarter past nine, he parked across the street from Mourning Hill.

He noted, with an ironic smile, that he was only a few feet away from the same ditch into which he had spun several weeks before.

Beyond the shoulder of the road, a large, white-tail deer perched at the edge of the forest. It watched him with onyx-black eyes.

Was this the same deer that he'd attempted to avoid hitting—resulting in his truck flipping over?

The animal stared at him for a beat, almost challengingly. Then it snorted and walked into the woods.

He frowned. Everything about this place was weird.

He looked across the road. Trees hid the house from view. Yet he swore he could *feel* Mourning Hill back there in the darkness. It radiated an aura of malignant energy.

He didn't want to get any closer. It was the last place in the world that he wanted to go. A night in a maximum-security prison would be preferable to this.

Coolness streamed over his lap. The driver's door popped open.

Sammy was prompting him to get out and do what he had to do. His son was in there against his will, and he was his son's last hope.

"Okay," he said. "I'm moving. Let's do this."

He opened the glove compartment, retrieved a pocket-size flashlight.

Then he reached to the floor. To get the axe.

Raymond used the axe to hack a path through the thick shrubbery that blocked the driveway. The branches cracked like bones under his blade. Clearing his way sapped his strength, though, and he prayed that he could summon a second wind before he made his main move on the house.

Crunching across the last of the felled bushes, he rested the axe on his shoulder and gazed at Mourning Hill.

Look up the word "spooky" in the dictionary, he thought, and this house would be featured. The mansion appeared unchanged since he had first visited, thirty years ago.

His hunch had been correct, too. Mika had come here.

The Rolls Royce was parked at the end of the driveway. Soft light glowed at several of the front windows.

The window of the upper chamber—where, in his dreams, he glimpsed the pulsating green light—was black.

What did that mean? Was their theory about the unearthly power in the house wrong?

He wasn't quite sure what to believe, and it frightened him.

Although he was afraid, endorphins flooded his blood, granting him the renewed energy boost that he'd hoped for.

And his sense of purpose—indeed, of destiny—had never been more acute. He was scared enough to piss his pants, but it was *right* for him to be here. No matter the ultimate outcome, he would never regret his decision to come here to rescue his boy. He was, in the truest sense, fulfilling his responsibility to his child.

If he died tonight, he'd die as a man who'd finally earned the right to call himself a father.

From his nightmares, he remembered that approaching the front door would lead him into a trap.

This time, the consequences were real, so why take a chance that the same thing might happen here?

Therefore, he walked to the north side of the property. He gripped the axe's long handle in both hands, ready to swing.

He heard a noise that grew louder as he walked. The sound came from an enclosed area along the side of the house—in his dream, the cemetery of unmarked graves.

It was the sound of shoveling.

Just like in his dream. Walter, undoubtedly, was digging a grave.

But for whom?

He recalled Walter tossing Carmen's body into the car's trunk.

Lord, please don't let it be what I think it is.

Tightening his hold on the axe, he sought cover behind a stout pine tree. He peered around the trunk.

Ahead on his left, there was a wrought iron archway, enwrapped in Spanish moss. A tall fence entwined with more moss enclosed the area beyond the entrance. He didn't see foot-high crucifixes jutting from the ground, however, as he had in his dream. He glimpsed, instead, tall stone statues standing within, veiled in mist and darkness. And the hulking shapes of boxwoods that begged to be trimmed.

Nevertheless, he knew what was really in there, underneath the surface. It was a garden, but a garden of death, not life. Seeded with the corpses of innocent people. Mika's victims.

Fear skittered down his back.

The shoveling continued with the cold repetition of a machine.

He didn't want to move any closer. But Walter was in there, and if he didn't take care of him, first, he would never make it inside the house to help Andrew.

Leaving the cover of the tree, he crept closer to the entryway. He peered around the corner.

Wearing a maniacal grin, Walter swung a shovel at his head.

Chapter 57

When Andrew returned to consciousness, he found himself lying on the bed in the master bedroom.

Mika dozed beside him, her arm covering him possessively. She had changed into a silky, crimson kimono. An empty champagne flute lay on the gold-rimmed nightstand.

On the wide, flat-screen TV across the room, a film played, the volume muted. It was one of his favorites: the first *Matrix* movie.

He remembered seeing flickering images before he passed out—shabby furniture juxtaposed with elegant surroundings—but as he looked around, the chamber was unquestionably luxurious.

He brushed his fingers across the sheets. They felt genuine.

What had he seen before he'd blacked out? Was he losing his ability to distinguish between fantasy and reality?

He didn't even know the time. He wasn't wearing his watch, and there were no clocks in the room. He had no idea how long he had been asleep. It could have been minutes, or hours.

It was still night, however; darkness filmed the window across the room. His throat tightened. He didn't dare glance out of that window again, lest he once more suffer a crippling emotional aftershock.

He carefully lifted Mika's arm and rolled away from her.

Her eyes fluttered open. "Feeling better?"

"I'm gonna take a walk around."

She yawned. "Good . . . get accustomed to our home."

This will never be my home.

He climbed out of bed and shuffled into the carpeted hallway.

The mansion was as silent as a mausoleum. He heard only the wind soughing through the eaves, and the creaking and settling noises typical of older homes.

But he felt as though he were being watched. He turned.

It was one of the cats. As motionless as a piece of sculpture, it sat at the end of the hallway, in front of the floor-to-ceiling mirror that covered the wall. It observed him quietly.

"Damn thing," he said. "Why don't you go away?"

The cat stared at him.

He ignored the feline and began to explore the house. It was vast, with eleven bedrooms, almost as many bathrooms, and a couple of dozen other rooms and sitting areas. Every room was immaculate and stylishly furnished with high-end, contemporary furniture and the latest and greatest technological gadgets.

It was as if Mika had discovered the blueprint for his dream home and brought it to magnificent life.

But it's not real, a voice whispered. *You had a glimpse of the truth before you blacked out . . . this place isn't what it appears to be . . .*

But everything he touched felt real; the jasmine in the air smelled real; and everything he saw was colorful and brand new, indisputably real.

Two things, however, captured his attention.

One: although there were numerous telephones, none of them had a dial tone. All of them issued only dead silence, as if they were mere props in a model house.

Two: a closer look at the oil paintings revealed that he and Mika were the featured subjects of each one. One work depicted them lying together in a grassy meadow under a summer sun, on the verge of a kiss. Another showed them riding a galloping black horse across a flowery countryside, her hands wrapped around his waist and her face pressed against his neck. Yet another piece had them sitting at a banquet table laden with fruit, feeding each other white grapes.

There were dozens of other paintings, but no matter the setting, the tone of all of them was the same: the celebration of a passionate romance.

She had created these works herself. On their first date, she'd told him that she was a painter. She was talented, imaginative.

But looking at the paintings made his stomach sour. Her obsession with him knew no limits.

I have to get out of here.

Downstairs in the foyer, he grasped the knob of the front door and twisted.

Surprisingly, the door opened. Cool, damp air drifted inside, carrying the sounds of nighttime creatures.

He thought of running out of the house, and dismissed the idea. She'd secured the boundaries with some kind of weird magic. Why waste more energy running in vain?

He had to accept the truth.

He was trapped. In a luxurious prison.

* * *

Mika awaited him at the crest of the staircase. One of the cats lounged on the balustrade, furry tail caressing her arm.

"Enjoy your walk?" she asked.

"My father said that he heard voices when he came here," he said. "Screams, footsteps—ghosts in torment, I guess. What happened to them?"

Her lips curled in disdain. "Those dreadful things would only distress you, baby. I've shielded you from them."

"Have you shielded me from anything else? Like the dust and junk I thought I saw around here, right before I passed out?"

"Dust and junk?" She spoke the words as if they tasted foul in her mouth. She swept her arm around them. "Do you see any of that, Andrew?"

"No, but I did, for a second."

She smiled. "Are you certain that you weren't dreaming?"

He shook his head. He wasn't certain of anything anymore.

"Where's the attic?" he asked.

"Why do you want to know?" Her gaze was sharp.

"Just curious. Place this big has to have an interesting attic, right?"

"Hmm. Curiosity can be dangerous. For your own safety, I've hidden the upper chamber."

"Sounds like you've hidden a lot from me."

"Does it? I apologize, but it is only to keep you happy. May I ask you a question?"

He shrugged.

She touched his cheek. By sheer force of will he kept

himself from pushing her away. He was on her turf. Pissing her off wouldn't help him.

"Do you remember our love?" she asked.

"No."

"Still?" She slipped her hand into the kimono's voluminous front pocket, fingered something there. "Remember how I promised to show you proof of our romance?"

"You said something about that, I think." What craziness was she going to bring out this time?

"Here it is." She dug something out of her pocket: a thick, worn, leather-bound diary. She handed it to him.

"I don't get it," he said.

"Open it."

He turned the brass latch on the diary, opened it.

The journal's ruled pages were yellowed, filled with elegant writing that could only be Mika's.

"Read the letters," she said.

Near the middle of the diary, he found a bundle of folded, age-softened papers. He unfurled one of them.

It was a letter, the careful penmanship—different from the cursive writing in the diary, somehow more masculine—done in dark ink. It was addressed to, "Celestina, My Love."

"Celestina was my birth name," she said.

He started to read.

By the time he reached the end of the page, his hands shook badly.

"You see?" Mika said. She smirked. "Proof, baby."

"This can't be real," he said. "You've made this up, had this forged or something."

"They're one hundred percent genuine, darling. I kept those letters because they kept you alive in my heart—and I knew you would come back to me one day, too. I wanted to have them as evidence to help you remember."

"This is bullshit."

"All of your running, all of your hiding from our love . . . see how pointless it was? You've always been mine, before you ever had any inkling of the truth—"

"Listen, this is bullshit!"

"Stop resisting the truth, honey—" She reached out to touch him.

He ran away from her. Bolted into the room across the hall: his so-called office. He slammed the door.

His legs felt weak. As if he were on the brink of passing out again. He dropped into the leather desk chair and drew deep breaths, to regain his bearings.

He clutched the diary and its unbelievable letters in his clammy hands. He wanted to throw it into a fire. But he couldn't. Because if she were right . . .

"Can't be," he said to himself. He shook his head, fat beads of sweat streaming down his face. *"Can't be."*

He would deny it forever. Accepting his connection to the letters was unthinkable.

She knocked on the door. "Let me in, Andrew. I know it's hard to accept the truth. But please don't shut me out like this."

Tensed, he sat still. He half expected the door to blow open. This was her lair, and she could do whatever she desired.

But she didn't force her way inside.

Was she trying some kind of reverse psychology tactic on him?

He waited another minute. Looked around the room anew.

If he ever got away from here and had an opportunity to build a dream home, his office would look nothing like this one. The fantasy had been ruined for him.

Finally, he rose. He opened the door.

He frowned.

Mika had vanished. Her loyal cat had departed, too.

At the end of the hallway, the long mirror rippled, like the surface of a lake. Then, it solidified.

The house was tomb-silent.

His frown deepened.

Something was going on.

Chapter 58

As the shovel whistled through the air on a direct course for Raymond's head, someone pushed Raymond out of the deadly blade's path.

He fell on his behind on the wet grass, the impact rattling through his pelvis.

A vortex of coldness spun around him.

Sammy. The kid had knocked him down—and saved his life.

"You have no business here," Walter said. He raised the shovel, preparing for a mighty downward swing.

Raymond grabbed the axe and logrolled across the ground.

Walter slammed the shovel against the earth in the spot that Raymond had vacated only a second ago, divots flying into the air and spraying the legs of a nearby goddess statue.

Raymond bounded to his feet.

He saw two bodies—Eric and Carmen—lying at the rim of a half-dug grave, like statues that had yet to be erected on bases.

Dear God. They were only kids.

Acid-hot grief boiled up his throat, and he choked it down. He didn't have time to get emotional. Allowing himself to lose focus would land his body next to theirs.

He brandished the axe like a baseball bat.

His steel-gray hair flopping on his head like a bad wig, Walter grunted and yanked the shovel out of the earth. He grinned, showing huge, straight white teeth that seemed misplaced in his weathered, walnut-brown face.

"I'll dig a hole for you next," Walter said. He came at Raymond, swinging.

The shovel sliced through the air. Moving away, Raymond almost slipped in the grass, but narrowly avoided the blade's swooping arc.

He swung the axe. Walter whipped the shovel toward him at the same time. The blades clashed together with a *clang*, the vibration rattling through Raymond's hands so violently that the axe jumped out of his fingers.

As he dove to the ground to retrieve the weapon, Walter struck his shoulder with the back of the shovel. Agony exploded through Raymond's arm. Crying out, he dropped onto the grass on his side.

"Too slow, old man," Walter said.

Tears of pain almost blinding him, Raymond rolled, found the axe, scrambled forward on all fours.

Move your ass, Ray. Ignore the pain and move.

In his mind's eye, he saw a terrible vision: Walter splitting his head open like a cantaloupe, his brains splattering the ground . . .

Don't think about that, Ray, don't you dare.

He crawled behind a thick maple tree. Using the trunk for support, he slid upward, until he was on his feet again. Gritted his teeth as intense pain fanned through his shoulder.

He saw graves around him, marked not by head-stones, but by clumps of summer flowers. Dozens of them, grouped around the boxwoods and statues. To anyone else, it might have appeared to be only an oddly arranged garden. But because of the insight his dreams had given him, he *knew* what lay only a few feet beneath the surface.

I'll be damned if it's my time to die. I'm not gonna be buried here.

His face a visage of fury, Walter thundered toward him. He swung the shovel at Raymond's head.

Raymond ducked out of the way.

The shovel thwacked against the tree, bit deep into the bark. Walter struggled to dislodge it.

Recognizing his opportunity, Raymond lifted the axe and brought it down on Walter's arm.

The axe cleaved through as if his limb were made of balsa wood.

Roaring, Walter fell to his knees. Blood spouted from his severed arm. He stared at it, stupefied.

Raymond froze, too. Stunned at the savage act he'd committed. Warm blood dripped down the axe handle, colored his fingers. He looked at the blood on his hand with an almost childish awe.

Shit, did I really do this? Did I really have to do this . . .

Walter forced himself to his feet. No weapon in his remaining hand, eyes afire, he lunged at Raymond like a rabid dog.

Raymond's conscience quieted and his survival instinct took over.

He stepped back like a baseball slugger and heaved the weapon toward Walter in a powerful arc.

The axe lopped off Walter's head with sickening, fluid ease.

The caretaker's decapitated body crashed to the ground. It writhed against the grass, legs kicking.

Raymond jammed his fist in his mouth to stem the urge to vomit.

Walter's head lay on its side, at the feet of a statue of Athena. The eyes blinked rapidly, like some macabre kewpie doll. The gaze honed in on Raymond. Hate burned in those eyes—eyes that should've been un-blinking and dead.

He was still alive. God in heaven, how?

Walter's torso twisted onto its stomach. Using its good arm, it crawled toward the head.

Raymond understood, with dreadful clarity, what was going to happen.

Walter was going to pull himself together. Like some horrific Humpty Dumpty.

Lying at the base of the maple tree, Walter's severed arm stirred—and began to creep like a tarantula across the grass, toward the body.

"Jesus, help me," Raymond whispered.

The task before him was more gruesome than any-thing he'd anticipated. But it had to be done.

He shuffled forward and grabbed a fistful of Walter's hair.

He refused to look down at the head dangling in his hand.

He cast the head into the unfinished grave that Walter had started digging. It thumped against the dirt, maybe three feet below.

Upside down, Walter's inhuman glare fixated on Raymond. Raymond shuddered, looked away.

Behind him, Walter's body scrabbled forward.

Raymond snagged an arm by the sleeve of the suit jacket. He dragged the body away from the grave.

Teeth gritted savagely, he went to work with the axe. He worked until he was convinced that Walter would be incapable of reassembling himself any time soon.

He finally plodded out of the garden on tired legs, soaked in sour sweat, blood streaking his hands and clothes, as if he were a butcher headed home after a long day at the slaughterhouse.

Once outside, he couldn't hold it back any longer. He dropped to his knees, bent over, and vomited.

If he ever lived through this night, the memory of what he'd been forced to do would haunt him until the end of his days.

He wiped his chapped lips with the edge of his shirt, and used the axe to help him stand.

"Okay, Sammy," he said. "That almost killed me, but I'm ready to go. What's next?"

A nudge in his back directed him to the rear of the mansion.

Chapter 59

At the back of the house, Raymond found a weather-battered pair of wooden storm doors. A padlock secured the entrance.

"Locked," Raymond said. "Got a key, kid?"

Sammy poked Raymond's hand that gripped the axe.

"It'll make a helluva racket," he said. "But I've probably lost the element of surprise by now."

Three clamorous whacks with the axe busted open the lock. The doors *eeked* as he pulled them open.

A concrete staircase descended into blackness. The stench of mildew assailed his nostrils.

He started to go in, then paused. Waited to see if something charged out of the darkness.

Nothing attacked him. Yet. He didn't know quite what to expect in this palace of horrors.

He fished the mini-flashlight out of his pocket and walked down the steps, shining the light beam in front of him.

He was in an enormous, dank cellar. Bric-a-brac, dressed in cobwebs, crowded the area; furniture and odds and ends were piled up to the ceiling in sloppy heaps.

The ceiling.

He recalled a book he'd read at his wife's insistence, entitled Dark Crevice or something like that; in one chapter, a clueless cop had walked into a cellar, only to find out—too late—that a bloodthirsty vampire clung to the rafters. He didn't want to be like that dumb policeman. He played the light across the ceiling.

Only frosty spiderwebs and rusted pipes up there. Nothing threatening.

Panning the light around the chamber, he located a staircase across the room. He weaved between the dust-covered furniture, arrived at the foot of the stairs. He flashed the light up there, too.

All clear. A door waited at the peak of the steps.

"This was almost too easy," he said. "Am I missing something, kid?"

The ghost did not respond. He no longer felt the chill in the air that indicated the spirit's presence.

Had Sammy left him alone to fend for himself?

Graveyard silence permeated the basement. He heard only the frenetic throbbing of his heart.

With or without his ghostly companion, he had to move forward.

He climbed the steps. At the top, he grasped the doorknob, turned it, and pushed open the door.

Three big, bluish-gray cats stood on the threshold, as if they had been waiting for him. Ears flattened, they hissed.

"Oh, shit," he said.

The animals attacked.

Chapter 60

Disturbed by the abrupt silence, Andrew returned to the master bedroom, looking for Mika. The room was empty.

Where had she gone?

He despised her and wanted to get as far away from her as possible, but her disappearance, especially at this moment, when she'd sprung a shock on him with the letters, troubled him. Something was going on. He wasn't sure whether the brewing incident was good for him. Or bad.

Behind him, the bedroom door whammed shut.

And opened.

But no one stood in the doorway.

"Who's there?" he asked.

A penetrating draft whisked inside and embraced him like an old friend.

"Sammy," he said. "Man, I'm glad you're here."

Sammy drifted away from him. The door closed, opened again.

Although they lacked the benefit of a computer or

Scrabble board to communicate, the message was clear: the ghost wanted him to leave the bedroom.

He walked into the hallway. "What's going on here, Sammy?"

A ghostly hand pressed against his back, urging him forward.

"I don't get it. What do you want me to do?"

A large, marble-topped table, adorned with a green vase, stood against the wall. Sammy guided him toward the vase.

Andrew touched the vase's flawless ceramic surface. He looked inside the vessel, lifted it and checked underneath, found nothing of interest.

"What do you want me to do with this?"

Small, cool fingers grasped his chin and turned his head.

He faced the end of the hallway. The long mirror—the one he'd earlier thought he'd seen ripple like a lake—hung at the end of the hall. It reflected the image of him, holding the vase, bewildered.

What was Sammy trying to tell him?

The ghost applied upward pressure to his elbows, causing him to lift the vase higher.

"You want me to throw this at the mirror," Andrew said, and knew he was right. He didn't know *how* he knew that it was the message Sammy was attempting to communicate to him. But he knew it as surely as he'd ever known anything.

He didn't know why Sammy wanted him to throw this thing, either, but he trusted that the child understood this house's secrets better than he did.

He hesitated—his mother's old teachings about breaking other people's property echoing in his head—then he hurled the vase at the mirror.

The vase struck the surface and shattered on impact.

But the mirror didn't break, as it should have; it didn't sustain any cracks at all.

"Weird," he said.

The glass shimmered, the surface swelling and ebbing, like a wall of water.

What was this?

He walked forward, his shoes crunching over ceramic shards.

"That's not a mirror," he whispered.

The entire mirror wavered . . . and then faded altogether, like watercolors washing away in a rainstorm.

It was a door.

Chapter 61

As the cats leaped to attack Raymond, he dropped the flashlight, startled. It clattered down the steps, leaving the dim light spilling from the room beyond the doorway as the only illumination to help him.

Goddammit, man, hold it together.

He didn't drop the axe, thank God. As the felines pounced toward him in unison, one feral mass of fur, flashing teeth, and glaring green eyes, he swung the axe.

The blade caught one of the cats in the middle, hacked it nearly in half. The animal emitted a blood-chilling screech.

The other two cats jumped onto his face and chest. Claws tore into him.

Losing his balance, the axe slipping out of his grasp, he tumbled down the stairs.

He slammed to the floor on his back, his head knocking against the concrete. A sea of blackness floated in his vision, threatened to tug him under into unconsciousness.

But terror kept him awake.

The creatures clawed and bit furiously. Ripped into his neck and chest.

He rolled around, trying to knock them off. Pulled at them.

The damn things were hard to get ahold of, their lithe bodies in furious motion. He finally seized a cat's head, went to twist it, and felt the animal's sharp teeth gouge his fingers. He shouted in agony.

The other feline pawed at his cheek, dangerously close to his eye.

To hell with this. He hadn't come this far to have his ass kicked by a bunch of cats.

Flipping over onto his back again, he jammed his elbows into the animals' skulls. Shrieking, they fell off him. They dispersed in the shadows, like phantoms.

He groaned, got to his feet.

He was slightly dizzy, and his body was a canvas of bloody scratches, but he had no time to dwell on his condition. The creatures were still alive and had some fight in them.

The axe lay at the base of the stairs, revealed in a fall of light and shadow. He picked it up.

On the steps above him, the cat he'd cleaved with the axe quivered, paws pedaling the air. It wasn't dead, either.

Didn't anything at this house ever die?

He heard the other two cats around him. Creeping across furniture. Angling for another attack.

"Come on, you bastards," he said under his breath.

One cat leaped off a dusty sofa.

Handling the axe like a sword, he swung the blade toward the creature and chopped it across the throat. Yowling, the cat dropped to the floor, head tethered to the body by a strand of fur and flesh.

He felt only a quick flash of nausea. After what he'd done in the garden, he'd acquired a cast-iron stomach for this gruesome work.

He picked up quick, stealthy movement in the shadows. The last cat.

He pivoted, following the rustling sounds.

"Not scared of you," he said.

Paws padded across cushions. Something clanged to the floor.

Then, silence fell over the chamber.

"Come on with it," he said.

The silence stretched on.

He felt the creature out there, watching him. Hesitant, maybe. It had seen how he'd cut down its buddies.

Perhaps he was giving these cats more credit than they deserved. He assumed that they were as supernaturally smart as they were resilient and vicious.

Turning to face the cellar, he began to climb the stairs backward. When he reached the step on which the first injured cat lay, he kicked it to the floor.

As he'd suspected, his attempt to leave drew the final cat out of hiding. It scampered toward him in a streak of gray fur and fiery eyes. Jumped at him from the bottom of the stairs as if bouncing off a trampoline.

He slashed the animal down the middle.

Screeching, it thumped down the staircase.

He surveyed the cellar below him.

The nightmarish cats writhed and whimpered, but they were far from being capable of mounting another attack soon.

He cleaned blood from his face with the back of his hand. He ascended the stairs and stepped into the room beyond.

Chapter 62

As the mirror dissolved, so did the rest of the illusory furnishings in the mansion.

The fresh, creamy paint on the walls faded to reveal tattered, patchy wallpaper. The thick carpeting in the hall transformed to scarred wooden floorboards. The overstuffed chairs, which had looked brand new, became ancient lumps with ruptured cushions. The crystal chandelier still dangled from the ceiling, but instead of sparkling, it wore a garland of cobwebs.

He shook his head, as if clearing away cobwebs from his own eyes.

This was the real Mourning Hill. Until now, he'd been wandering through a stylized fantasy version of the house, overlaid on the reality like a glossy varnish. He'd seen a glimmer of the true house a short while ago, before he'd lost consciousness in the bedroom— but this time, the images around him were solid, permanent. The truth was here to stay.

The silence had ended, too. On the fringes of his hearing, he detected incoherent whispers. Muffled footsteps came from within rooms along the long corridor.

From somewhere distant, a childlike wailing reached him.

The tortured sounds of restless souls. Mika's victims. He faced the door.

There could be only one reason why Sammy had led him to this point. This door must lead to the attic. Where the great power within the house, Mika's energy source, resided.

A soft hum vibrated from behind the doorway, as if an actual motor purred inside the room.

Mika's warning replayed in his thoughts: *Curiosity can be dangerous. For your own safety, I've hidden the upper chamber.*

A lie, probably. Intended to keep him under control. Just like the extravagant illusions throughout the house.

He put his hand on the doorknob.

A current of energy, like electricity but different, sizzled through him and blew him backward several feet. He sprawled on his back, strange heat rushing through his nerves, dizziness swimming through him.

Slowly, he sat up. He examined his palm. A red arc burned on his skin from where he had touched the knob. It hurt like a burn, too.

Either Mika had somehow rigged the doorknob to shock anyone who tried to turn it. Or something inside didn't want to let him in.

Chapter 63

Carrying the axe in hands crusted with dried blood, Raymond moved through the rooms on the first level of the mansion.

Although he had last explored Mourning Hill over thirty years ago, the place was as he remembered it, as if he were wandering through a palace of his memory and not an actual physical structure. The dusty rooms were vast, museum like, full of antique furniture that looked as if it hadn't been dusted in decades. Fat white candles burned in various areas, supplying a modicum of light.

Then there were the paintings. In the flicker of candle-light, he studied a painting that portrayed a black woman, and a young black man who could only be his son, lying together in a meadow under a warm sun.

Another one depicted Andrew and Mika riding a horse across the countryside. Yet another showed them sitting at a table full of fruit, feeding each other grapes.

The painter, whomever it was, had undeniable talent. But seeing the pieces sickened Raymond nearly as much as the blood he'd spilled earlier. This woman was dangerously obsessive. Taking into account her inhuman abilities, he wasn't sure how he was going to get Andrew away from her.

And where were they? He hadn't seen or heard anything to indicate that they were in here. He felt as isolated as if he were crawling through an ancient crypt.

He left a living room area, and walked through the arched doorway, into the main hall.

The woman exploded from a shadowy room across the corridor.

Clothed in a bloodred kimono, she might have been a beautiful Angel of Death come to bear him away to the afterlife.

She attacked him before he could react. She crashed into him, drove him back with the strength of an angry rhino. His shoulder smashed into the wall, chips of plaster crackling onto his head. But he kept his grip on the axe.

Hissing, the woman bared her teeth. Curly locks of her black hair hung in her face, which had transformed from a vision of exotic beauty into an ugly mask of fury.

She really hasn't aged at all, he thought, in a frozen moment of terror. *Sweet Jesus, she looks the same as when I met her at that party thirty-some years ago . . .*

Then he broke his paralysis, and fought back.

He pushed her away and took a chop at her. The blade sang through the air, but she bounced to the other side of the corridor, easily eluding him.

"You look good for your age, Raymond," she said. "But you're awfully slow."

"Where's my son?" He struggled to catch his breath.

"What does it matter to you? You abandoned Andrew to grow up on his own. He doesn't need you."

Her words touched an emotional live wire. Yelling, he charged at her.

He swung. She evaded the weapon's arc and darted to the other side of the hall.

He attacked again, swinging in a wide circle.

She leapt out of harm's way. The axe bit into the wall, sank deep into the plaster and got embedded there.

He cursed, realizing the irony of his predicament. Walter's shovel had been stuck in a tree when Raymond had shorn his arm off.

Nevertheless, he strained to yank the axe free. Without a weapon, he was defenseless against her.

Clucking her tongue, Mika shoved him aside. She tore the axe out of the wall with a single jerk of one hand. She twirled the weapon like a baton.

Raising his arms protectively, he dipped into a defensive crouch, but she was way too fast for him. She rammed the axe handle into his groin.

He grunted, doubled over.

Want to disable a man, aim for the family jewels.

She clubbed the back of his skull. He dropped to the hardwood floor on his face.

Grimacing, he floated on a raft of pain.

He'd been a fool to think that he could fight this woman, all on his own. He hadn't had a chance in hell.

Where was Andrew?

Mika turned him over. Placing her slippered foot on his chest, gazing down at him, she held the axe high, like a statue of a goddess of war.

"Why are you here?" she asked. "I find it hard to believe that you've come for your son."

"Taking him home," he said in a brittle voice. A knob on the back of his head pulsated, dispatched couriers of pain throughout his body.

She mashed her foot harder against his chest. He gasped.

"So that's true? You trespass on my property, butcher my caretaker and my cats, all in the service of some ludicrous effort to take Andrew away from me? After how long I've waited for him to return to me?"

Her eyes were crazed. There would be no reasoning with her, no talking her out of her obsession. She was as insane as he'd feared she would be, and the only way to end this was to end *her*, permanently.

But he was beginning to doubt that he was the one who would do it.

Chapter 64

As Andrew wandered the cluttered rooms on the second floor, searching for another doorway that might lead to the upper room, he heard a commotion. It came from the main hallway, downstairs.

One of the voices sounded like his father.

Hope sparked in him. Was this another cruel hallucination?

He ran into the hall and peered over the railing, to the floor below.

He couldn't believe what he saw.

Chapter 65

Raymond lay spread-eagled on the floor, pinned beneath the woman's foot. He didn't dare move. She could lop off his head with the axe as easily as chopping through a cord of hickory wood.

He couldn't believe that it was going to end like this. All of the dreams he'd had the past few weeks . . . none of them had foretold that he'd die at the hands of this madwoman, that he'd be fated for an ignominious burial in an unmarked grave near this hell house.

What about the unearthly power they believed existed in this mansion? Couldn't it—whatever *it* was—intervene to help?

Maybe they hadn't known what the hell they were talking about. Maybe they had misinterpreted his dreams and all the records they'd discovered. Maybe coming to this house had been a fatal mistake.

It didn't matter anymore. This was where he had wound up. And he was out of options.

"I won't enjoy this," Mika said, and sounded genuinely sad. "You fathered the man that I love, and I'm grateful for that. But I can't allow you to take him away from me, I simply *can't*."

"Let me go," he said. "I'll leave both of you alone, won't ever come back."

He was lying, merely stalling for time. If she let him get away, he'd return all right—with enough firepower to blast this place to Mars.

"I can't do that," she said. "I know your thoughts—you would tell others, and return. My baby and I would never have any peace."

"Listen, I wouldn't do that. Promise."

She smirked. "Considering how many false promises you made to Andrew when he was a child, I don't believe that your word is worth much, Raymond."

He shut his mouth. Her statement cut him deeper than any blade could have.

She raised the axe.

Praying fervently, he closed his eyes.

Lord, please, I'll do anything if you stop this from happening. Don't let me die like this, God, please. I'm sorry for everything I've done, I'll do better, please, God, please, LET ME LIVE—

"Mika, stop!"

It was Andrew.

Raymond's eyes snapped open. His son rounded the newel post at the bottom of the spiral staircase.

Thank you, Jesus.

Then Andrew spoke words that convinced Raymond that the hell in which he found himself had just gotten a hundred degrees hotter.

"Let me take care of him myself," Andrew said.

Chapter 66

Let me take care of him myself. . . .

Raymond searched for a secretive gleam in Andrew's eyes, a wink, anything to convince him that his son was playing a joke. Surely, he had heard wrong.

But there was no such signal. Andrew's face was grave.

What in God's name was going on? Had this woman brainwashed him?

Mika, too, appeared puzzled. "You want to murder your own father, Andrew?"

"Asshole's never done a damn thing for me," Andrew said. He rubbed his hands on his jeans, as if preparing for hard work. "I want to pay him back. Like you paid back *your* father for what he did to you, Mika."

Raymond remembered the newspaper account of how Dr. George Mourning had murdered his wife with a shotgun, and then committed suicide. Evidently, it had been Mika's punishment for him taking away her lover.

Mika's eyes shone, as she considered his son's proposition. Slowly, she smiled.

"Yes," she said. "That's how it should be. This is indeed your responsibility."

Andrew stepped closer. Mika offered him the axe. Andrew held it, tested its weight.

"Please, Andrew, don't do this," Raymond said. "Jesus, what the hell's wrong with you? I'm your father, I know I haven't been great but I've been trying to do better! Please forgive me, son, don't do this. Forgive me!"

"Too late for that forgive me shit." Andrew spread his legs like a lumberjack.

Raymond tried to get up. Mika scowled and kicked him sharply in the ribs, knocking him back to the floor, gagging.

Andrew lifted the axe high.

"God, help us both," Raymond said.

Andrew swung the axe.

Into Mika's chest.

Chapter 67

Andrew drove the axe into Mika with such force that it shattered her breastbone and sank several inches into her chest.

Her mouth opened, a faint croak escaping her lips. She wilted against the wall and thudded against the floor. The axe protruded like a wooden limb from her torso.

She lay still as a department-store mannequin, glazed eyes staring at the chandelier.

Andrew wiped his hands on his shirt.

Perhaps it made him a bad person to admit it, but whacking her with that axe was the most pleasurable thing he'd done all day.

Dad cowered on the floor, gaping at him, as if unsure of what he had seen. Swollen red scratches marked his face, like tribal scars. No doubt, he'd endured a battle with Mika's infamous felines.

"Come on, Dad." Andrew offered him his hand. "I haven't killed her. We don't have long before she gets up again."

"You scared the shit out of me, man." He took

Andrew's hand, and got to his feet. "Thought you were gonna put me down for good."

"All writers are closet actors." Andrew smiled briefly.

Dad watched Mika. "She looks dead to me. You sure she isn't?"

"Ever seen a horror flick? She's like the creature that won't die. Come on, we've gotta get upstairs."

Andrew hurried to the dust-covered staircase and began to climb, taking the creaky steps two and three at a time.

Dad pulled his attention away from Mika and followed him.

"What's upstairs?" Dad asked. "Did you find . . . it?"

Andrew knew what he was talking about: the nameless power that dwelled in the upper room.

"Sammy showed me a door," he said. "I think it's what we want."

"So that's where the kid's been. He'd been with me on the way here. Saved my ass when I was out there with Valter."

"He may have saved all of our asses," Andrew said.

As though they sensed trouble coming, the spirits in the mansion had become agitated. Along the hallway, doors flew open and slammed shut. Footsteps pattered through rooms. The chandelier swayed on its rusty chain, as if blown about by a violent wind.

At another, earlier time, the poltergeist phenomena would have scared the shit out of Andrew. But he ran down the corridor, unfazed by the supernatural activity around him. He'd seen so much in the past few days that it would take more than some agitated ghosts to frighten him.

They arrived at the attic door.

"I couldn't open it," Andrew said. "I got something like an electrical shock when I tried to go in. What do we do now?"

Dad scrutinized the door. When he looked at Andrew, his eyes were sober. "I go in."

"But we can't *go* in, Dad, that's my point."

"The door's meant for me, not you, young buck," Dad said softly. "The thing in there . . . it's been calling me, in my dreams."

Dad reached for the knob. Andrew grabbed his hand, pulled it away.

"Are you sure about this?" he asked his father.

"Son, I know you don't trust me, never have. And that's my fault. But this time, you've *got* to trust me."

Dad had honed in on the exact conflict that divided him. Trust. He didn't trust his dad to know what he was talking about, didn't trust him to do the right thing. He felt as though he needed to be hovering over his father's shoulder, to supervise his actions and make sure he didn't screw up.

"I've *got this*, son," Dad said. He squeezed Andrew's hand. "Trust me. Please."

"But—" Andrew started, and stopped himself when he noticed his dad's eyes. They were iron, determined.

Dad was going to go inside. Even if he had to knock him down to do it.

Andrew swallowed. His feet were heavy as sandbags. But he stepped out of the way.

Dad closed his hand over the knob. Andrew nearly flinched, fearing his father would get a terrible jolt.

Nothing happened.

Dad turned the knob, and opened the door. It came open smoothly.

Impenetrable blackness waited inside. The engine like vibration that Andrew had heard earlier grew louder.

Before going in, Dad glanced at Andrew.

"This was meant for me," he said. "But I did it for you."

He stared at Andrew for a beat, then walked into the darkness and closed the door behind him.

Andrew slumped against the wall.

Somehow, he understood that he would never see his dad again. If his father emerged from that room, he wouldn't be the same man that Andrew had despised for his entire life and then finally begun to love. The thing in that attic, whatever it was, was going to take his father away from him forever.

The most difficult part to accept was that he realized it could be no other way. This was the tragic hand that fate had dealt them.

He pressed his fingers to his eyes, to stop the flow of tears.

Downstairs, Mika awakened. Howling in rage.

Chapter 68

Raymond walked through the doorway and into the most perfect blackness that he had ever known. It was like plunging into an ocean of warm, pitch-black water miles beneath the surface and the reach of the sun.

A low hum permeated the air. As if a massive generator of some kind were stored in the room. Whatever it was, it radiated a field of energy that lifted the hairs on his arms and neck.

Fear stirred in his gut.

What am I doing in here? I don't know what I've done . .

Like a blind man, he extended his arms, searching for a wall, anything. His hands found a smooth length of wood, examined it. It felt like a staircase railing.

He lifted his foot, edged it forward. It landed on a step.

Good, some stairs. Now just go on up.

The chamber had a clean, faintly antiseptic scent. He smelled nothing like the mildewed, dusty attic that he'd expected to find.

Slowly, gripping the railing, he navigated the stairs

As he moved upward, the humming increased in volume. His teeth thrummed in sync with the steady drone.

There were thirteen steps. At the top, his feet found a firm floor.

Although the view from outside the mansion indicated that there should be a window up here, the darkness was complete, as if the glass were coated with thick, black paint.

He ventured forward, closer to the source of the vibration.

Lord, I hope I'm doing the right thing. I'm stepping out here on nothing but faith.

As he neared the nucleus of the energy, the buzzing, suddenly, was no longer outside of him.

It was *in* him, resonating in the cavity of his chest, as if it had taken over his heart.

His body, numbed by the increasingly frequent vibrations, began to shake.

And visions flooded his consciousness. Exploded in his mind's eye like supernovas in the darkness of space.

Verdant, primeval woods, disturbed by a rumbling in the air that climaxed with an orb of fiery energy erupting out of the very atmosphere . . .

Wild animals wandering to the area, basking in the power they sensed but could not see, their bodies rewarded with unnatural vigor . . .

Brown-skinned people arrayed in splendid, ceremonial garments, conducting tribal rituals here in foreign tongues . . .

A scholarly looking white man, Dr. Mourning, stealing into the chamber at night and drinking of the energy for short sips, sufficient to allow miraculous workings to flow from his fingers . . .

A doe-eyed, beautiful black girl, known as Celestina

and later as Mika, sneaking into the upper room and absorbing the power that would change her life forever . . .

There were more images, some of which he understood, and others which he did not. A visual record of those who had used—and abused—the power over the centuries.

Knowledge came, too.

He knew what he could do with his power. The miracles he could work. The evil he could destroy. The good he could do for his son.

And he knew that to use the power as he desired would kill him. Would overload the capabilities of his physical body, perhaps induce a major heart attack.

But it had to be done.

Even as that bitter knowledge washed over him green light flared in his vision, an all-consuming brightness that blasted away the darkness as effectively as the sun vanquishing the night.

And then the brilliant radiance was no longer outside of him.

It was in him, too.

Chapter 69

Mika had risen.

Hiding behind the hallway balustrade, Andrew watched her pull the axe out of her chest as casually as someone plucking a splinter from a finger. Her head swiveled around. Then up.

He ducked away, but too late. She had seen him.

He heard her footsteps racing to the staircase.

He looked to the attic door. His father had been inside for a couple of minutes. What was going on in here?

He wanted to check inside, but his painful memory of touching the knob kept him away.

Mika pounded up the stairs. Shouting his name.

What if Dad had collapsed and died up there in the upper room, his heart stopped by the alien energy?

Mika bounded onto the landing. A slash in her kimono revealed that the axe wound had faded entirely.

"You've pissed me off now, Andrew," she said. "But I'll deal with you after I've dealt with your father. Where is he?"

Andrew didn't answer. But his gaze flicked across the door.

Mika's eyes widened as large as saucers.

"He couldn't have," she said.

The door opened.

Andrew's father emerged from the darkness.

Throughout the mansion, the spirits shrieked.

Chapter 70

Something about Andrew's father was different. Although he looked the same, in a physical sense, as he had when he had entered the room, when he walked out of the darkness, an inexplicable change had come over him.

It was, Andrew decided, a transformation in his aura—an invisible field of energy that surrounded him like a second skin.

Andrew could feel the energy blazing from his dad's aura, like heat waves from a fire.

Glaring hatefully at Andrew's father, Mika coiled, preparing to attack.

His father strode past him, paying him only a reassuring glance, as if to say, *I've got things under control.*

Andrew backed against the wall and got out of the way.

Screeching, Mika attacked his dad.

Dad calmly thrust his arm forward and clamped his hand over her throat.

Gagging, Mika batted her arms at him, but she couldn't break his powerful grip.

Dad lifted her in the air, her legs kicking.

He swung her around, to dump her over the balustrade.

Driven by desperation, Mika wrapped her legs around Dad's waist.

Dad didn't lose his chokehold on her throat, but he lost his balance.

Together, they flipped over the railing and fell to the floor below.

Chapter 71

The sound of Dad and Mika striking the hallway boomed through the house.

The mansion was alive with restless spirits. They banged doors. Hammered walls. Overturned furniture. Flung vases and sculpture. Screamed as if they had withheld all of their misery to be released at that penultimate moment.

Ignoring the chaos, Andrew sprinted downstairs.

Although they had fallen almost fifteen feet, neither Dad nor Mika had lost consciousness. They wrestled on the floor, bodies interlocked in what would have been an intimate manner if their angry grunts had not betrayed the true nature of their struggle.

Andrew found the axe lying near a table leg. He picked it up, though he was unsure whether he would need it. He moved closer.

Dad gained the advantage. He pinned Mika beneath him and pressed both of his hands over her throat.

Mika thrashed wildly, as if her body were a sack of writhing snakes. But she could not break free.

"Give it back," Dad said over and over. "Give it back."

He was talking about the power, Andrew realized. The power she'd stolen from the upper room and the souls of her victims.

He watched over his father's shoulder.

"Give it back . . ."

He throttled her savagely.

Mika arched her back and released a garbled scream.

Dad pressed his mouth over hers, as if to administer mouth-to-mouth resuscitation.

But as Mika's body buckled like a wind-blown sheet and began to shrivel, he realized that Dad was sucking the life *out* of her.

Her black hair lost its luster, turned bone-white at startling speed, and then fell away from her scalp in brittle sheaves. Wrinkles streamed across every centimeter of her skin as if poured on her from a jar, running over her in deep, saggy furrows. Her taut muscles deflated like balloons losing air; her curvaceous figure atrophied to a gnarled, stick-thin body that almost vanished in the red kimono's billowy folds.

Drained of the power that had sustained her, she was reverting to her true, old age.

Her gaze found Andrew. Tears carved down her sallow cheeks.

He heard her voice in his mind, clear as a clarion: *I'll always love you, soul mate eyes.*

Then, the brightness faded out of her gaze, and milky cataracts clouded her vision.

Andrew looked away.

He hadn't loved her. He had feared her, and he despised her for what she had done. She had acted out of an unwavering but misguided love for him. It sickened him that she'd never realized how wrong she was.

But she had loved him to the end, as she'd promised she would.

Chapter 72

Wearily, Dad rolled away from Mika, and lay on his side.

All that remained of Mika was a corpse that appeared to have lain in a grave for decades. Andrew averted his gaze and went to his father.

Dad clutched his chest. He sucked in short breaths.

"Can't hold on . . . much longer," Dad said. "Power's . . . too much for me. Help me up."

"Listen, you're gonna be okay, Dad." Andrew grabbed his father's arm and helped him to stand. Energy crackled through his fingers where he touched his father, a pleasant tickling sensation. But he was starting to cry, and he couldn't stop. "Everything's gonna be all right."

"Take me to your friends . . . outside," Dad said. "Fast, son."

Although Andrew didn't understand his father's request, he didn't question him. He threw open the front door. Keeping a steadying arm around his father's waist, they hurried off the veranda and across the lawn, to the moss-wreathed archway that enclosed the garden.

A thin mist hung over the area, but Andrew spotted

the bodies of Eric and Carmen, lying beside a mound of raw dirt, not far from the watchful statue of Aphrodite.

Grief speared his heart. He nearly lost his balance.

"Here," Dad said. He knelt beside the bodies. He gestured for Andrew to move away.

Andrew stepped back. "What . . . what're you gonna do?"

Dad placed one hand on Eric's head, and his other hand on Carmen's forehead. He closed his eyes. He began to shudder.

Understanding came to Andrew.

"Oh, Jesus," he said. He sank to his knees in the grass.

He didn't believe what might happen.

But he wanted to believe, more than he'd ever wanted anything.

Hands pressed firmly against their heads, Dad shook as if experiencing a mild seizure. Eyes shut. Face contorted in a rapture of miraculous power.

The cool air around them grew warm. The bracing scent of ozone reached Andrew's nostrils, and he looked to the heavens, half expecting to see a bolt of lightning sizzle to the earth.

Movement came from the dead bodies.

Carmen's fingers twitched.

Eric's folded leg straightened.

Oh, my God. Am I really seeing this?

He crawled across the ground, closer.

Dad moved away from Carmen and Eric. He raised his hands and face skyward, as if in supplication. Whispered words came from his lips. Prayers.

Carmen sat up.

She rubbed her eyes, blinked as if she'd been napping.

The fatal knife wound in her throat had vanished. Not even a scar remained.

Yawning, Eric rose, too.

He frowned at the house robe he wore. His flesh also was unmarked.

Carmen looked at Andrew. "Drew, what happened?" Her voice was clear, blessedly normal.

"Yeah, what's been going on?" Eric said. "Why am I wearing this thing?"

Tears running down his face, Andrew opened his mouth. But he couldn't speak.

Dad collapsed.

Andrew cradled his father's head in his arms. Eric and Carmen huddled around him.

Dad's breaths came slow and ragged.

"Brought 'em back," Dad said softly. "Least I could do . . . 'fore I check out."

Andrew held his father's hand.

"We're taking you to the hospital," Andrew said. "They're going to take care of you there, you'll be back to normal in no time, wait and see, Dad, we'll be back on the links before you know it."

Dad's eyes were watery. "You forgive me?"

Andrew was crying so hard that he could barely manage to speak the words.

"Dad, yeah, I forgive you. Yes. For everything . . . everything."

Dad smiled. "Always loved you, young buck."

"You're not gonna die. No, you're not gonna die on me, not now, Dad . . ."

His father's eyes slid shut. His shallow breaths ended, lips slightly parted.

He was gone.

Andrew buried his face in the crook of his father's neck, and wept.

* * *

When Raymond died, his physical vessel breaking under the pressure of containing a prodigious amount of psychic energy—the totality of the power that had thrived in the land for eons—he unconsciously pierced a hole in the atmosphere of the spirit, the same dimension from which the energy had originated.

The power, drawn like a magnet to its home, poured out of him, and into its rightful realm.

Mourning Hill, once an estate built on an ancient, sacred place of power, instantly became merely a dilapidated mansion that stood on a large plot of ordinary, red Georgia clay.

Eric and Carmen pulled Andrew to his feet and held him in a tight, group embrace.

For a long time, none of them said a word.

Then, someone tapped Andrew's arm. He looked around.

The translucent apparition of a child greeted him.

Sammy.

The ghost regarded Andrew's father, and offered a bittersweet smile.

"Thank you, Sammy," Andrew said, his voice raspy.

Sammy floated in the air like a kite, toward the house.

Like a giant whirlpool in the sky, warm white light swirled in the air above Mourning Hill. Glowing ethereal bodies poured out of the mansion, like smoke, and drifted into the light.

The spirits, freed at long last, were advancing to their proper place in the afterlife.

Sammy gave Andrew a final wave, and then he melted into the light, too.

Six weeks later . . .

As Andrew's house was gradually reconstructed from the charred ruins, so he worked to rebuild his life, too.

Having Carmen and Eric—who had been through the fire with him—helped.

Neither of his friends consciously remembered the experience of death—perhaps a blessing. But the memories returned to them in nightmares that mercifully faded into the blackness of forgetfulness when they awakened.

Andrew had his own nightmares to deal with, and figured that he would, for a long time.

And there were the hallucinations, too.

In the weeks afterward, he saw Mika no less than twenty times: while browsing at the bookstore; cutting his mother's grass; dining at a restaurant; driving his car. Other places, too. Every time, a closer examination revealed that, of course, Mika was not there.

She was dead. Unquestionably. They had buried her in the estate's cemetery, beside the caretaker.

Afterward, for good measure, they had set fire to the mansion. A perusal of the news stories the next day uncovered the headline: "Historic Mansion Burns to Ground, Arson Suspected."

Destroying the house was the only thing that his father hadn't done for him.

Andrew visited his dad's grave often. To keep it adorned with fresh flowers and to pay his respects.

He hadn't known his father well. But he hadn't died a stranger to him.

That, Andrew reflected, was blessing enough.

After leaving the cemetery one cloudy Saturday afternoon, Andrew returned to Carmen's town house. They lived together while Andrew waited for work to be completed on his house. It was a temporary living arrangement that would soon transition to something permanent. He planned to propose to her by the end of the summer.

Carmen met him at the door. They kissed, held each other.

"How're you feeling?" she asked him.

"Blessed," he said, which was how he always responded to the question these days.

She indicated a pile of mail on the kitchen table. "This mail's been around for a while, Drew. You up to going through it yet?"

For years, he'd used a post office box for his personal and business correspondence. Carmen had dutifully retrieved the mail a couple of times a week. He had yet to open any of it. He'd been known as a creature of obsessive habits. But part of him resisted a return to the routines of everyday life.

"I guess I should," he said. He managed a chuckle. "Might be a check buried in there, right?"

"You never know." She smiled and handed him a letter opener.

Standing at the table, he began opening mail. Most of it was junk: offers from magazines and credit card companies; postcards for products that held no interest for him; past due bills . . .

Then, he stopped.

It was time to admit it. There was something far more important than opening junk mail that he needed to resolve.

He went into the guest bedroom, where he kept most of his clothes in the chest of drawers, and pulled out the bottom drawer.

Underneath a package of T-shirts, he located the

padded, nine-by-eleven envelope. He took it to the kitchen, opened it.

He slid out a collection of letters.

These were the only things—other than sorrowful memories—that he had taken from Mourning Hill.

He perused the delicate, time-yellowed papers.

They were missives of love, written to Celestina.

All of them were signed by the same man.

Mark Justice.

The bold, looping signature was identical to the one with which Andrew autographed his pseudonymous novels.

Each time he examined the letters, which he had done at least a dozen times since the night at the mansion, he experienced the same curious and deeply troubling sensation.

Painful throbbing, concentrated at the back of his skull.

As if remembering the bullet to the head that had killed Mika's lover . . .

He had been delaying this, but he finally had to answer some tough questions.

Was Mark Justice more than a pen name?

Was he Andrew's alter ego?

What would Mark Justice do in this situation . . .

His repressed, past-life identity?

He shook his head firmly. No. He would not allow Mika this final victory. He wouldn't let her memory haunt him for the rest of his days.

He bundled the letters and took them to the stove. He switched the gas burner on high.

He fed the papers to the flames.

Carmen entered the kitchen. "Drew, what in the world are you doing?"

"Forgetting the past." He washed the remaining ashes down the sink, and walked toward Carmen.

And his future.

After publishing his fourth thriller with the Mark Justice pseudonym, Andrew ended the series and began to write young adult novels under his own name. Whenever anyone asked him what had become of Justice, he replied, in a solemn tone, that Mark Justice had died while rescuing a young boy from a terrible place. He was laid to eternal rest somewhere in rural Georgia, in a humble grave beside his long-deceased fiancée.

SUBSCRIBE TO BRANDON MASSEY'S TALESPINNER

Here's a sneak peak at
Brandon Massey's new title,
The Ex,
coming July, 2007!

When Cecil Jackson saw the tall black man walking on the shoulder of the road, he had to stop for him.

No sane man would be outdoors in this kind of weather by choice, Cecil realized. The man walking on the side of the road wore black boots, blue jeans, a black ski jacket, and a gray woolen skullcap. His hands were shoved deep into his pockets. A green knapsack hung from one of his broad shoulders.

Cecil gently tapped the brakes, slowing gradually, lest he skid across a patch of ice and spin into a ditch himself.

Cecil was a devout Christian, a deacon at his hometown Baptist church. He'd spent the past two hours delivering holiday goodies to the sick and shut-in members of the congregation. It was a week before Christmas, and Cecil was committed to doing his part to spread holiday cheer.

Perhaps that explained why he decided to stop for the brother. Cecil did not normally drive around picking up strangers. But it was Christmas time. If he couldn't do a good deed now, well, then when could he?

As Cecil neared the man, he tapped his horn.

The guy looked over his shoulder. He had the wool cap pulled so low over his head that Cecil could barely make out his face. Frosty tendrils of air puffed from his mouth, further obscuring his features. Cecil had an impression of brown skin, a mustache, dark eyes.

Cecil extended his hand and beckoned him inside. The man nodded, opened the door.

Icy air slipped inside, and then Cecil could see the man's face. He was young—compared to Cecil, anyway—perhaps in his mid-thirties. Strong jaw. Alert eyes.

"Get in, brother," Cecil said. "Bitterly cold out there."

"God bless you, sir," the man said, with a crisp voice. He sounded like an educated man, and a godly one at that. Cecil's tension eased out of him.

Cecil cranked up the heat another notch and offered his hand. "Cecil Jackson."

"Dexter Bates." His hand was still cold, but his grip was firm.

Comforted by these things, Cecil pulled back onto the road, snow and ice crunching underneath the tires. "Where you headed, Brother Bates?"

"I'm going to visit my in-laws," Dexter said. "They live in Zion. It's been about four years since I last saw them."

"Four years? Long time to go without seeing family."

"Sure is. Are you married, Brother Jackson?"

"Forty-two years." Cecil raised his ring finger, showing the gold band.

"Now that's what I'm talking about," Dexter said. "Commitment. Taking the vows seriously. Till death do us part. These days, you don't see enough of that in the younger generations."

Cecil nodded sagely. This Brother Bates had a fine head on his shoulders. Young brothers like him gave Cecil hope for the next generation of men.

"How long you been married?" Cecil asked.

"Nine years, eleven months, and nine days."

Cecil laughed. "I bet you don't ever miss an anniversary."

"Never. I certainly won't miss our tenth. I've been looking forward to it for a long time."

"Got something special planned, eh?"

"Yes." Dexter nodded, smiling as if amused at some private joke. "Why did you stop for me?"

"It's Christmas time," Cecil said. "And it was the Christian thing to do."

"Not too many people would have stopped for a tall, athletic-looking young black man. They would've been afraid."

"When God is on my side, no weapon formed against me shall prosper."

"I'm impressed." Dexter chuckled. "You sure know your Bible, Brother Jackson."

"I've been leading men's Bible study at my church for seventeen years—I better know it."

"What does the Good Book say about death?"

Cecil glanced at him. What an odd question. But Dexter appeared to be genuinely curious.

"Well, it says a lot," Cecil said. "For example, before Christ resurrected Lazarus, the crowd told him that the man was dead. Christ answered that Lazarus was merely sleeping. Some folk believe that death is like that—like sleeping."

"Sleeping, huh?" Dexter pursed his lips. "So good night, Brother Jackson."

Cecil turned in confusion as the man drew something out of his jacket. Something sharp and shiny.

A knife.

Oh, Jesus.

He drove the blade through Cecil's parka, into Cecil's

kidney. Deep. A small gasp of pain escaped Cecil's lips, his fingers grew slack on the steering wheel, and his foot slid off the gas pedal.

"There, there now, we don't want to have an accident," the man said, his voice coming to Cecil as if from the end of a long, dark tube. Cecil sensed rather than felt himself being pushed between the front seats and into the back. He sprawled across the bench seat, leaking blood.

The man had climbed behind the wheel. The vehicle had never veered off the road.

Brother's smooth, Cecil thought dimly. *He's done this before.*

Then Cecil noticed the tremendous quantity of blood coming out of him, gushing out him, it seemed. His coat was soaked. The seats were wet. His blood was forming a puddle on the floor.

He groaned, tried to move, but couldn't. It was as if a slab of concrete lay atop his body.

Lord, help me. Help your humble servant.

"I've got to find somewhere to bury your body," Bates said, as calmly as a best buddy stating that he was looking for a spot to fish. "All these deep snowdrifts, so many choices. We'll find a nice one for you, Brother Jackson. That's the least you deserve for the good deed you did today. A comfortable place for you to lay your head.

"Until the carrion eaters find you."

Cecil closed his eyes, and offered a final, desperate prayer.

Let me die soon, oh, Lord. Let me die soon . . .